KI-GOR

THE COMPLETE SERIES VOLUME 3

KI-GOR

ᵀᴴᴱ COMPLETE SERIES VOLUME 3

WRITTEN BY

JOHN PETER DRUMMOND

INTRODUCTION BY

HOWARD ANDREW JONES

ALTUS PRESS

2016

EDITED AND DESIGNED BY
Matthew Moring

PUBLISHING HISTORY
"Introduction" appears here for the first time. Copyright © 2016 Howard Andrew Jones. All rights reserved.

"Tigress of T'wanbi" originally appeared in the Winter 1941–42 issue of *Jungle Stories* magazine (Vol. 1, No. 12).

"Slaves for the Renegade Sultan" originally appeared in the Spring 1942 issue of *Jungle Stories* magazine (Vol. 2, No. 1).

"Blood Priestess of Vig'Na" originally appeared in the Summer 1942 issue of *Jungle Stories* magazine (Vol. 2, No. 2).

"The Cannibal Horde" originally appeared in the Fall 1942 issue of *Jungle Stories* magazine (Vol. 2, No. 3).

THANKS TO
Gary A. Buckingham

TABLE OF
CONTENTS

INTRODUCTION BY
HOWARD ANDREW JONES

TO ENJOY KI-GOR WE have to let go of the conceptions of the present and seek the same vicarious thrills as the magazine's reading audience in the 1940s. In the best Ki-Gor tales they're not that difficult to find. The jungle is a different place from what we know: it's strange and mysterious and brimming with hidden dangers and great unmapped regions where, as Edgar Rice Burroughs already showed legions of readers, decadent remnants of lost civilizations still flourish in crumbling glory. Ki-Gor's fated to stumble across more than a few of those himself and the best stories in this collection chronicle two of those adventures.

It's not the "lost valley" aspect that makes these stories stand out. After all, by this time, Ki-Gor's encountered a lost valley or two already. It's that Ki-Gor and his supporting cast have experienced a subtle evolution of character and pacing has been ramped up. While I enjoy many scenes and characters in the Ki-Gor adventures collected in the first two Altus Press volumes, as far as I'm concerned the winter of 1941 is where Ki-Gor's tale spinners really started hitting their marks.

Ki-Gor's speech pattern has varied, but by this time the editors had nixed his use of faux primitive man talk, just as they have almost completely abandoned George Spelvin's step-and-fetch accent. Before too much longer they'll completely cease reminding readers of George's backstory and refer to him only as Tembu George, leader of a tribe of Maasai warriors.

We can't know why these changes were made, but I like to think that the editors behind Jungle Stories understood that the earlier presentations might have been objectionable to readers, or, in the case of the "Me Ki-Gor, You Helene" speech pattern, have come off as a little silly.

From this point forward we'll more and more frequently see Ki-Gor displaying a natural, commanding nobility of spirit and greater measures of cleverness and cunning. With increasingly regularity Tembu George and N'Geeso show independence and capability and it grows more and more clear that Ki-Gor cannot succeed without them. Plots, even if recycling some favorite themes, grow more elaborate (and occasionally bizarre) and start clicking along at greater speed—all of which usually results in grand pulp excitement.

It should hardly be expected that the popular entertainment of previous generations would reflect our own values, and Jungle Tales is rife with depictions that, while acceptable in previous decades, are hardly nuanced. Issues of race are where modern readers are apt to have the most trouble with Tarzan archetypes. Like all jungle men heroes, it's a given that the white Ki-Gor is the superior to every native when it comes to jungle lore, and I'm not sure there's a single Arab to be found in these tales who isn't in league with an evil slaver.

On the other hand, Ki-Gor displays genuine color-blindedness and has both friends and enemies among the natives; black men and white can be villains or heroes. Ki-Gor's two closest friends are black. As mentioned above, as the series begins to hit its stride they end up being far more resourceful and intelligent than might be expected, particularly Tembu George. While sidekicks, N'Geeso and Tembu George are trusted confidants, not servants, and beloved by both Ki-Gor and Helene. Speaking of which, despite a propensity for being kidnapped or captured when the plot demands it (a propensity, it must be said, shared with Ki-Gor himself) Ki-Gor's wife is herself no helpless pushover—she's deadly with the bow and is an even finer swimmer than Ki-Gor.

In short, then, while Ki-Gor stories have many elements of their time, they also show us that the people of that time were not so backward as we can sometimes assume. We should know better. Yes, there was all manner of racism, both subtle and overt, in American society of the '40s. Yet the fact that *Jungle Stories* continued to sell speaks to evidence that a wide reading public found the ideas of white and black men who pledged love and brotherhood to one another perfectly acceptable, and that a woman with some independence and skill, like Helene, was not so far from societal norms.

Taste is subjective of course, but "Tigress of T'wanbi" is the first Ki-Gor, chronologically, that makes my personal best-of list, and

"Blood Priestess of Vig'Na" ranks among my absolute favorites. Both are tightly paced yarns with plenty of action and surprises.

I think you'll find "Blood Priestess of Vig'Na" especially enjoyable. It's always read a little to me like what would have happened if Robert E. Howard had written a Tarzan story—it's chock full of great action sequences and moments of pulp grandeur. In some ways it's the most fantastic of Ki-Gor's adventures yet, although even more supernatural exploits await him, as you'll see in upcoming volumes.

STORY XII
TIGRESS OF T'WANBI

CHAPTER 1

THERE WAS NO SOUND except the monotonous dreeing of insects. Birds and beasts alike were sunk in torpor under the baking heat of the brassy, noonday sun. But far down on the jungle floor, protected from the fierce glare by layers of leafy canopy, Ki-Gor, White Lord of the Jungle, strode along a tiny trail.

On his powerful shoulders was balanced a freshly killed antelope that would weigh not an ounce less than two hundred pounds. But Ki-Gor padded swiftly along with it as if it weighed no more than a jungle fowl. Indeed, so rapid was his pace that his friend, little Ngeeso the Pygmy, traveling the tree-route above him, was hard put to it to keep up.

Ordinarily, Ki-Gor would not have carried off the entire carcass of such a big buck. One quarter, or even a few good steaks would be all that he and his mate, the beautiful red-haired Helene, could consume before the meat spoiled. But because Ngeeso had been near when he felled this buck, and had looked so longingly at the plump legs and fat ribs, Ki-Gor had decided to take the whole beast along so that Ngeeso's people could have a feast.

In the remote, secluded glen which was Ki-Gor's home, his only human neighbors were the Pygmies. And from old, wrinkled-face Ngeeso, the Chief, down to the tiniest solemn child, they were devoted to Ki-Gor and Helene. The jungle man and his mate reciprocated this affection by just such gestures as killing fresh meat for the tiny forest denizens.

Now, as Ki-Gor strode tirelessly along, the drone of the insects took on a deeper undertone. That would be the waterfall, and Ki-Gor knew he was not far from home, that lovely sanctuary on the island in the rapids below the falls. Helene would not be expecting him home so soon. Unconsciously, Ki-Gor's steps hastened a little. They always did when Ki-Gor got close to home. For, of all the things in heaven and on earth, nothing counted for so much as a single red hair on the head of his beautiful mate.

"Hai!" squeaked Ngeeso, considerably to the rear. "Art thou carrying the antelope, O Big Brother—or it thee?"

"What's the matter, Little One?" Ki-Gor laughed, stopping and turning around. "Art thou getting too old and decrepit to keep up a normal pace any more?"

"A normal pace!" Ngeeso raged. "Aye, I can keep up a normal pace—even when the trees grow far apart in spots as they do along here. But I never was able to keep up with one who lunges along the ground like a charging leopard!"

The little man swung himself to a bough above Ki-Gor, his tiny bow and quiver flapping against his wrinkled torso. There he sat for

a moment puffing and blowing indignantly, while Ki-Gor laughed up at him. Then, Ngeeso's beady little eyes, scanning the forest restlessly suddenly fixed themselves on a spot ahead on the trail.

"Speaking of leopards," Ngeeso said in a voice suddenly lowered, "unless my eyes mistaken me there is one not far away."

The laughter disappeared from Ki-Gor's bronzed face, and he watched Ngeeso's seamed face.

"Where, Little Brother?" he murmured, "in front of us?"

"Aye," Ngeeso muttered, "and it's as well I saw him. He is at some distance. The leaves are thin between us—else I had not seen him at all. I think—" the little man craned his neck—"I think he is stretched out on a bough directly over the trail."

"Aha," Ki-Gor murmured, "that is not too good."

He shifted the buck on his shoulders and prepared to drop it on the ground, but Ngeeso spoke.

"Nay, Big Brother, leave him to me. It is a long bowshot but—" he plucked a tiny arrow from the quiver—"I think I can reach him."

"As thou say," Ki-Gor shrugged. "Thy bow hand is still steady, but—"

"Oh, I will not miss him," Ngeeso said confidently, "as long as I can reach him. These arrows of ours have only to pierce the fur and make the veriest scratch. It will take a little while for the poison to travel through the veins. But when it does—no one will be troubled by *that* leopard any more."

"Those are dangerous things, those arrows of yours," Ki-Gor observed humorously. "I hope thou wilt always be quite sure of what thou shoot at. For instance, I wear a breechclout of leopard skin. It would be most awkward, O Little One, if one fine day thou shot me by mistake thinking I was a leopard."

Ngeeso giggled as he raised the bow.

"Thou art forever joking, Big Brother, and mocking me. Be still now, for a moment while I take aim. This is no easy shot."

He squinted along the tiny arrow, then suddenly lowered the bow again to giggle.

"Imagine," he snorted, "mistaking thee for a leopard!"

ONCE AGAIN, he aimed the arrow, his beady eyes narrowing to deadly slits. It was a difficult shot only because of the distance involved. The little patch of spotted fur which he saw through the light screen of leaves did not budge. It was a motionless target. The brown claw which was his right hand drew the bowstring back steadily. Back, back it went until the bow was bent almost double.

Then two fingers of the claw flew open. There was a little *ping!* The tiny arrow flittered away through the air, carrying on its tip enough poison to kill an elephant if it struck an unprotected spot—the eye, for instance, or the inside of a nostril.

Ngeeso leaned forward from the bough following the flight of the little arrow. His mouth and eyes were wide open. Seconds went by, then the Pygmy gave a squeak of triumph.

"Got him!" he exclaimed. "A little high on the back, but I wanted to be sure the arrow wouldn't fall short—"

Suddenly, the Pygmy's voice died away with a little groan.

"Why—what's the matter, Little One?" Ki-Gor demanded.

Ngeeso's eyes were bulging with horror.

"Aie, me!" he whispered, and began beating his breast slowly. "Ai! Big Brother, what have I done!"

"What, what?" Ki-Gor cried fiercely in sudden alarm.

"It—it is no leopard!" Ngeeso sobbed, "I see—I see—white flesh!"

Just then there came a piercing scream from down the trail, and another—and still another.

"Ki-Gor! Ki-Gor! KI-GOR!"

It was Helene's voice.

For a second, Ki-Gor was numb. Then horror began to roll up and down his back in great ripples. Helene wore leopard skin, too.

"Thou murderous little monkey—" he bellowed, in a strangled voice. He flung the antelope from his shoulders and pounded up the trail, moaning.

To Ki-Gor every step seemed an eternity. Actually, it was scarcely six seconds before he was standing under a tall baobab tree looking upward.

Helene was stretched out on a bough twenty feet over the trail, staring down with bloodless face, her fingers clutching the bark of the limb spasmodically.

"Oh, Ki-Gor!" she moaned, "thank heavens you were near! One of the Pygmies shot a poisoned arrow at me... I'm sure it was a mistake—"

"Where did it hit?" Ki-Gor demanded, tensely.

"The small of my back," Helene replied. "Hit the leopard fur a half inch away from my own skin."

"Did it go through?" Ki-Gor hardly dared listen for answer.

"I—I don't know," Helene stammered. "I felt a slight bump. Then I looked back over my shoulder and saw the arrow...."

"Don't move a muscle," Ki-Gor commanded, and started up the tangle of vines that coursed twistingly up the huge tree trunk.

His mind was numb, and his hands and feet worked purely automatically to hoist him up to the bough on which Helene was outstretched. It could not be! He told himself, it must not be! The arrow must not have penetrated the leopard skin! The veriest scratch, Ngeeso had said, and it would take but a little while for the poison to go through the veins.

Ki-Gor hauled himself up to the bough and crept out toward the prone body of his mate. Another wave of horror swept over him as he saw the arrow. The tiny, deadly shaft, hardly a foot long, was slanting into the back of Helene's abbreviated leopard skin garment at the small of her back. A half inch to the right, and it would have penetrated Helene's own fair skin. But chance—or Ngeeso's fine shooting—had sent it into the leopard skin.

It was that fact that enabled Ki-Gor to get a grip on himself. It remained to be seen whether the point had gone through and scratched Helene's skin beneath. While there was a chance that it had not—there was hope. Ki-Gor bent over his mate's still form.

"Keep perfectly still," he said gently, and calmly. His right hand went down to the edge of the leopard skin garment just above the arrow. Slowly, ever so slowly, he drew the leopard skin up and away from Helene's tanned skin.

A thrill of joy went through Ki-Gor as he perceived that the leopard skin lifted away without resistance. Warily, though, his left hand went to the feathered butt of the arrow and drew it out of the leopard skin. Then he lifted the garment higher—and now his hands began to tremble a little—and peered at, Helene's skin underneath. Long and carefully, his keen eyes searched the smooth velvety surface. Then he took a deep breath and dropped the leopard skin back into place.

The arrow had not so much as touched Helene's skin.

Thanks to the angle at which it had struck, it had not penetrated the leopard skin. Ki-Gor's head began to swim a little. He quickly dropped the deadly little arrow to the ground, and moved backward carefully along the bough.

"It is all right, Helene," he said and his voice was trembling a little. "It is all right. The poison didn't touch you—there is no danger."

"Oh!" Helene gasped. "Oh, thank heaven!"

She turned her head and looked back over her shoulder with a wan smile. But the smile began to broaden immediately, the blue eyes twinkling.

"Why, Ki-Gor!" she chuckled. "Your face is positively gray! Oh! and look behind you—behind your right shoulder."

Ki-Gor quickly twisted his head around. On the branch just above him sat Ngeeso. His seamed little face was set in agonized lines, and his right hand clutched one of his own arrows half way down the shaft. The poisoned tip was a scant inch away from Ngeeso's own leathery neck.

"What did thine eyes see, Big Brother?" the Pygmy said quaveringly. "Did the tip…?"

"The tip did not touch her, Little One," Ki-Gor interrupted quickly. "Put down that arrow!"

"Art thou positive, O Big Brother?" Ngeeso persisted. "Because if I caused the death of thy mate—even unwittingly—then must Ngeeso decently die as soon as possible."

"Nay, nay, Little Friend, no harm has been done."

"Ai-ee!" Ngeeso wailed, moving the arrow down from his neck, but still holding it in his hand. "But suppose—suppose—"

"Forget it!" Ki-Gor commanded, and quoted a Pygmy proverb. "If the arrow fail to hit the bird, it is as if it had never been fired."

"Ai-ee!" Ngeeso moaned disconsolately, "Thou art too kind, Big Brother. I cannot bear it!"

It took Helene and Ki-Gor at least ten minutes to persuade Ngeeso that he should not punish himself for the accident which came so near to having fatal consequences. But at the end of those ten minutes Ngeeso finally replaced the arrow in his quiver, and both Ki-Gor's and Helene's nerves had returned to normal.

"You know," Helene said, as the trio resumed the journey toward the island home, "we really ought to know some sort of antidote to whatever poison they use on those arrows."

"Yes, we should," Ki-Gor agreed grimly. "But there isn't any that I know of. Or that the Little People know of either."

"Why that's terrible!" Helene observed. "Suppose one of them accidentally scratched himself…"

"That has happened," Ki-Gor said. "And when it did—there was no hope. The little man died."

Helene shivered.

"That's why I nearly went crazy," Ki-Gor said simply.

"Well, that's not right," Helene declared. "Somewhere there must be an antidote. I suppose they get the poison from a plant, don't they?"

"Yes," Ki-Gor said, "I know the plant."

"You do?" Helene said thoughtfully. "You know—there is someone who I'll bet would know the antidote. He was a great herb doctor-that Hindu doctor that helped you escape from the slave traders."

"Hurree Das," Ki-Gor murmured. "Yes, he might. He knew a great deal about all kinds of plants. Yes, Hurree Das might know."

"Why don't we make a trip sometime up north and visit him?" Helene suggested.

"All right," Ki-Gor said. "The next time we go up to see Tembu George. Hurree Das is about a week's journey northwest of George. We will do it. But not for several weeks."

CHAPTER II

KI-GOR DID NOT KNOW it then, but he and Helene were destined to be traveling northward much sooner than several weeks from then. Destiny was, in fact, awaiting them just a hundred yards up the trail, in the person of a tall, uneasy Kara-mzili youth.

The Kara-mzili had a right to be uneasy. He was crouching, eyes rolling, under the great tree which supported one end of the rope bridge to the island. And above him in the tree, a half dozen of Ngeeso's Pygmies had arrows trained on him.

"Hai, Bwana Ki-Gor!" the youth cried breathlessly as the jungle man and his mate came into view. "Tell the Little People I come as a friend! They have threatened me with the poisoned death in their little arrows for too long. We Kara-mzili are brave—but that is a horrible death."

"Calm your fears," Ki-Gor said. "They will not shoot until you do something unfriendly. Why did you come here?"

"I bring a message, O Bwana Ki-Gor," the young black said. "An urgent message from Dingazi, King of the Kara-mzili, Protector of the Race, Emperor of the World."

"Dingazi!" Ki-Gor exclaimed in astonishment. "Dingazi sends me a message!"

"Aye, that he does!" the youth cried. "The great King is troubled by things that are happening in Kara-mzililand. He desires your advice. He begs you to make the journey to Dutawayo as fast as you can come!"

Ki-Gor stared at the messenger. Dingazi was a tremendously powerful potentate. He ruled over a large territory with a population of not less than four million souls. He had a magnificent army of nearly thirty thousand men, well-disciplined and drilled in Zulu tactics. What possible trouble could Dingazi be in that he should call upon Ki-Gor to help him out?

Yet, if Dingazi *were* in some trouble and needed Ki-Gor's help, Ki-Gor could not refuse it. It was not too many months before that Dingazi bad, almost single-handed, dared his own subjects' hysterical blood-lust to protect the lives of Ki-Gor, Helene and Tembu George— all of whom were then at Dingazi's court.

"What is the trouble?" Ki-Gor bluntly asked the messenger.

"I do not know," the youth said. "I am but a messenger. There are rumors about invaders from the north."

"Invaders?" Ki-Gor said incredulously. "Who dares to invade Kara-mzililand? Not the Maasai—for they are friendly, and are connected by marriage. Who else is there to dare the might of Dingazi's *impis?*"

"I don't rightly know," the youth confessed. "But it is said that there is some sort of mighty ju-ju being performed. The rumors say our border guards are slain before they could see the enemy. They say also that the subject tribes in the north are rising."

"I can't believe it," Ki-Gor said slowly. "Why does not Tembu George and the Maasai come to Dingazi's aid?"

"Maybe he has sent for them," the messenger suggested. "I only know that Dingazi sent me to bid you hasten to him."

"Very well, then," Ki-Gor said, with decision. "We will come." He turned to the Pygmies in the tree. "Hai, Little Brothers, have you seen aught of the great gray elephant? Is he hereabouts?"

"Aye, Big Brother," the Pygmies chorused, "that he is—just above the falls stuffing himself with the lush grass beside the water."

"It is good," he said and turned to his mate. "I will go after Marmo. Will you go across and collect my war-gear and some food? The Little Ones will help you bring them back over the bridge. We will start for Kara-mzililand as soon as I come back with Marmo."

DUTAWYO, THE capital of Kara-mzililand, was in a ferment of excitement by the time Ki-Gor, Helene, and the messenger arrived. Well-trained and docile as old Marmo was, he would obey Ki-Gor only up to certain points. He did not like towns and crowds, and he had, therefore, stopped of his own accord in the outskirts of Dingazi's capital and let his passengers off.

As the trio walked through the crowded, noisy streets, an excited throng gathered in their wake and followed them up the hill to Dingazi's kraal. Ki-Gor was quick to notice one thing about the crowd, and that was that they were excited without knowing exactly what they were excited about. They were bewildered and uncertain. Whatever the menace on the northern border was, the Kara-mzili had heard only rumors—they had been told no facts.

At the gateway to the royal kraal, a young warrior stepped forward and informed Ki-Gor that Dingazi would receive him immediately. This was unusual. Dingazi loved his pomp and ceremony as well as any other African monarch, and out of sheer autocratic whim he would keep his dearest friend waiting for two days for an audience. It was an indication, therefore, of the extreme urgency of the situation, that Dingazi did not stand on the usual ceremony now, but wished Ki-Gor to come and see him without delay.

As Ki-Gor and Helene walked into Dingazi's large circular throne room, the old king was lost in thought, staring at a piece of parchment in his hands. A tense silence prevailed among the score and a half persons in the room, as Dingazi sat motionless on his throne—a vast, thick-shouldered, pot-bellied man, naked to the waist and wearing the yellow-and-black striped kilt of his own bodyguards.

Ki-Gor stepped forward unafraid and spoke.

"Greetings, O Dingazi!" he intoned. "Emperor of the World, All-Conquering Lion!"

Dingazi's massive head jerked tip.

"Hail, Ki-Gor!" he roared. "White Lord of the Jungle—whose Kingdom lies in the direction of the Four Winds! Right glad am I to see thee and thy slender wife! Come, we will go to my apartments and talk over the strange happenings up on the Border. By the Gods! I don't know whether to laugh about them or fly into a rage!"

Dingazi stood up, a huge figure, and slowly stepped down off the throne-dais. Four of his guards hastened to his side. There was a party of strangers in front of the throne—Arabs, by their dress. Three men and a heavily veiled woman, they were, and they drifted to one side as Ki-Gor and Helene came toward the King. Dingazi clamped a huge hand on Ki-Gor's wrist and led him off to a doorway on the right side of the room. In the other hand, the king still held the piece of parchment.

It was a strange story Dingazi had to tell....

ABOUT TWO weeks before, a messenger had arrived from the north, bearing a report from the leader of a small military outpost on the rugged, broken frontier. This leader had noticed smoke rising from behind the hills to the west of his post. He had taken a squad of men to investigate. He had eventually come upon the smoking ruins of a village. And they were truly ruins. The village had been completely destroyed, and every single inhabitant had been killed or abducted. There was not one living thing in the village.

The messenger went on to say that the only clues as to the identity of the raiders were footprints. There were all manner of footprints, indicating a considerable force. Among the prints were some which looked like zebra tracks except that they were much larger. And there were other tracks that were unmistakably elephants' spoor.

The conclusion of the message was to the effect that the leader of the patrol intended to follow the tracks northward and catch up with the raiders.

However, there was no word from that patrol leader for two days. As a matter of fact, he and his patrol were never heard from again. The next messenger came from a different patrol farther to the east.

This messenger had much the same story to tell. A village desolated with no survivors to tell of the disaster or of the perpetrators. This time, there was less evidence left. The raiders had driven off the cattle of the villagers and had covered most of their own tracks in doing so.

Dingazi had dispatched reinforcements to the frontier posts with orders to keep him informed. But five days went by without a word from the frontier.

Finally, a small trading safari of Arabs had come to Dutawayo and delivered to Dingazi a roll of parchment which they said had been given to them by a mysterious veiled horseman.

"A horseman!" Ki-Gor interjected.

"That is what the Arabs said," Dingazi replied. "And here is the parchment. What language is the writing on it? I cannot read it."

Ki-Gor took the parchment wonderingly. "It is written in English," he said, after a moment.

"What does it say?" Dingazi demanded.

Ki-Gor studied the parchment without speaking for some time. When he looked up again, his face was perplexed.

"O Dingazi," he said. "This message is hard to believe. If it were not for the other things that have been happening, I would say it was an impudent joke."

"A joke?" Dingazi said grimly. "My destroyed villages are no joke, or my frontier guards who have vanished without a trace."

"I will read it to you," Ki-Gor said, "and you may judge for yourself."

Helene moved over beside him and looked curiously over his shoulder. Her face, too, took on a perplexed expression. Slowly, Ki-Gor translated:

"To Dingazi, Chief of the Kara-mzili—"

"Chief!" Dingazi exploded. "Who dares to address a King—an All-Conquering Emperor as a petty chief!"

"I am but reading you the message, O King," Ki-Gor said patiently. "There is much worse to come. It goes on, 'Know then, Dingazi, that your days as a ruler are numbered—'"

Dingazi splattered wrathfully, but subsided as Ki-Gor continued.

"—'unless you make due amends for the crimes committed against me by your stupid subjects!'"

"Crimes!" Dingazi gasped. "What crimes?"

Ki-Gor shrugged and went on, " 'First some villagers wantonly attacked my people who were passing peacefully through their village. When we punished them for their impudence, you sent soldiers after us. My people well know how to take care of them. Your insolent troops have been annihilated. Any others you think to send against me will meet a like fate. Be warned, Dingazi! My patience is nearly exhausted! Stop this insolent aggression against my peaceful people! If you cease your senseless resistance, and agree to pay an indemnity, then you will not be harmed. You may continue to rule the Kara-mzili until you die.

"Upon payment of one hundred pounds of gold, five hundred tusks, one thousand pounds of salt, and every tame elephant in your kingdom, I will agree not to wage war against you during your lifetime. Failure to make this payment will result in a lightning invasion of your lands. The Sword of Hannibal as wielded by me, his descendant, will fall on the Kara-mzili with unexampled ferocity, killing and enslaving! The tribes subject to you will rise against you. Your power will be shorn from you! And you, Dingazi, will be dressed in chains! Be warned, Dingazi!—in time! (Signed) Queen Julebba—the Tigress of T'wanbi."

Having finished the translation of this extraordinary ultimatum,

Ki-Gor handed the parchment back toward Dingazi. The old man struck it to the floor in a fury and stood glaring at it in rage.

"Who—" gasped the king, finding his voice at last—"who is Queen Julebba? Who dares to send *me, Dingazi,* such a monstrous message? What sort of people are these who slaughter peaceful villagers in the dead of night!"

KI-GOR SAT down while Dingazi's fury blew itself out. At last, the old king fell silent. His eyes rolled at Ki-Gor and something close to a grin appeared on his broad, black face. "This is silly," he declared. "It is silly for me to be upset by such a thing. Queen Julebba!"

Dingazi snorted. "Still, I suppose I'd better send an expedition after these raiders right away, before they do too much damage. What do you think, Ki-Gor?"

"I don't know what to think," the jungle man replied. "Tell me, O Dingazi, is there no one who has brought you firsthand information about them?"

"No one," Dingazi replied promptly. "There are plenty who have come with rumors, but no one to tell me how many of the raiders there are—or even what they look like. Much less does anyone know of this woman who calls herself Queen Julebba."

"What about the Arabs who brought this parchment to you?" Ki-Gor persisted. "Do you believe that they saw only a single horseman?"

Dingazi looked thoughtful for a moment, then he barked a command to one of his guards. A moment later, one of the Arabs was led into the room, and Dingazi began questioning him. The Arab maintained that he had seen only a single horseman. It was in the evening when the light was poor, but he had seen that the man's face was wrapped in cloth. However, the Arab said that he had talked with some villagers who had seen a good-sized force near the place where the veiled horseman had stopped the safari.

Dingazi finally dismissed the Arab and sent for his companions who were brought in one by one and questioned singly. The other two men corroborated the first Arab's story about the villagers seeing a foreign army, although these later versions increased the size of that army considerably.

But the last person to be questioned held different views on the subject. It was the woman, tall and slender under the voluminous outer garment which veiled her from her head to her toes. Ki-Gor caught just a glimpse of flashing eyes behind the narrow slit in the cloth, and he sent a quick glance at Helene at the sound of the Arab woman's deep dramatic voice.

"How can I speak of an army which I scarcely saw?" she said contemptuously in Swahili, "and yet I saw more than my father and brothers. I saw a few veiled horsemen, a few black spearmen. There may have been more—there may not. But they have caused great destruction up in the north, so much that my father and brothers think it is a large army. I think not, but then I don't know."

Dingazi stared at her in puzzlement for a moment, then turned to Ki-Gor.

"Wah!" he said. "How can I get at the truth? One says one thing, another says another. I'll send up five *impis*. That should be enough to smoke out the dogs!"

"Five *impis!*" It was the Arab woman, with a voice full of scorn. "Five thousand men to beat off a border raid! What a joke on the mighty Kara-mzili! Why, that would be like sending out an elephant to destroy a cockroach!"

Dingazi looked at the woman, startled.

"What do you know of *impis*, O Veiled Woman?" he demanded.

"Who does not know of Dingazi's *impis!*" she retorted. "The fame of the Kara-mzili war-might knows no bounds! For many moons have I crossed back and forth through your domains with my father and brothers, and nowhere else have I seen the equal of a Kara-mzili *impi.*"

Dingazi sent her away with a pleased smile. "Who would have thought," he observed, "that an Arab woman would notice such things? I am glad I talked to her. It was quite true what she said. If I sent five *impis*, we would be a laughingstock."

The old king turned to a guard. "Bring Lotoko in here," he commanded. Then to Ki-Gor he said, "Lotoko commanded my armies when I originally conquered that northern territory. I will send him up with half an *impi* to capture this impudent Julebba."

Ki-Gor was silent while Lotoko came in and received his orders and instructions from the king. The jungle man was much less satisfied than Dingazi to accept the opinion of the Arab woman over that of her father and brothers. For one thing, Ki-Gor wondered why there should be a difference of opinion among the Arabs at all. They had presumably seen the same things and had the same opportunity to form an opinion. Yet the Arab men thought Julebba had a formidable force, and the woman thought she had not. It was very confusing.

Another thing bothered Ki-Gor, too. As his mind went back to the message from the mysterious Julebba, he realized that in a strict sense, it was not an ultimatum, Julebba had made specific demands, but she had laid no time-limit on the satisfaction of those demands. Furthermore, and this seemed very important to Ki-Gor, *she had made no provision at all for Dingazi's answering the ultimatum!* Was that an oversight? Ki-Gor wondered. Or was it intentional? In other words, could it be that the message was not really intended to be answered, but was designed only to terrorize an aging monarch?

Ki-Gor was roused from his thoughts by Dingazi.

"Accept my gratitude, O Friend," the king said, "for coming so promptly to read the writing on the parchment. I thought it looked like English, therefore I sent for you as soon as I received it. I hope now that you and your woman will visit with me for many days."

As a matter of courtesy, Ki-Gor accepted the invitation. But even as he did so, he knew that before the day was over he would probably volunteer his services and go northward with Lotoko's punitive expedition.

For Ki-Gor was discovering within himself an overpowering curiosity concerning Queen Julebba.

EARLY THE next morning, Helene took her place with Ki-Gor beside Lotoko at the head of five hundred kilted Kara-mzili who were to march north to deal with the mysterious Julebba. There was still a glint in Helene's eye, and Ki-Gor's face wore a look of resignation. Helene had flatly refused to be left behind at Dutawayo as Ki-Gor had proposed, while he went away with the column. But it had taken some time to convince him that she could take care of herself perfectly well on the expedition.

"You know I can, Ki-Gor," she had argued. "I've learned so much since that day when my plane cracked up in the middle of the jungle. If you hadn't come along and protected me, I wouldn't have lived the day out, probably. But that was a long time ago, Ki-Gor, and I'm no longer a spoiled darling of Society."

Ki-Gor had not been able to dispute that. From the very beginning Helene had been an apt pupil in the jungle lore in which Ki-Gor schooled her. She could keep pace with Ki-Gor's long tireless strides along the elephant trails; she could travel the tree-route; she could read spoors, and stalk small game, and she could even handle a light spear well.

"It isn't that you would be in the way," Ki-Gor had said, finally, "but I don't think this expedition is going to be so easy as Dingazi does. There is something very peculiar about these raiders, and the way they work. I smell danger up there in the north, somehow."

"Well, then, that settles it," Helene had said firmly. "You can't deny me the right to share any and all danger with you. I always have shared it, and I always will."

And so Helene went north with Ki-Gor and the Kara-mzili expedition.

CHAPTER III

LOTOKO EXPECTED TO ARRIVE on the frontier in three days' time. But even before the end of the first days' march, the expedition began to run into evidence that the raiders were perhaps more powerful than they had originally been estimated. Just before sundown, the force marched into a good-sized village and found its inhabitants in a ferment. They were all making preparations for immediate evacuation and flight toward Dutawayo.

The village headman informed Lotoko that the mysterious invaders were already far into Kara-mzililand, striking secretly and swiftly at night, burning and slaying, and leaving hardly any survivors. The headman said the invaders had hundreds of men, perhaps thousands. There were horsemen, terrifying creatures in turbans and with their faces swathed in cloth. There were elephants, too, trained to war, and even hundreds of apes who climbed over village stockades with lighted torches.

When Lotoko asked the headman how he had learned these things, the man answered that the information had come from some people from the next village. Lotoko looked thoughtful. He knew that there was no way of keeping this news from spreading through the ranks of his little force.

The next day the expedition went through two more villages and even more discouraging reports about the size and ferocity of Queen Julebba's raiders. In fact, if the stories were true, the enemy could hardly be called raiders—they must be an army of invasion. Lotoko called Ki-Gor and Helene to one side.

"I don't like this," Lotoko confessed. "Dingazi did not give me enough men to fight an army of that size."

"You have heard only rumors," Ki-Gor pointed out. "You still don't know the actual size of the enemy."

"No, but the rumors all point in the same direction," Lotoko said gloomily. "We Kara-mzili are brave. But the bravest of men don't like to be sacrificed because of someone's mistake."

"Then send a messenger back to Dutawayo for more men," Ki-Gor suggested. "But remember one thing—not one person who has talked about the size of the enemy force has seen it. Every report you have heard has been at second hand."

Just at that moment, there was a great hullabaloo among the warriors, and presently several of them dragged a strange black up to Lotoko. Here, the warriors said, was a man who had actually seen the enemy and could give first-hand information. Lotoko began to question him.

At first, the man seemed too frightened to talk, but gradually he grew more confident and readily gave information. The story he had to tell was even more discouraging than the rumors they had heard from the villagers.

There were, the man said, at least two thousand in Queen Julebba's army. There were spearmen, bowmen, and horsemen. Yes, there were elephants, too, he said, and trained apes. And what was more, the army was perfectly led and fought like demons. In fact, the man added shivering, there could be no doubt that this Queen Julebba was a strong ju-ju herself and could infect her troops with that quality.

All during this questioning, Ki-Gor was studying the man. He was not at all the physical type of Kara-mzililand. He was blacker, shorter-legged, more powerfully built. Ki-Gor had seen his type in Nigeria, far to the northwest. The man had said that he came from one of the border villages that was destroyed, and was—as far as he knew—the only survivor. He had climbed a tree, he said, and had lain unseen while the ferocious invaders ravaged and slaughtered. After they had razed the village, they were gone as suddenly as they came, and after a long time, he came down from his tree and fled southward warning the other villagers on his way.

It would have been a plausible story, even to Ki-Gor, if it had not been for his race. But the jungle man kept wondering what a Nigerian would be doing in a Kara-mzili village. And the more Lotoko questioned the man, the more Ki-Gor suspected that he was not quite what he pretended to be. His information was too complete, too detailed.

After Lotoko had finished with the man, he ordered his release, and turned to Ki-Gor with an apprehensive face.

"This is very bad," he admitted. "I cannot turn back. It would lower the prestige of the Kara-mzili tradition. Besides, Dingazi would probably have me killed. And yet, to go forward against such superior forces is not wise. To be sure, we would probably give a good account of ourselves—"

"One moment, Lotoko," Ki-Gor said. "I wouldn't believe everything that fellow said if I were you."

"Why—what do you mean?" Lotoko demanded.

"I'm going to follow him," Ki-Gor said. "I want to see where he goes and what he does. I might even decide to have a talk with him."

"What for?" Lotoko said, wonderingly. "He is just a simple villager with good powers of observation—"

"Maybe he isn't just a simple villager," Ki-Gor said. "At any rate, I'm going to find out. When you order the march resumed, I'll stay behind, I'll rejoin you sometime tomorrow."

It took Ki-Gor several minutes to persuade Helene to go ahead with Lotoko and the column, but she agreed when he pointed out that he would be gone only a day and a night.

WHEN THE force moved off behind Lotoko and Helene, Ki-Gor stayed behind—inconspicuous in the foliage beside the trail. Then he drifted back to the last village the column passed through. The Nigerian was just leaving it on his way southward. Ki-Gor skirted the village unseen and picked up his trail.

The man seemed to be in a considerable hurry, and at first Ki-Gor found some difficulty in keeping up with him and still keeping out of sight. After a while, though, the man's very haste convinced Ki-Gor that he did not suspect he was being followed. So without troubling much to stay hidden, Ki-Gor maintained a steady pace about three hundred yards behind the Nigerian.

In this way Ki-Gor followed his man nearly four miles. Then the trail temporarily deserted the jungle for the short grass of the veldt. Ki-Gor could see ahead of him a considerable distance. His Nigerian was nowhere in sight.

What had happened to him? Ki-Gor asked himself. Had the man

suddenly decided that he was being followed—and dropped down beside the trail to let Ki-Gor pass him? Or had the Nigerian simply left the trail and gone away in another direction?

Ki-Gor searched the dust of the trail, and clearly saw the man's spoor. He continued his tireless, ground-covering gait, but kept his eyes fixed on the Nigerian's footprints. If it seemed that the Nigerian had stepped off the trail to let him pass, Ki-Gor intended to go on past him and do the same thing himself farther along.

But then it occurred to Ki-Gor that the Nigerian might read the tail of footprints just as well as he did. So the jungle man suddenly and completely changed his tactics.

Just as the Nigerian's footprints swerved off the trail, Ki-Gor halted abruptly and called out in an injured tone.

"Hai, Brother!" he said, "What is the trouble? Are you hurt? Or are you avoiding me? For the past four miles I have been trying to catch up with you, so that we could keep journey together. But you have traveled a mighty pace."

There was no answer to this overture, but Ki-Gor could see the tops of the two-foot grass quiver about twenty feet away.

"Hai, Brother!" Ki-Gor said in a louder voice. "Why do you hide from me? I am not your enemy. I am no man's enemy. And I ask nothing of you except your company for as long as you intend to travel this path."

There was another long silence. Suddenly, the Nigerian sprang out of the grass and came toward Ki-Gor. His hands were empty, and he wore an exceedingly sheepish expression on his wide face.

"I—I—er—thought you were following me," the man said. "I didn't know what your intentions were. Nowadays, you can't be too careful. Anyway, I saw you with the Kara-mzili warriors."

"Yes," Ki-Gor said amiably, "I came back to carry the warning to the villages between here and Dutawayo. Down here about a mile, the trail branches. I thought I would take one branch and you the other."

"It is good," the Nigerian said, relief spreading over his features. "The people must be warned. You will help. It is good."

Ki-Gor noticed that the man's Swahili was not very good. He was half tempted to say something in Hausa, or some other northwestern language, and observe the effect on the man. But he decided against ft. He was after bigger game than this one Nigerian.

The Nigerian was not especially disposed to talk—perhaps he realized his Swahili would not stand up under close observation—and after a while Ki-Gor gave up any attempt at a continued conversation. When they arrived at the fork in the trail, the Nigerian brightened.

"I will take the road to the left," he announced. "Fare thee well."

"Go in peace," Ki-Gor smiled and swung off down the right hand path. He was well satisfied to be taking this branch. It turned and went straight back into forest country, whereas the left fork continued over the open rolling veldt.

As soon as he was out of sight of the Nigerian, he began to consider his next move. Although he doubted the Nigerian's talents for stalking, he had to allow for the possibility that the man would follow his trail for a while to make sure he had gone. He moved along at a swift pace for a half a mile—until he was well within the woods. All the way he stayed consistently on one side of the trail close to the grass and underbrush.

When he thought he had traveled a safe distance, he simply stepped off the path. He went straight to the nearest large tree and climbed into the lower branches. Then, traveling the tree-route, he back-trailed some four hundred yards. It was as well that he took care to go silently. For he caught sight of the Nigerian standing in the middle of the trail indecisively. The man was looking down at the ground and then up the trail.

Finally, the Nigerian decided, apparently, that Ki-Gor had really gone on to the next village. He turned around and began to lope away in the direction in which he had come.

Ki-Gor gave him a fair headstart, and then set off to follow him. But this time, Ki-Gor was going to keep himself well out of sight.

THREE HOURS later, just before sundown, Ki-Gor watched his Nigerian cautiously enter a narrow, wooded kloof at the base of a range of low hills. Scarcely had the man entered the wall of trees before he stopped and began to talk out loud, in the Kanuri dialect of northeastern Nigeria. But Ki-Gor quickly realized that the man was talking to someone who was hidden nearby.

"I do not see you," the Nigerian said. "Do you see me? It is Yako, the Spearman."

There was a moment's silence, then a voice from somewhere answered.

"Pass, Yako the Spearman," the voice said, and Ki-Gor could nowhere see the owner of the voice.

Yako went on into the kloof, but Ki-Gor stayed where he was. It would be unwise to follow until he had located the unseen watchman. Darkness would come within an hour, and Ki-Gor decided to wait for it, rather than blunder into trouble.

In a very short time, another figure entered the woods, announced himself, and was permitted to pass. Then two men came along together. After that, there was a space of fifteen minutes or so when nothing happened. Then Ki-Gor felt a slight vibration of the ground. It slowly increased, and after a while, he could make out the sound of horses' hooves.

At first, Ki-Gor thought it was a single horse at a gallop. Then, in the gathering dusk, he perceived that there were several horses coming into the kloof at a slow walk. They were in single file, and Ki-Gor blinked incredulously when he saw that it was the group of Arab traders he had seen in Dingazi's house at Dutawayo.

The leader of the file was the veiled woman.

As she came to the place where Yako the Spearman had been challenged, she reined in her horse. Dropping the reins, then, she lifted the skirts of the long outer garment, and drew it up over her shoulders and head. A moment later, the garment was lying across the pommel, and the daughter of the Arab trader sat her horse bareheaded and unveiled.

Ki-Gor stared in amazement. She was without doubt one of the most beautiful women he had ever seen in his life.

She tilted her firm, exquisitely modeled chin upward, and flashed huge black eyes up toward the trees.

"Do you see me, O Watchman?" she demanded, in the deep thrilling voice Ki-Gor had already heard in Dutawayo.

"I see you, O Queen!" the hidden watchman declaimed. "Pass, Mighty Conqueror, Spotless Virgin, Gracious Queen! Your devoted army awaits your coming, O Julebba!"

Ki-Gor just did suppress an involuntary gasp of amazement. Julebba! The daughter of the Arab trader! What magnificent audacity!

As she moved away under the trees followed by the three Arabs and the half dozen or so black spearmen that formed the guard, Ki-Gor pondered the extraordinary situation.

WHO THIS astounding young woman was, and what had brought her down from the north to make unprovoked war on such a formidable nation as the Kara-mzili—all that was beside the point. The most important fact was that she was at war with Dingazi, and that she was carrying on that war with the most unbelievable originality and daring. Just how big her army was Ki-Gor did not yet know—he intended to see it that night—but it could not be so very large to be contained in a comparatively small mountain kloof. But, however large the army was, she was supplementing its striking force with two other tremendous weapons. They were Terror and Confusion.

She had annihilated border villages, taking care that there were no survivors to tell of the deeds. The only persons who told the Kara-mzili of the invaders were her own men whom she had sent throughout the northern areas with tall stories of the invaders. That these agents had succeeded in spreading terror and confusion among the Kara-mzili Ki-Gor had already seen. Even Lotoko was worried before he had so much as laid an eye on Julebba's army.

Then as a brilliant cap to the climax, she had disguised herself as an Arab woman and coolly gone before Dingazi to confuse the old king completely as to the nature and strength of her forces. Ki-Gor had to shake his head admiringly when he recollected that she had herself persuaded Dingazi to send not five *impis* but only one-tenth of that force—five hundred men, instead of five thousand.

Ki-Gor guessed the fate that Julebba planned for Lotoko's little force. She would probably try to destroy it without a trace, and by the very mystery of its disappearance throw all the Kara-mzili into such a state of terror that they would no longer have the will to fight.

His course of action became clear. He must get past that hidden watchman, go into the kloof, find out as much as he could about Julebba's army, and then hasten off to rejoin Lotoko and Helene.

The first problem, that of getting past the watchman, he decided to leave until dusk had faded out entirely. If the watchman could not see him, he could not challenge him. To be sure, it might be possible to crawl off to one side and slip into the kloof through the tangle of undergrowth. But the entrance to the ravine was very narrow, and he would not really be far enough away from the path at any event. So, he settled himself to wait for another twenty minutes or so.

But, just at that moment, Ki-Gor heard a scraping sound. He fixed his eyes on the tree in which he suspected the watchman was concealed.

There, coming slowly down the trunk, was a huge black. Puzzled, Ki-Gor watched the man descend to the ground. He was carrying something in one hand—just what it was, there was not enough light to see. But from the man's subsequent actions, Ki-Gor got a very good idea of what it was.

It was fine rope or string of some kind, and the man was stretching it across the path, securing both ends at the base of two trees on either side. It was a neat trap for any stranger who might creep along in the dark and try to enter the kloof unseen.

IN VIEW of this complication, Ki-Gor decided to wait no longer, but to take direct action. Knowing the string was there, he might successfully locate it and step across it without disturbing it. But then again he might not. Furthermore, he might have to leave the kloof in a hurry, in which case it would be better not to have a string stretched across the path.

Very seldom did Ki-Gor kill a man in cold blood, but he knew he would have to do that to this guard. It would not do to allow him a chance to cry out and bring down Julebba's entire army on him.

The guard was bending over now, tying one of the strings, his back to Ki-Gor. The jungle man gathered his legs under him. Then he shot up and forward as if his great body were released from a bowstring. He covered the ground between him and the watchman in three heartbeats.

The watchman gave a little cry of alarm and half-turned. By that time, Ki-Gor was upon him. His left arm went around the man's neck, bending him backward. His right hand closed over the watchman's mouth, stifling his outcry to a gurgling groan. Ki-Gor thought of the hundreds of innocent Kara-mzili villagers that Julebba's men had slaughtered—and tightened his hold.

Suddenly there was a wild yell from above. An ugly shock of alarm went through Ki-Gor. At the same moment, the man in his arms bounced—as if something had hit him. Ki-Gor looked down over the man's shoulder and saw a long arrow sticking into the black chest. The watchman went limp. In the meantime, the yelling continued from the tree above.

Ki-Gor cursed himself for not thinking of the possibility that there were two watchmen. A second arrow whizzed past his ear. Something had to be done about that second watchman, and right away. Shifting his grip, Ki-Gor lifted the limp man in his arms, using him as a shield, and staggered forward toward the base of the tree from which he had come. Still another arrow smacked into the ground beside him, and the watcher in the tree continued to bawl out.

With a sudden, quick movement, Ki-Gor flung the body of the first watchman on the ground. Simultaneously, he rolled away in the other direction. An arrow smacked into the inert body of the first watchman. But Ki-Gor was climbing the trunk of the tree, now, snaking up like a monkey before the archer could notch a new arrow and aim.

He just made it to the lowest limb when the bowman shot again. But Ki-Gor swung his body under the limb a fraction of a second before the arrow sang past him. The jungle man knew he was in a desperate position, but his very danger spurred him to more furious action. Almost automatically, his right leg swung over the bough and his body followed through. Hardly had he gained his feet, before he was leaping up the trunk to the next limb above.

Not until that moment did Ki-Gor see that the bowman was sitting astride that limb. There was an arrow already notched in the man's hands—an arrow that was meant for Ki-Gor's up-lifted throat. But before that arrow could be released, Ki-Gor's right hand had closed over a black ankle. Swiftly, relentlessly, he had jerked downward. Down fell bow and arrow as the black strove desperately to save himself. But the iron grip on his ankle never relaxed, and hauled him down inexorably, until he was hanging legs down from the bough. But now Ki-Gor was hanging by his hands, too, and he gathered his legs up under him and shot them forward. His feet hit the bowman's chest like twin battering rams.

The black gasped and groaned. His fingers relaxed their hold, and he dropped. It was nearly thirty feet to the ground, and he hit with a sickening thud and lay still.

Ki-Gor lost no time in getting down the tree. The bowman had undoubtedly been heard down in the kloof, and there would probably be very little time to escape. Ki-Gor hit the ground running and sped toward the spot where he had left his own bow, quiver and assegai. As he paused to scoop them up, he heard the drumming of horses' hooves. The pursuit had begun!

KI-GOR HESITATED a bare second while he made up his mind which was the most promising avenue of escape. His first impulse had been simply to run away out to the veldt, and trust to the darkness to swallow him up. But then he realized that he would not get far before the horsemen would overtake him. Furthermore, if he did somehow escape from them, he still would not have the information about this strange army that he wanted to take to Lotoko.

He whirled around with sudden decision and ran back toward the kloof. Thirty seconds later, a score of horsemen pounded down the path and reined in, shouting, around the bodies of the two watchmen. But Ki-Gor was already traveling the tree route thirty feet above and to one side of the path—toward the interior of the kloof. Burdened with his war-gear as he was, and traveling in almost pitch darkness, his progress was necessarily slow. But taking infinite care to avoid discovery, he worked his way to the edge of a small clearing in the middle of the kloof, and eventually stared down at a sight which Dingazi, King of the Kara-mzili would have given a great deal to see.

The first objects that caught Ki-Gor's eye in the torch-lighted scene below were the elephants. There were four of them, splendid bulls. They were uniformly big—almost as big as Marmo—and they were evidently well trained. They stood in a row on one side of the clearing, a score or so of black boys squatting on the ground in front of them. The dress of the blacks showed them to be Balubas from the elephant-country of the Belgian Congo.

Next, Ki-Gor's eyes traveled to the center of the clearing, to a pile of rocks on which had been placed a high-backed wooden throne. On that throne sat Julebba, a picture of barbaric splendor. Her beautiful head was lifted proudly high, the night-black hair falling straight and shining to her shoulders. An ivory necklace fell from the splendid column of her throat toward the jeweled breastplates which crowned her high tawny bosom. Below them her torso gleamed bare down to the narrow golden girdle, and her beautifully molded thighs were boldly outlined under the sheer white ankle-length skirt.

Completing the barbaric picture, she wore wide bands of dull gold on each upper arm, and her right hand gripped an efficient-looking, light spear.

There was a subdued murmur of many voices filling the clearing, but Julebba sat detached, aloof. It was as if she were waiting for something to happen, or someone to arrive. Perhaps, Ki-Gor shrewdly guessed, she was awaiting news about the disturbance at the entrance of the kloof.

Looking beyond her, he perceived that not all of her horsemen had ridden away down the path. There were still some twenty drawn up in a row behind her throne, and strange and fearsome they looked to Ki-Gor. He had never seen any such horsemen in his life. They looked a little bit like some Arabs he had seen, in that they wore turbans. But the turbans were a different shape from those worn by the traders and slaverunners of the East Coast. Furthermore, men of Julebba's had covered their faces, so that only narrow slits were left for them to see through.

To the left of Julebba's throne were massed about fifty rugged blacks armed with heavy spears. They were very likely fellow-Nigerians of Yako's. And on the other side of the throne, there were another fifty blacks—from the Ubangi country by their looks—and they were armed with longbows.

Ki-Gor counted the men in the clearing once again, remembering that there were probably about twenty horsemen absent. Then he marveled. Could this, he asked himself, be *all* of the dreaded army of invasion? The mysterious force that had ravaged and burned the northern border of Kara-mzililand, struck terror in the hearts of one of the stoutest-hearted races of Africa—could this be it? Less than a hundred and fifty men plus four elephants and their Baluba boys! It was truly unbelievable!

No wonder Julebba, in her Arab disguise, had persuaded Dingazi to send only five hundred men after her! She could not have successfully attacked one *impi*—much less five *impis!* As it was, Ki-Gor wondered how this handful could beat Lotoko's five hundred stout warriors. He began to understand why Julebba had so carefully laid her groundwork of confusion and terror, and spread the stories of great numbers of horsemen, spearmen, bowmen, elephants—and trained apes. Where, Ki-Gor suddenly asked himself, were the trained apes?

CHAPTER IV

JUST THEN A HORSEMAN galloped into the clearing from the path. The quiet hubbub ceased, and Julebba turned her head inquiringly. The horseman was not veiled, and Ki-Gor recognized the Arab who had posed as Julebba's father at Dingazi's court. The Arab reined in before the throne and spoke briefly to the queen. The language he used sounded like Arabic, which Ki-Gor did not understand, but as he held up two fingers, Ki-Gor guessed he was reporting two casualties at the entrance to the kloof. Julebba then asked some questions, to which the Arab seemed to reply negatively.

Ki-Gor began to get an uneasy hunch that it was time for him to think of leaving the scene. Just how he would get away he was not sure, although there was a possibility that he might be able to scale one of the steep sides of the kloof. It would be dangerous enough, for both sides were nearly perpendicular and consisted of rough, shaly rock. But dangerous or not, Ki-Gor decided to swing himself to the nearest bank and explore it.

But a new development in the clearing below caught his interest. He decided to stay a few more minutes and watch. It was a decision he very soon regretted.

The rest of the veiled horsemen were returning down the path, their horses at a walk. An angry murmur went over the Ubangi bowmen squatting beside the path, and Ki-Gor very quickly saw what caused it. The first two horsemen each bore one of the two sentinels that Ki-Gor had felled.

Julebba stood up suddenly, eyes flashing. She shouted a brief order in the Hausa dialect, and a half dozen of the Ubangi ran to the foot of her throne. The horsemen drew up beside them, whereupon the Ubangi lifted the two bodies gently down to the ground. Julebba swung around and shouted:

"The doctor! Where is the fat doctor?"

An indistinct figure rose up from the shadows near the elephants, and waddled toward the throne. Ki-Gor recognized him, and nearly fell out of his treetop with astonishment.

It was Hurree Das, the Hindu.

It was the very man Ki-Gor and Helene were talking about when Dingazi's messenger came to them. How Hurree Das came to be in Queen Julebba's army, Ki-Gor had not the faintest idea. The Hindu was a curious, and very droll character who by his own admission was a rascal. Ki-Gor had first encountered him among a gang of notorious slave-dealers. The Hindu had been a partner in the gang and shared in the profits which he earned as medical adviser. Yet when Ki-Gor had lain a prisoner of the gang, Hurree Das had saved him from a dreadful tortured death, even at the risk of his own life.

And now once again Hurree Das had come into Ki-Gor's life—and once again he was associated with a murderous gang. Only this time, the gang dignified itself with the title of "army," the chief a self-styled "queen."

Ki-Gor leaned forward fascinated as Hurree Das knelt down beside the bodies on the ground. He had not changed at all. There was the same plump, soft figure in the long black coat, the flimsy white cloth draped around his fat legs, the round black pillbox cap on his back curls.

"Well?" demanded Julebba, "What do you say, Doctor?"

Again Ki-Gor's mouth opened in wonderment—for Julebba had spoken in English! Then he remembered that her "ultimatum" to Dingazi had been written in English. Who was Julebba?

Now, Hurree Das was straightening up. "Beg to inform Your Majesty," he said in his sing-song tenor voice, "that both patients are indubitably dead. One has neck—other has arrow through left ventricle of heart. It is Ubangi arrow fired at close range. Would venture guess that two sentinels were in disagreement over some private matter and did each other in—so to speak."

"Silence!" Julebba exclaimed in a terrible voice. "They were killed in line of duty while defending their Queen!"

"Ah, yes! No doubt, no doubt!" Hurree Das replied hastily. "Fearful act of aggression by conscienceless Kara-mzili, no doubt!"

"Exactly!" Julebba said sternly.

She lifted her head then and began speaking to her army in Hausa. It was lucky for Ki-Gor that she did—or so he thought—because he suddenly discovered that he had gone too far out on his bough in his desire to watch the proceedings below. It had bent downward and he had begun to slip along it.

HE CAUGHT himself just in time and carefully dragged himself back nearer the trunk. If the men below had not fixed their attention on their queen they might possibly have noticed the slight rustle and sway of the leafy branch. As Julebba's voice rose oratorically, Ki-Gor searched the up-lifted faces below and was reassured.

"This very moment we are tracking down the murderers!" Julebba was shouting. "And tomorrow you will all taste the sweet wine of vengeance!"

There was a concerted rasping snarl of response from the army and Julebba raised her voice over it.

She spoke: "In a few moments we will depart on our appointed assignments! The spearmen will hurry to make contact with Lotoko's force and will lead it toward the trap which the rest of us will have set. And when the hated Kara-mzili have been maneuvered into position for the kill—"

Julebba paused dramatically and a tense silence hung over the kloof. In spite of himself, Ki-Gor was spellbound by her voice. He knew that he should be taking the opportunity to steal away, but the situation gripped him so that he lingered on, telling himself that he might learn more specifically the battle plans of the invaders.

Almost in the next second, however, Ki-Gor felt a terrific, burning intuition that something was very wrong. Was it something he heard? Or smelled?

It was both!

There was a faint rustle right in the tree behind him. At the same time, he caught a whiff of a heavy animal scent. He whipped his head around and stared into the murk of the tree. Then his blood ran cold, as a shrill chattering broke the silence over the kloof. He saw the dark form crouched against the trunk of the tree—saw other forms clamber near. Dark as it was in the tree, Ki-Gor knew they were large apes.

The other apes picked up the loud awful chattering and Ki-Gor knew that they had tracked him through the trees. The sudden bedlam below in the clearing confirmed it. Julebba was screaming and the Nigerians scampered toward the foot of the tree bearing torches aloft.

Ki-Gor swung himself around with a bitter snarl and faced the ape. It was too late to bother about staying concealed now. He would be lucky if he escaped at all. He sprang to his feet and stood balanced precariously atop the limb. Then he leaped toward the trunk of the tree. The ape rose upward with a harsh squeal. Ki-Gor's assegai was poised. He lunged with it, and impaled the ape through its hairy throat. The creature gave a horrible half-human cry, and Ki-Gor sprang over it and seized the next branch above him.

Just as he drew up his legs, he felt each ankle gripped by a horny paw. He kicked out frantically. There was a snarling grunt, and one ankle came free. But the other leg was held fast, and in a split-second the horny paws had him around the knee. Ferocious fangs slashed at his calf. There was nothing to do but let go the branch above and drop down to throttle the creature.

Ki-Gor dropped fighting. But even Ki-Gor could not land on the limb below and fight and keep his balance. He teetered for an awful moment and felt himself going. He shot a hand toward the vines growing up the tree-trunk, but there was another ape, snapping and clawing. His hand clutched thin air and he felt himself falling.

In the brief moment of consciousness left to him, he gauged the next limb far below him. He wondered whether his body would fall across it. If that happened, it would break his back. He twisted his body. But the ape was still clinging to one leg snarling and biting, and he could not straighten himself out.

Then there was a crash and Ki-Gor knew no more.

WHEN HE came to, Hurree Das was bathing his face with water. Julebba stood behind him, bending slightly and looking down, her beautiful face distorted with ferocity.

"Aha!" Hurree Das murmured. "Eyes opening with returning consciousness. We meet again under most unfortunate auspices, Ki-Gor! Most dreadfully sorry, but what can do?"

"Silence, Doctor!" Julebba commanded, "Stand away."

Hurree Das hurriedly removed himself from Ki-Gor's side. Julebba came forward a step and stared down malignantly.

"Who are you?" she demanded, "and why do you come spying where you have no business and killing those with whom you have no quarrel?"

Ki-Gor raised himself on his elbows without replying. How he had survived the fall he did not know. He must have twisted enough to have struck the bough below with his head instead of his body. He had then probably dropped limp to the ground. And because he had been limp he had broken no bones.

"Answer me!" Julebba cried savagely. "Answer me, strange White Giant! Who are you?"

Ki-Gor looked up coolly.

"You have seen me before," he replied slowly and insolently. "I do not sneak around in disguise."

"A-a-a-!" Julebba screamed. Her right hand lifted and a dagger glinted. Ki-Gor grinned up at her contemptuously. The hand with the dagger in it did not descend. Julebba stood with it upraised, an incredulous expression creeping into her lambent eyes.

"No one," she said in a voice suddenly lowered, "no one insults me and lives long."

"And Ki-Gor," said the jungle man coolly, "fears no man—or woman."

With that, he very deliberately sat upright, and equally deliberately gathered his legs under him and stood up. He swayed dizzily and took the weight off his right leg which pained fearsomely where the ape had bitten him. But he managed another nonchalant grin, his eyes boring straight into Julebba's.

"Ki-Gor!" she whispered, and although she was tall she had to look up at Ki-Gor now. "Yes, that is what Dingazi called you. He called you 'White Lord of the Jungle' and said your kingdom lay in the direction of the Four Winds."

Her right hand holding the dagger dropped to her side, and she stepped back.

"Why have you come here?" she said in a tone that was more reproachful than angry. "Why have you killed two of my bowmen and three of my apes? You have no quarrel with me."

"I am Dingazi's friend," Ki-Gor said sternly, and added, "Besides I don't like women who make war."

"Oh, don't you?" Julebba glowered. "Men make war. Why shouldn't women?"

"Because women make a treacherous, cruel kind of war," Ki-Gor replied, "full of tricks and deceits. They use innocent people to carry out their designs. The most terrible kind of war is the kind a woman makes—or that a man makes who is like a woman himself."

A gust of anger swept over Julebba. She stamped her foot and tossed her black locks.

"Why am I standing here listening to a stupid hulk of a man while he insults me?" she said. "You should be on your knees, begging for mercy! You apparently don't realize who I am. I am Queen Julebba, don't you understand? Julebba, descendant of Hannibal! If I make war like a woman then I make war better even than Hannibal did! With this tiny army I will shatter Dingazi's mighty hosts! And *then* I'll be Queen Julebba of Kara-mzililand!

"And after I've trained the Kara-mzili to fight my kind of war—there will be no army, *no nation*, in Africa, that can withstand me! Why, these spearmen—" she gestured toward the Nigerians—"and these bowmen and the horsemen—they will be the officers in my all-conquering army of Kara-mzili! And you—*you*, who call yourself White Lord of the Jungle—standing there smiling at me! I'll make you smile at me! I'll have you torn into shreds. I'll have every bone in that huge stupid body of yours broken and crushed! Then, let us see whether you will smile at me!"

She glared.

"Who," said Ki-Gor promptly, "will tear me to shreds? Your spearmen? Big men from Bornu, they are, but it will take all fifty of them to conquer me. And I promise you that if they attack me, I will barehanded kill ten of the fifty! Can you afford to lose one-fifth of your spearmen?"

Julebba stared at him in speechless amazement.

"Or perhaps you will set your apes on me," Ki-Gor went on vigorously. "I don't know how many you have left, but remember—I killed three of them even though they came upon me unawares. Or your bowmen—there are about fifty of them—line them up with arrows notched. Let me have my bow—and in a fair fight I promise you I will kill *twenty* of them before I die! Why, even your elephants—" Ki-Gor leaned forward, eyes blazing—"I have one elephant who is so big that he would only need to flap his ears—and your four would turn tail and run from him!"

Ki-Gor drew himself up scornfully.

"Do your worst, Queen Julebba!" he said coldly. "You cannot frighten Ki-Gor. What a shame it is that a woman so beautiful as you should make war. You were meant for better, pleasanter things than tricks, and deceits, and disguises, and the slaughtering of innocent people. Perhaps you will have a change of heart after you have met Lotoko's force. They are five hundred against your hundred and fifty, and they are thirsty for vengeance."

KI-GOR FOLDED his arms as an indication that he had finished speaking. His blue eyes were fixed on Julebba's smoldering black ones. There was a long pause while the jungle man waited to see the effect of his boldness. It was the only possible tack for him to take. His position was so desperate that only the most desperate device could even postpone a lingering death. He had, therefore, deliberately insulted Julebba, hoping thereby to shock her into an indecisive frame of mind.

Abruptly, Julebba spoke.

"You talk just like a man," she said calmly. Her eyes narrowed and her mouth twisted in bitter lines. "According to all men, beautiful women exist only to make love to. But I have another purpose—and that is to show men how wrong they are. If I am beautiful, it doesn't mean anything to me. I want to rule—to direct—to wield power. I want to show all men that there is a woman who can do anything they can and do it better. I want to show them that a woman can *even make war* better than men! I will *show you, Ki-Gor!* Tomorrow, or the day after, you will see for yourself how an army led by a woman will trap and annihilate a force over three times its size!"

Ki-Gor's face did not betray by so much as the twitch of a muscle the relief that was spreading through him.

"I will decide what to do about you," Julebba said, "after I have attended to this other business. And now," she added mockingly, "I know you are big and strong—but please be quiet and not kill any of my men while they tie you up. I will really have to do that, I'm afraid. I really can't spare half my cavalry just to guard you."

She swung away toward her throne issuing a string of orders. One of the veiled horsemen dismounted and held a long knife at Ki-Gor's throat while two Nigerians pinned his arms to his sides and then went around and around him with strong rope until he was thoroughly trussed from his shoulders to his hips. Then he was rudely thrown to the ground, and an elephant-boy armed with a wicked-looking curved knife was apparently assigned to guard him, the horsemen and the two Nigerians rejoining their own groups.

With the postponement of his fate, Ki-Gor felt a prodigious physical letdown. His whole body ached from his fall, and his right leg began to hurt cruelly where the ape had bitten him. Bruised and ailing though he was, he nevertheless began to consider ways and means of escaping his bonds and his guard so that he could find Lotoko and warn him of the trap Julebba boasted of setting for him. The outlook for that escape was not promising, because the army was evidently getting ready to move from the kloof very soon. Then Ki-Gor glanced down at his right leg when some torches came near him, and by their flickering light he saw that he had been badly bitten, and that the wounds ought to be attended to quickly to prevent blood-poisoning.

To his great relief, Hurree Das appeared beside him carrying a little black bag.

"ONCE AGAIN it devolves on Doctor Hurree Das," the Hindu said humorously, "to preserve you for postponed execution. Well—on the other occasion, you lived to fool your would-be executioners. Here is hoping your luck keeps up! I say, old fellow!" he said, staring at

Ki-Gor's leg, "that is a nasty wound! Very nasty, indeed! It will require some prolonged and delicate treatment to insure against septicemia. Ticklish job working around tendons of calf. My dear fellow, I am afraid it will hurt like fury! I think possibly small intravenous injection is indicated." He frowned.

Still muttering, the Hindu reached into his bag and brought forth a curious metal object the like of which Ki-Gor had never seen. It was cylindrical and came to a sharp point at one end. The Hindu brought forth two small bottles, and proceeded to dip the pointed end of his cylinder into first one and then the other bottle. Then he poised the point of the instrument over Ki-Gor's arm.

"Shall now proceed to prick you with my hypo," he said. "Please do not jump or you will break end off bally thing. Ready?"

"What is it?" Ki-Gor asked uneasily, although he trusted the plump doctor.

"Purpose of easing pain in leg. Steady on, old fellow." Then Hurree Das's practiced hand jabbed downward, while Ki-Gor wondered. How something applied to one's arm could help the pain in one's leg was hard to understand. Hurree Das muttered solicitously, pulled the needlelike point of the instrument from Ki-Gor's arm, and then busied himself with other instruments which he brought out of his bag. Presently he got up and waddled off to one of the campfires, and Ki-Gor turned his attention to the scene around him.

Evidently, the army was preparing to leave the kloof very soon. There was a constant subdued bustle and movement, both of men and animals. After considerable shifting around, the Nigerian spearmen came over in a body and lined up in front of Julebba's throne. Ki-Gor twisted his head around far enough to see that Julebba was standing up. Her right hand swung up over her head and the torch-light glinted on a short broad-bladed sword.

"Soldiers of the Ever-Victorious Army!" she chanted. "The Sword of Hannibal is raised up against your enemies!"

The waving, flickering flames seemed to distort Julebba's passionate face and her eyes seemed huger and blacker.

"To you men of Bornu," she went on, and now her face, her head, her whole body seemed to wave with the torchlight. "To you is the honor of making the first approach—"

Julebba was speaking to these men in Kanuri, and Ki-Gor knew Kanuri as well as any African tongue. Yet he found it hard to follow her words. Her voice seemed at once muffled and yet clear and metallic as a bell—seemed close in his ear and at the same time too far away for him to hear aright.

And now the slim tense figure in front of the throne seemed to dance around jerkily. Ki-Gor blinked his eyes hard and then found it hard to open them again. He heard the Nigerians roaring but it sounded fantastic and unreal. The whole scene began to fade out. Then Hurree Das's voice sounded conversationally from a great distance.

"Ah! How is patient doing? Resting easy, I trust?"

Ki-Gor tried to answer but his tongue and lips felt so thick that all he could produce was an inarticulate mumble. It alarmed him for a moment, and he forced his eyes open. But all he could see were dancing figures and leaping flames, and then enormous weights gathered on his eyelids and forced them shut again.

There followed now a period of wildly improbable happenings. Scores of beautiful women with cruel red mouths hovered over him. They had blue-black hair that seemed to writhe about their necks. After a while, Ki-Gor could see why the blue-black locks writhed—they were tiny blue-black snakes, and each little snake had a cruel red mouth. Then there came a man who was half man and half horse, and his face was swathed in red bandages. And this creature stood over Ki-Gor with a Pygmy poisoned arrow and kept digging it into the calf of Ki-Gor's leg. Ki-Gor struggled to get at the horrible creature, but a python was coiled around his chest pinning his arms to his sides and he could not get his hands free.

But suddenly it was not a python coiled around him but an elephant's trunk. Ki-Gor could not see very well but he thought it was Marmo and he talked to him. Marmo answered him—which was very strange, because Marmo had never answered him before. Stranger still, Marmo spoke in two voices. One of them was familiar—it sounded like Hurree Das. The other voice was a woman's voice, deep and thrilling. Ki-Gor thought it was a great joke that Marmo should talk with the voice of a woman and he told Marmo that. Whereupon Marmo answered him using both voices at once.

Finally, Marmo seemed to be ashamed of his woman's voice because he did not use it any more, and there was only the voice of Hurree Das droning on in flowery English. Then something about that voice made Ki-Gor suspicious and he opened his eyes.

TO HIS astonishment, he was lying stretched out under a tree beside a great rock. It was broad daylight but quite cool indicating that it was still early morning. There was no sign of Marmo, but Hurree Das was sitting cross-legged beside him.

"Where are we?" Ki-Gor demanded. "What is this place?"

"Most likely it is first balcony seats for watching impending hostilities," Hurree Das replied. "Ah, my friend! You have been dreaming quite considerable time. Most delicious morphine jag you have been enjoying, don't you know? How does injured leg feel to you?"

It did not feel bad. It ached and smarted somewhat but Ki-Gor was accustomed to that sort of pain. He lifted his right leg experimentally, and saw that it was well bandaged below the knee.

Now Ki-Gor really began to take stock of his surroundings. He and Hurree Das were apparently on the steep side of a hill overlooking a wide stretch of veldt. Low branches from the tree above swept downward providing an effective screen, so that they could see without being observed by anyone below on the veldt.

As Ki-Gor stared down, waiting for a complete return of consciousness, he noticed a curious and significant conformation of the line where veldt met the wooded base of the hills, just below him the veldt jutted inward into the hills in the form of a wedge several hundred yards long at its deepest apex. The hills sloped steeply down on all sides and extended out like the arms of a chair to form a base for the wedge about a quarter of a mile across. Ki-Gor stirred uneasily, his mind going back to Julebba's words to her army, "We will set a trap—" Was this where the trap was to be laid?

He stirred again, and suddenly realized he was lying on his arms. He struggled to free them and discovered that his wrists were securely manacled behind his back. And manacled they surely were—not merely fastened with rope—he could feel the metal bands on each wrist, now, and a stout chain pressing into his back.

He turned his head and looked at Hurree Das. The Hindu was apparently sorting out and inspecting the instruments in his bag.

"Hurree Das," Ki-Gor murmured, "are we alone?"

"Oah, by no means positively not," the Hindu replied without looking at Ki-Gor. "There is a nasty looking customer squatting behind your head with homicidal weapon held in position ready for malice aforethought."

Ki-Gor thought that over and then said, "The elephant boy?"

"Yess," Hurree Das replied with a smirk. "Toomai of the Elephants. That is joke. His name not really Toomai, he being African blackfellow. Toomai was name of character in story by Mistah Rudyard Kipling, don't you know! Hence joke!"

After a pause, Ki-Gor said, "There are times, Hurree Das, when I don't understand everything you say."

"Oah! How can you saying so!" Hurree Das said indignantly. "Please to know I was graduated cum laude from Bombay University, everybody commenting on most extensive vocabulary."

Ki-Gor had only the vaguest idea of what a university was, but he had more important things to think about at that moment. For one thing, he wondered exactly what status Hurree Das enjoyed in Queen Julebba's army.

"When," Ki-Gor said carefully, "did you join Queen Julebba?"

"Less than a fortnight past," the Hindu replied.

"Where?"

"On upper reaches of Ubangi River. I was making extensive tour for purpose of botanical research when contact was made by pure happenstance."

The doctor picked up a tiny knife and stared at it critically. Ki-Gor frowned. He still had not found out what he wanted. Was Hurree Das going to help him, or not?

"If Julebba should—" Ki-Gor began, then decided to rephrase his question. "I mean, what reward did Julebba promise you to come with her?"

"Oah, no positive proposition was propounded. My decision to join her army as Army Medical Corps was based on purely negative considerations. Her Majesty graciously informed me I could enlist with her and stay in good health. Alternatively, I could refuse and be tortured to death. I have, like most Hindu people, constitutional aversion to torture, so I accepted offer of service."

"Ah!" Ki-Gor sighed, "I'm glad to hear that."

"OAH HEAVENS!" Hurree Das ejaculated, looking at him sharply. "You did not for one instant think I was willing tool of this bloodthirsty monarch? Oah Heavens, no! People can say truly that Hurree Das is great rascal, that he is always and forever looking out for Number One, that he is not above violating certain ordinances for personal profit, that he is—in short—monumental rogue! But there is not slightest justification for supposing Hurree Das would be voluntary accomplice in such systematic mass-murder as this Julebba is engaged in! No person who has taken Hippocratic oath could ever be that!"

By now Ki-Gor was grinning. "Good," he approved. "As a matter of fact, the only person I ever heard call Hurree Das a rascal was— Hurree Das, himself!"

"Possibly," the Hindu shrugged. He added dryly, "Although you should sometime meet some of Civil Authorities in city of Nairobi, Kenya Colony, which place I one time evacuated in great hurry."

"Yes, but now listen, Hurree Das, you must help me to escape. I don't know just how, yet, but I'll work out a way."

There was a long pause. Ki-Gor glanced sharply at the Hindu. Hurree Das was looking mournful.

"Oah dearie me!" he said at length with a heavy sigh. "Much as I would like to do all in my power to help you—I am afraid it is entirely out of question and impossible."

"Why?"

"For simple reason that if my complicity should be discovered, this amiable queen, this Julebba, would have me tortured and killed. I do not mind in the least being killed—that is merely one more step toward achieving Ultimate Nirvana—but I hate like deuce being tortured. It hurts so, don't you know, old fellow!"

Ki-Gor gazed off glumly toward the veldt. For a moment, he had high hopes only to have them speedily dashed to the ground. In time he might be able to persuade the Hindu to change his mind. But escape from such a ruthless captor as Julebba could only succeed by the most resolute and daring methods. A timid and half-hearted partner might prove to be worse than no partner at all.

"I am filled with shame," said Hurree Das contritely, "to disappoint in such a manner. But what can do? And please to remember this blackfellow behind you is also guarding me."

"You mean Julebba doesn't trust you?" Ki-Gor said.

"Most certainly not," Hurree Das said emphatically. "And if you somehow got away—even if I did not help you in any way, shape, or manner—Julebba would most likely accuse me of aiding and abetting such escape. And with dire consequences to yours truly, Hurree Das, M.D."

"Oh, but you wouldn't be around," Ki-Gor said quickly. "If I got away I would take you with me."

"Clah, not understanding that part—so sorry," the Hindu said. "That might change aspect of things—hist!" he broke off and stared up the hill behind him. "Ah! Someone is coming! Might possibly be Her Majesty coming to make sickcall."

There was a considerable rustling in the undergrowth up the hill, a rustling which swiftly became louder and nearer. Presently, one of the giant chimpanzees could be seen, swinging along on his knuckles using his long hairy arms like crutches. Close behind him and flanking him slightly came two more of the beasts. They came downhill in an aimless meandering fashion, but still in the general direction of Ki-Gor. Then Julebba appeared and behind her were four more of the apes.

There was nothing meandering about Julebba. She came directly and purposefully toward Ki-Gor. He struggled up to a sitting position and watched her coming. She was dressed in the costume of the night before and carried the light spear.

As she drew closer, Ki-Gor had to admit that she was fully as beautiful by daylight as she had been under the torches. Her flawless, cream-colored skin gleamed in the dappled sunlight that filtered through the foliage and her tall magnificent figure moved with sinuous majesty through the undergrowth.

BOTH HURREE DAS and the Baluba boy stood up long before she came up to them, but Ki-Gor stayed as he was, in a sitting position. But when she stood beside him she seemed not to notice anything wrong about that. She said nothing for a long moment, but looked down at Ki-Gor with burning eyes that traveled from his yellow hair the length of his great bronzed body down to his feet.

"It will not be long now," she said finally, "before you will see your Kara-mzili friends slaughtered like sheep."

Ki-Gor glanced up in surprise. Her opening gun had been milder than he expected. Moreover, it had been directed at the Kara-mzili and not at him personally.

"I have just received word," she continued, "that my spearmen have already seen Lotoko's force and have been seen by him. My spearmen are retreating, of course"—she smiled vindictively—"and in this direction. They will be in sight in two hours."

"Where is the rest of your army?" Ki-Gor asked bluntly.

"They are already at their battle stations."

Ki-Gor looked down at the wedge-shaped tract of veldt below

him, and then at the wooded slopes that reached out like arms on either side.

"I don't see them," he said briefly.

"You won't," Julebba said, "and neither will Lotoko—until it is too late."

Ki-Gor smiled. "You are just fooling yourself, Queen Julebba," he said. "If you have five hundred men you would still have a hard time beating five hundred Kara-mzili. Next to the Maasai, the Kara-mzili are the finest fighting men in Africa, just because you hide a few elephants and horsemen and bowmen, don't think they will prevail long against such overwhelming odds."

"I will bet you," Julebba, said coldly, "that not a single Kara-mzili escapes!"

"How can I bet—what can I bet?" Ki-Gor queried.

"Your life," the queen said.

"My life?" Ki-Gor said frowning. "Spoken just like a woman. My life, just now, is not mine to bet. You can have me killed whenever you feel like it. In fact, you have already promised to kill me after the battle."

"Well, perhaps I've changed my mind!" Julebba snapped. "Perhaps I shan't have you killed. That is my decision to make, and I shall do exactly what I please!"

Ki-Gor was beginning to feel a little bewildered.

"It might help your fate a little," Julebba went on accusingly, "if your attitude toward me were less insolent."

She swung around and faced Hurree Das.

"Have you treated his leg properly?" she demanded. "Will it heal soon?"

"Oah, yess!" Hurree Das stammered. "Indeed, I have done everything possible to prevent infection, oah yes, indeed!"

"Very well," Julebba said. "Your post is down below ready to treat the wounded as soon as the battle begins. You had better go down immediately and make your arrangements."

"Yes, Madame!" Hurree Das cried. "I am going now. I am hurrying like anything!"

His plump body went crashing through the undergrowth toward the foot of the slope. Julebba turned back to Ki-Gor.

"I will see you after the battle," she announced. "After you have seen how a great general does what you say is impossible—maybe—maybe you will be more humble."

With that she turned and stalked away across the slope, the seven apes shambling after her. Ki-Gor studied her diminishing figure until she was out of sight.

What an extraordinary woman! What had caused the comparative mellowing of her attitude toward him?

Ki-Gor put that line of thought away for a while, and concentrated on figuring a means of immediate escape. Although he hardly dared admit it even to himself, he was a little impressed by Julebba's confidence over the outcome of the impending battle. It seemed inconceivable that her tiny force could defeat, much less annihilate the Kara-mzili half an *impi*, and yet—if Lotoko's men were taken completely by surprise....

KI-GOR LOOKED around at his guard. If he was going to escape he had to do it soon, so that he could get to Lotoko and warn him of Julebba's trap. Helene, after all, was with Lotoko, and if there was the slightest chance of Helene being endangered, he must get away and prevent the battle from taking place.

Escape should not be too difficult to accomplish now. His only bonds were the ones on his wrists. His powerful legs were free, and he had used them as effective weapons many times before during his adventurous life. To be sure his right leg was wounded—how badly, he was not sure. He rolled over on his stomach with a groan and spoke to the guard.

"Oh, I'm stiff, brother," he said. "I must stand up a moment and stretch. You need not be alarmed. You are armed and I am chained."

"Why should I be alarmed, O White Giant?" the elephant boy said surlily. "As you say—I am armed and you are chained."

Ki-Gor lay on his stomach and looked at the Baluba.

"Are you not homesick?" he said, "being so far from your country?"

"Nay, why should I be?" the Baluba growled.

"What are you getting from this warlike adventuring and risking of your life?"

"There will be rewards," the elephant boy said.

"They are promises only," Ki-Gor pointed out, "and promises are cheap."

"Promises are better than nothing," the Baluba retorted.

"Are they—I wonder," Ki-Gor said reflectively. "Down to the south where I live, there is a wonderful place for a man like you. There is a fine village set on fertile soil near a river with pure, clean water that is teeming with fish. The men in the village are kind and gentle, the women are handsome and strong and hard-working."

"Why do you tell me this, White Giant?" the guard said.

"If you came with me," Ki-Gor said simply, "you could live in that place. You could have ten goats and twenty cows and twenty wives."

"Wah!" the Baluba spat on the ground. "You yourself just said that promises are cheap. And even your promises don't approach the ones our Queen makes. Why, after we have conquered Kara-mzililand, I am to be chief of a whole village! I will have *fifty* cows and *fifty* wives!"

Ki-Gor fell silent. Evidently, the elephant boy would be hard to bribe on the basis of mere promises. Perhaps, it would be better after all to attack the man. He arched his back with a groan and twisted his head with a futile gesture.

"I would like to get up on my feet," he complained, "but with my wrists chained behind my back like this, I can't do it alone. Would you help me up?"

"Help yourself," the Baluba grunted. "Roll over on your back and draw your legs up under you."

"Ah, yes, maybe I can do it that way," Ki-Gor said, hiding his disappointment. If the Baluba had done what he asked and come and bent over him, it would have been easy. Now, something else had to be figured out.

He rolled over on his back, as the Baluba had suggested, drew his legs under him and staggered upward. He stood swaying and gasping for a moment. He was considerably weaker than he had realized. He covertly tested his right leg, resting his full weight on it. The pain that shot through his calf was fearful. It was not very encouraging.

However, Ki-Gor decided that whether his leg pained or not, it would hold him up while he swung his left leg in a prodigious kick. He took a step forward uphill toward the guard.

His heart beat a little quicker as he noticed that the Baluba was not even looking at him, but was staring off at something in the distance.

"Hai!" the Baluba exclaimed. "Here they come, I think! They made quick time!"

"Here who come?" Ki-Gor said.

"Our spearmen," the Baluba said, still looking off toward the veldt. "No doubt the Kara-mzili are in hot pursuit! Wah! They'll walk into the trap like elephants into a pit!"

In spite of himself, Ki-Gor looked over his shoulder. Far off on the veldt, there was a dust cloud rising slowly into the air. Shading his phenomenally keen eyes, Ki-Gor could just make out black specks under the dust cloud. He turned his head back quickly.

"CAN YOU see any of them yet?" he asked the Baluba. The elephant boy shook his head and squinted his eyes toward the horizon. If ever there was a guard vulnerable to attack, it was this one now. Ki-Gor shifted his weight to his right leg, and swept the Baluba with one all-embracing glance. The man seemed to be oblivious of all danger, his right hand carrying the curved sword hanging loosely at his side.

One tremendous kick into the man's stomach would knock his breath out, knock him down—might even knock him unconscious. If he were still conscious, Ki-Gor would kick the sword out of his hand, and swiftly kneel on the man's throat. A swift, resolute attack would prevent the man from making a sound to summon help.

Ki-Gor dug the toes of his aching right leg into the ground to give him a sure purchase. The muscles of his left leg tensed—then his ears caught the sound of rustling undergrowth behind him. He shot a glance over his shoulder—and his heart died within him.

Julebba, accompanied by her seven apes, was coming rapidly toward him.

To attack the Baluba now would be worse than futile. With his hands chained behind him, he could not possibly fight off so many giant chimpanzees, and besides Julebba would scream for help.

The Baluba boy stepped around him waving his sword in a salute, and Ki-Gor sadly watched Julebba hasten toward them.

"They are coming!" she cried exultantly, "Do you see?"

Ki-Gor nodded wearily, and she smiled triumphantly up into his face.

"In a short time now," she said, "the fun begins. This, you see, is our first test. Up to now we have only met frontier guards—small groups. But here, finally, we are going to meet a real force. Not a big one, but they outnumber us more than three to one. And you will see! Not one of them will escape!"

Ki-Gor looked off anxiously at the dust cloud. If Julebba, by any mad chance, were right, what would happen to Helene? He wondered whether he should mention the fact that Helene was with Lotoko. Then he dismissed the idea in disgust. Julebba couldn't be right! It was ridiculous.

"You still won't believe me, will you?" Julebba said, eyes narrowed in a derisive smile. "Let me tell you something you don't know—or have forgotten. Those Kara-mzili are beaten now—already—before they even reach us here. Why? Because they are so completely confused about my strength. They have been told we are few in numbers, and they have been told we number thousands. They don't know which stories to believe. Now, finally, they have caught sight of us-the spearmen. There are only fifty of them. No doubt, Lotoko thinks that is all there are. Think of the shock it will be to him and to his men when—thinking they have penned up a handful of men in this place below—suddenly they are assaulted on three sides by new forces. They have underestimated us for so long, that when the attack comes, they will overestimate us. It will be a terrible shock."

Ki-Gor knew that there was a great deal in what she said. But Julebba had not finished. She pointed out on to the veldt where Ki-Gor, by now, could make out running black figures quite distinctly.

"They have been running a long time now," she said. "My spearmen retreating and the Kara-mzili pursuing. They are all going to be out of breath and tired. But only a *part* of my force will be tired. The rest will burst forth fresh on the Kara-mzili."

Ki-Gor essayed an indulgent smile, although he did not feel like smiling.

"You have figured everything very closely, haven't you?" he said. "But have you figured out a way to make Lotoko send his *entire army* into that little wedge of veldt? He is too good a general to do that. He will send fifty or more men in to chase your fifty. The rest he will hold in readiness."

"Don't fear," Julebba said calmly. "He will send every man he has into the wedge. For one thing, he won't suspect a trap. For another, he will be over-anxious. This is the first time he has seen the mysterious invaders of Queen Julebba—he will strain every nerve to kill or capture them."

"Well," Ki-Gor shrugged. "We'll see what happens soon enough."

His face was blank as he gazed out on to the veldt, but his mind was in a turmoil. This extraordinary woman by his side had apparently not overlooked a thing. Her imagination and ability to read human nature, and moreover, her skillful and daring application of that faculty to military problems—was frightening. By now, Ki-Gor was getting genuinely worried that Lotoko and the Kara-mzili might actually meet the fate that Julebba was so confidently predicting for them. And Helene was with Lotoko!

IF THERE was ever a time that he needed to be free, it was now. And yet, he knew in his heart that escape was completely impossible, as long as he was surrounded by those powerful apes trained to do the bidding of the strange and beautiful woman who stood next to him.

And now the three Arabs came through the undergrowth toward them, the old Arab who had posed as Julebba's father, and the two younger ones who were supposed to be her brothers. From the conversation that followed Ki-Gor gathered that they each commanded a unit of the little army.

The old Arab spoke in Arabic but Julebba for some reason answered in English.

"No," she said, "Take no prisoners. Wait a minute, though—there should be one man saved. We will release him later to take the news to Dingazi that we have an enormous army. It will seem enormous when we first burst out on them. So do this—take one prisoner as soon as possible and put his eyes out immediately. We'll let him go then and he can tell of his impressions of the Ever-Victorious Army."

She switched back to Arabic then and Ki-Gor could not understand what she said next. But he knew now that he had to tell her about Helene and plead for her life in advance. It would be risky enough to have Helene a captive to this bloodthirsty woman, but it was better than having her killed outright.

The Arabs seemed to have finished the talk with Julebba and were backing away. Ki-Gor took a deep breath and was about to speak to Julebba, when all three Arabs suddenly jumped on him. Manacled as he was, and taken completely by surprise, Ki-Gor could not put up an effective resistance.

But the assault was quickly over, and the Arabs had jumped away from Ki-Gor's thrashing legs before he realized what it was all about. Then the purpose of the attack was demonstrated by the thick, evil-smelling turban cloth that was bound tightly around Ki-Gor's mouth.

"Just in case," Julebba told him calmly, "you tried to shout out to your Kara-mzili friends and warn them of the ambush."

Ki-Gor's heart sank. He had held that idea in the back of his mind as a last desperate resort. But this woman thought of everything.

"Ah! You look so fierce!" Julebba mocked him. "If your head were covered as well, you would look like one of my Tuareg horsemen."

So the veiled cavalrymen were Tuaregs, Ki-Gor thought dully. He had heard of Tuaregs and knew that they lived on the great deserts far to the north, but he had never seen any before. How they happened to be so far south out of their element was no greater a mystery than was Julebba herself.

But now Julebba's Nigerian spearmen were panting into the wedge, Lotoko's Kara-mzili shouting triumphantly scarcely three hundred yards behind them. Ki-Gor's eyes strained for a glimpse of Helene somewhere in the black mass of Kara-mzili, but they were too far away as yet. He still hoped against hope that Lotoko would use common prudence about sending his entire force into the ambush.

But just at that moment, the Nigerian spearmen did some very fine acting. Half way into the wedge, they stopped and looked around them in great agitation as if they had just noticed that they were hemmed in. Then they pretended to decide on a last stand. They closed their ranks and faced the Kara-mzili with shouts of defiance.

Apparently, Lotoko could not resist that bait. The entire half-*impi* ranged itself into the solid phalanx which was the basis of Kara-mzili infantry tactics, and marched resolutely into the wedge.

Ki-Gor groaned behind his gag. Julebba had predicted accurately.

CHAPTER V

FROM THEN ON THE action proceeded like a bad dream exactly as Julebba had planned it. The spearmen, once again acting, fell back right into the tip of the wedge drawing the unsuspecting Kara-mzili in with them. At the psychological moment—when the Kara-mzili were all well into the wedge—but still a hundred yards away from the decoying spearmen—Julebba struck.

From the woods on both sides of the Kara-mzili phalanx there suddenly came a shower of arrows. They were great archers, those men from the Ubangi. Half a dozen volleys poured into the vulnerable Kara-mzili before they realized what was happening and swung their long shields about to protect them from the unexpected arrow attack on their flanks. By that time, nearly three hundred arrows had poured into the serried masses at point-blank range, and while not every arrow had killed a man, the death toll was fearful.

But the Kara-mzili wheeled bravely and charged the deadly woods. They were still in overwhelming numbers and apparently with unbroken morale. But now Julebba played her second card—the elephants.

They erupted suddenly from the woods—again on both sides—two on each flank. Each elephant carried on its back a large shallow howdah loaded with fifty-pound rocks. The Baluba boys hurled these rocks down on the defenseless heads of the Kara-mzili. Behind the elephants, the Ubangi archers streamed out keeping up an incessant shower of fearsome arrows.

As the Kara-mzili recoiled at the flanks, the Nigerian spearman hurled themselves on the original front rank. The elephants bored bloody pathways through Lotoko's kilted warriors cutting the phalanx in half.

In a very short time the Kara-mzili were no longer an *impi*—they were merely a crowd of demoralized individuals. Panic swept through the shattered ranks. With one accord, the Kara-mzili broke and ran.

Safety seemed to beckon from the open veldt, away from the cramped slaughter of the wedge, and the Kara-mzili fled with screams of terror away from the wooded slopes.

But now Julebba climaxed her ambush. The Tuaregs poured out of the leafy screen at the apex of the wedge. With curved swords raised high they galloped around the Nigerian spearmen and fell on the doomed Kara-mzili. Before Ki-Gor's horrified eyes, Julebba proceeded to demonstrate the truth of the military theory that cavalry is never so dangerous and effective as when it is unleashed in pursuit of an already beaten enemy.

The battle had been so fast and so furious that not until this moment did Ki-Gor's searching eyes finally locate his wife. As the rear ranks dissolved into flight, he saw a tiny white figure left behind. Ki-Gor wondered whether Julebba saw it, too, but he did not dare turn his head to look, for fear he would lose sight of Helene.

Apparently, Helene had not lost her head like the Kara-mzili. She moved not out toward the veldt but toward the wooded side of the wedge. Ki-Gor, knowing that all of Julebba's men were out in the open now, and that therefore the woods were the safest place, held his breath while Helene threaded her way through the fugitive blacks.

She all but made it.

With sickening horror Ki-Gor saw a single Tuareg horseman bearing down on her when she was only a few yards from the line of trees. In the next few seconds Ki-Gor thanked the fates for providing his wife with a keen mind, an athletic body, and undaunted courage. She apparently heard or saw the Tuareg galloping down on her, and instead of losing her head, she swerved and came to a standstill facing the oncoming horseman. Ki-Gor could just make out the light spear in her hands. She stood perfectly still until the horse seemed to be almost on top of her. Then she sprang to one side and the horse pounded past her. The Tuareg rider, evidently astonished that she had not perished under the hoofs of his steed, reined in sharply and swung the horse around. He must have been further astonished when he found that his prey instead of running away had pursued him. Helene had run swiftly after him, her spear poised in her right hand. While the Tuareg was reining the horse around, Helene reached out and hauled at his left stirrups, away from his sword-hand.

KI-GOR COULD hardly believe his eyes as Helene thrust upward twice with her frail spear. But the Tuareg's head jerked backward as if the second thrust might have caught him in the throat. At the same moment, the horse reared up high in the air. The Tuareg brought his sword around and slashed downward wildly. Then, suddenly, he seemed to be sliding back down on to the horse's crupper—apparently he had lost the reins. A split-second later, the Tuareg was down on the ground prostrate, and Helene was hanging on for dear life to the bridle of the plunging horse.

Julebba, sitting beside Ki-Gor, gave an angry cry.

"That is a white man down there!" she exclaimed. "He has killed one of my Tuaregs!"

She leaped to her feet shouting imprecations. But Ki-Gor did not look at her. He was watching Helene—who had been a fearless rider long before she came to Africa—mount the Tuareg's horse and ride hell-for-leather out toward the veldt and safety.

Julebba screamed at the Baluba boy and sent him scampering down to the field of battle carrying orders from her that the Tuaregs should pursue and capture the mysterious "white man" at all costs. But by the time the Tuareg leader received the orders, Helene was far away and out of sight on the veldt.

Julebba whirled around at Ki-Gor. "Who was that white man?"

she demanded. Then she realized that Ki-Gor could not answer her with the great gag tied around his mouth. She whipped out her dagger, knelt down and cut the bandage away. Ki-Gor thus received a few precious seconds to decide on his answer.

"Who was that white man who was with Lotoko?" Julebba repeated grimly.

"It was a woman," Ki-Gor said, guessing that she would probably find that out anyway later. Then he added, "The woman is my wife."

"Your wife!" Julebba screamed. Then she remembered. "Of course!" she said slowly. "The red-headed woman in the leopard skin outfit that was with you at Dutawayo. Well—as soon as we catch her"—Julebba's eyes flashed—"you will no longer have a wife."

"Why?" Ki-Gor said sharply. "Why should you kill a woman who has done you no harm?"

"She killed one of my precious Tuaregs!" Julebba replied hotly. "That's why!"

"You don't know yet that he is dead," Ki-Gor said, and his face was dangerously bleak.

"Well, then, I have a better reason for killing the woman!" Julebba shouted. "No woman shall have you for a husband but me—Julebba, the Conqueror!"

Ki-Gor stared at her aghast. Before he could organize his whirling thoughts enough to make some answer, she spoke with a beckoning sweep of her arm.

"Come! We will speak of this matter later. Now, we will go down the hill. There is much to be done."

Ringed by the giant chimpanzees, Ki-Gor followed Julebba's sinuous figure down the slope. Judging from the rapidly diminishing sounds from the field, the battle was nearly over. And when Ki-Gor reached the foot of the hill, he saw that that was so. A few Tuaregs were still hunting down and killing the last survivors of Lotoko's five hundred stalwart kilted warriors. But groups of Nigerians and Ubangi archers were already searching the field for their own wounded.

Hurree Das had a rough dressing station set up and was hard at work patching up the wounded as they walked or were carried to him. The casualties were preposterously small, considering the overwhelming numbers of the enemy. There were twenty-one wounded in all—seven of them severely—and the dead numbered exactly five. Three

Nigerians, one Baluba, and the Tuareg who had ridden down upon Helene. Her spear had caught him in the throat, severing his jugular.

As Ki-Gor looked out over the shambles he marveled that such a holocaust could have been contrived by a beautiful young woman. For a moment, he wondered whether she really was the brain that conceived this brilliant strategy... or whether she was a figurehead behind which someone else worked—someone like the old Arab, perhaps. But Ki-Gor's doubts in this direction were soon dispelled by Julebba's own actions.

WHILE THE vultures slowly wheeled downward out of the sky, Julebba organized her victory. Her orders were given to and carried out by the three Arabs, and she issued them in Arabic, so Ki-Gor did not understand her words. But he saw how swiftly the Nigerians went among the dead Kara-mzili gathering up their weapons, and how another party went around stripping the blue-and-white kilts and feather headdresses off dozens of Lotoko's lately fallen men. The purpose of that latter action Ki-Gor did not quite understand, but he had no doubt Julebba had an excellent one in mind. Then the Baluba boys carried the severely wounded on to the howdahs of the elephants, the Ubangi bowmen were assembled and dispatched up over the hills in a body, and finally the Tuaregs gathered around to form an escort for Julebba herself.

Ki-Gor's manacles were removed, to his great surprise, and he was given a horse to ride beside Julebba. Any sudden hopes of escape that rose in his heart swiftly died, however, as he saw that he would be completely ringed about by Tuaregs. And as the cavalcade moved off, Ki-Gor no longer had the slightest doubt that Julebba herself was the guiding genius of her "Ever-Victorious Army."

The route of the cavalcade led out of the wedge on to the veldt, then turned leftward and bore along the base of the range of hills. They traveled at a moderate pace for about four hours, and Ki-Gor was not surprised when their destination turned out to be the hidden kloof of the night before. Evidently this was the secret rendezvous of the army. What did surprise Ki-Gor was the fact that the Ubangi archers had arrived at the kloof ahead of them. Evidently there was another route into the ravine over the hills—a route too rough for horses and elephants but passable for agile men on foot.

Ki-Gor's mind had been furiously busy during that four-hour ride, and although he arrived at no definite course of action, he had considered a host of ideas, some of which might crystallize into concrete plans with more thought. For one thing, he became interested in the two younger Arabs who rode on either side for the entire distance.

He had not been able to place them in Julebba's scheme of things. They looked enough alike to be brothers, and they looked enough like the old Arab to be his sons. But they did not resemble Julebba, they being typically Arab, swarthy and hook-nosed. Julebba was comparatively pale and her nose was straight and exquisitely beautiful by any standards except possibly those of the Guinea Coast.

Who were the Arabs, then? Ki-Gor asked himself. But then, he sighed, who was Julebba?

He had tried to converse with the young Arabs during the ride, using Swahili. But they had both answered his overtures with such rude grunts and ferocious looks that Ki-Gor did not pursue the attempt. He did not quite understand that enmity. It went beyond the fact of his being a prisoner of war—there was something directly personal in it.

Beyond the clearing in the middle of the kloof, there were three tents hidden away among the trees. The largest and most ornate of these tents was, of course, Julebba's. The other two were alike in size and appearance and were used by the Arabs. About an hour after the arrival in the kloof, the two young Arabs escorted Ki-Gor to the large new tent.

"Sit down," Julebba said. "We are going to talk personally. My Arabs will remain to ensure your good behavior, but we will talk English so that they cannot understand what we say."

She flashed a brilliant smile and Ki-Gor tried to keep the bewilderment out of his face. What an unpredictable woman!

"First of all," she said, "you are truly a white man, aren't you? You couldn't possibly be anything else, in spite of the way you are dressed. When did you come to Africa?"

Her tone was one matter-of-fact friendliness. Ki-Gor used the same tone and described his origin, the death of his missionary father in the jungle, and his own self-upbringing.

"Magnificent!" she exclaimed softly when he had finished. "What a husband you will make me! I may even let you be king, instead of just a consort."

Ki-Gor eyed her and said bluntly, "Who are you?"

SHE SMILED indulgently at him and then said, "It is a long story. My father was a white man. He captured and trained wild animals for European circuses, and he spent most of his life in Africa. My mother was a circus performer from Malta, originally. And while the Maltese are considered Europeans, they are actually descended from the ancient Carthaginians. That is why I say I am a descendant of Hannibal.

"When I was young my mother died, and I lived a tawdry, degrading life traveling with my father in little circuses. Then he took me to Africa with him and I began to live. I had done a lot of reading as a child, and was particularly interested in the life and military campaigns of Hannibal. The first time I saw a tribe of Tuaregs, I thought how irresistible they would be if they were properly led in warfare.

"How I became their leader is not important, but I did it with the help of Mohammed, here"—she indicated the old Arab—"who had been a friend of my father's. I led them down from their desert home and headed southward, skirmishing on the way and learning my art of war. I recruited among a few of the tribes I fought with. The army you see is the result—small, but of marvelous quality.

"By this time, I decided I would not only be a general, but I would be a queen. And rather than spend years carving out a kingdom for myself, I decided to look for an already established realm, and take it over. Kara-mzililand answered my problem. It is a mighty nation to conquer, but conquered it can be, and I am well on my way to doing it. When Dingazi receives the news of the fate of Lotoko's force, he will be so terrified that his fine army will be useless—he being unable to direct it. Within two weeks-maybe much less—I will be Queen of Kara-mzililand."

Ki-Gor kept his face grave and his eyes on Julebba throughout this remarkable recital. But his thoughts were racing, and he was ready for her next gun.

"I thought there could be no greater happiness than being Queen of Kara-mzililand," she went on, "until I saw you, Ki-Gor. And when that happened, I could look into the future and I could see—that I would be a very lonesome queen, indeed, without you at my side."

Her great eyes seemed to devour him as she said the words. He remained silent, principally because he was not at all sure what he ought to say.

"Well!" she exclaimed. "What have you to say?"

"What can I say?" he said soberly, "Except that I cannot be your husband because I am already married."

"Forget the red-headed woman!" Julebba snapped. "She is as good as dead, already. As soon as my Tuaregs catch her—and they will not fail—I will have her quickly put away. Then you will no longer have a wife and will be free to marry me."

"But suppose," Ki-Gor said gently, "that I don't *want* my wife to be killed?"

"Ki-Gor, do not make me jealous of the red-headed woman!" she cried wrathfully, "Or—instead of putting her out of the way mercifully, I will have my apes perform the execution!"

An icy chill traveled up Ki-Gor's back, and he had to remind himself that Helene had not been captured yet. But if she were....

"What is the matter with you, Ki-Gor!" Julebba cried in exasperation. "Am I not beautiful? Am I not three times as beautiful as that sunburned savage? Will you not be the husband of a mighty queen if—"

"Wait a minute, O Julebba!" Ki-Gor said diplomatically. "You have given me no chance to say how tempting your offer is—how flattering. And if I were single, I would have a far different answer to make—"

"Then I will make you single!" Julebba shrieked. She suddenly quieted down and gazed calculatingly at Ki-Gor. "Suppose—" she said at length, "I sent her away—suppose I did not kill her—"

Hope surged through Ki-Gor, then, only to be dashed away with Julebba's next words.

"No," she said abruptly, "that wouldn't do. You are still in love with her, I can see that, If she were sent away safe, you would marry me, but you would run away the first chance you got—run away to her. No. The woman must die."

"If she dies," Ki-Gor said stonily, "then guard yourself, Julebba. Because I will surely kill you."

"Oh! You beast!" Julebba screamed, springing to her feet. The three Arabs also sprang up, but she waved them back and stepped over to Ki-Gor. Before he realized what was happening, she had knelt beside him and kissed him full on the mouth. Then she drew back, face contorted with rage, and slapped him hard on the face.

"GO AWAY!" she raged. "Go and think—think hard on what you should do! You will spend the night with Ahmed and Ali. And if you have an idea of escaping"—she flashed a cruel smile—"you may as well forget it. Both of your guards are already furiously jealous of you and would like nothing better than an excuse to kill you. Especially Ahmed, the older one, because Ahmed would like very much to have the position you are refusing."

As Ki-Gor left Julebba's tent and walked slowly away, he felt two knife points in his back. But he felt no fear of the two Arab brothers. And Julebba's parting shot had the reverse effect on him than she intended, because it crystallized one of the ideas which had been in his head vaguely for the past two hours.

Just after the evening meal, Hurree Das came to Ahmed's tent to change the dressing on Ki-Gor's leg and inspect the wound. The Hindu, for once, was quiet, had very little to say. Whether that was because he was very tired from his work on the wounded, or whether he was terrified of the beetle-browed Ahmed who sat in the tent glaring—Ki-Gor could not say. He peered at the bites on Ki-Gor's leg and murmured:

"Remarkable healing job going on, old fellow. Don't know how you are doing it."

Ki-Gor bent over and looked at his leg and spoke casually—for Ahmed's benefit—as if he were commenting on the wound. "The needle that you used to put me to sleep with—is it in your bag?"

"Yes," Hurree Das replied, "but, gracious! Why do you ask?"

"Then, when you leave," Ki-Gor said, "leave the bag behind, as if by accident."

"Oh lordy! What is your intention?"

"I have to escape," Ki-Gor said, still keeping his voice matter-of-fact so that nothing in his tone would arouse the suspicions of Ahmed—who did not understand English.

"Oh! Fearful risk for poor Hindu doctor with no possible pretensions to heroism."

"Nobody will know you had anything to do with me. You simply forget to take your bag with you when you go. I'll do the rest. If you come back very early in the morning, you can be the one who discovers that I have gone and give the alarm."

"Oh! Dearie me!" Hurree Das moaned. "Am frightened like the devil—but I cannot refuse you."

With flying fingers, the Hindu put on a fresh bandage. When he had finished, he tossed the surgical scissors into the bag and stood up.

"Happens to be full load already in syringe," he said in English to Ki-Gor. Then he turned to Ahmed, said a polite goodnight in Swahili, and turned and half ran out of the tent.

"WHAT WAS all that talk about, Nasrani?" Ahmed demanded in Swahili.

"We were talking about my leg," Ki-Gor replied.

"The Hindu looked frightened," said Ahmed, suspiciously.

"He was," Ki-Gor agreed. "The leg is not healing rapidly, and he is afraid Queen Julebba will blame him and punish him."

"Wah!" Ahmed said bitterly.

"She is young, your queen," Ki-Gor carried on smoothly. "She has girlish whims."

The Arab glowered at Ki-Gor without answering.

"This whim concerning me, for instance," Ki-Gor went on serenely. "Who am I to have the honor of marrying her? I merit no such wonderful fate."

"If she wants you, she will have you," Ahmed said bitterly.

"It is not right," Ki-Gor said shaking his head. "There is one person who should marry the queen—one person who has earned that right—"

"Who?" snapped Ahmed, leaning forward and whipping a dagger from his girdle. "Who do you think has the right, dog of a Nasrani! Speak! Or by the—"

"Nay! Cool down!" Ki-Gor said good-naturedly. "The person I speak of is none other than yourself!"

Ahmed glared in silence for a moment. Then he said ominously, "Do you mock me, Nasrani?"

"I do not," Ki-Gor said calmly. "Does she not look with favor upon you, O Ahmed?"

"She did," Ahmed admitted, "but never enough. And now since she has seen you—"

"Wait," Ki-Gor said. "Have you ever tried a love-philter?"

"Aye, many of them," Ahmed growled, "but they did not help."

"What were they-the kind you drink?"

"What other kind is there?" Ahmed said.

"There is a philter I know of," Ki-Gor said, lowering his voice, "and it never fails. You do not drink it, but instead, you inject it in your veins through a hollow needle."

"I do not believe you," Ahmed said, then added. "Where is such a philter and such a hollow needle?"

"There happens to be one within arm's reach of you," Ki-Gor said. "It is in the bag the Hindu left behind."

Ahmed shot a glance at Hurree Das' bag lying near Ki-Gor.

"Is this a trick to get me within reach of you?" Ahmed demanded.

"Nay, it is no trick—I'll push it over toward you."

A moment later, Ahmed held the hypodermic syringe gingerly in his hands. Ki-Gor explained how it worked.

"How do I know it is not a deadly poison?" Ahmed demanded.

"Would a *hakim*, a doctor, carry deadly poison in his bag?" Ki-Gor said patiently, and Ahmed was silenced.

"By injecting the philter into your blood," Ki-Gor explained, "you will become so desirable to her that you will be irresistible. She will come to you, possibly, in your dreams. With some persons though, it works more slowly and takes several days to make its effect."

Ahmed put the needlepoint in the crook of his elbow, experimentally moved it until he felt the vein underneath as Ki-Gor had directed him. Then he threw a terrible look at Ki-Gor.

"There is something wrong here," he accused. "Why should you give her up—a queen, beautiful and mighty—"

"I cannot marry her myself," Ki-Gor explained patiently. "I am already married, and we Christians are only allowed one wife."

Ahmed stared long and hard at Ki-Gor. Finally he snarled, "Absurd religion!" and pressed the needle into his arm.

A little more than an hour later, Ki-Gor lifted the back flap of the tent and went searching through the pitch-black woods for the back way out of the kloof.

CHAPTER VI

TWENTY HOURS LATER, KI-GOR limped up a little hill, exhausted from lack of sleep and food, and racked with the pain in his right leg. He had not stopped once since he left the kloof in which Julebba's army was hidden. He had pressed ever onward toward Dutawayo, unable to rest until he knew that Helene had not been captured by Julebba's Tuaregs. He had come now about half the distance to Dutawayo, and had seen no sign of her, although he had kept to the route taken by Lotoko's ill-fated expedition. But, he told himself, that was possibly good news, and meant that she had safely gone all the way to Dutawayo.

He had nearly reached the crest of the little ridge he was climbing, when he thought he heard voices in the distance. He stopped a moment to listen, and now if he heard one voice he heard hundreds. He hurried to the top of the hill and stared in amazement.

At a distance of about a half a mile in front of him, there stretched an immense long line of twinkling campfires. There could be nothing less than an army camped there, and a big one. And the only big army in Kara-mzililand would be a Kara-mzili army. Ki-Gor ran down the hill, regardless of his aching right leg.

He was recognized at the first campfire and greeted. It seemed to him that the warriors were very quiet, if not actually depressed and fearful.

"Have you seen aught of my wife, the Red Headed One?" he asked immediately.

"We did not see her," was the answer, "but we heard that she rode into the camp early this morning on a horse."

Ki-Gor's heart sang a joyful cadence.

"I must find her quickly," he shouted. "Where would she be?"

"Most likely with King Dingazi," they answered.

"Dingazi!" Ki-Gor exclaimed. "Is he here, then?"

Quickly, he sought out the royal tent, and was immediately received. Relieved and happy as he was at the news about Helene's safety, he was a little shocked by the appearance of Dingazi. The old king looked ten years older, his great shoulders bowed with discouragement, and fear lurking in his bloodshot eyes.

"I did not expect to see you away from Dutawayo," Ki-Gor said.

Dingazi shook his head. "The very day Lotoko left, villagers came to Dutawayo from all sides running away from the great army of invaders. I collected ten *impis* as fast as I could, but there were delays. And I could not reach Lotoko in time to save him—or try to save him," the old man amended. Then he said, "You heard about what happened to him?"

Ki-Gor said, "I was there when it happened, and saw the whole thing."

"You saw it!" Dingazi cried. "Ah, thank the gods for something. Tell me what happened!"

"Yes," Ki-Gor agreed, "but first of all, where is my wife? I expected to see her with you."

Dingazi raised his head slowly. "When did you see her last?" he demanded.

"During the battle," Ki-Gor said. "She killed a Tuareg and fled on his horse. I didn't know until tonight that she had escaped them."

"She escaped them," Dingazi said. "She came here this morning, thinking you would be with me. When she found you were not, she cried out that you must be a prisoner of Julebba's and she rode away again immediately to look for you."

Ki-Gor felt a great weariness go over him. If she had *only* stayed! They would now both be safe with this great host of Kara-mzili. As it was, who knew where she might be? She might even have fallen into the hands of the Tuaregs.

"I *was* a prisoner of Julebba's," Ki-Gor said with a sigh.

"Hah!" Dingazi exclaimed. "Tell me about her and her monstrous ju-ju army! Ai-ee! I don't know what to do! What will become of my poor people!"

"What do you mean monstrous ju-ju army?" Ki-Gor demanded.

"I asked Helene about the massacre," Dingazi said, "but she said she was in the rear ranks and did not see much until our men were already badly cut up. She said it was an ambush, but she could not estimate the number of the enemy. Fortunately, tonight another survivor arrived—one of the *impi*. He was blinded at the beginning of the fight, but he was in the front rank. He said it was fearful the way the ju-jus poured out of the ambush by the many thousands—horses, elephants, everything!"

"Now, wait a minute, Dingazi," Ki-Gor said soberly. "I spent a day and a night as a prisoner of those jujus, and I can tell you to a man how many they are, and how, they fight. Listen!"

WHEN KI-GOR finished his account of Julebba, and her army, and her tactics, and how they prevailed over Lotoko, Dingazi leaned back pop-eyed.

"I—I can't believe it!" he gasped. "A hundred and fifty men did *that!*"

"And one woman," Ki-Gor added. "And she doesn't need men to fight with, Dingazi—she uses ideas. Her greatest weapon is fear, just think how skillfully she has used that weapon. Here you are with ten thousand of the best fighting men in Africa, and you were afraid to do battle with one hundred and fifty."

"No longer am I afraid," Dingazi said grimly. "The *impis* will start at dawn. I will send for my commanders now—I want you to tell them how to find this kloof if you can."

"I can," said Ki-Gor. "I can draw a map of those hills by now and they cannot go wrong. But let your commanders hurry, because I must go as soon as possible to try and find Helene."

"But you can't find her until daylight," Dingazi expostulated. "And then she is on foot. The horse she came on is still here. You can take that. But now you should rest a little and eat a little before you start."

The horse changed matters somewhat and Ki-Gor decided to take Dingazi's suggestion. Food was brought, and while Ki-Gor ate, he discussed with Dingazi and his commanders various plans of action, plans which depended on whether or not Helene was a captive of Queen Julebba. In the meantime, Dingazi had finally convinced himself of the importance of the psychological element in this bizarre crisis. He had sent runners throughout the immense camp repeating Ki-Gor's story, and very soon the depressed and fearful Kara-mzili left their forebodings behind, and the drums began to beat out loud victory dances.

And when Ki-Gor would have fallen over dead asleep, Dingazi asked him to make a special visit to a certain unit, the five hundred men of the Blue-and-White *Impi*. The other five hundred of this *impi* had perished with Lotoko. Ki-Gor told them briefly the story of the ambush, and when he finished a roar came from the warriors and they demanded the right to strike the first avenging blow.

Now, finally, Ki-Gor was allowed to sleep. Three hours sufficed to recoup his strength, however, and he woke up of his own accord with the first rays of a full moon. Dingazi had ordered the horse made ready, and weapons were provided. There were a bow and quiver of arrows, two throwing sticks, and a fine Kara-mzili assegai.

The camp was still wide-awake as Ki-Gor threaded his way between the campfires. One wide section was empty, the fires down to smolder-ing embers, indicating that at least one *impi* had moved out and was padding northward through the moonlight.

Although there was a full seven hours before dawn, Ki-Gor pushed the horse along as fast as he dared. He wanted to get back as soon as possible to the big veldt near the hills in which Julebba lay hiding.

He reasoned that if Helene were safe back in the jungle, he could do no harm by getting between her and the secret base of Julebba's army. And if she were captured he might still be in time to intercept her as she was being taken to the kloof.

He had been riding for nearly four hours when he got a scare, reining in the Tuareg horse sharply. He was just leaving the trail when he realized that the dark figures on the trail ahead were the rear guard of one of Dingazi's *impis* on the march. He walked his horse with the commander of the unit for some distance, and finally, coming to an open run of several hundred moonlit yards, he kicked the horse forward and left the *impi* behind.

The sun was well on its way to the zenith by the time Ki-Gor came within view of the range of hills which was his ultimate destination. The horse was tired and so was Ki-Gor but he was well content. Two hours before he had caught a glimpse of two horsemen in the distance. They were going disconsolately in the same direction he was. There could be no doubt that they were Tuaregs, and Helene was not with them. He had chuckled to himself, Helene had learned well the ways of the jungle. She was as smart and resourceful as a Pygmy.

SEEING THE Tuaregs empty-handed had almost convinced Ki-Gor that Helene had evaded capture. And unless she had rashly gone up into the range of hills, she should be perfectly safe by now. She might have returned to Dingazi to see whether he—Ki-Gor—had come in. Or she might have caught sight of some of the Kara-mzili advance guard, who would have told her that he was free.

But just to make doubly sure, Ki-Gor decided to patrol that part of the veldt for a couple of hours before returning to Dingazi himself. In case Julebba decided to move her little army, Ki-Gor would be there to see and report it.

He dismounted to reduce his visibility and led the horse forward until he was about a mile away from the entrance to the kloof. If Julebba's men came out in any numbers he could see them, and he himself would only be a speck on the veldt. He sat down for a while in the shadow of the horse and gazed at the peaceful hills in front of him. Presently, the sun had climbed so high that there was no more shadow except right under the horse's belly. Ki-Gor stood up and glanced behind him.

He grunted with surprise and swiftly mounted the horse. There was a party of men a quarter of a mile away from him out on the veldt, and they were coming straight toward him. He watched them carefully for a moment, then rode toward them. They were spearmen in the gaily-striped kilts of the Blue-and-White *Impi*.

He had gone hardly a hundred feet toward them, when he gave a glad cry and set his horse at a gallop. Walking in front of the company was Helene!

Just as he had surmised—he told himself exultantly—she had caught sight of them and been told that he was safe. They had made wonderful time, he thought to himself, those men of the Blue-and-White *Impi*. He tried to remember whether they had still been in the camp when he left there.

Now he was riding full tilt at them, waving his arm gaily at Helene. But she did an odd thing. She held up both arms straight over her head and then gestured toward him with a sort of pushing motion of her hands. It was as if she were telling him to go away. Then he heard her voice.

"No, Ki-Gor!" she shouted. "No!"

The men in the blue-and-white striped kilts on each side of her put black hands over her face. Ki-Gor reined in the galloping horse and the cold sweat started out all over his body.

The men were Julebba's Nigerians dressed in dead men's kilts!

They yelled and brandished their spears as Ki-Gor swung the horse out of spear range to consider the situation. Helene had been fooled by the striped kilts just as he had been just now. She had come out of her safe hiding place and walked right into the arms of the Nigerians, thinking they were Kara-mzili. But now, what was to be done?

Ki-Gor rode around the party seething. The entire company of Nigerians was there—at least forty-five men. Could he, single-handed, rescue Helene from them? The only way that could be done would be to kill nearly every one of them. How could he do that? Ki-Gor considered his weapons. He had a tremendous advantage with the horse—and with the Kara-mzili bow. His arrows could outrange their spears. He could circle them on the horse and pick them off one by one with his arrows from a safe distance.

He glanced down at the quiver lashed to the saddle—and groaned. The quiver was full, but still there were barely twenty arrows in it. Suppose that every arrow killed a man, there would still be twenty-five stalwart spearmen left after he had shot them all. He had two throwing sticks—they could account for two more. Still, twenty-three men would be left. And twenty-three spearmen of the caliber of these Nigerians would be too many for him to handle—too many, that is, for him to take a prisoner from.

Another thought struck him. While he was attacking them with arrows, what would be happening to Helene? The chances were that the Nigerians would simply kill her in reprisal for their own dead.

No, he regretfully decided, he could not take Helene from them by force. One other tactic suggested itself, but it had only a remote chance of succeeding. That was to ride down on them hard, depending on the weight and momentum of the horse to carry him through to Helene. He would sweep her up on to the saddle and cut his way out. It was a desperate resort, but he decided to try it.

He rode warily around the company, picking the spot to charge. They had dragged Helene into the middle of the group. Possibly they anticipated the very move he was about to make. With a muttered imprecation, Ki-Gor bent low over the horse's neck and banged his heels against the horse's ribs.

LIKE A bullet the beast shot forward at the shouting mass of Nigerians. But as the horse thundered down on them, they galvanized into action, and flung themselves into a set formation. A dozen men knelt, forming a front rank, and they held their spear butts to the ground, points leaning forward at an angle. Another dozen stood behind in a second rank, and their spears paralleled the front ranks. It was an impregnable defense—the classical maneuver of spear-armed infantry against attacking cavalry, and as old as organized warfare.

Ki-Gor groaned and hauled the head of the speeding horse around. Derisive shouts followed him as he sheered away. He might have known, he told himself, that Julebba would train her men in that formation.

He dragged the horse to a stop and dismounted with a heart of stone. Knowing Julebba's vindictive jealousy and hatred of Helene, he dare not let her be carried into the kloof without him. As long as he could not rescue her by himself, or get help for some time to come—he would go in with her. He would be a helpless prisoner, too, but he would be there to plead, cajole, or threaten Julebba against harming Helene.

"Hai! Brothers!" he called out in Kanuri, holding up his hands so that the Nigerians could see that they were empty. "I will not resist.

You had better not kill me, though, because your queen wants me alive."

They came forward warily, but as soon as they were convinced Ki-Gor was playing no trick, the scowls left their faces. They tied his arms without resentment, and even seemed pleased with him for speaking such fluent Kanuri. They chaffed him good-naturedly for being beaten and captured, and boasted of their queen's cleverness in dressing them in the uniform of the enemy. Most important of all, they let him go straight to his wife.

"Oh, darling!" Helene cried, throwing her arms about his neck, "I guess I ruined everything! I thought maybe you'd fallen into their hands. You didn't come back to Lotoko and me, and you weren't at Dingazi's camp—so I felt I just had to go out and look for you!"

"I know, I know," Ki-Gor said gently. "I was captured, but I got away all right."

"Oh, and now you're captured again!" Helene wailed, "and it's all my stupidity! Why don't I ever learn to trust you to get out of your own difficulties!"

"I wish you had trusted me this time," Ki-Gor said ruefully. "But then, you can't be blamed for thinking these men were Kara-mzili. I was fooled by their dress, too."

"Come on, Brother," one of the Nigerians said. "We have to get along. You can walk with your woman, if you want. But no tricks, now. We will be watching you. One false move and you're a dead man."

"There is nothing I can do, Brother," Ki-Gor replied good-naturedly, as he and Helene fell into stride. "And speaking of dead men, that's what you'll all be when the Kara-mzili catch you in those kilts."

"First they have to catch us," the Nigerians laughed. "We will have killed many of them, and be away before they get over their surprise."

"But there is a day of reckoning coming for you," Ki-Gor said. "Did you know there was a great army coming after you? Not just five hundred this time, but thousands upon thousands!"

"Aye, we heard they were coming," the leader of the Nigerians said carelessly. "But they stopped a day's journey away. They were afraid to come farther. It is a rich joke—they think we are ruled by a ju-ju. All we have to do is to make faces at them and they will break and run. We will be in Dutawayo; in three days, you'll see."

Ki-Gor smiled to himself. Evidently the Nigerians had seen none of the Kara-mzili advance-guard that had been streaming northward from the encampment during the night.

Helene tugged at his arm. "Tell me what's been happening to you," she begged. "How were you captured, and how did you escape?"

BRIEFLY, KI-GOR outlined his adventures from the time he left her with Lotoko's column until he rejoined her as a captive of the Nigerians.

"And now," he concluded, "we are in a desperate spot. Julebba has sworn she is going to kill you, and I have told her that if she kills you, I will kill her. She doesn't seem to be moved by ordinary considerations—I don't know how to appeal to her to do even the things that are in her interest to do."

"Well, I don't know," Helene said. "I think you handled her pretty well when you were first captured. You said she was on the point of having you killed on the spot."

"I don't think I had much to do with changing her mind, though," Ki-Gor said wearily. "She just seemed to develop a sudden—sudden—love, no, love isn't the word—she doesn't love me—"

"Infatuation," Helene supplied.

"Infatuation, then," Ki-Gor said. "Although, I think it was really that she suddenly realized that I was white. And she, being a white woman, decided that she should have a white husband." He smiled at her.

"My dear," Helene said dryly, "if she'd been coal-black, she would still have wanted you. Don't be so modest. Any girl would want you."

"Well, anyway, that's the situation," Ki-Gor said ignoring his wife's remark. "I don't know just what we're going to do. Wait and see, I suppose. By the time we are taken in front of her, she may have changed her mind about killing you, who knows? But sooner or later, the Kara-mzili are coming. They will surround the kloof and they'll force their way in, no matter how many of them are killed. Dingazi promised me that. But how soon they can get there, I don't know. We may both be dead before they go, or we may be killed as soon as the attack begins."

Helene walked silently for a few seconds, eyes on the ground. Then she looked up at Ki-Gor.

"Darling, I wouldn't be honest," she said, "if I didn't admit that I've got a dreadful sinking feeling in the stomach. I've faced death before, but I don't ever recall walking in to it—"

"I had to tell you," Ki-Gor said defensively. "You couldn't go in without a little warning—"

"Oh, I don't mean that, darling," Helene responded quickly. "Of course you had to tell me. All I wanted to say was this—it's been nice knowing you, darling—and—and—if we've got to die now, thank God we're together!"

She smiled at her mate, then looked away quickly before he could see the tears roll out of her blue eyes. Characteristically, Ki-Gor scowled ferociously.

"We're not dead, yet, Helene," he growled. "Not yet!"

As Helene looked back at him, she noticed that he was limping slightly.

"Darling!" she cried, "is your leg hurting you terribly?"

"No," he replied calmly, "it doesn't hurt very much. But I want our enemies to think I can hardly walk."

By the time the little company entered the kloof, Ki-Gor was limping so heavily that he had to be supported on each side by a derisive Nigerian.

There was tremendous excitement in the clearing within the kloof when the Nigerians swaggered in with their two prisoners. Their arrival evidently cut short some ceremony or spectacle of some sort. Julebba was on her throne, her seven apes squatting about on the rocks which formed its pedestal. On the ground in front of her stood Mohammed and his two sons. In front of them a tall thick stake had been driven into the ground, and leaning up against that stake, his wrists lashed to it high above his head, was Hurree Das.

The Hindu's body was bare except for the voluminous *dhoti* that draped over his legs from his plump waist, and his lemon-colored back was striped with red welts. Evidently, Hurree Das was being punished for something. However, the punishment had not been too severe, because the skin of the back had not been broken.

Julebba shouted some commands. Hurree Das was freed and staggered away to one side, and the Nigerians paraded before the throne with their prisoners.

Julebba's huge eyes rested in silence for a moment, first on Helene and then on Ki-Gor. Finally, her red mouth curved in a cruel smile.

"GREETINGS, KI-GOR," she said, her deep voice ironic. "This should show you how useless it is to try to run away from us. You are recaptured and brought back even before we have finished punishing the stupid dolt who was responsible for your escape."

"If you mean that Hurree Das helped me," Ki-Gor said—he certainly owed this to the Hindu—"you are wrong. He just forgot his bag."

"Oh, I know he didn't intentionally help you," Julebba said contemptuously. "He wouldn't dare. But if he hadn't forgotten his bag, you wouldn't have escaped. But, let's get to more important matters. How far away did you get, Ki-Gor? Did you see your friend Dingazi?"

Ki-Gor hesitated a second, frantically trying to decide what to answer. Finally he said, "Yes."

Julebba's answer was a hearty laugh. "I'm sorry," she said, "but I don't believe you. You didn't have time." She turned to the leader of the Nigerians. "Where did you catch him?" she asked in Kanuri.

Ki-Gor held his breath as the man told her. By a miracle, the Nigerian forgot to mention the horse.

"Very funny, Ki-Gor," Julebba said. "What did you tell Dingazi and what did he tell you?"

"He told me," Ki-Gor said carefully, "that he would surround this place with ten thousand men."

Julebba laughed again. "A pretty bluff, Ki-Gor," she said. "Only I happen to know that Dingazi, after coming half the distance from Dutawayo with an army, stopped dead. Because he and his men were too terrified to come any farther. By now they are probably flying back to Dutawayo. Your bluff won't work, Ki-Gor. You should learn from me never to bluff unless you have some means of backing it up. Now, here is what I propose to do with you. You have refused my heart and hand which I offered you. That hurt me for a moment, but I got over it, I am completely indifferent to you now. So much so that I wouldn't even trouble myself to kill you in revenge. From now on, I am completely uninterested in you or this redheaded woman whom you seem to be so attached to. You could go your way this minute— if I did not see in you an instrument. I can use you to make a swift and final conquest of the Kara-mzili. Dingazi is afraid, but he still has thousands of soldiers. He must make them swear fealty to me. To get him to do that, I must have him personally in my power. Dingazi must come here to me. And, you, Ki-Gor, must bring him!"

Again Ki-Gor had to admire the woman's ruthless cunning, her reckless daring. He guessed what was coming next.

"So," Julebba went on, "I am going to turn you loose. You will find Dingazi and you will bring him back to me. You will bring him back alone—he must have no soldiers with him. How you will accomplish that, I don't know. That is your problem. But you are clever, you will find a way. Because your little wife is going to remain here as a hostage. She will be perfectly safe—remember, I have no personal feelings one way or another toward you, now—she will be perfectly safe until you come back with Dingazi alone. If you betray me, if you attempt to rescue her by force—she will be dead long before you can fight your way in here."

"If I fight my way in here," Ki-Gor said evenly, "and find her dead—you will not live long."

"We will not be here, my friend," Julebba said. "You forget there is a back way out of this kloof—a route you have never traveled."

Ki-Gor decided to let her continue to believe that.

"Well then," he said, "suppose I can bring Dingazi here, and you get what you want from him—then what happens to my wife and me?"

"You go free, of course," Julebba said calmly. "I might even make you some sort of reward for your services."

Ki-Gor sank his chin in his collarbone, as if considering the offer. Actually, he was delighted with it. Anything that would gain time was to his advantage—time to allow the Kara-mzili to surround the kloof in such force that Julebba could not escape. When he could show her that, he could bargain with her. Her life to be spared, if Helene was set free unharmed.

"All right," he said, finally. "I haven't much choice. But to find Dingazi and bring him back will take time—four or five days perhaps. More, perhaps, because I am very lame."

"I will give you three days," Julebba said. "I will lend you a horse. You will start immediately. Ahmed and Ali will ride with you a short distance to see that you go in the right direction. But if I know you right, and I think I do, you will not try any tricks. You are too much in love with your wife."

HELENE'S FACE was bloodless as she watched the Nigerians take the ropes off Ki-Gor, and as he came to her and put his arms around her in farewell.

"Ki-Gor!" she whispered in his ear, "What on earth are you going to do now?"

"Don't be afraid," he murmured, "This is good for us—gives us the time we need."

"But—do you think when you come back—you'll—you'll find me alive?"

A cold finger touched Ki-Gor's heart. "Yes," he said. "As long as you are more useful to her alive, you will stay alive."

He was sure that was true, but he nevertheless felt an unpleasant uneasiness as he mounted the horse that was brought up, then.

"Good-bye," he said looking down at Helene, "and be brave." Then he looked up at the throne and said, "Good-bye, O Queen, keep your promises and I'll keep mine. I'll see you in three days—maybe sooner."

He rode in silence out of the kloof, Ahmed on his left side, and Ali on his right. Not until the trio had issued out on to the veldt did anyone speak. Then Ahmed said through clenched teeth, "Do not think for a moment, dog of a Nasrani, that I forgive you your trickery! Do not think that Ahmed ben Mohammed forgives the lying son of a pig who gulled him, with soft words of a philter—!"

Ki-Gor looked at the hateful mask which was Ahmed's face. What was this all about? Were these two Arabs going to try and kill him?

"Oh, do not fear for your miserable life, Nasrani!" Ahmed snarled. "You are safe enough—for the moment. Our beloved queen has ordered it so, and so it shall be. Otherwise I would never be riding with you in peace like this. If I could have my way, you would be on the ground, my knee on your chest, my knife at your throat—"

"Nay, calm yourself, my brother!" exclaimed Ali, on the other side of Ki-Gor. "There is plenty of time for your revenge."

"Aye, there is," Ahmed grumbled, "but it wears hard on a man's pride to delay collecting—"

"You can wait," Ali said soothingly. "After all, there is a terrible revenge already taking pl—"

"Silence! You fool!" Ahmed shouted. And Ki-Gor's blood froze.

"I—I—mean, I—" young Ali stammered.

"You have said enough!" Ahmed stormed.

By sheer will power, Ki-Gor kept his face composed, as if he had not understood Ali at all. But the two Arabs stared at him with embarrassment and suspicion. Ki-Gor assumed a mildly puzzled frown.

"What do you mean?" he said finally, as if he had not the remotest idea of Ali's involuntary revelation. "What revenge?"

Now Ahmed had a story ready. "Revenge on you, Nasrani! Your friend the Hindu hakim is just about now being thrown to the apes!"

Ki-Gor stared incredulously, then laughed out loud. "My friend!" he shouted, then laughed again. "What typical Muslim stupidity! The Hindu is no friend of mine! Why he couldn't even heal my wound properly!"

He laughed some more to cover up the furious workings of his brain. The covert, malicious smile on Ahmed's thin face was unnecessary confirmation of that which he was already convinced of. That somebody was being thrown to the apes, but that that somebody was not Hurree Das. It was Helene!

"Ow!" Ki-Gor yelled, reining in his horse. "My leg! I hope the apes do a good job on that fool of a hakim! Here, I have to stop a moment and rest this leg."

Then he acted.

He drew his bandaged right leg up double, putting his foot on the saddle. Then, before Ahmed realized what was happening, he had disengaged his other foot from the stirrup and sprung from the horse. He went through the air like a panther, hit Ahmed shoulder-high, and in the same breath wrenched the scimitar out of his right hand. His momentum carried him across the back of Ahmed's horse. He landed lightly on the ground on his feet beside the screaming Arab who was hanging head down out of the saddle.

One ruthless blow of the scimitar nearly decapitated Ahmed. The frightened horse plunged away dragging its bloody burden. Ki-Gor, not wasting a motion, bounded straight at the shrieking younger brother. And even though Ali had some warning, he was helpless against the murderous assault by the jungle man.

IT WAS the matter of a moment to strip Ali's bloody robe and headdress off and hastily throw them over himself. Then still grasping the scimitar, he caught the nearest horse and started back for the kloof at full gallop.

Would he be in time? The agonizing question asked itself over and over again in his tortured brain as the horse pounded over the two miles that separated him from the kloof. Gradually, his mind cleared a little, and he asked himself what he would do if he *were* in time. A sweeping glance of the horizon showed no evidence of the Karamzili being near enough. It was still early to expect them, he admitted with an inward groan. And yet the *impis* had been on their way since midnight, and they were burning for revenge, hastening to the kill. There was the remote possibility that the advance guard had circled northward to come down the back way into the kloof. But that was a hope Ki-Gor hardly dared to entertain. For a while at least, he was on his own. He would have to save Helene—if she still lived—singlehanded.

He blamed himself endlessly for falling into Julebba's trap so easily. He should have been instantly suspicious, he told himself, of her airy renouncement of interest in him. It was out of character. He should have known that she would wreak a terrible revenge on Helene the moment he had gone.

He was nearing the entrance to the kloof now, and he still had no concrete plan of action. But the vague impulse which had prompted him to put on the Arab burnoose and turban suddenly pointed to an impromptu course of action. As he thundered toward the narrow leafy gateway, he began shouting in Hausa to the unseen Ubangi sentinels in the trees.

"The Kara-mzili!" he yelled, as if panic-stricken. "All is lost! The Kara-mzili are coming! Thousands upon thousands of them! All is lost! Save yourselves!"

Without slackening pace, he plunged down the path toward the clearing still shouting his warning of a fictitious enemy at his heels. As he burst into the clearing, a fearsome, bloodstained apparition, he saw that he was barely in time.

Helene was tied to the stake in front of the throne, tied by her wrists above her head, the way Hurree Das had been. But she was facing outward, her back to the stake, and staring with horror and loathing at the two black apes who stood in front of her. The other five hairy creatures were crouched on the rock pedestal below Julebba's throne. By their attitudes, they expected soon to join their fellows around the stake, around that fair, tender body....

When Ki-Gor first appeared, Julebba and her men were too shocked and astounded to move. The clearing was a small one, and the galloping horse carried Ki-Gor across it to Helene in a few seconds. The chimpanzees nearest Helene dodged chattering away from the horse's flying hoofs. Ki-Gor sprang from the horse's back, his bloodstained burnoose flying. He hit the ground just behind one of the scrambling apes. Down flashed the scimitar on the flat, brutish head. Ki-Gor snarled with pure unleashed rage as he felt the blade bite into the hard skull—felt it snap off at the hilt under the terrific impact of the blow. He flung useless hilt aside and whirled to meet the next brute.

Through a red haze he saw the other five shambling down toward him, heard Julebba's piercing shriek, heard the confused babble of her army. Instinctively, he shucked off the loose burnoose and the head-dress. The nearest ape was charging him now. Ki-Gor flung the burnoose full at him, then leaped after the burnoose. The ape struggled in the folds of the robe—struggled only a few seconds, though. Ki-Gor leaped over him, launching a furious kick as he did so, and the ape collapsed quivering.

Through a red haze Ki-Gor saw five huge chimpanzees scuttling toward him, jaws a-slaver. Without hesitation, he swept down upon the nearest one, seized an arm and a leg, and swept the chattering, snapping beast high in the air over his head. Then he flung him squarely at the next nearest ape. Like a cat that tosses a mouse in the air and then runs after it, Ki-Gor was on the ape again. Seizing a limp black arm, he danced backward, raising the squealing beast off the ground. Then he began to whirl the heavy, black body around his head by that one arm.

"A-a-a-r-r-r-gh!"

Ki-Gor roared his defiance and hardly realized he did it. Three chimpanzees charged him in a body now, and the broken half-dead carcass that was whirling over Ki-Gor's head went crashing into them. He pounced on one of them, lifted it by its short legs, dashed its brains out on the pedestal of Julebba's throne.

ALL THIS time, there had been a mounting roar in the kloof, but Ki-Gor had had eyes only for apes. He whirled now, looking for the next one to tackle. Just as he did, something prodigiously heavy hit him on the back of a shoulder. He stumbled forward, nearly fell down, with a biting, clawing brute trying to reach his throat. Ki-Gor jabbed his right fist back over his left shoulder, caught the brute just under the round black ear. Then, seizing a hairy wrist, he hauled the stunned ape off his shoulder, and hurled him to the ground.

One more ape remained on its feet. He had been knocked down when Ki-Gor threw the body of one of his fellows at him. He stood now ten feet from Ki-Gor chattering with terror. The jungle man took one step toward him, and the ape wheeled and ran away like the wind.

Ki-Gor shook the red haze out of his head and looked around him.

An extraordinary silence hung over the clearing. He saw that his mad combats had carried him far to one side away from the throne and the stake that Helene was still tied to. Standing a safe distance away a mixed mob of Balubas, Nigerians, and Ubangi archers gazed at him in awestricken silence.

The silence was broken by Julebba.

"Cowards!" she screamed. "Craven wretches! Catch that man and kill him!"

Ki-Gor looked back at her. Beyond her, far beyond her, by the tents among the trees, something moved.

"It is too late, O Julebba!" he cried. "Your murderous career is over!"

But Julebba did not even hear him. She was climbing down from the throne, mouthing imprecations, and brandishing her royal spear. Still screaming, she leaped to the ground and sped straight toward the helpless figure of Helene tied to the stake. Ki-Gor was a split-second late divining her intention. And when he started running, he was afraid he would be too late to prevent the mad queen from running Helene through with the spear.

Then from nowhere appeared the paunchy figure of Hurree Das. He was still naked to his loincloth, and his round face shook with terror. But he stood squarely in Julebba's path. In his right hand a metal cylinder gleamed.

Julebba tried to swerve around the Hindu. But he shot out a pudgy hand, seized her accurately by one elbow. There was a quick struggle, then Julebba flung away, screaming and holding her elbow.

Ki-Gor reached Helene's side, looked back at the advancing mob of Julebba's men—and prepared to die. Then he threw a glance over his shoulder to the other end of the clearing where the tents stood among the trees.

"Hurree Das!" Ki-Gor shouted, "come over to me quickly and get out of the way! The Kara-mzili are here!"

Like a horde of dark avenging angels, the kilted warriors of Dingazi poured into the clearing from the back way. Without a shout or any clamor of any kind, they padded down silently for the kill. The Ever-Victorious Army recoiled, then broke and ran for the narrow path leading out of the kloof. They well knew the revenge the Kara-mzili would take. But they did not know that there were more kilted warriors waiting impatiently for them.

The Kara-mzili slew quietly and purposefully. They were a mighty fighting race, and they were avenging the blow to their pride as well as the death of their comrades who had marched with Lotoko. And here the tables were exactly turned. Here, the Ever-Victorious Army was demoralized, showing that the best discipline in the world can be cracked by shock and surprise. A few of the Nigerians attempted to organize a defense, but they were too few and were soon swept away in the tidal wave of blood. The Tuaregs rode around in a panic until they were swallowed up in the black mass of Kara-mzili. The Balubas and the bowmen from the Ubangi fled in all directions.

Less than a half-hour after the first kilted warrior had entered the kloof, the last of Julebba's men was hunted out of a tree and dispatched. Julebba was dead, too, but she had died from the deadly poison in Hurree Das' hypodermic needle.

THE PLUMP doctor was still trembling three hours later. Dingazi had just arrived with his main army, disgusted because they had not been in time to participate in the triumph of the advance guard. But a camp was promptly set up out on the veldt, and a victory feast was promised as soon as some food could be brought up.

"Oh, dearie me!" said Hurree Das. "Am not at all positive I can eat any food for some time to come!"

"By the time the food is ready," Ki-Gor smiled, "I think you'll be hungry."

"Oh, but you don't seem to realize!" the Hindu said. "This is positively first time I ever intentionally killed anybody.

"Any doctor may 'lose a patient,' don't you know? But, here I simply walked up to a poor woman and did her in!"

"I wouldn't call her a poor woman," Helene said with a reminiscent shiver.

"No, no," the Hindu said. "That, I'm granting you, is most horrible inaccuracy. More correctly let us denominate her—homicidal maniac. No, what is so remarkable is simply that I, Hurree Das, a Gujerati Brahmin, should be elected as Instrument of Fate. I—whose ancestors were vegetarian and who never killed so much as a chicken in four thousand years!"

"Incidentally," said Helene, "what was the poison you used in the syringe?"

"Vegetable poison distilled from plant of Genus Strychnos," said the doctor. "Same like Pygmies use on their arrows—exactly same."

"For heaven's sake!" Helene exclaimed. "That is extraordinary!"

"How so, dear lady?" Hurree Das inquired.

"Why, before Ki-Gor and I had ever heard of Julebba—or even knew that Dingazi was in trouble, we were talking about coming up to pay you a visit."

"Delighted, I'm sure," said Hurree Das. "What was occasion of such conversation?"

"I had just missed being hit accidentally by one of the Pygmy's arrows. I was simply terrified, because if I *had* been hit, I wouldn't have known what to use for an antidote. What is the antidote, Hurree Das?"

"Absolutely and positively no antidote," Hurree Das said cheerfully. "It is most marvelous poison."

"Ki-Gor!" Helene looked around her brows at her huge mate. "Do you think you can make the Pygmies stop using poisoned arrows around us?"

Ki-Gor sighed and nodded. He did not relish the idea. Ngeeso had a quick wit and a sharp tongue, and Ki-Gor would rather battle the Ever-Victorious Army single-handed than have a battle of words with Ngeeso, who was three feet, eleven inches tall.

STORY XIII

SLAVES FOR THE RENEGADE SULTAN

THOUGH IT WAS YET early morning, a malevolent sun glowed balefully through a stifling haze which was so thick that Ki-Gor could scarcely see the edge of the bamboo forest a mile down the mountain side. Beyond that forest endless miles of khaki-colored plains stretched eastward, but Ki-Gor sensed rather than saw them through the murk. He and his wife, the red-haired Helene, had paused momentarily beneath the drooping withered leaves of an ironwood tree. Beside them was the almost dry bed of what was once a fair-sized mountain river. All that was left of that river now was a small brook muttering impotently down the middle of the sandy water course.

Ki-Gor turned his head and gazed southward and a little westward to the tumbled peaks of Ruwenzori barely outlined through the gauzy veil of haze. Then he looked forward again to the east and shook his head.

"This is bad," Ki-Gor said. "What's the word—when there is no rain? And everything dries up?"

"Drought," Helene supplied.

"Drought—oh yes," Ki-Gor said. "They are having a bad one over here. The rains should have come long before now. I wonder what the Ngombi-Maasai are doing about their cattle."

"What can they do?" Helene asked. "I guess maybe we picked a poor time to come and visit George."

"Maybe we did," Ki-Gor admitted. "But we don't have to stay long. We'll tell him how things are with Dingazi, and then go along toward home. The big *minyata* is not far from here—we'll be there soon. We'll spend the day, and stay tonight maybe, and then start off tomorrow morning." He turned and looked at the river bed again. "Teh! The water is low. I once floated down this river on a raft. Now we can walk down it."

They moved on down the slope along the river bank, the bronzed yellow-haired giant and his slender red-haired mate. Helene was proud nowadays of the fact that Ki-Gor no longer needed to adjust his pace to hers—or if he did, it was very little. She had picked up the ways of the African wilderness remarkably well since she had joined her life with Ki-Gor's. Her already athletic body had become even further hardened, and she had acquired some of Ki-Gor's supreme self-confidence in the savage jungle and trackless veldt.

Ki-Gor stopped abruptly and her eyes quested keenly for the reason. "There!" she told herself, that's how self-confident I've become! Once upon a time I would have been scared silly at those vague shapes looming up through the haze over there!

The ground here had leveled off for a little distance, forming a small plateau, an upland meadow. The river, shrunken though it was, flowed more slowly and widened out into good-sized pools. The vague shapes Ki-Gor was watching were moving slowly about the pools a half a mile away. For a moment, Helene could not make them out—their outlines being blurred by the bamboo forest beyond. But Ki-Gor's astonishing eyesight was un-baffled.

"Cattle," he said briefly. "Maasai cattle—with the big horns and the little feet. How did they get up here?"

HIS LEFT hand felt behind his neck and eased the hunting bow which was slung across his broad bronzed back, then his right hand slid up the haft of his mighty spear and took a new grip. Then Ki-Gor moved forward.

"They're perfectly gentle and tame, those cattle, aren't they?" Helene murmured inquiringly.

"Oh yes," Ki-Gor replied, blue eyes twinkling. "They are when the Maasai drive them. They will not be accustomed to having Ki-Gor drive them, though."

"Oh?" Helene murmured, and waited for Ki-Gor to explain.

"They shouldn't be up here without someone watching them," Ki-Gor went on. "They probably wandered up the river bed looking for more water, or this green grass up here."

"But you think they shouldn't be here?" Helene asked.

"If cattle like green grass," Ki-Gor said, "lions like cattle."

"I begin to understand," Helene smiled.

"There!" Ki-Gor whispered sharply. "We are just in time! Look—creeping over the bank toward the cattle."

Helene's eyes opened wide. An indistinct tawny shape, almost the color of the bamboo canes, was oozing out of the grass at the raised bank of the river bed. Without Ki-Gor to point him out, however, Helene would never have noticed the lion.

Ki-Gor slid down on to the sand of the river bed. The lion was about three hundred yards away.

"Stay with me," Ki-Gor directed quietly, "but not too close. If I don't move fast, our friends the Ngombi-Maasai are going to lose some cows."

Then Ki-Gor was sprinting down the river bed. Helene, following as fast as she could, marveled how swiftly and silently he carried his giant frame. He needn't have worried, she reflected, about her staying too close to him. When he ran like that, she never in the world could keep up with him. In a few seconds, he had far outstripped her.

When he had covered half the distance toward his goal, the lion still had not seen him, but the Maasai cattle had. They raised their heads from the pool they were drinking from, and stared uneasily. Here and there great horns tossed, and tiny hoofs shifted. The lion's muscles knotted tensely as he prepared to spring before his prey moved out of reach.

Ki-Gor, a hundred yards away now, had a fast decision to make. Would the lion spring before Ki-Gor could reach him? Ki-Gor hoped he would not. But if he did—there! The tawny brute crouched suddenly.

Without hesitation, Ki-Gor roared a challenge. The lion checked itself just as it was about to launch through the air. It fell forward awkwardly and rolled scrambling down the bank to the river bed. For a split second, the beast sprawled on its chin, all four legs thrashing and clawing. Just as it scrambled to its feet, and before it had quite discovered what had distracted it from its spring, Ki-Gor was upon it.

Without slackening his furious pace, Ki-Gor took off in a prodigious leap. He left the ground fifteen feet from the bemused lion. The brute gave a strangled bellow, started to rear on its hind legs, and then finally ducked and rolled over on its back like a frightened house cat.

Ki-Gor, sailing five inches over the raking claws, plunged his mighty spear straight downward into the twisting, tawny body. The razor-edged, trowel-like blade bit through the thick dirty-yellow fur. All of Ki-Gor's might had gone into that prodigious downward thrust. The blade sheared through a rib over the lion's heart and plunged on through the beast's vitals and out the other side, pinning it to the sandy earth.

As Ki-Gor hit the ground on the other side of the lion, he skipped a few paces forward and turned. The lion uttered a fearsome screech, arched its back convulsively, and finally straightened out in a frantic rolling leap. Snapping and clawing, it dislodged the impaling spear-blade from the loose sand and flung its tortured body from side to side. The Maasai cattle, thrown into sudden panic, were bellowing to the heavens.

Because of the bedlam of noise, Ki-Gor did not hear Helene's warning shriek. Only his own extraordinary intuitive sense of danger impelled him to fling himself to the ground. Another roar was added to the frightful welter of sound, and a lioness hit the sand just in front of the jungle man.

SHE HAD evidently crouched unseen behind her mate up on the bank, then had leaped at Ki-Gor as his back was turned toward her. She swerved to face Ki-Gor with incredible agility. At the same time, he gathered his feet under him and flung himself toward her tail. His knife was in his right hand, but it was a poor weapon against an enraged lioness. The great spear was spitted through the dying male lion, and it would take more than a few seconds to disengage it. But until he could get hold of his spear, Ki-Gor was in appalling danger from the lion's mate.

As he darted for her hind quarters, she circled with him, coughing and snarling. He dug his feet in the sand and dodged backward. It was imperative that he keep the lioness off balance. If she gained a second to set herself for a spring, he would be in a bad way.

Cursing himself for having forgotten that lions often hunt in pairs, Ki-Gor threw himself into a dance for life. The muscles of his great thighs rippled as he feinted one way and then the other. The lioness moved swiftly with him. So fast was she, and so nimbly did she follow Ki-Gor's lightning movements, that the jungle man felt a sick dread begin to steal over him. He had faced other lions before now armed only with a knife and somehow survived. But each time he had been cruelly mauled. Every wound from a lion's claws or jaws must be drastically cauterized, and he had been laid up for days after those other fights.

He felt reasonably sure that he could kill this lioness before she could kill him, but it would cost him a lot in blood and pain, and he

quite reasonably wished he could avoid it. Then, suddenly, he thought of Helene.

What was she doing? In his grim concentration on the lioness, he had lost sight of everything else about him. He had to see what Helene was doing. Yet he dared not look away from the lioness for even a fraction of a second. So he proceeded by a daring series of leaps to circle the lioness. Gradually, twisting and shifting, he had maneuvered himself and the lioness so that he was facing upstream and could look over her shoulder. What he saw appalled him.

Helene was standing over the lion he had mortally wounded. She was dodging the raking claws of the brute as he twisted in his death agony. She was trying to wrest Ki-Gor's spear out of his writhing, blood-soaked body.

"Helene!" Ki-Gor yelled. "No! No! Stand away from him—"

Just then the lioness leaped. For the flicker of an eyelash, Ki-Gor's attention had been distracted from her, and that fraction of a moment nearly cost him his life. As it was, he was just able to duck under the lioness' hurtling body. A heavy forepaw whistled past his head. If the blow had connected, it might have broken his neck. But the blow did not connect, and the lioness overshot her target. She landed sprawling again, her hind claws raking the ground an inch from Ki-Gor's thigh. This time, however, the lioness recovered her balance quicker than Ki-Gor did.

With a fearsome roar she swung around and saw her enemy sprawled helpless on his back. Ki-Gor had just time to double his knees and bring them up over his stomach when the snarling beast was on top of him. Grimly he shielded his throat with his left arm and struck upwards furiously with the knife in his right hand. Whatever happened, he was resigned to a bad clawing.

But by some miracle the lioness was not clawing him. Her body rested heavily on his doubled up knees, but it began to dawn on Ki-Gor that her great forepaws were curled inward and twitching aimlessly on his chest. Then a well-remembered voice boomed out over the bedlam of sound, and something was hauling the limp carcass of the lioness to one side. Ki-Gor blinked and looked incredulously up at Tembu George.

The big American Negro dropped to his knees beside Ki-Gor, anxious-eyed.

"Y'all right, Ki-Gor?" he demanded. "My lawd, that was reelly sumpin'. A man takes on a li'ness without nuthin' but a little bitty knife to go with. Is you *crazy*, Ki-Gor? Is you out of yo' mind?"

SLOWLY THE jungle man got to his feet, while Tembu George rumbled on. At their feet the lioness lay still, an ax buried deep in her flat skull. Helene came and laid her head silently on Ki-Gor's shoulder for a moment. Ki-Gor shot an anxious look at her face. Then he saw that she was not going to cry, and relaxed with a smile. He held out a hand to Tembu George.

"Thank you, friend," he said. "I think you saved my life."

"Shucks!" George retorted. "I nevuh did no such a thing. You prob'ly been all right. But you mighta got some claw-mahks. An' seein's how you was p'tectin' ouah cows—why I thought I ought to kind of take a hand."

"But—but where were you?" Ki-Gor demanded.

"Down the rivuh a spell," George said. "Me and some of the boys"—he waved a hand toward four gigantic Maasai coming toward them—"seen these-yere cow-tracks down below, so we come on up to git 'em. We was away down yonder by the bamboo trees when we see you take on them li'ns. We come along as fast as we could—but, shucks!"—he broke off and stared at the lioness—"you didn't need no he'p with that fust one, anyways."

Helene now lifted her head from Ki-Gor's breast, her self-control restored. She smiled and thanked George, while Ki-Gor fell silent. In truth, Ki-Gor was acutely embarrassed. He did not regret having gone to the rescue of the Maasai cattle. It was quite likely that the lions would have destroyed the entire group of them, which would have represented a considerable loss. What embarrassed Ki-Gor was the fact that he had so disregarded ordinary caution in attacking the first lion that he had found himself in terrible peril of life from the lioness. Ki-Gor was, of course, utterly brave, and he never hesitated to take fearful chances. But his daring was always calculated. He prided himself on never endangering his life unnecessarily. But here was one occasion when he had impetuously gone beyond the limits of his usual prudence. And his displeasure with himself was increased by the knowledge that his friend, Tembu George, had risked his own life to save him.

He stared down at the bloody head of the lioness, at the ax that had split her skull. Then he bent down for a closer look. Ki-Gor had never seen a tooled ax before. His hand closed over the helve and jerked. Then he straightened up and gazed curiously at the gory bit.

"What is it?" he finally asked George.

The big American Negro smiled. "Don't you know, Ki-Gor?" he said. "Why that there is a sho'nuf ax. I jest bought it last week f'om

a trader in f'om the Coast. Mighty useful thing when a man is fixin'
to cut down a tree or somepin'. Nevuh thought I'd be killin' li'ns with
it. But that goes to show you. You nevuh know whut you goin' to be
doin' day after tomorrow."

"An ax," Ki-Gor murmured, with a pleased smile, and handed the
implement to George. "It is good. You must show me how to use it."

"I'll have to practice up some musse'f," George admitted with a
grin. "I used to be right handy with one when I was a kid down in
old Kaintuck'—but say! How come you two way ovuh this side of the
mountains?"

"Why, we were coming to call on you, George," Helene said.

"Is that a fact?" George beamed. "Well, I kinda hoped mebbe that
was on yo' mind. Yessuh, that there is good news fo' me. Well, c'mon
then, le's get on down. I bet y'all could do with somepin' to eat."

As the group walked down the river bed beside the shrunken
stream, George and Ki-Gor and his wife exchanged news.

"We all kinda bothered with this yere drought," George confided.
"It sho' nuf has dried us all out down yonduh. We all has been kinda
wonderin' if we hadn't oughta do somepin' about it."

He went on then to explain that the regular seasonal rains were a
month overdue, and that the question of pasturage for the great herds
of the Maasai was getting serious.

"An' it ain't only us that is sufferin'," George said. "Eve'ybody fo'
hundreds of miles 'round is in a bad way. An', you know, tha's whut
stahts trouble. You take one tribe, say, ovuh here an' they run outa
water—why they begin lookin' ovuh the fence onto the next tribe's
land. An' if the next tribe got a little water left, why they is goin' to be
a fight about who-all is goin' to use that water. Fust thing you know,
you got a war on yo' hands."

"Ah!" Ki-Gor said, "have you been having trouble with your old
enemies, the Nandi?"

"No," said George, "the Nandi ain't bothered us none. But fust off,
the Nandi ain't my *pussonal* enemies. They is old enemies of the Maasai,
and I is livin' with the Maasai—"

"And the Maasai do what you tell them?" Ki-Gor interrupted
shrewdly.

"WELL," GEORGE grinned. "It's a funny thing. Here's this cullud
fella, an American Negro, call George Spelvin, an' he is ship's cook
on this boat comin' into Mombasa. Well, it's the fust time this fella

evuh been to Africa, an' he jest leaves the ship an' takes a walk for
hisse'f inland. An' he gets along real well with all the African boys,
an' fust thing you know, he ain't George Spelvin no mo'. He is Tembu
George", an' he is permanent guest of these yere Maasai."

"He isn't the Headman—yet," Helene grinned.

"Oh, no!" George corrected. "An' he ain't nevuh goin' to be. Ol'
Shafara is still Headman down yonder. But whut I'm tryin' to tell
you—sometimes the boys will ask me whut-all I think about somepin'
that has maybe come up. An' nine times out of ten, why they'll go
ahead like I tell 'em."

"Why that's wonderful, George," Helene remarked. "That means
you have all the influence without any of the responsibility."

"Yeah, tha's about the size of it," George admitted with a twinkle.
"Only thing is, of co'se—whut I tell 'em better be right, or I ain't goin'
to have the influence very long. So far, I has been lucky. Now take
with the Nandi. Fo' years and years, the Maasai and the Nandi has
been mortal enemies—an' fo' no reason that I c'n figger out. The Nandi
is blood-cousins of the Maasai. They look like 'em, only they ain't quite
so tall. They act like 'em, only they ain't quite so tough in a battle—the
Maasai usually beats. But here they go—both sides carryin' on like a
bunch o' little boys wearin' chips on they shoulders. 'Come on, boy.'
says the Maasai, 'knock 'at chip off an' see whut it gets you.' The Nandi
says, 'I hear you talkin', but all you got is a lotta big-mouth.' An' away
they go, hammer and tongs! An' they ain't no need for it. The Nandi
is hunters, and the Maasai is cattle-raisers—they ain't no reason for
'em to get in each other's way."

"Don't tell us you were able to convince your friends that war with
the Nandi was unnecessary," Helene said.

"Well, I kinda postponed it, anyways," George said. "I don't know
how long they'll hold out—but it's been all quiet 'long the Potomac
fo' some time now."

"That's good," Ki-Gor said. "Then the drought has not caused—"

"Well, I'm 'fraid it has," George interrupted. "Tha's one thing about
Africa. If it ain't one thing, it's anothuh. We got peace with the Nandi,
but lawd! trouble starts comin' up maybe f'om anothuh direction."

Throughout this conversation, the trio had been progressing down
the river-bed, picking their way among the boulders and fallen tree
trunks that lined the almost dry water-course. Part of the way had
been through the belt of bamboo forest, and Ki-Gor was thankful

they could go along the river bed rather than through the forest itself. For the great canes grew so close together that it would have been slow and difficult going for human beings, and it would have been impassable for the cows that the Maasai boys were herding along behind.

Presently, the bamboo gave way to a narrow belt of hardwood forest which diminished into parkland, and finally to a dry, treeless prairie. From there it was only a short distance over the withered grass to the great *minyata,* or kraal, of the Ngombi-Maasai.

Evidently George's guests were spotted from afar. For scores of gigantic Maasai came streaming out of the *minyata,* laughing and waving their arms gaily and made for George and his two friends. Ki-Gor and his lovely mate were extremely popular with the Maasai. And Ki-Gor, in turn, liked and respected the tall, superb warrior-herdsmen.

Shafara, the Headman, and young Merishu, the seven-foot War Chief, greeted the jungle man and his mate with thunderous shouts and hospitable exclamations, and the last lap of the journey into the *minyata* was made with a joyous escort consisting of most of the tribe. Once inside the gates of the kraal, Ki-Gor and Helene followed George to his house while the villagers hastened preparations for an impromptu banquet to be held later in the day.

ANOTHER WARM welcome awaited the travelers inside the house of Tembu George. His handsome wife, Princess Shaliba, greeted them heartily and took Helene into another room to hear the news of her father Dingazi, King of the Kara-mzili.

"You spoke of trouble from another direction," Ki-Gor suggested, when he and George were alone.

"Yeah," George replied. "Did you ever heah of a fella called Black Mike?"

"The slave-runner?" Ki-Gor said sharply, "with the fort down toward Lake Tsaga?"

"That's the one," George affirmed. "Great big white man—"

"He is bad," Ki-Gor said.

"He is poison," George said. "Then you know him?"

"I have met him," Ki-Gor nodded his head gloomily. "Some years ago, I was in that fort. He'd captured the son of a Manyema chief, and I went there to ransom the boy. I had some trouble, because you can't trust the man. What is your trouble with Black Mike?"

"Same thing that is happenin' all ovuh this side of the mountains," George said. "The drought has hit Lake Tsaga bad. And Black Mike wants to move ovuh into ouah country."

"Don't let him," Ki-Gor said emphatically.

"We don't want to," George replied. "We know the man is poison. He would make a very bad neighbor. You know what I and the Maasai think about slavery, anyways—we hate it. We don't want any part of a slave-runner anywheres near us. And this Black Mike, he don't jest run slaves—he plays 'round with smuggled ivory and di'monds, too. He's a real bad white boy."

Ki-Gor shrugged. "If you don't want him to come here, you don't have to let him."

"Well," said George. "He's a smaht one. This message he sent was real polite. He ask *our permission*—get it? Our permission fo' him to move in yere *temporary*—ontil the rains come. Oh yes, he's real polite an' no mistake. But he's the kinda fella, whatevuh he make up his mind he wants—he gits! Or tries awful hahd to git!"

"You aren't afraid of him, are you?" Ki-Gor asked.

"The Maasai ain't afraid of him," George said. "But the Maasai ain't afraid of nobody. But I know this much—if Black Mike wants to come in yere, I and the Maasai is goin' to have kind of a time keepin' him out. He's got him a bunch of tough Somali boys. Now they don't worry me, them Somalis. The Somalis is tough, but the Maasai is twice as tough. But the only thing is—*they got guns.* Black Mike smuggles guns along with everything else. And you know the British nevuh did let the Maasai have guns. I guess they figure if the Maasai had guns, there wouldn't be no livin' with 'em."

"And right now," Ki-Gor said thoughtfully, "the British are too busy to help you—"

"Sure," George shrugged. "The British got their own war to fight. Besides, the Maasai would nevuh ask fo' no he'p. Can you imagine Merishu hollerin' fo' the British to come and fight a war for 'im?"

Ki-Gor smiled.

"No, that ain't it," George pursued. "Merishu will fight—if I advise him to. But by golly, I don't care how brave a man is—if all he got is a *spear*, and th' othuh fella has got a *gun*—the odds is all against him. He is gamblin' with loaded dice. Now I don't know how many Somalis Black Mike has got—but my lawd, if he only had ten, just ten of them boys, and they had plenty of ammunition, why they could stand off out of spear range and kill off a hundred Maasai tryin' to get to grips with 'em. Of co'se, in the end we could prob'ly keep Black Mike out, but it sho' would cost a lot of lives an' I'd hate to see that happen."

"Don't forget one thing," Ki-Gor pointed out. "Black Mike knows the Maasai and how they can fight. He probably doesn't want to fight them any more than you want to fight him."

"Tha's right," George conceded. "Tha's why he is bein' so doggone polite. He is askin' 'permission' to come ovuh yere."

Ki-Gor stared at the floor in silent thought. Then he said, "What are you going to do?"

"What do *you* think?" George asked.

"I think," Ki-Gor replied, "that Black Mike is too smart to fight the Maasai. But he will bluff down to the last minute."

"Yeah, he'll do that, all right," George nodded.

"He may have—"

But whatever it was that Ki-Gor thought Black Mike might have remained without expression for the time being. A sudden commotion outside caused the jungle man to break off in the middle of his sentence. He and George both rose and went to the door of the house. The villagers were milling around in great excitement, not unmixed with alarm. Merishu came running toward George's house.

"Horsemen!" the young war chief shouted, "They are galloping toward the gate!"

"How many?" George demanded.

"Five or six. White men and Somalis."

"Let them in if they come in peace," George said. To Ki-Gor in English, he said, "Looks like Black Mike has come to get his answer in person."

CHAPTER II

WHATEVER ELSE KI-GOR MIGHT think about Black Mike, he was forced to admire his brazen courage. The slaver came riding into the *minyata*—crowded with a murmuring, hostile throng of Maasai—attended by one other white man and three Somalis. Two dwarfish Wandarobo trackers trotted alongside the Somalis. It was true that Black Mike and his party were all armed with rifles, but they gave away that advantage to some extent by coming within the walls of the *minyata* within spear reach of a large group of tall Maasai warriors.

George and Ki-Gor hurried toward the center of the *minyata* where Shafara and Merishu were standing awaiting Black Mike. Shafara turned his stern old face toward George and made a gesture indicating that he wished George to speak for the tribe.

George nodded and without hesitation strode forward toward the horsemen.

"Black Mike," he called, in a tone that was both pleasant and courteous, "will y'all please dismount?"

The strapping, broad-shouldered man in advance of the others sat his horse in silence for two seconds. Then he swung a leg over the saddle and dropped lightly to the ground. His dark handsome face creased in a smile, showing flashing white teeth.

"Are you the one they call Tembu George?" he inquired, in a voice almost as deep as George's.

"Tha's me," George said. "Will you please dismount your men, Black Mike?"

"I think not," the slaver said, still smiling.

"Well, I think they better," George said, his broad face expressionless. "They can either dismount, Black Mike, or they can turn right round and ride right out of that gate."

The smile died on Black Mike's face. He turned and swept the silent crowd of towering Maasai with an all-embracing stare. Then the smile returned to his chiseled countenance.

"If you insist," he said to George, and barked an order over his shoulder. The Somalis and the other white man slipped off their mounts and stood beside them, their guns cradled in their arms.

Now some Maasai youths had brought out a good-sized table and set it in the center of the compound. Others set up a huge umbrella over the table. George waved a massive hand at the chairs beside the table.

"Be seated, Black Mike," he rumbled, "be seated. This yere is my friend Ki-Gor."

"Yes, I've met Ki-Gor," the slaver said, moving to the table with easy poise. "Aren't you far away from your hunting grounds, Ki-Gor?"

"Yes," said Ki-Gor, "like many others this season."

The slaver flashed an inquiring glance at the jungle man, then sat down. Ki-Gor had rarely seen a man with as compellingly handsome features as Black Mike. Whatever the man's ancestry was—Portuguese, Dutch, Irish, or perhaps a little of all of them—his thin, high-bridged nose, smooth brow, and jutting chin gave him a markedly aristocratic look, that was somehow at variance with his big, burly body. And handsome as his face was, there was a lack of unity there, too. His eyes and mustache did not match his olive skin and black, wavy hair, the eyes being pale gray and the mustache being almost blond. The combination lent a mongrel, almost sinister quality to his face.

"I understand, Tembu George," the slaver said directly, "that you are not a native African. Is that right?"

"Tha's right," George rumbled.

"Well then, I won't beat around the bush with you and go through a lot of ceremonial. I'll get right to the point. This damned drought has been playing the deuce over our way, and we've got to get out for the time being. I can see you've been hit, too, although not quite so badly. You at least have *some* water left in your river. Our river is bone dry."

He paused and looked at George. But the big Negro made no comment, merely inclining his head as if waiting for Black Mike to continue.

"I thought of all the open pasture land that your friends the Maasai control over here," the slaver went on, "and it occurred to me that for a good consideration, we might occupy a small part of it—temporarily, of course. I sent a message over here to that effect, but of course, there has hardly been time to get an answer. So, as I happened to be out scouting today, I thought I might drop in and see what your general opinion of the idea was."

The slaver leaned back in his chair with an inquiring smile on his handsome face. For the first time, George smiled.

"I SEE," he said noncommittally, and turned as a Maasai youth came up bearing a container of native beer and gourd cups. "I c'n recommend this beer, Black Mike," he said. Several moments went by in silence while the gourds were filled, and George and the slaver drank slowly. Ki-Gor left his gourd untouched.

"Well?" Black Mike said finally. "What about it?"

"Well, I'll tell you," George said, ponderously. "It's like this. You got a drought ovuh yo' way—we got a drought right yere. And all around, ever'body has got a drought. Fo' miles an' miles, they just plumb ain't enough water to go around. But you know how it is with the Ngombi-Maasai. They is cattle raisers. I don't know *how* many head of cattle they got to take care of—anyways, it's a pow'ful lot, a pow'ful mess of cows. They all got to get water and green grass, and green grass don't grow without there ain't some water around."

"Yes, I realize that, of course," Black Mike said, and his face began to lose a little of its pleasant expression.

"Well now," George leaned forward confidingly, "we ain't got us enough land right now to take care of all them cows the way they ought to be took care of. So we just kinda wonderin' how we could spare any land—"

"Wait a minute!" Black Mike exclaimed. "That's ridiculous! We have no cows—and right now, we haven't even many slaves. I got rid of most of them a while back. There's just the few we have left, and my twenty-five Somalis. We would take up less than an acre of ground altogether."

"I know, I know," George said patiently. "*You*-all wouldn't take up so much land. But they is othuh people roundabouts that would sho' take a *passel* of land!"

"What do you mean?" Black Mike demanded imperiously.

"Why I means this yere," George said. "Supposin' we consents to you-all comin' ovuh yere and settin' down for a spell. Why, they is a whole mess of othuh neighbors we got would want to do the same thing."

"Well, you wouldn't have to let them," Black Mike snorted.

"If we let one man come," George said, "we got to let all the yothuh men come, too."

"Certainly not!" Black Mike cried. "It isn't as if my people were a large tribe—"

"That ain't the point," George said, still patient. "It jest wouldn't be fair and square."

"Rubbish!" the slaver growled. "Since when—"

"Oh, now hold on!" George said good-naturedly, "We-all yere in this *minyata* aims to play fair and square with ever'-body—"

"Well, come to the point!" Black Mike snapped. "Are you telling me I can't move over on to Maasai territory for a short time?"

"I is plumb sorry, Black Mike," George said sorrowfully, "but I guess tha's how it stands."

THE SLAVER'S black eyebrows beetled over his pale eyes. "You realize, of course," he said in a dangerous monotone, "that I have stretched a point in being so courteous as to ask permission before moving?"

"You has been real courteous," George acknowledged.

"You realize, don't you?" the slaver's voice rose, "that I could march right in here any time I felt like it?"

"Well," George weighed the idea, "you could try it."

"Your Maasai are supposed to be great warriors," Black Mike snarled. "But you realize that they wouldn't stand a chance against rifles?"

"Well, they might be what you'd call a diffunce of opinion about that there," George said gently. "Yessuh, a li'l' diffunce of opinion."

"Wah!" Black Mike rose to his feet "I don't know why I waste time talking to you! You are no Maasai to begin with. Where is the Headman?"

"*I* is speakin' fo' the Headman, Black Mike," George said softly. "I has full powers to speak fo' the Headman. You try to speak to him direct, Black Mike, an' you jest get yo'se'f into a pack of trouble."

The slaver's handsome face contorted with rage.

"If you think," he blazed, "that I'm going to let any black tribesman stand in my way—"

"Jest a minute. *Jest a minute!*" George drawled, his eyes narrowed to slits.

As if by magic, an eight-inch knife had appeared in his huge black hand.

"Keep yo' hands away f'om yo' belt, man!" George directed. "I is in command, right now. Don't you get a wrong idea an' go to grab yo' gun. You ain't got a chance of throwin' down on me—I is jest too fast with my li'l' shivaree! Befo' you could even begin to fill me up with lead, I could fill you up with eight inches of steel! Now if you want to talk to me, set down! And fust thing you do, you 'pologize fo' that name you called me!"

Black Mike stared in amazement at the giant Negro. Then a calculating look came into his pale eyes, and finally he gave a short laugh and sat down.

"Why," he said, jocularly, "I didn't know you were so sensitive. I assure you I meant no offense—"

"If you didn't mean no offense," George snapped, "don't give any!"

"How could I know what would offend you—" the slaver began.

"I ain't heard no apologize, yet!" George roared, raising his voice for the first time. "Let's have it man, or I'm goin' to start carvin'!"

"All right, all right!" Mike said hastily. "You win. I apologize. There—you satisfied?"

"I heard you 'pologize," George growled.

Mike laughed again. "You realize, of course," he said, "that if you had attacked me, my Somalis would have shot you dead."

"By the time they got around to it," George retorted, "it would nevuh done *you* no good, Mike."

"Let it go," Mike said, briefly, "—for *now*. But don't think I'm going to forget this in a hurry."

"I didn't intend you should," George said dryly. His look wandered as he stared straight into Black Mike's pale eyes.

All through this clash of wills, Ki-Gor had sat watchfully silent. In one way, he had admired George's sturdy independence. In another, he felt that George might be overplaying his hand. Ki-Gor was sure that Black Mike was trying to run a colossal bluff. At the same time, he believed that the slaver was too smart a man not to have some aces hidden up his sleeve. However, for the moment Ki-Gor had to admit that George was triumphant. Black Mike had been definitely faced down.

The slaver suddenly threw back his head and laughed.

"This is pretty silly," he announced, after a moment. "Here we are, a couple of grown men, quarreling like twelve-year old boys."

"Sho' is silly," George agreed, but he did not smile.

"Instead of this silly bickering," the slaver said, "why don't we try to get together? Now, I'll grant that you're the man I should talk to. I'll grant that you don't want me to move into your territory. But supposing *you* grant me a couple of things."

"Such as?" George said.

"Grant me that I'm in a rotten position from the drought," Black Mike said reasonably. "I've got to do something, I've got to move somewhere. And I'd like to move here. Now, instead of my threatening you with force, let me put it this way. You don't want to admit me, because then all the rest of your neighbors would feel they had a right to move in. Is that right?"

"As far as it goes, tha's right," George conceded.

"And some of your neighbors could be quite troublesome, couldn't they?" Black Mike pursued. "The Nandi, say?"

"The Nandi ain't goin' to trouble us none," George said.

"They have in the past," Black Mike pointed out. "They're tough boys, the Nandi. Now, look. You let us move in here temporarily, and I will guarantee to take care of any other people that think they can follow my example. The Maasai won't have to take a day off from their cattle to worry about invaders. How about it? Isn't that fair enough?"

George's reply was in the negative, but Ki-Gor did not hear it. He was deep in thought. Black Mike's remark about the Nandi worried Ki-Gor. He thought he detected a hidden ace. His mind moved swiftly for a few seconds, then his attention returned to the scene in front of him. Black Mike was speaking.

"But surely," the slaver was saying, "even the Maasai could use a military alliance against the Nandi, could they not?"

Before George could reply, Ki-Gor spoke.

"George," he said, and the big Negro swung around in surprise. "It is none of my affair, George," Ki-Gor went on, "but I've been listening carefully to everything you and Mike have said to each other—"

"Yeah," George said anxiously. "Whut's on yo' mind, Ki-Gor?"

"This much," Ki-Gor said. "If I were in your place—and I am not—but if I were, I would let Black Mike move in here!"

TEMBU GEORGE stared at his old friend in stunned amazement.

"You—you would *what?*" he gasped finally.

"I am sorry," Ki-Gor said, "if what I say does not please you—"

He broke off feeling uncomfortable under George's accusing gaze. The big Negro was the picture of a man suddenly stabbed in the back by his most trusted friend. He threw a glance at Black Mike—who was wisely keeping still—and then looked back at Ki-Gor. Finally, he cleared his throat.

"Ki-Gor," he said softly, "what are you talkin' about, man?"

Ki-Gor rose to his feet, frowning.

"I've already said," he said stiffly, "that this is none of my affair. But if you took my advice, you would try and work out some agreement with Black Mike. It is useless and stupid to oppose him blindly this way."

Ki-Gor stared over George's head. He devoutly hoped that that last statement would jolt George out of his mute, sorrowful attitude. Evidently it did, for George rose out of his chair, eyes narrowed suddenly.

"Useless an' stupid, is it?" he said, with a rising inflection. "Well, look yere, Ki-Gor—when I need yo' advice, I'll come round and ask you for it! I don't know whut's come ovuh you, all of a sudden—"

"There is no need for you to be quarrelsome with me," Ki-Gor said swiftly, hiding his gratification that George was at last quarreling with him publicly. Ki-Gor had decided that it was very necessary for him to quarrel with George. He took two paces away and turned.

"I will go now," he said stiffly. "I could not stay here any longer after—after this. But think over what I've said. Think over what you have told Black Mike. Maybe you'd better change your mind."

As he turned away, Black Mike came swiftly after him, pale eyes gleaming with a feral light.

"Ki-Gor," the slaver called, "wait a while. I don't think I shall be staying here much longer. We could join forces."

"I cannot wait another minute," Ki-Gor replied coldly. "And if I were you I would stay here until I got what I wanted. George *may* change his mind!"

With that the jungle man wheeled and stalked through the uneasy crowd of Maasai toward George's house. Helene and Shaliba had been standing in the doorway, and now Helene hastened anxiously toward her mate.

"Ki-Gor!" she exclaimed. "What got into you! Why are you quarreling with George?"

Ki-Gor took both her hands in his and murmured for her ears alone, "This is for George's good, but he doesn't know it yet. I must get away from here—alone. Take sides with George against me—refuse to leave with me. Then try to keep Black Mike here for the rest of the day. Do your best. Remember it is for George's good."

Helene stared uncomprehendingly into Ki-Gor's urgent face.

"Come!" he whispered. "Say joist loud you won't leave with me!"

"I get it," she whispered in return, then she backed away. "I don't understand you at all, Ki-Gor!" she cried then. "I can't imagine that you would turn against George!"

"I haven't turned against George!" Ki-Gor said in a tone loud enough for George and Black Mike to hear. "He is the one who has quarreled with me because he didn't like the advice I gave him. I am going now. I will be back in a few days when everyone's tempers have cooled off."

With that, he turned on his heel and stalked out of the *minyata*. Once out of the gate, he turned to his right and headed ostentatiously for the highlands to the west, climbing up toward the hardwood forest in full view of the silent assemblage in the *minyata*.

But when he reached the shelter of the trees, and could no longer be seen from below, he turned abruptly and headed due north. He spent the rest of that day and all the ensuing night heading at top speed for the country of the Nandi.

CHAPTER III

ASHWANA, HEADMAN OF THE Nandi, scratched the gray wool on his long head and contemplated his long, skinny shins in perplexity. Then his eyes rolled up under his wrinkled forehead and gazed at the bronzed giant squatting opposite him.

"We know of Ki-Gor, we Nandi," he offered, "and from all we have ever heard, Ki-Gor always speaks truth. But—"

"I don't ask you to believe me," Ki-Gor said patiently. "You will find out for yourself in due time. This slaver will come to you—if not tomorrow, then soon after. He will have another white man with him, three Somalis, and two Wandarobo. He will invite you to make war against the Ngombi-Maasai. He will promise to help you against them with his twenty-five Somalis armed with Italian rifles."

"Slavers!" old Ashwana spat out the word. "The veriest scum of the world! We Nandi don't hold with slavers."

"Then what will you answer this scum of a slaver?" Ki-Gor asked.

Ashwana fell silent a moment. "It would be a wonderful opportunity to get revenge," he said. "The last time we fought the Ngombi-Maasai, they tricked us out of a great victory. If we had twenty-five rifles on our side—"

"Do the Nandi require help to carry on their wars?" Ki-Gor said dreamily.

Ashwana glared. "No!" he snapped.

"Do the Nandi require the help of *slavers* to—"

"No!" screamed Ashwana, leaping to his feet. "Never! We Nandi fight our own battles! We are afraid of no one! We will conquer the earth if we feel like it! In a fair fight, we will always beat the Ngombi-Maasai! Big cows that they are!"

"Then what will you tell the slaver?" Ki-Gor demanded.

Ashwana ignored the question. "Did the Maasai send you here to beg us not to attack them?" he demanded.

"I told you that the Maasai don't even know I'm here," Ki-Gor said.

"We Nandi," Ashwana brooded, "we Nandi hate slavers—but it would be a wonderful opportunity! We would take their women, we would slaughter their precious cattle, while their backs were turned!"

"What would you say?" Ki-Gor countered, "if I told you that the Maasai had agreed to let this slaver set up camp on their land?"

"To stay, you mean?" Ashwana asked.

"To stay," Ki-Gor said.

"I would say the Maasai were cowards," Ashwana declared promptly. "And whatever the Maasai are, they are not cowards. They will not let the slaver stay on their land."

"You are right," Ki-Gor smiled. "They will not let the slaver stay, no matter if he had five times twenty-five rifles to fight them with. Now, would you punish brave men for being brave? Would you thus attack them while they are defending themselves against rifles?"

Again Ashwana brooded. He shook his head. "It would be a wonderful opportunity," he sighed, and Ki-Gor groaned inwardly.

HE HAD been sitting with the old Nandi chieftain for four solid hours, and he was exactly where he was when he started. Ashwana would concede the truth of everything Ki-Gor said, and then irrationally dwell on the joyous prospect of a successful campaign against a possibly beleaguered tribe of Maasai. Ki-Gor decided to try one last approach.

"O Headman of the Nandi," he began, "you hate the Maasai?"

"Certainly we do," Ashwana replied promptly.

"And you hate slavers?"

"Certainly we do."

"Tell me, O Ashwana," Ki-Gor said, closing his eyes as if in deep thought, "which do you hate worse, the Maasai or the slavers?"

Ashwana thought it over.

"How can I say?" he finally said. "The slavers are like venomous snakes to be killed whenever they are found. The Maasai are like lions that we Nandi hunt for the sport of it. How can I say—it is impossible to say which we hate worse."

It was all Ki-Gor could do to control his exasperation at the old man and his traditional hatreds. Then he suddenly got an idea.

"Wait!" he cried. "You fight the Maasai as you would go lion-hunting—for the sport of it?"

"Exactly," the old man replied.

"Then," Ki-Gor said triumphantly, "what would you do for sport if there were no more Maasai?"

"If—if there were no more Maasai?" Ashwana repeated, bewildered.

"Yes. Suppose that there were no more Maasai at all—who would you have any glorious wars with?"

"Why—why—" Ashwana scratched his head. "But there will always be Maasai."

"Not if they are beaten by the slavers' rifles," Ki-Gor warned. "Those that aren't killed will be carried away in chains to the Coast. Then there will be no more Maasai for you to fight with."

"No Maasai!" he muttered to himself, pulling at his thick lower lip. "I can't imagine it!"

"Well, there you are!" Ki-Gor leaned back in triumph. "The slaver is a coward. He doesn't want to fight the Maasai, even though he has rifles and they haven't. He will not fight the Maasai, if you Nandi do not help him—he will be afraid to. But he will come to you with fair words and promises. He will try in every way possible to get you to join him against the Maasai. He will make the mistake of thinking you are so stupid as to believe him."

"We Nandi are not stupid!" Ashwana declared hotly.

"I know that," Ki-Gor replied, "but the cowardly slaver does not. He will come to you and promise you everything if you will go with him and wipe out the Maasai."

"But we Nandi don't want to *wipe out* the Maasai!" Ashwana cried. "Because if the Maasai were wiped out, then who would we fight?"

Ki-Gor breathed easy at last. When the old man began to express as his own ideas which Ki-Gor suggested, the battle was as good as won. A faint blue-grey luminance showed through the doorway of Ashwana's hut, heralding the coming dawn. Ki-Gor sighed and blinked. He had been sitting arguing with the old man since a little after midnight.

"You are sleepy. So am I," Ashwana stated. "Lie down and sleep."

"A hundred thanks," Ki-Gor replied getting to his feet, "but I must go. My woman is with the Maasai. I must get her and take her back to my own country far away. Now, O Ashwana—what will the Nandi say to the slaver when he comes to ask help against the Maasai?"

"He will not be allowed inside the village," Ashwana declared stoutly. "I will post an armed guard to watch for him and turn him back. We will not even talk to the scum."

"It is good," Ki-Gor nodded. He knew he could depend on the old man. "The Maasai will not forget."

"The Maasai!" Ashwana said scornfully. "Here—bear a message to the Maasai for us. Tell them to send us word when they are no longer in danger of being attacked by the slaver and his rifles."

"You will know that without any word from the Maasai," Ki-Gor said, and went to explain. "The slaver is desperate because of the drought. When the rains come, he will no longer need to move. He will not attack the Maasai after the rains come."

"Ah," said Ashwana. "Then take this message to the Maasai. Tell them to beware when the rains come. For as soon as the first raindrop falls, the Nandi will be on their way over to thrash them!"

Ki-Gor grinned and hurried out of the indomitable old man's presence.

HE HAD spent precious hours among the Nandi, but he had gained his point. He had accomplished his self-appointed mission better, in a way, than he had originally thought possible. If the Nandi would not even speak to Black Mike, they would not reveal to him that Ki-Gor had been there ahead of him.

Just how far ahead of Black Mike he actually was, Ki-Gor had no way of knowing. But as a matter of ordinary caution, he loitered a moment at the edge of the village before crossing the clearing that surrounded it. There was no sign of approaching horsemen in any direction, however, and Ki-Gor slipped across the clearing into the jungle beyond, picked up the trail to the south and settled down into his loping ground-eating travel pace.

As he pounded along the winding trail, a humiliating idea crossed his mind. Supposing he had overestimated Black Mike! Supposing Black Mike had never thought of going to the Nandi to enlist their aid against the Maasai! Ki-Gor blushed at the thought. If that were so, then he would have taken this grueling trip for nothing. He would have made a fool of himself to the Nandi. He would have contrived the elaborate quarrel with George for nothing.

Ki-Gor stopped dead in the middle of the trail, appalled at the idea. But as he thought about it, he realized that even if he had misread Black Mike's mind, he could not have done otherwise. Perhaps Black Mike was not so smart as he gave him credit for being—but he could not have afforded to take the chance that he wasn't. There was too much at stake. No, he decided—if he had it to do all over again, he would act in the same way.

Ki-Gor stepped forward. He wished now that he had not stopped. It had brought home to him how tired he was. His eyes itched from lack of sleep and his powerful legs felt heavy. He moved along slowly, trying to make up his mind whether to stop for a while and get a little sleep.

It was unfortunate that Ki-Gor chose that section of the trail to go slowly. It made him a much easier target.

He did not see the net until the lower edge of it was already falling down below his waist. He dropped to his knees quickly, but he was not quick enough. His reflexes, slowed down by fatigue, could not save him. A shrill cackle of Wandarobo laughter broke the jungle silence and Ki-Gor was jerked off his feet, thrashing and grunting in the toils of a hunting-net.

Ki-Gor groaned and cursed himself for forgetting Black Mike's Wandarobo trackers. He kicked his great legs furiously but it was in vain. The net, cunningly wrought from the toughest lianas, was snubbed close. And Ki-Gor, White Lord of the Jungle, lay helpless on his shoulder blades, his ankles writhing four feet in the air.

He stopped struggling for a moment to take stock of his situation. He knew the Wandarobo hunted birds with nets, and he had heard vaguely that they sometimes went after bigger game with larger webs, made out of stronger vines. But he had never thought that he himself would be caught in the toils of those primitive savages. This net that had been dropped so neatly over his head was strong enough to hold a lion. A rope reeved around the open end of the net acted as a drawstring and effectually closed the net. In this case, it acted as a hobble, binding Ki-Gor's ankles tightly together. The rope stretched straight upward to a thick bough overhanging the trail.

It was a matter of only a few seconds while Ki-Gor took these details in. But already the grinning Wandarobo was scrambling down the tree trunk to the ground, a wicked-looking knife flapping against his bare buttocks. Frantically, Ki-Gor jabbed both his elbows outward against the tough woody meshes. The pressure around his waist was not so strict as at his ankles. But even so, Ki-Gor found that his arms were effectively pinned to his sides.

The net had been perfectly cast, but it was sheer bad luck for Ki-Gor that the three-inch meshes had slipped unhindered over the spear blade, rendering that weapon useless, at least for the moment. Quickly, his right hand relaxed on the shaft of the spear and groped for the knife on his right hip. But with sinking heart Ki-Gor realized that the knife was inches away from his clutching fingers. He could not draw his elbow back far enough.

HE TWISTED his head around just in time to see the Wandarobo drop lightly to the ground. The squat little savage, hardly bigger than a Pygmy, paused just long enough to free his murderous curved blade from its skin scabbard. Then he scuttled toward the helpless giant in the net.

Up to now, Ki-Gor had not uttered a sound. But he suddenly realized his appalling danger, and accordingly he found his voice.

"Aaarrgh!" he roared. "What do you think you are going to do?"

The Wandarobo kept coming forward until he was six feet away from Ki-Gor. Then he stopped, and his flat, brutish face wrinkled in a crafty smile.

"What—" he said—"does any hunter do when he catches a lion in his net?"

"Spawn of a baboon!" Ki-Gor snarled. "You have caught something more dangerous than a lion today!"

The Wandarobo cackled. "Even a white rhinoceros would not look dangerous if he were strung up by his hind quarters."

"Stupid monkey!" Ki-Gor raged. "Do you know who I am? I am Ki-Gor. Why did you cast your net at me?"

"Aye, I know well enough," the Savage retorted. "The white bwana ordered me to follow you. 'Watch him,' says the white bwana, 'and if he acts suspicious, why take him in the net. And then,' he says, 'hang on to him until I get there.' So that's what I did."

"Why do you say I acted suspiciously?" Ki-Gor demanded.

"You left the *minyata* of the Maasai going in one direction," the Wandarobo leered, "and then you circled and went in another direction. You came over here to the Nandi. I call that suspicious."

"Brainless fool!" Ki-Gor stormed. "That was not circling. I just changed my mind—"

As Ki-Gor railed at the Wandarobo, his left hand was creeping stealthily across his stomach toward the knife hilt which he could not reach with his right hand. He hoped his loud words would distract the savage's attention long enough for him to get hold of the knife. Then he would slash the lianas and roll free to cope with the Wandarobo.

But the savage was alert.

"Hai!" he cried, his button eyes darting a glance at Ki-Gor's left hand. "What is this?"

Ki-Gor threw caution to the winds, stabbed desperately at the hilt of his knife. The grasping finger tips barely grazed the hilt. The Wandarobo yelled and swung his short sword up. Ki-Gor doubled his legs up convulsively. The back of his head dragged along the ground for a fraction of a second, and then his body swung free, suspended from the ankles by the rope over the tree-branch. There was a disappointed yell and a clang as the Wandarobo's sword hit the ground where Ki-Gor's head had lain a half a heart's beat before.

Now Ki-Gor had no plan to follow. His precious knife slipped out of its sheath as he hung upside down in the air. He was unarmed, tied-up and helpless while a murderous little savage swung a two-foot sword at him.

The next few minutes remained a blur ever afterwards in Ki-Gor's memory. His only possible hope of survival was to keep moving somehow. The only way he could move was by bending his knees and then straightening them out again. He gained one initial advantage which he did not realize for a moment. The Wandarobo had dropped his sword on that first tremendous swing at Ki-Gor's head. The savage had then leaped to recover it. And Ki-Gor, on the return of his pendulum spring, banged into the slight, black body, and hurled it three feet away.

Now, by a titanic effort, the jungle man twisted his body around, and straightened his knees so that his chest and not his back rested on the ground. The Wandarobo was picking himself up wrathfully.

Frantically, Ki-Gor's hands were groping through the net for his knife which he estimated must be lying directly under his body. The savage darted forward to retrieve the sword that was sticking in the dirt scarcely three inches in front of Ki-Gor's nose.

The Wandarobo was fast, but Ki-Gor's leg muscles were faster.

Once again, the jungle man kicked himself forward. Once again, the Wandarobo was bowled over, screaming with frustrated rage.

DIMLY, KI-GOR felt himself drenched with sweat. He was still alive, and he would stay alive as long as he could keep the Wanda-robo away from his only weapon. But he was not foolish enough to think that he could keep up that maneuver indefinitely. Sooner or later, the darting little savage would get his hands on that sword. And then it would be all up with Ki-Gor.

And now, in the few seconds respite before the Wandarobo could come at him again, Ki-Gor clawed desperately beneath him for his knife. For a moment, he thought he had it. A finger and the thumb of his left hand closed over the blade. But then the Wandarobo was flying at him again and had to be fought off.

Again, Ki-Gor's mighty legs kicked. But to his horror, he swung short of that all-important sword. The brutish savage would get it—! Ki-Gor kicked again, frenziedly. He nearly screamed with the pain at his ankles as the tough rope bit into them. But then something happened.

Before he quite realized it, he was lying on top of the Wandarobo. *And his legs and feet were lying on the ground!*

That last superhuman kick had broken the rope!

The Wandarobo wriggled snarling out from under him. Ki-Gor could not stop him. But the jungle man was flaying his legs free of the entangling bottom of the net. The savage saw what had happened. With a wild cry he flung himself at Ki-Gor, black hands clawing at his throat. The ferocity of his charge rolled Ki-Gor over on his back. The jungle man still could not free his arms, but he flung his legs up high over his head, and then twisted his torso violently to one side.

His legs crashed to the ground, left knee first. Another spas-modic jerk and both of Ki-Gor's knees were on the ground. With one swift motion, the jungle man swung his body off the ground and shook the snarling Wandarobo off. Then the muscles on his lean stomach corded and his body jack-knifed. A second later and Ki-Gor was standing upright. But he was by no means out of danger yet.

His hands were clawing the meshes of the net upwards, when the Wandarobo flung himself with a howl of despair in a last attempt to kill Ki-Gor before he could get free. This time, the little savage had recovered the sword. An early sunbeam flickered on the curved blade as it swooped over the Wandarobo's bullet head. If that blow had landed, the razor-sharp blade would have sheared away the net and both of Ki-Gor's hands. But the jungle man brought up his right leg with fearful violence and uncanny precision. The ball of his foot caught the plunging savage accurately under the heavy jaw.

There was a muffled *snap*. The Wandarobo uttered a gurgling scream. His feet left the ground, and his filthy body seemed to hang on empty air for an eternity. Then the savage crashed to the ground in a limp heap and lay twitching feebly.

With trembling fingers, Ki-Gor shucked the net off over his head. The Wandarobo lying at his feet, broken neck grotesquely twisted, did not look dangerous now. But Ki-Gor knew that he had never been nearer death than he had during the last few frenzied minutes. Small as the Wandarobo were, they were fearless implacable savages, cunning in the lore of the jungle and as quick to deal death as a cobra. Ki-Gor shivered and turned to look at the frayed end of the rope still dangling from the overhanging bough. The rope was two inches thick and skillfully woven of the toughest of lianas. Ki-Gor marveled a little that he had been able to break it. It had been designed to withstand strength greater than any human being was supposed to possess.

However, Ki-Gor was not one to waste time over post mortems. He threw the net over the still form of the savage, and moved southward along the trail. He permitted himself one reflection on the recent struggle which had so nearly cost him his life. And that was—supposing there had been *two* Wandarobo! If there had been, Ki-Gor privately conceded that nothing could have saved him.

Then he put the thought out of his mind and quickened his steps.

But the thought refused to stay out of his mind. Ki-Gor remembered that there had been two Wandarobo in Black Mike's party at the *minyata*. Had only one of them followed him to the Nandi village?

THE SUN was up just high enough so that here and there some stray beams filtered through the less densely foliaged portions of the trail. Ki-Gor slowed his travel-gait a little and kept his eyes on the dust of the path.

Sure enough!

He halted abruptly and stepped back a few paces. His trained vision caught the fresh spoor entering the trail from the side. The small splayed footprints were headed southwards—in the same direction he was going.

There had been two Wandarobo all right. But only one had stayed to prepare and execute the ambush, while the other had scurried back to inform his master, Black Mike.

Once more Ki-Gor moved along the trail. But no longer did he travel at his easy travel-gait. Now he moved at a dog trot, in spite of bruised weary legs and a tired brain. If possible, Ki-Gor had to catch that other Wandarobo before the little tracker could get to Black Mike. Ki-Gor did not want the slaver to know that he had been to the Nandi village.

How much of a head start the Wandarobo had on him, he of course had no way of knowing. He could only trust to luck and his own brawny legs.

For four hours, Ki-Gor sped on his way, never relaxing his grueling pace. Then, while the sun had yet to climb to the zenith, the jungle man swerved and stopped. The Wandarobo's spoor left the trail. It was the matter of a moment to figure out that the tracker had climbed into a tree to sleep. How long he had slept there was not revealed, of course, but at any event, his head start was cut down by some degree. Ki-Gor picked up the spoor again a little farther along the trail— evidently the Wandarobo had gone several yards through the trees before returning to the path—and set off again in hot pursuit.

Two hours farther along the trail, the Wandarobo's footprints again disappeared. Ki-Gor investigated again very carefully. It was entirely possible that the cunning little savage had back-trailed. This proved not to be the case, this time, however. Apparently, the Wandarobo had caught and killed a jungle fowl and had then sat down and eaten it raw.

Once more Ki-Gor set off, nerves tingling. His chances of catching the tracker seemed better and better. To still the clamor of his own empty stomach, he had eaten some fruit from an old baobab tree, the astringent juice having a refreshing and reviving effect.

High as his hopes had been of catching the Wandarobo, they began to dim as the hours passed and the little savage did not come into sight. By now, Ki-Gor was nearing the Maasai country, and the jungle began to thin out. Other trails began to cross the one he was following, and at each crossing he had to stop and make sure that the Wandarobo had not turned aside. And when sunset came on with the Wandarobo still unseen, Ki-Gor began to wonder if his incredible day-long marathon was going to prove fruitless. Dusk would swiftly follow the sunset, and then he would no longer be able to see the Wandarobo's spoor in the dust of the trail.

The sun finally went down behind the western highlands, and Ki-Gor slowed to a stop just about ready to confess himself beaten. His legs ached as though they had been pounded by giant hammers, and his eyes felt as if he had been through a sandstorm. He looked around at typical Maasai country, rolling grassy pasture land, dotted here and there with small copses of trees and thick bushes. Fifteen or twenty feet ahead of him, the trail skirted just such a copse. Wearily, the jungle man moved ahead. There was no longer any point in continuing his mad race after an unseen quarry. He would step off the trail into the bushes and lie down to sleep for a while. Somewhere, not far away, he could hear thundering hooves. Eland, probably. But Ki-Gor was too tired to be interested. He parted the nearest bushes with his hands and silently—from force of habit—stepped into the copse.

Precisely at that moment, he heard the rustle of bushes not far away. He froze in his tracks. The rustle continued and there came another sound—a very human yawn. A man was stepping out of the same copse. Soundlessly, Ki-Gor parted the bushes and peered out.

Standing on the trail not ten feet away was a Wandarobo.

THE SAVAGE'S back was to Ki-Gor, and he was evidently staring ahead to where the trail swooped upward over a little rise. Ki-Gor's heart pounded, and he gathered his muscles. His luck was in after all, just when he had given up. A grim smile formed on his bronzed face. To think that he should find his quarry all unsuspecting in the very place he had selected to go to sleep!

The pounding hoof beats of the unseen herd of eland or whatever they were sounded nearer. The Wandarobo was evidently listening to the sound. Ki-Gor hesitated. The Wandarobo did not seem disposed to go away from there in a hurry. Perhaps it would be as well to wait until the eland had passed by, before he tried to catch the savage. Eland are big brutes and not to be underestimated. It would be as dangerous to stand in front of them as it would to stand in front of a herd of stampeding cattle.

Nearer and nearer sounded the drumming hooves, and still the Wandarobo loitered on the trail beside the copse. Ki-Gor regretted now that he had not immediately stolen through the bushes until he came up beside the savage. Then one spring and he would have had him. Perhaps there was still time, he reflected. If he inadvertently rustled a leaf, the sound of the hoofbeats would cover the noise.

He was just about to act on that idea when the Wandarobo galvanized into motion. The savage gave a wild yell and started running up the trail. Ki-Gor cursed his indecision and sprang out of the copse in pursuit.

At that moment five horsemen came galloping over the rise. It was Black Mike.

Quick as thought, Ki-Gor swerved and dived headlong back into the bushes. There he lay panting, cursing himself and wondering whether the slaver had caught sight of him, or whether the gathering dusk had masked his brief appearance out in the open.

He heard shouts up the trail and the hoofbeats slowed and stopped, as the horsemen evidently reined in their mounts. Then Black Mike's voice sounded, curt and demanding, speaking the Wandarobo dialect. The savage's voice answered, high-pitched and whining, and Ki-Gor breathed easier.

"Well, did you keep his spoor?" Black Mike demanded.

"Aye, we did not lose it," the tracker replied.

"Have you got him?"

"By now he is in the net," the tracker announced.

"Dead or alive?"

"How do I know?" the Wandarobo said. "I started back before he came out."

"Came out?" the slaver's voice was hard. "Came out of what?"

"The Nandi village, Bwana."

"The Nandi village! Curse him!" Black Mike snarled. "I should have suspected that! The sly devil! Heaven knows what he was doing there! But whatever it was, it wasn't helping us!"

There was a moment of silence. Then Black Mike spoke in English, evidently to his henchman. "What do you think, Pereira? Is it any use to go ahead? Or shall we turn and ride straight back to the Maasai. Curse! It makes my blood boil to think of the time we've been wasting at that *minyata* while this Ki-Gor has been playing the devil behind our backs with the Nandi!"

"How do you know what he has accomplished with the Nandi?" Pereira asked.

"I don't, of course," Black Mike snapped, "but I can guess. Think back and see how he slipped away from the *minyata* after he had the disagreement with Tembu George. And by the way, that quarrel begins to look trumped up to me, now. And the way this Ki-Gor's wife was so friendly— Look here, Pereira, I think we'd better go right back and renew our demands. Play our hand as strong as possible."

"But why guess?" Pereira pointed out. "Somewhere near the Nandi village, our Wandarobo probably has the fellow trapped. He'd make a fine hostage."

"If he's alive," Black Mike grunted. He switched back to Wandarobo and questioned the tracker. "Will the white ape be alive by the time we get there?"

"How do I know?" the savage leered. "My brother who stayed behind with the net—he sometimes get a terrible blood-lust."

Ki-Gor, crouched in the bushes scarcely five yards from Black Mike, permitted himself a grim smile. How well he could testify to the "terrible bloodlust" of the tracker's brother!

THERE WAS silence now among the group on the trail, and Ki-Gor held his breath. It all depended now on whether Black Mike went on to the Nandi village or turned back to the Maasai *minyata*. It was unfortunate that the second Wandarobo had escaped Ki-Gor and delivered his message to the slaver. Unfortunate—but not irretrievably so. If Black Mike went on, the situation would be saved. If he turned back, he could of course beat Ki-Gor to the Maasai, and the situation then would not be good. Ki-Gor's political move toward the Nandi would have gone for nothing.

"Look here, Pereira," Black Mike said suddenly in English, "why don't we just go back and tell Tembu George that we saw the Nandi and got the promise of their help?"

"Try and run just a pure bluff, you mean?" the henchman said, doubtfully.

"Certainly. He'll have no way of knowing that we haven't seen the Nandi."

"If you'll permit me to say so, I think it would be quite useless," Pereira said. "It's not like you to run a bluff that you have no way of backing up."

There was another long silence, during which Ki-Gor could hardly contain himself for suspense. Then Black Mike spoke with finality.

"You're right, Pereira," he declared. "Come on. We'll ride all night if this tracker of ours can keep the trail in the darkness."

Ki-Gor laid his weary head on the ground and carefully let out his breath as the group of horsemen moved away down the trail toward the Nandi country. It had been a close call all around, but it was working out for the best. The jungle man thanked his stars for the miracle which had kept Black Mike, riding over the brow of the hill, from seeing him diving back into the bushes. If the meeting had occurred twenty minutes earlier, there would have been daylight enough so that the slaver could not have missed seeing him.

As the hoof beats of the slaver's horses died away in the distance, the jungle man sat up. He was tired almost to the point of stupefaction, but he knew he could not take time to rest—yet. He must get back to the *minyata* and tell George everything that had happened. Then only could he lie down and get the sleep for which his body and brain cried out.

CHAPTER IV

FOUR HOURS LATER, KI-GOR walked into the brilliantly fire-lighted *minyata* of the Ngombi-Maasai.

"Ki-Gor!"

The cry went up on all sides, and George and Helene hastened toward him.

"Man, I sho' am glad to see you!" the big American Negro rumbled. "Where-at have you been, anyways?"

"I'll tell you," Ki-Gor said. "But, first, did Helene explain to you about—?"

"About ouah big public quarrel?" George supplied, laughing. "Yeah, she did, an' I was sho' glad to git the low-down. You had me kind of on a peg there for a while, Ki-Gor—you really did."

"Did you think I was really quarreling with you?" Ki-Gor asked with a smile.

"Man, I didn't know *whut* to think!" George exclaimed. "Fust off, I couldn't b'lieve my ears! Then I got so aggravated I wanted to slap yo' face. Why, I thought you'd gone a little crazy there—settin' yo'se'f against me like that! That ain't like you, nossuh! An' I nevuh begin to catch on that you was puttin' it on until sometime aftuh you'd gone on away. Miz Helene come ovuh and sit with me talkin' to Black Mike an' kinda layin' herse'f out bein' nice to him—an' that struck me as kinda funny too. Then Miz Helene, she tip me a big wink, an' I saw the whole thing. The way Miz Helene was stallin' around with Black Mike, I see that was whut you wanted I should do, so then *I* begun stallin'. Why, we kep' that fella hangin' round all night and all day today. He only went away f'om yere a few hours ago."

"Yes, I know," Ki-Gor said, "I saw him."

"You saw him?" George cried. "Whereat? And, anyways, where you been? C'mon, talk!"

"I've been to the Nandi country," Ki-Gor informed him.

"Nandi country!" George echoed. "Whut you been doin' ovuh yonduh?"

Ki-Gor explained his whole strategy then and the reasons for it.

"Well, fo' the land's sakes!" George murmured. "Who would evuh of thought of a thing like that! But you say you fixed up the Nandi so they ain't goin' to go along with Black Mike?"

"I don't think so," Ki-Gor said. "Ashwana told me they would not even talk to Black Mike when he came to see them."

"And you is sure he is goin' ovuh there?"

"I am sure," Ki-Gor said. "And when he comes back here, he will be in an ugly mood—"

"Does he know you went to the Nandi?" George asked.

"Yes, his Wandarobo saw me." Ki-Gor paused, then decided not to tell of his near-catastrophe with the net-thrower. It would only worry Helene.

"Well, you is prob'ly right, Ki-Gor," George said. "That Black Mike goin' to come steamin' back yere some time tomorrow, an' we bettuh be ready for him."

"You know"—it was Helene who spoke—"I wonder if you aren't both a little wrong about Black Mike."

"Wrong?" Ki-Gor said blankly. "How do you mean?"

"Well, it seemed to me that he was quite a reasonable person," Ki-Gor's wife went on. "After you went away, Ki-Gor, all during the long conversations he had with George, he wasn't threatening or didn't offer violence. He was—well, he was just reasonable."

George giggled. "I'll say he was reasonable," the big Negro chuckled. "He had an idea he was goin' to talk me around to his way of thinkin'. Nossuh, Miz Helene, don't git a wrong idea of Black Mike jest because he talks fair with his mouth. That fella is strictly poison."

"Maybe so," Helene shrugged. She did not seem entirely convinced.

"WELL, KI-GOR," George turned to the jungle man. "You got any ideas?"

"I have one idea," Ki-Gor replied. "I will tell you that idea and then I am going to sleep, for I am very tired. If Black Mike decides to try and fight his way into your country, this *minyata* is a poor place to defend. There is no cover around, and his men can ride around and keep your warriors off with their rifles. There would be no chance to come to close quarters with them, and in the meantime they could kill your cattle or drive them away."

"I think you is thinkin' about the same thing I am," George said, nodding. "You mean we should move up the river?"

"Yes. There is still green grass above the bamboo forest. You could drive the cattle up there, and you could keep Black Mike's Somalis from following you up. They would have to come up the river bed— there is no other way they can get past the bamboo jungle."

"It's the best idea," George declared emphatically. "We'd ought to be able to defend a narrow pass like the river bed, no mattuh how many rifles they has. Only thing is—that pasture ain't goin' support all the cattle very long. They isn't enough grass."

"I thought of that, too," Ki-Gor said. "But supposing you made a little dam across the stream?"

"A dam?"

"Just above the bamboos," Ki-Gor explained, "where the ground slopes off steeply again. If you dammed the stream at that point, what little water there is would back up along the level stretch behind and flow out on to the pasture. There is enough water to fill up the banks in a day. In two days it would overflow, and in a few days more there would be more green grass on both sides."

"Why, that don't sound like a bad idea, at all," George admitted. "An' we could make a framework for that dam out of bamboo sticks. That new ax of mine ought to come in real handy cuttin' them sticks down."

"Well!" Ki-Gor smiled and got to his feet. "Now, I think I'll go to sleep."

"Jest one mo' thing," George begged. "Here is sompin' that has kinda worried me. It's goin' to take some time fo' the boys to round up all their cows. Supposin' Black Mike comes back befo' we is any-wheres near finished movin'? He might try and pull a fast one on us, someway or anothuh."

"He wouldn't try anything with only three Somalis," Ki-Gor objected. "He would go and get the rest of his men before—"

"Well now, you cain't nevuh tell," George said. "A fella like him would know he could get away with an awful lot as long as he is out of spear range of the Maasai. He knows he could keep 'em off with rifles."

"I see," Ki-Gor said. "What we need, then, is some way of surrounding him with warriors close to him. So that he wouldn't dare fire a shot?"

"Tha's exactly whut we need," George confirmed.

"Very well," Ki-Gor sat down again. "Here is one idea."

IN SPITE of fearsome heat and a morning filled with the noise of a tribe packing up to move, Ki-Gor slept straight through until noon. Shaliba and Helene fed him a light breakfast and then the three of them went out of the *minyata* up the slope along the bank of the shrunken river. On an open knoll below the beginning of the hardwood forest, George was standing with Merishu and a handful of warriors. They were staring off across the open plains.

"So far, Black Mike has not appeared," Ki-Gor commented.

"No, he hasn't," Helene confirmed.

"Maybe they can get the cattle up out of danger before he comes," Ki-Gor said hopefully.

Helen made no response for a brief time. Then she said, with just a hint of challenge in her voice, "Why do you say 'out of danger,' Ki-Gor? Do you really think Black Mike will cause any trouble?"

"Certainly he will," Ki-Gor said, and looked at his wife in surprise.

Helene stared at her feet as they climbed the slope. "Well, I don't know," she said finally. "I don't often disagree with you, Ki-Gor, as you know. But it seems to me there is something to be said for this Black Mike."

"How?" Ki-Gor was interested.

"Well, he's suffering more from the drought than the Maasai are. He has to move somewhere until the rains come. Wouldn't it save a lot of trouble if the Maasai—sort of gave in generously, and let him move in? As long as it's just temporary?"

"Are you pretending?" Ki-Gor said in amazement, "the way I was?"

"No, I'm not," Helene said, sharply, "I've just been thinking about it. Really, Black Mike impressed me as being a most reasonable man."

"Helene, Helene!" Ki-Gor exclaimed. "He is a slave trader—a dangerous man."

"Well, anybody is dangerous who is driven to desperation," Helene said. "If Black Mike were not *forced* into fighting, I don't think he would. If both sides just got together and discussed their difficulties in the right state of mind—if each side was willing to concede a little—there wouldn't be any need to fear trouble. You wouldn't have to go into all this strategy."

"Ah, Helene," Ki-Gor said, "You're wrong! You don't know Black Mike."

He was on the point of recounting his narrow escape at the hands of the net-casting Wandarobo, but thought better of it. It should convince Helene completely of her error in judgment concerning Black Mike and his minions, but—Ki-Gor decided against telling her the story anyway.

"He's a human being like anyone else," Helene was still defending the slaver. "And it's about time that human beings—even in Africa— found some solutions to their differences without always resorting to force. I bet you that if George were just willing to negotiate a little, instead of saying flatly 'No'—that this whole business could be settled peaceably."

"There's only one way to settle this peaceably," Ki-Gor grunted, "and that is to show Black Mike that the Maasai are too smart and too dangerous for him to try to attack."

"To that kind of a statement," Helene said tartly, "there is no answer."

They climbed on in silence. Ki-Gor made no attempt to explain Helene's strange attitude. As she had said, they rarely disagreed. But every now and then, Ki-Gor had found that Helene had a mind of her own and was not hesitant about expressing her opinions.

Shortly afterward, they joined George and Merishu on the knoll. Off to the east, a good-sized herd of cattle was moving toward them along the moss-covered river bank.

"Well, here come part of the cattle," George remarked, "and no sign of Black Mike yet. It's kind of a slow job roundin' up all them cows, but maybe we'll git 'em up the mountain in time, yet. You sleep well, Ki-Gor?"

"I slept too well," Ki-Gor responded with a smile. "I'm still sleepy. But"—he shielded his eyes and gazed off toward the north—"I am not too sleepy to see some horsemen coming fast."

George swung around hastily.

"By gollies, you're right!" he exclaimed. "Tha's Black Mike, all right! And I'll bet he is fit to be tied!"

THE FIVE horsemen came at full gallop along the slope just below the lower fringe of hardwoods. If they continued without deviating in that same direction, they would reach a point on the river considerably above George and his friends. The big American Negro watched them for a moment, looking away to the herd of plodding cattle below now and then, and then looking back.

"They ain't much we c'n do, I guess," he said at length. "We'll just wait an' see how things turn out."

The five horsemen were getting close enough so that Black Mike could readily be recognized in the lead. They reined in at the top of the river bank and seemed to be taking in the situation. Then Black Mike put his horse down the sandy bank on to the river bed, followed by his men. They splashed across the little stream and up the other bank. They were now on the same side of the river as the little group around George. Then the five horses lined up abreast and came slowly down the slope.

Merishu stiffened and barked some commands at the half dozen warriors around him. But George murmured a cautionary word, and Merishu and the warriors relaxed again, albeit uneasily.

Two hundred feet away, Black Mike and his men reined in.

"That was a fine trick you played on me, Ki-Gor!" the slaver shouted. "But it didn't do you much good."

"He'd say that anyway," George murmured, "don't pay him no mind."

"You thought," Black Mike shouted, "that if you could get in ahead of me, you could queer me with the Nandi. Well, let me tell you you failed! Right this minute, the Nandi are ready to move against their old enemies, the Maasai, the moment I give the word."

He paused, waiting for a response from Ki-Gor or George. There was none forthcoming. The slaver threw up an angry arm.

"With the Nandi coming in on one side," he shouted, "and me and my men blasting through on the other—the Maasai haven't a chance! You will be slaughtered like sheep!"

Again he waited. And again there came not a word from George or Ki-Gor.

"If you think I'm not telling the truth," the slaver cried, getting apparently angrier by the minute, "you'd better think again. Because you can't afford to be wrong!"

Black Mike paused. And when he spoke again, his tone was altered. Now it was not angry, it was regretful, almost sorrowful.

"I gave you your chance," he said, "I was perfectly ready to be reasonable. I even offered you protection against the Nandi—those same Nandi that now will be harrying your rear while my riflemen cut your warriors to pieces!"

All this time, the herd of cattle had been climbing steadily up the slope. They were coming quite close to the scene of the parley. Gentle, docile creatures they were, their big horns bobbing and their little hooves kicking puffs of dust from the dry turf. About a score of tribesmen were driving the herd, most of them at the rear. Two or three drivers ran up to the van of the herd to head them off a little to the south, so that they would not disturb the group around George.

"Preparing for war, are you?" Black Mike cried. "Too bad. It will be the last war the Ngombi-Maasai will ever wage!"

Again the slaver waited in vain for some sign that his words were taken seriously.

"What's the matter with you?" he cried passionately. "Can't you realize your danger? Don't you know you're liable to be exterminated? Are you so stupid that you can't see that?"

He moved a little closer to make himself heard over the increasing noise of the approaching cattle.

"Tembu George!" he called. "I'll give you one last chance to settle this thing peaceably. I'm still willing to call off the Nandi—"

Ki-Gor suddenly stepped forward a pace.

"Save your breath, Black Mike!" he said. "Your man, Pereira, said to you yesterday that it was unlike you to run a bluff that you could not back up."

BLACK MIKE and Pereira flung astonished looks at each other. Then Black Mike turned flushing.

"Why—why what do you mean?" demanded.

"You didn't see me, Black Mike," Ki-Gor said, "but I was with you. What did you think of your Wandarobo with the net?"

The slaver's face was blank.

"You didn't find him, then?" Ki-Gor said. "That means you did not get as far as the Nandi village. You were turned back. You didn't even talk with the Nandi, at all!"

The slaver's dark face went pale with rage. He urged his horse forward a few steps and raised his rifle high above his head in a furious, threatening gesture.

"You think I am bluffing, Ki-Gor!" he shrieked. "Then you'd better hurry away from here. Your friends, the Maasai, will be the ones who will suffer by your bad guessing."

Ki-Gor merely smiled for an answer.

"Tembu George!" Black Mike shouted. "This is positively my last warning! And don't think it will do any good to drive your cattle into the hills. I'll be back with all my men long before you can get half of them out of the way. I have a good mind to pick off a few right now, just to show you what's in store."

"I wouldn't do that," George shouted back.

"Don't come any nearer!" the slaver commanded. "And tell your herdsmen to keep their distance—no matter how close the cattle come to us. Keep their distance! As long as none of your men come within spear range," he added, flashing white teeth triumphantly, "they won't get hurt. But if any of them come closer, we'll knock them off like pigeons! You can't beat guns with spears, you know!"

"Is that right, Mister Black Mike?" George shouted. He threw a calculating glance at the herd of cattle. The leading cows were far up the hill beyond the slaver's party, the main herd being more or less abreast with Black Mike himself.

Tembu George gave a deep chuckle. He thrust two fingers into his mouth and blew a long shrill whistle. Then he waved a hand out to the passing herd.

"There you are, Black Mike!" he shouted. "An' they is a good many of them that is within spear range!"

Black Mike stared slack-jawed at the cattle. Sprouting up all through the herd were tall Maasai warriors, fully armed. Scores of them straightened up from the deep crouching position they had been maintaining amongst the cattle. In that manner, two hundred of them had been able to come up unseen to within two or three hundred feet of Black Mike and his men. Guns might still have a tiny advantage— but not nearly enough!

"I wouldn't shoot, if I was you, Black Mike," George advised. "If you was lucky you could kill jest five of us. You could fire jest one round. And then, by gollies, you'd get a bellyful of Maasai steel."

For a moment, Black Mike sat as if in a trance, staring at those warriors who had seemed to have materialized out of thin air. Then he suddenly laughed—a long, rich, infectious laugh.

"Well, by golly, Tembu George," he roared, "you win! You and Ki-Gor. You've outsmarted me at every turn. I have to admit it, much as I hate to. And I'll have to admit I was just bluffing when I threatened to fire at your warriors. I wouldn't dream of doing any shooting with ladies present!"

He swept off his hat and bowed in the direction of Helene.

"Now, I am not quite sure what I shall do," he said, straightening up. "Heaven knows, I have done my best to avoid bloodshed. From the very beginning, I hoped to come to a pleasant agreement with the Ngombi-Maasai. After all, I wanted very little—just a temporary asylum until the rains come. And you'll have to admit, Tembu George, that you have been extremely stiff-necked about the whole matter—but that's your affair. Now, as I say, I don't quite know what I shall do. One thing is sure—I've got to move. And the Maasai country is the only place within reach that I can move to. So—I suppose it will come down eventually to force of arms. It's unpleasant, it's wasteful. I will lose a lot of men—the Maasai will lose a lot more. But, I guess it can't be helped. Well, thanks for a pleasant and instructive afternoon, and I think we'll be off. I trust—"

"WAIT!"

Ki-Gor couldn't believe his ears.

It was Helene.

"Wait!" she cried again, and began to run toward Black Mike. "Why do you go away talking like that?" she stormed. 'You could find a peaceful way out—if you only tried!"

Ki-Gor stared aghast at his wife. She had run more than half the distance separating him from Black Mike. His brain told him frantically to run after her, yet somehow he was momentarily incapable of moving a finger. He saw the look of astonishment on Black Mike's face change to swift calculation, and then to incredulous delight.

"Helene!"

The word choked itself out of Ki-Gor's throat, and he flung off the paralysis that had chained his limbs. He sprang forward. But already he knew he was too late.

Black Mike had slogged his horse around—was making straight for Helene. She drew up short in horrified surprise. The horse was upon her in three bounds. Black Mike hauled its head around and bent low in the saddle. His reins and rifle were in his left hand. With his right hand, he scooped Helene up off the ground. Then with brutal efficiency he flung the girl face down across the horse's withers, and spun the horse around.

"Stand back, Ki-Gor!" the slaver cried. "If you want your wife to live another moment—stay where you are!"

Ki-Gor dug his heels into the ground and halted with a groan. The rifle was now in the slaver's right hand. The right elbow was drawn back, finger on the trigger, and the muzzle of the gun prodded Into Helene's armpit.

George took in the situation and shouted a command at the Maasai who were leaping toward the slaver and halted them in their tracks.

"As you can see," Black Mike cried in a voice tight with desperation, "this is a very awkward position to hold a gun. It would go off at the slightest excuse. So, no one will make a motion of any kind—if Ki-Gor's wife is to live!"

"Don't shoot her, Black Mike!" Ki-Gor's voice was careful. "Because if you do—I will tear you to pieces with my own hands!"

"I hope I don't have to shoot her," the slaver retorted. "But so help me, if anyone advances so much as a half inch on me or on any of my men, I'll be squeezing this trigger!"

"You had better put her down," Ki-Gor said. "You will never get away with this."

"Oh, don't think I won't!" the slaver returned. "This is the finest hostage I ever had hold of."

"You are wrong, Black Mike," Ki-Gor said. "She is not your hostage—you are her hostage. As long as she is alive, you live. The minute she dies, then you are finished!"

"You can put it that way if you want to," Black Mike said with an unpleasant smile, "but the fact remains that if you want your wife alive you will leave me very much alone. If she's dead you can kill me, but that won't bring her back to life. Now look here—I'm going to clear out of here. I'm going to order my men to surround me, and then we are going to go at a walk right down the river bank. All the time, my rifle will be aimed at your wife's heart, and my finger will be on the trigger. And a very nervous finger it will be, I may add. I don't think I have to say any more, do I?"

"Yes," Ki-Gor said. "Where are you going?"

"Where am I going?" the slaver echoed. "I don't think that concerns you, does it? Or, in a way, I suppose you are interested. Well, I'll tell you—I'm going on back to my little fort. Once I get there I may change my mind, but a rough plan of action would be that I'll gather up my entire organization and bring them back here during the next few days. I shall expect the *minyata* to be evacuated, and I shall simply march in and occupy it. I will still have my pretty little hostage, of course, to ensure the good behavior of anybody who might otherwise try to kick up a fuss. Does that answer your question?"

Ki-Gor nodded slowly.

"And bear in mind," the slaver added, "that I shall be very watchful until final arrangements are concluded. For instance, I shouldn't follow us, if I were you. And I shouldn't attempt any sort of ambush— in fact, any sort of hostilities of any kind. Because in the event of there being any, the first person to die would of course be your wife. Is that clear? So—you will see or hear from me very shortly."

A hateful silence hung over the scene as Pereira and the Somalis edged their horses close to Black Mike. Then slowly the little knot of mounted men moved past Ki-Gor, past George and Shaliba and Merishu, past the lower end of the herd of cattle, down the river bank and out on to the plain.

MUTE AND horrified the Maasai followed the slavers with their eyes. When they seemed a safe distance away, the warriors made swiftly and silently for George. He muttered something to Merishu who in turn gave quiet orders, and the warriors subsided. Then George walked over to Ki-Gor.

"Whut we goin' to do, Ki-Gor?" he said, putting a hand on his friend's shoulder.

The jungle man stared down on to the plain and shook his head.

"There is nothing you can do," he replied in a low voice. "Nothing that would not be more dangerous than useful. Whatever is to be done, I will have to do alone."

"Well, I sho' wish I could he'p out—but I know how it is. There is times when mo' than one person is a handicap."

"Yes," Ki-Gor said soberly. "This is one of those times. I am going to Black Mike's fort. I don't know what I'll do when I get there—I'll decide that when I see what conditions are. If luck is with me, I'll be coming back in a great hurry—with Helene."

George's huge hand squeezed Ki-Gor's shoulder gently. "We-all will go ahead and move up the river-bed, so's we'll be ready for Black Mike's next move."

Ki-Gor nodded. "Don't forget the dam."

"We won't," the Negro replied. "Now, Ki-Gor, you sure you want to do things this way? You don't think you better take some of the boys along jest in case?"

Ki-Gor considered a moment, and then shook his head. In some ways, it might be a good idea to take along some of the warriors. But this was a situation which called for speed and secrecy. The Maasai were unquestionably the finest fighting men in Africa, but they were not woodsmen. They made indifferent bushwhackers, and were notoriously poor stalkers. No—their presence might be costly at a critical moment.

"Okay," George said. "Say, you ain't plannin' to follow the footsteps of them fellas, is you?"

"No, I know a shorter way across the foothills," Ki-Gor replied. "There is nothing I can do until they get back to the fort—and I may get there as fast as they do by taking the short cut."

CHAPTER V

KI-GOR'S ESTIMATE OF RELATIVE time and distance was—as usual—accurate. Just after sunset of the next day, he crouched behind a small boulder and watched a little knot of horsemen move across the barren plain in front of him toward the dun-colored blockhouse that was Black Mike's fort. The jungle man's eyes hardened, and his fists clenched involuntarily as he imagined what was going through Helene's mind, as she was borne along helpless, the victim of her own trusting impulse. Black Mike would pay, Ki-Gor resolved, and pay to the limit for his treachery. But first, Helene had to be rescued and carried safely away from any chance of reprisal.

Black Mike had chosen well the site for his fort. A small river had cut a winding channel across the plain, a channel so winding and tortuous that at one spot it virtually doubled on itself. On the inside bank of this hairpin bend, Black Mike had built his fort. The site had the virtue of a peninsula, the river furnishing a water moat on three sides. And for at least a mile in every direction, all cover had been systematically removed. During daylight hours at least, it would be impossible for anyone to approach the fort and remain unseen by the watchers on the walls.

The fort itself consisted simply of an open square of ground enclosed on all four sides by a thick wall roughly ten feet tall. At each corner there was a small house with a second story rising above the wall to form a watch tower. It was by no means an impregnable stronghold, but manned with warlike, rifle-armed Somalis, and with the additional protection of the water barrier, it was a sufficiently hard nut to crack for even such fighting men as the Maasai.

The drought had of course removed one defense, the river. The gravelly, boulder-strewn bottom of the river bed was now as dry as the parched plain on either side. It was that factor, added to the shortage of drinking water, that was forcing Black Mike to abandon the fort for the time being.

As the hazy daylight faded into gloomy twilight, Ki-Gor stole toward the river bed. It was the natural avenue for him to take to the fort, for by hugging the steep bank nearest the fort he would be almost completely hidden from the watch-towers, even though night had not yet set in.

But before Ki-Gor had traversed half the distance to his objective, a burst of activity in the fort indicated that Black Mike fully expected visitors that night, and did not intend to be caught napping. On top of each of the four walls of the fort, bonfires were built and lighted. And shortly afterwards, men carrying torches issued forth from the gate and went out in four directions from the fort.

One of these torchbearers came straight for the place where Ki-Gor was lurking. The jungle man moved down the river bed toward the fort, so that he would be beyond the range of light shed by the torch. But by some curious fatality, the torch-bearer changed his own direction and once again made straight for Ki-Gor.

Ki-Gor was about to go still farther to avoid being seen by the Somali, when an idea struck him. He had as yet devised no plan to get into Black Mike's fort. Why not simply attack this torchbearer as he crossed the river bed, dress in the man's clothes and stroll back through the gate of the fort unchallenged? If the man were armed, it would probably be with a rifle, and a rifle was not an efficient weapon of defense when one hand is already employed carrying a torch.

As the Somali came closer and closer, Ki-Gor sank down behind a low boulder close to the bank. It was not perfect concealment, the boulder not being large enough, but it would suffice until the torch-bearer came so close that Ki-Gor could be at his throat in one great, sudden spring.

Nearer and nearer came the man until his torch began to throw an eerie yellow glow over the dry river bed. He reached the bank about fifteen feet away from where Ki-Gor was crouching. There he paused, holding the torch high, and staring out into the darkness.

Ki-Gor held his breath. If the man did not see him down there, huddled by the boulder, it would be a miracle. But evidently it never occurred to the Somali to look for danger in the river bed. He continued to gaze out across beyond the other bank. Never once did he look down. Finally, he dropped to a sitting position and dropped his legs over the bank preparatory to sliding down. Ki-Gor gathered his muscles.

BUT THE Somali hesitated. Then he turned his head and called out into the darkness behind him. Ki-Gor stiffened. A voice answered. And as the torchbearer slid down the rubbly bank to the river bed, another Somali emerged from behind him and stood at the top of the bank. The second Somali carried no torch. He did carry a rifle ready for action.

Ki-Gor forced back a sigh of disgust and made himself as small as possible while the torchbearer, followed by his bodyguard crossed the river bed, climbed the farther bank, and disappeared from view.

Ki-Gor went morosely down toward the fort. As in the case of the Wandarobo whom he almost but did not quite catch, he was not sure whether he had been lucky or very unlucky. Certainly, if he had jumped the torchbearer, the bodyguard would have shot him, or at least raised the alarm. In that sense he was lucky. But his scheme for getting inside Black Mike's fort had gone glimmering, and now he would have to devise some other means of accomplishing that task.

As he drew nearer to the fort, he was encouraged by one thing. That was that Black Mike's men were making a tremendous amount of noise. Evidently the slaver had ordered immediate preparations for moving. The whole fort was in a ferment of activity.

That fact would prove of great service to Ki-Gor. He would not have to worry about dislodging some stray pebbles as he moved down the river bed, for they would never be heard over the tumult that reigned in the fort.

In a very short time, Ki-Gor stood under the wall of Black Mike's stronghold. Standing close to the bank under the wall, he was completely in the shadow. The light from the bonfire on the wall above falling short of him. Having come thus far, he paused to consider his next move.

He tried to recall the interior arrangements of the fort as he had seen them on his other visit to the place. He remembered clearly that each corner of the quadrangle contained living quarters. One of them Black Mike had set aside for his own exclusive use. But which corner that was, Ki-Gor could not remember.

It seemed probable that the slaver would be keeping Helene close by him. Therefore, however he got inside the fort, Ki-Gor decided to make his entrance as close to Black Mike's quarters as possible.

But in which corner were those quarters located?

The jungle man racked his brain. But it had been more than three years since he had been to the place, and his memory failed to give him a trustworthy picture. Keeping his face tilted upward, he proceeded to go along the base of the wall. It was with increasing concern that he noted how well guarded the place was. Two Somalis patrolled the top of each side of the quadrangle past the bonfires, and on each watch tower two more Somalis were posted. Ki-Gor began to wonder whether he would be able to climb and cross any part of that bastion.

He rounded the first corner and went along the next section. Just the matter of scaling that smooth elevation was problem enough in itself, without the added complication of the alert Somali guards. Furthermore, the river bank was about eight feet high, and the walls rose up another ten feet.

A dull rage began to creep over the jungle man as he continued along the second section of wall. The shouts and the laughter of the fort's inhabitants seemed full of derision directed straight at him. Ki-Gor clenched his great fist over the shaft of his Maasai spear. For the moment he seemed to be frustrated. But he vowed it would not be for long. There was a long night ahead of him to find a solution to his problem.

He continued catlike along the river bed, and turned the second corner. He looked up and his heart gave a great bound. Half way to the top of the watch tower a square of yellow light showed. A window!

The watch tower on the other corner had shown no light, in there had been no window breaking the smooth surface of the wall. This corner must be Black Mike's!

For a long moment, the jungle man stood with his head tilted back studying that square of light. The window was about three feet square, he estimated, and there were two stout bars placed vertically in it about a foot apart. As nearly as Ki-Gor could judge, the lower edge or sill of the window was about eighteen feet above the river bed where he was standing. It struck Ki-Gor as obvious that if he could somehow manage it, that window offered the most promising entrance to Black Mike's stronghold of any that he had seen so far.

JUST HOW he would scale eighteen feet of smooth river bank and wall, he did not know—nor how he would overcome the obstacle of the bars if he could get up to the level of the window. But if he did find some means of climbing up there, he would not be in plain sight of an unknown number of aggressive Somalis.

Finally he dropped his chin thoughtfully and looked around him. How could he get up there?

He had no rope. And even if he had, he was not sure it would do him any good. He considered the possibility of leaning his eight-foot spear against the river bank and somehow shinnying up it—then quickly discarded the idea as impracticable. His wandering eyes lighted on a large boulder lying well out toward the middle of the dry river bed. It was a good five feet high. The jungle man went through some rapid calculation. If he could take off in a flying leap from the top of that boulder, he might—might be able to reach the sill of the window with his fingertips. Say the distance was eighteen feet. The boulder was certainly five feet. His own height was well over six feet and his arms reached up nearly another two feet over his head.

He added his figures together, reckoned that if he stood on the boulder and reached upward, his fingers would be some five feet short of the window sill. Could he leap up five feet? He could try.

The first thing to be done was to roll that boulder over to the bank under the precious window. Ki-Gor appreciated that that would be a job. Fortunately the river bed there was hard gravel, and the boulder was approximately spherical—but even so it would be a prodigious weight to budge. And worst of all, the boulder was half in, half out of the light shed from above by the nearest bonfire. He would have to expose himself to possible discovery when he got on the other side of the great rock to push toward the bank.

The jungle man did not hesitate. In spite of the uproar going on within the fort, he crept silently to the boulder. Then he ducked swiftly into the firelight and out of it again behind the sheltering rock. There he waited for an alarm to sound from the top of the wall. None came. Evidently he had moved too fast for anyone to have caught sight of his bronzed body as it flashed out of the shadow of the wall to the shadow of the rock.

Carefully he extended his feet and leaned a shoulder against the boulder. Then his muscles bunched as he gave a gentle heave. The rock did not budge. Again he heaved. The boulder seemed to give a fraction of an inch—then dropped back to its original position. Now, Ki-Gor set himself. His feet well braced, he lunged at the rock in a titanic effort.

The boulder moved reluctantly for an inch or two, then halted. Desperately Ki-Gor pushed. With straining muscles, he held the boulder poised for a moment and then set it rolling. An inch, two inches, five inches, it rolled—then stopped abruptly. And Ki-Gor knew that it must have rolled on to a flat surface, and that he might as well try to move Ruwenzori any farther. The only thing he had accomplished was to move the boulder almost entirely into the shade of the wall. But to move it another inch, he realized he would have to try some other means.

An idea struck him. He slipped around the rock to the bank. His right hand closed over the iron-shafted Maasai spear he had left on the ground. He returned with it to the boulder and found a smaller rock to move near the base of it. Years before, Ki-Gor had discovered for himself the principle of the lever. He was about to apply that element of engineering now, although he was a little doubtful of how good a crowbar the slender spear-shaft would make. Worse yet, when he inserted the butt end of the spear under the boulder, the broad blade would protrude out behind into the firelight. There would be an excellent chance that a watcher on the tower or the wall would see the glinting reflected light. However, that could be remedied and quickly. He spat vigorously on both sides of the blade, and then smeared clay on them from the bank. A cautious test showed no reflection.

Now Ki-Gor went to work. For the first few minutes, his progress was slow. He could not use the full length of his improvised lever, because that would put him out in the firelight. Also he was chary of bending the spear-shaft by putting too much weight on it. But gradually he inched the boulder toward the bank and farther into the shade. After a while he could use the full length of the spear, and then his progress was limited only by the amount of noise caused by the boulder and the lever on the gravel river bottom. One extra operation was required to bring the boulder close up under the window—a space had to be excavated in the bank. But this was accomplished with the broad spear blade. And finally, Ki-Gor stood on top of the boulder ready to try leaping upwards to catch the window sill with his fingers.

THE ENTIRE operation had taken a remarkably short time—less than an hour, Ki-Gor estimated—but it had been finished none too soon. For some reason the noises within the fort diminished quite suddenly, as if the inhabitants were tired or talked out. Here and there, a Somali jabbered or laughed, but generally speaking quiet descended over the fort. Ki-Gor thanked his stars. If he had to move the boulder now, he could not have done it without being heard.

He considered his next problem. At least the leap upward from the rock would be comparatively noiseless. The real problem was whether he could make it. He bent his knees in a preparatory crouch, and swung his arms from his shoulders. Then he sprang.

But as his feet left the rock, he knew he would not make it that trip. His palms hit the wall a foot below the window sill, and he pushed himself away and dropped down lightly on to the boulder. His second attempt was no better—perhaps not even as good. After a third spring fell short, Ki-Gor stood still a moment to consider the situation.

Somewhere in the fort, he could hear a door being opened. The door sounded close by over his head—it might have been in the room with the window. He heard a bolt or hasp being drawn, then a faint squeaking as of rusty hinges. The sound of heavy footsteps could be heard, followed by the squeaking hinges again, and the rasping of the bolt. Somebody had come into that room, closing and bolting the door behind him. Then a man's voice sounded in conversational tones, and the skin along Ki-Gor's spine rippled.

"Well, my dear," said Black Mike, "are you in a pleasanter mood, now?"

There was no answer, but Ki-Gor had no doubt about whom Black Mike was addressing in that room.

"Oh, come now?" the slaver's voice was indulgent, coaxing. "Why not be reasonable? You're a prisoner in my fort. There isn't a chance in the world of being rescued. You won't be released to Ki-Gor until I say so. Why not make the best of something you can't do anything about? You might as well be philosophical. Being belligerent and scratching my face to ribbons won't help you any—you know that."

"That's where you're wrong!" Helene's voice was low, but it was intense. "It helped a lot! It did me a world of good to get my fingernails into that beautiful brown face of yours!"

Black Mike laughed good-naturedly.

"Quite a tigress, aren't you?" he chuckled. "Or perhaps I should say leopardess, considering that your attractive costume is made of leopard skin. Tell me, how long have you been ranging Africa in that outfit, scratching the faces of admiring males?"

"There is to be only one admiring male in my life," Helene replied, "and that is my husband. The first day he saw me, he saved my life. I was making a solo airplane flight across Africa. My motor conked out over the jungle, and by great good luck I made a crash landing practically on Ki-Gor's doorstep. If he hadn't taken me under his protection I wouldn't have lived out the day."

"Oh yes!" Black Mike remarked. "I remember hearing about that at the time—hearing about your attempted flight, I mean, and about your disappearance. I took to the bush soon after that, and never did hear about your being rescued. Well, well! So you're the rich American society girl, are you?"

"I am Ki-Gor's wife," Helene said stonily.

"Oh, come—you're not really married to him!"

"We were married at Fort Lamy two years ago. Perhaps you won't believe me—but sooner or later you will believe Ki-Gor when he tells you. Ki-Gor can be very convincing when he wants to be."

"HAH!" THE slaver gave a short laugh. "I'm afraid you can't frighten me with Ki-Gor. He may be big and strong—but then, so am I."

"And you have a gun," Helene said bitterly.

"Oh—even without my gun, I wouldn't be afraid of Ki-Gor," Black Mike said airily.

"I hope you get an opportunity to back up your boast," Helene said. "And the sooner the opportunity comes, the better I'll like it."

"I wouldn't hang on to any false hopes if I were you, my dear. Ki-Gor has about as much chance of getting through my outposts tonight as a rhinoceros would. And even if he did, he would be cut down by a bullet long before he came near me. And I'll say this much for Ki-Gor, he is smart enough to know that. So don't go hoping he'll do something foolish. You'd better resign yourself to staying in my hands until you have served my purpose."

"I resign myself to nothing," Helene said.

"So foolish," Black Mike chided. "You might as well make your sojourn pleasant for—yourself, as well as me. You said yourself I had a handsome face."

"I loathe your face!" Helene cried. "And if you come any nearer to me—I'll spit in your face!"

"At least that's better than scratching it, anyway," Black Mike jeered. "That was so silly. How much more comfortable you'd be if your hands weren't tied with that rough rope! Such pretty hands! Such pretty arms, too—nice and rounded—"

"Go away! You swine!"

"And the nicest legs I've seen in Africa—ah? You *are* a little leopardess, you—"

Helene screamed a long, bitter, outraged scream that lasted for several seconds.

But at the first sound, Ki-Gor took off from the rock. Blind rage surged through him, sending super-human power to his leg muscles. He roared upward as if he had been shot from a catapult. Steely fingers clutched at the window sill and held, while his feet and knees churned against the wall. Before gravitation had begun to drag his body downward, he swarmed up far enough so that one hand grasped one of the window bars. The sinews of the forearm started out as he crooked the elbow and dragged himself upward. Now, the other hand grasped the second bar. A moment later, his mighty chest rested on the window sill, and he was staring with hate-filled eyes at the scene within.

All he could see of Helene was her flailing legs. Black Mike's broad back hid the rest of her. But she was evidently lying on a rough bed, and the slaver was bending over her. Black Mike's hands were hidden from Ki-Gor's view, but Helene's scream was suddenly choked off, as if a great hairy hand had closed over her mouth.

Ki-Gor reached both hands up, achieved a grip higher on the bars. Then he flung himself upward, until both knees rested on the narrow window sill. His body was automatically following the lightning decisions of his mind now, as if he had long ago planned and rehearsed every step.

The bars were only a foot apart, leaving an opening too narrow to permit his huge body from going through. Then the bars would have to be removed! He lifted his right hand and dealt two hammer blows with the tough heel against the base of the bar. The thick iron gave out a soft, dull ring. Inside the room, Black Mike straightened up and seemed about to turn around. But Helene started to scream again, and once more he bent over her and shut off the scream.

Ki-Gor wasted no more time trying to remove those bars—they were obviously too well rooted. But if they could not be removed, they would have to be bent apart—enough so that a space wide enough to admit Ki-Gor's body could be made. Swiftly, he twisted his body to the right, and extended his right leg until his foot was braced firmly against the side of the window. Then both hands grasped one of the window bars close together half way between the top and bottom. Ki-Gor's muscles corded as he dragged at the tough iron. All his strength went into one prodigious tug.

FOR A moment, Ki-Gor began to think he had attempted the impossible. Then a wild hope shot through him as it seemed to him that the iron had given a little—and continued to give. And his eyes confirmed it. The bar was bending toward him, slowly and reluctantly—but bending! Ki-Gor threw everything into one last furious pull.

There was a sudden noise—a dry crackling sound. The bar sagged in Ki-Gor's hands, bent steeply with him so that he almost lost his balance. To his astonishment, he saw that the top of the bar had pulled out and away. There was no time to conjecture the reason why it had torn away from its mooring at the top and not the bottom of the window. There was an ominous sound from within the room.

Shifting his weight, Ki-Gor looked in and saw Black Mike staring at him. The huge slaver still had his back turned, but his handsome face was turned and he was looking over his shoulder in horrified amazement. Quick as a snake, Ki-Gor threw his legs across the window sill. There was room to spare between the sound bar and the one which he had wrenched and bent out of position. But Black Mike was quick, too. He wheeled his heavy body around like a top, groping with his right hand for the revolver at his belt. Could he draw the gun and have time for a shot before Ki-Gor could get through the window and leap across the room at him?

Ki-Gor saw in a flash that he could. The gun was out of the holster before Ki-Gor's feet struck the floor. In another quarter of a second a bullet would slap into Ki-Gor's plunging body. At such short range there would be no missing.

As in a dream, Ki-Gor saw Helene roll her body on the bed—saw her legs come up. And as Black Mike's hand brought the muzzle of the gun up, Helene's right foot kicked it savagely. The gun all but flew out of the slaver's hand. A curse twisted out of his mouth, and his hand jerked crazily trying to recover the revolver. But Ki-Gor was upon him in two jumps.

As he charged, Ki-Gor hooked left and right hands in succession at Black Mike's head. Only the fact that the slaver was falling forward at the time prevented the blows from landing with positive effect. Both blows landed high on the slaver's head.

Ki-Gor, being self-taught, always fought with his hands open, hitting with the palms like a gorilla. It was a fortunate circumstance at this moment, for if his fists had been balled he might have damaged his knuckles against Black Mike's hard skull. As it was, the slaver fell groggily against Ki-Gor's legs and knocked him temporarily off balance. In trying to regain his balance, Ki-Gor fell forward across the slaver's burly body. At the same time, he felt thick arms wrapping themselves about his legs.

He rolled to one side, kicking furiously. Managing to wrench one leg free, he twisted around to slash at the back of the slaver's thick neck. But Black Mike, hanging grimly on to Ki-Gor's left leg, suddenly rose up. Before Ki-Gor could land a blow, he was lifted off the floor and thrown heavily on his back.

And now Ki-Gor knew that he was up against one of the most formidable opponents he had ever in his life tackled. He had barely time to draw back his one free leg and drive it against Black Mike's barrel chest. The slaver was trying to fall on top of him, trying to pin him to the floor. And he nearly succeeded. But Ki-Gor's desperate kick deflected his huge body sufficiently so that most of his prodigious weight hit the floor beside the jungle man.

Now Ki-Gor's left hand flailed short blows at the slaver's head. Mike had to release his hold on Ki-Gor's leg to bring his arms up to ward off that stinging left hand. The jungle man wrenched himself out of the disadvantageous position on the floor and rolled over and up on to his feet.

A sensation of relief swept over Ki-Gor as he attained his feet. He had been for a moment in serious danger. He must not allow the slaver to get a wrestling grip on him. Mike's extra weight would give him too heavy an advantage.

All this flashed through Ki-Gor's mind in a fraction of a second as he wheeled to dash at the recumbent slaver. But now Black Mike was yelling—yelling for help at the top of his voice.

"Pereira! Quick! *Pereira!*"

WITH LIGHTNING decision, Ki-Gor whipped out his knife and darted toward the bed where Helene was rolling and tossing. It took a precious second to sever the rope at her wrists. He whirled then to see Mike, still yelling, scramble across the floor toward his revolver. The slaver saw Ki-Gor leap at him, knife in hand, and he reared up to meet the charge.

As Ki-Gor stabbed downward, a hamlike fist flashed out, hit the knife-hand on the inside of the wrist. Then a terrific blow crashed between Ki-Gor's eyes. He staggered back, momentarily stunned, his right wrist numb. He heard his knife clatter to the floor, and instinctively he ducked another blow at his jaw.

If Helene's life had not been concerned, Ki-Gor would have felt a degree of admiration for Black Mike's fighting prowess. It was decidedly an equal fight. Black Mike evidently thought so, too, for he stopped shouting for help.

But Ki-Gor knew that his first shouts must have been heard, and that in a few moments, Black Mike's minions would be swarming through the door. It would no longer be an equal fight then.

"Helene!" he shouted. "Get out the window! Tie the rope to the window bar!"

A pile driver blow landed on his chest and Ki-Gor gave ground. But as Black Mike shuffled in to deal another one, Ki-Gor shook the fog out of his head and began hooking both hands at the slaver's dark face. It was Ki-Gor's best fighting style. A half dozen furious punishing cuts stopped Mike's murderous advance and restored the balance of the battle.

"Go on, Helene!" Ki-Gor cried, seeing out of the corner of his eye that she had not moved.

Mike seized the moment to give a bull-like rush, arms extended to grapple Ki-Gor's waist. He almost caught the jungle man. But the lean hips in the leopard skin twisted aside, and Ki-Gor slashed at Mike's ear as he went by. The slaver's head was traveling with the blow, or it might have knocked him out. As it was, he staggered three steps before he regained his balance. Ki-Gor should have leaped in for the kill. But there was Helene. He hesitated and flung a glance at her. She stood beneath the window, rope in hand.

"Go! Go!" he pleaded. "You can't help!"

Helene turned with a sob, and Ki-Gor wheeled toward Black Mike.

The golden opportunity had gone. The slaver was poised on the balls of his feet, arms extended. A sudden babble of voices sounded outside and swelled louder. Mike's men had heard him.

The slaver and Ki-Gor both glanced quickly at the great hardwood door to the room. It was securely barred from the inside. Mike's men could not get in until the bar was drawn.

The slaver was a foot closer to the door than Ki-Gor. He flung a lightning glance at Ki-Gor and feinted a rush at him. Instead of continuing the rush, however, the slaver whirled and sprang toward the door. But Ki-Gor had read his mind. He ignored the feint and leaped toward the door with Black Mike.

The slaver half turned and hit the door with his shoulder. At the same instant, his leg lashed out in an incredibly swift kick at the oncoming form of Ki-Gor. The heavy boot struck Ki-Gor's hip with paralyzing force. The jungle man flinched momentarily, and Mike fumbled with the iron bar at the door. Ki-Gor leaped again. Again the slaver kicked.

This time, Ki-Gor was prepared. Both hands seized the thick ankle, and he threw himself backward. The slaver hopped forward, help-lessly shouting and pumping the trapped leg. Ki-Gor dropped one hand to the toe of the boot and twisted the foot downward.

The slaver fell just in time to save his ankle from being broken. As he crashed face down on the floor, Ki-Gor took off. The jungle man landed on the prostrate giant's shoulder blades. Both hands rained heavy slashing blows at the slaver's ears. The slaver buried his head between his beefy shoulders, and heaved his body upward trying to throw his enemy off. Ki-Gor stopped hitting and slipped both hands around the thick neck seeking a strangle hold.

There was a tremendous uproar outside the room now, and some-body was dealing bludgeon-like blows against the heavy door. It was time Ki-Gor was leaving, if he was ever going to leave. Mike thrashed his heavy shoulders and arms trying to break Ki-Gor's hold. And he did, in fact, dislodge one hand partially. The jungle man knew he had to resort to other, quicker tactics.

BACK ON to the giant's neck went the dislodged hand, and quick as a cat. Ki-Gor slipped off the heaving body. With both feet braced on the floor, the jungle man dragged his adversary's head upward—up and up, until the slaver's knees swung clear. Bellowing incoherently, Black Mike scrambled wildly to get his feet under him. The moment he did, Ki-Gor let go his hold on the neck. And before the slaver had regained his balance, Ki-Gor poured blow after smashing blow into the handsome face.

Reeling sideways, Black Mike could only paw the air feebly and turn his head from side to side to try and escape that rain of right and left hooks. Then the shouts died away to gurgles as Ki-Gor continued to slash murderous blows at the face. The feeble motions of his arms grew feebler, and his eyes began to glaze over. One last furious cut on the jaw, and he lurched to one side off balance and crashed headlong to the floor.

Ki-Gor sprang to his side and bent over him. But the slaver was completely unconscious. The jungle man hoped he had killed him. But the door to the room was straining at the hinges under the battering from the outside. There was no time to make sure Black Mike was dead. Ki-Gor leaped across the room and threw a leg over the window sill.

The rope was there, tied to the one sound iron bar where Helene had left it. It was a short length, but sufficiently long so that there was only a short drop from the end of it to the top of the boulder.

"Ki-Gor!"

Helene had to whisper several times for Ki-Gor to hear her over the noisy alarm going on up on the parapets of the fort. But eventually, he found her and seized her by the hand.

"Oh, Ki-Gor," she whispered, "will you ever forgive me?"

"When there is more time," Ki-Gor retorted, "I will forgive you anything. Now, we must run—run for our lives!"

Black heads lined the parapet above them, as Black Mike's men strained their eyes toward the protective darkness of the river bed. It was only a matter of moments before they would inevitably be discovered. Ki-Gor wasted no time in trying to decide which way to run. Leading Helene back up the river bed in the direction from which he had come, he rounded the first corner just before some resourceful Somali tossed a burning brand down from the top of the wall. A second earlier and the flickering torch would have revealed the jungle couple escaping. But they were already scrambling along the second walk out of range.

Ki-Gor knew that he had one advantage. Until Black Mike's men broke down the door to his room, they would not know exactly what to look for. They would have to see the bent window bar and the rope to get any clue as to what had happened in that room. If Black Mike was dead, which Ki-Gor devoutly hoped he was, they would be without adequate leadership. Pereira did not seem like a very commanding personality. So—until the door to Black Mike's room was forced, he and Helene could race up the river bed under the shadow of the bank without fear of pursuit.

Only one serious obstacle might show up. If one of the slaver's outpost bonfires was close to the river bed, the fleeing couple would be seen. But as they left the fort with its excited inhabitants behind, Ki-Gor could see up the dark channel of the dry river far enough to satisfy himself that there was no outpost near either bank. He slowed down a little bit for the benefit of Helene, who was stumbling breathless along the unfamiliar route.

"It would be easier going," he told her, "up on the bank. But we might be seen there. So we'll just have to keep on as fast as we can down here. Just follow close behind me, and I'll lead you around the boulders."

"Yes, Ki-Gor," Helene whispered in reply.

CHAPTER VI

A **HALF AN HOUR** later, Ki-Gor halted under the vague shadow of a great tree. There was precious little light to see by, the only illumination being the haze-obscured stars, but Ki-Gor knew he had arrived at the edge of a forest belt above and to the westward of Black Mike's arid plain.

"Up the tree," he commanded Helene.

"We'll stay here a little while and decide what to do next. Go up as high as you can—I think we may be able to see the fort."

Sure enough, from the swaying tree-top, they could make out the twinkling lights of the fort two miles or more below them. A ring of lights far outside the fort showed that the outpost bonfires had been augmented, and that an impromptu search was going on. The impression was strengthened when a group of bobbing lights separated from the fort and moved out over the plain.

"Hm," Ki-Gor murmured. "They are very busy down there. I wonder whether Black Mike recovered."

Helene stared out into the night without responding.

"Aha!" Ki-Gor chuckled. "They are going down the river bed in the other direction. They couldn't have found any tracks. It would be hard to see a spoor on hard gravel with just a torch. It will be hard enough tomorrow morning by daylight. And by tomorrow morning we will be far away."

He turned restlessly to his silent mate: "What's the matter, Helene?" he demanded. "You are so quiet. You say nothing."

Helene heaved a great sigh. "Oh, Ki-Gor," she said humbly. "I don't know whether I can talk without bursting into tears."

"Oh don't!" Ki-Gor said in quick alarm. "Please don't cry."

Nothing agitated Ki-Gor more than Helene crying.

"I'll—try not to!" Helene sniffed. "But I'm so—so ashamed, Ki-Gor! I thought I was doing such a smart thing—and all I did was to get into a terrible jam—and put you in awful danger—"

"That's all right, Helene," Ki-Gor said, in distress. "You meant to do the right thing."

"Oh, but I was so wrong!" Helene wailed, "and you were so right! Never in my life did I misread a character so awfully! In spite of all you said, I was sure Black Mike was decent at heart! And it was just sheer pig-headedness that got us into a terrible mess!"

"Forget it," Ki-Gor said. "We don't have to worry about Black Mike now—I hope. Anyway, we got you away from him. He wasn't decent, was he?"

"I should say he wasn't!" Helene said fiercely. "I'll probably have a black eye in the morning from where he hit me. But he's going to bear the marks of my finger nails for some time to come."

"Good," Ki-Gor applauded. He said then, reflectively, "I wish there had been time to make sure I killed him."

"That's why I wanted to stay in the room with you," Helene said. "I thought I might be able to get my hands on his revolver. I would have shot the brute without the slightest compunction."

"Hm," Ki-Gor murmured again. "That would have been a good idea. I was wrong not to let you stay. Now, you see—you made a mistake. But then, I made a mistake. Everyone makes mistakes—but if they come out all right, why it doesn't matter, does it?"

"Oh Ki-Gor! You're just trying to make me feel better!"

"Well, do you?" said Ki-Gor. "Do you feel better?"

"I'm ashamed to say I do," Helene replied.

"Good," said Ki-Gor, and he dropped his legs preparatory to climbing down the tree. "Because we should travel for a while. In the morning, the Wandarobo tracker may find which way we did go. We are not far from thick jungle—if we get well into it now, they will never be able to follow us through it. Particularly, those Somalis on horses."

Helene's spirit was willing to continue the trek for an indefinite length of time. But after a couple of hours of slogging through dense underbrush in pitch darkness, her knees began to give way. Once again that night, the couple climbed a tree, but this time they stayed there to get some much-needed sleep.

Just before Helene dropped off, she suddenly remembered something she had meant to mention to Ki-Gor.

"About the Wandarobo tracker," she said, "we don't have to worry about him picking up our trail back there."

"Why not?" Ki-Gor asked.

"Because he wasn't at the fort tonight."

"No?"

"No. Black Mike sent him off on some errand as soon as we arrived at the fort. I remember feeling sorry for the little man. He had traveled all the way beside Mike on foot, and here he was being sent right out again."

"So much the better," Ki-Gor said, dismissing the incident. "Where did Black Mike send him, do you know?"

"I'm not too sure," Helene said, "I can't speak Wandarobo, you know. But I thought I heard the word, 'Nandi.'"

"Nandi!" Ki-Gor exclaimed. "Then Black Mike hasn't given up trying to make friends with them!"

"As I say, Ki-Gor," Helene said, apologetically, "I can't be sure that was it. But I don't think Black Mike was still trying to make friends with the Nandi. More likely just the opposite. Because he gave the Wandarobo a brand new rifle."

"A rifle!" Ki-Gor exclaimed. "That's very funny. I never knew of a Wandarobo who could use a rifle."

He mused for a moment on the oddity of the situation, and then dropped off to sleep.

JUST AT daybreak the jungle couple climbed out of the tree and renewed their trip back to the Maasai country. It was rough going and the two of them could not make as fast a time as had Ki-Gor alone when he was coming over the foothills to rescue Helene. It had taken him, then, about twenty-four hours altogether. But that was all traveling time, as he had not stopped to rest anywhere on the way. Therefore, the return trip would take at least that long—and probably longer—with several hours taken out for rest. If they rested at night, Ki-Gor reckoned that it would take them two full days and nights to get back to Tembu George and his people.

But during the first morning, Ki-Gor dwelt on the thing which Helene had told him the night before. Why would Black Mike send the Wandarobo to the Nandi armed with a rifle that he very probably had no idea how to use? The more Ki-Gor thought about the matter, the less sense could he make out of it. And the more puzzled he grew about it, the more uneasy it made him. Unconsciously, he quickened his pace through the rough upland jungle until Helene was put to it to keep up with him. But Helene had no intention of protesting about going so fast. She felt so guilty of her folly in walking into the kidnap-ing, that she vowed to herself she would follow Ki-Gor implicitly until they got back to their snug home in Central Africa.

The result of the brisk rate of travel was that the couple arrived at a point only four hours away from the Maasai *minyata* by noon of the second day—hours ahead of their predicted schedule. Ki-Gor stopped to consider their route. They could go by either of two ways. One of them led straight up over a considerable mountain. It would be rugged going, through tangled undergrowth and up steep slopes. It would bring them out eventually some distance above the new Maasai camp. They would in fact strike the shrunken river and follow it down to the grassy plateau above the bamboo forest.

The other route was slightly longer but much easier going. They would simply go down a ravine to their right and come out onto the rolling plain. Once arrived there, they would turn north skirting the edge of the forest until they came to the river. Then they would go upstream through the bamboo forest to the plateau. Ki-Gor decided on this second, easier route mainly because Helene showed that the pace he had maintained was wearing her down, even though she had not complained.

They picked their way down the ravine without incident and then turned to their left as they came out into the open just above the

Maasai plain. Here it was pleasant walking. They stayed just within the fringe of parkland or hardwood forest, benefitting by the shade of the majestic old trees. Presently, they could see the deserted *minyata* swimming in the haze far away on the plain.

"It isn't far now," Ki-Gor remarked. "George will be glad to see us."

"Yes," Helene returned, "I guess he's been a little worried."

"I think he wondered how I would get you back," Ki-Gor smiled. "I don't blame him—I didn't know myself until I stopped under that window."

"I still don't know how you ever moved that great boulder over," Helene said, then stopped in surprise. Ki-Gor was standing stock still staring out toward the distant *minyata*. "What's the matter?" she demanded.

"There are some people coming out of the *minyata,*" he said briefly.

"Really? Well—why shouldn't there be? Maasai, aren't they?"

"They are warriors—carrying long spears," Ki-Gor said slowly, eyes focussed on the distance. "But they are not Maasai."

"Not Maasai?" Helene echoed blankly.

"What are they, then?"

"They are not dressed in red cloth like the Maasai," Ki-Gor said. "They are wearing brown buckskin robes, as far as I can tell—like the Nandi."

"Nandi!" Helene exclaimed. "Heavens! What are they doing over here, I wonder!"

"We will soon find out," Ki-Gor announced grimly. "They are coming up along the river. If we hurry, we will cut them off from going up too far."

THEY HURRIED, and were sitting at the lower edge of the hardwood belt as the group of Nandi sauntered up the river bed. Old Ashwana was in front of the party—there were some twenty altogether—and the headman was carrying a rifle. Ki-Gor began to guess what the errand of the Wandarobo had been.

"Peace to you, O Nandi," Ki-Gor called out, standing up.

The Nandi looked startled, but answered his greeting civilly enough.

"You have come to make war on the Maasai, after all?" Ki-Gor asked.

"No." Ashwana looked faintly sheepish. "No, not at all. We come to make an *indaba*."

"With the Maasai?" Ki-Gor pursued.

"With Black Mike, the slaver," Ashwana corrected him.

"How," said Ki-Gor, "can Black Mike arrange an *indaba* in somebody else's country?"

"Ask him," Ashwana shrugged. "How would I know?"

"But look," Ki-Gor said, frowning. "If some Maasai should happen to see you here, there would be trouble. They would not stop to inquire whether or not you came in peace."

"We are not afraid of the Maasai!" Ashwana declared. "If they attacked us, that would be their lookout!"

"Don't you suppose," Ki-Gor said, "that Black Mike arranged an *indaba* here on purpose—just so that you might accidentally meet some Maasai and get to fighting with them?"

Ashwana considered the question. "He might have," he admitted after a minute. "But he said otherwise."

"Of course, he wouldn't tell you his real reason for bringing you over here," Ki-Gor said scornfully. "But you already knew that Black Mike wanted you to go to war with the Maasai, so that he could have allies in his war against them."

"He made no conditions in his message," Ashwana said sulkily. "All he said was that I should bring some men and meet him at this place and he would bring our presents."

"He is giving you presents?" Ki-Gor asked. "What do you have to do in return?"

"Nothing, I said," Ashwana cried petulantly. "And they are splendid presents, too."

He gazed pridefully at the Mannlicher rifle in his hands.

"He is giving you rifles, Ashwana?" Ki-Gor said.

"Yes—twenty of them," Ashwana said triumphantly. "Isn't that worth risking war with the Maasai for?"

Ki-Gor looked at the rifle, thinking hard. Black Mike had played a trump card. It all depended now on whether Black Mike was still alive and able to come and reap the benefit of his smart play.

"I know nothing of rifles," Ki-Gor said, walking up to Ashwana and staring down at the weapon.

"Nor do we," Ashwana admitted. "But Black Mike will teach us how to make them go."

"My woman knows all about them," Ki-Gor offered. "Show her your gun."

"Ah! Does she?" Ashwana said eagerly. "Tell her to show me!"

The Nandi dialect is sufficiently close to Maasai for Helene to have followed the conversation pretty well. She came up and took the gun from the old man. She pointed against the river bank and squinted through the sights. An admiring sigh went through the watching Nandi. Then she lifted it from her shoulder, drew back the bolt and inspected the breech. The gun was unloaded.

"Where are the little eggs to go into it?" she asked Ashwana.

"What eggs?" said the old man.

"You must have some little slender eggs," Helene said, holding her thumb and forefinger apart, "about this long. They come tied together in packages of five."

"Can't you make the gun go without them," Ashwana demanded, his face falling.

"No," Helene said, "This gun without the eggs is like a bow without arrows. It is useless."

"DO YOU see?" Ki-Gor proclaimed to the crest-fallen headman. "The gun is worthless. Black Mike's presents are as worthless as his promises! What will you tell Black Mike, now, O Ashwana, when he comes to the *indaba?*"

"There will be no *indaba!*" Ashwana exclaimed wrathfully, "we will go—"

The old man was suddenly interrupted by several of his men.

"Here they come! Black Mike and his Somalis!"

Ki-Gor looked quickly out over the plain and saw a long line of horsemen galloping toward them.

Black Mike, then, was still alive!

"Helene!" he commanded. "Go up the river, quickly! Tell them what has happened, and to be ready for an attack!"

"All right," Helene said with questioning eyes. "But aren't you coming, too?"

"I'll come in a minute," Ki-Gor said. "I must do something here first. Hurry!"

Helene handed the rifle back to Ashwana and hurried away up

the river bed. The old man gazed sourly at the rifle, then turned and stared at the oncoming horsemen.

"Shall we kill the deceiving dogs of slavers?" he demanded of his men. There was an immediate growl of assent from his men.

"Wait!" Ki-Gor cried. "They all have rifles which will go! They will stand off at a distance and kill everyone of you before you could get close to hurt them."

"What shall we do, then?" Ashwana asked.

"One of two things," Ki-Gor said. "You can follow me up to where the Maasai have gone—I will explain to them that you come in peace."

"No," said Ashwana. "We want to settle accounts with the slavers."

"Then fool them," Ki-Gor urged. "Pretend that you will hold the *indaba*. And then when they are close enough, go after them with your long spears. Kill them and take their rifles."

"Aye, we will do that," Ashwana said. "We will kill every last one of them."

Ki-Gor melted backward to the cover of a tree trunk, congratulating himself on his quick thinking. It was fortunate that there had not been a chance meeting between these trespassing Nandi and some Maasai. As it was, there was a good chance that the outraged Nandi might conduct a fine slaughter among the unsuspecting men of Black Mike. And such an outcome would weigh very lightly indeed on Ki-Gor's conscience.

Events began to move swiftly now, and several things happened which Ki-Gor had not counted on.

To begin with, not only was Black Mike alive, but he was at the head of his mounted Somalis. And Black Mike was nobody's fool when he dealt with African natives. He halted his force some two hundred feet away from the group of Nandi and hailed them.

"You have come, O Nandi!" he shouted. "And so have I!"

Now came another thing which Ki-Gor had not counted on. He had not realized that the Nandi would be such poor actors. If they were supposed to be pretending friendly feeling toward Black Mike, they would have fooled no one—least of all the astute slave trader.

"Aye, we have come," Ashwana growled, while his men scowled ferociously at the Somalis. "Why did you give us no eggs?" Black Mike was still for a moment, his scarred puffed face thoughtful.

"What do you mean by eggs?" he asked quietly.

"You know well enough," Ashwana said, surlily.

"I came with guns for you, not eggs," Black Mike stated carefully. "What is this talk of eggs? And why do you look at us in this unfriendly way?"

"We are perfectly friendly!" Ashwana snarled. "Even though you bring us worthless guns without eggs, we are friendly."

"Wait a minute!" Black Mike's eyes narrowed. "Who has told you about eggs?"

"Why, Ki-Gor did," Ashwana replied, naive to the last. "Only a few minutes ago. Do you know Ki-Gor?"

"Yes, I know Ki-Gor," Black Mike replied. "Where is he now?"

"Why—" Ashwana waved an arm, "over behind that tree."

BUT SEVERAL seconds before that Ki-Gor had set off up the slope on a dead run, dodging from tree to tree. So that he was perhaps five hundred feet away from Black Mike's men when the slaver shouted orders and bullets began to scream by his ears. It was just enough of a head start to save his life for the moment, for he was able to keep tree trunks between himself and his enemies for several precious minutes.

And the Nandi finally did make up to some extent for their stupidity. For Mike had commanded his entire force to gallop up the river bed in hot pursuit of Ki-Gor, and as the Somalis urged their horses forward, the Nandi charged them valiantly. Oblivious of the rifle fire, the lanky warriors flung themselves headlong at the Somalis. It was a hopeless thing to do—for not only were the Nandi out-weaponed, but they were outnumbered. Black Mike had mustered nearly fifty men.

But the Nandis folly saved Ki-Gor's life. Black Mike had to stop and dispose of them before he could pursue Ki-Gor in earnest. And by the time the first rush of the Nandi had been bloodily beaten off, Ki-Gor was up to the lower edge of the bamboo forest.

Here the jungle man was faced with a choice of action. He could dive into the bamboos and trust to the thick cover for a temporary hiding place. Or he could come out into the river bed and hope to arrive at the Maasai camp without being picked off by a rifle bullet. He quickly chose the second course. Helene, to be sure, would have warned George and the Maasai about Black Mike's presence. But when no Ki-Gor appeared, they might come down and run into the well-armed Somalis themselves.

As the jungle man leaped off the bank to the boulder-strewn river bed, he glanced downstream and saw that a dozen or so Somalis were urging their horses uphill less than a hundred yards away. And behind them came Black Mike with still more riflemen.

Ki-Gor ran boldly in the open without regard for cover. He reasoned that as long as the Somalis were on horseback they could not shoot accurately. It was only when the going got too rough for horses that they would dismount, and then he would be in danger.

The Somalis stayed mounted much longer than Ki-Gor thought they would and in spite of the rocky river bed began overtaking Ki-Gor rapidly. One man in particular outstripped the rest and was within fifty feet of Ki-Gor when he fired wildly. The bullet whizzed unpleasantly close to the jungle man. He scooped up a good-sized stone, whirled suddenly and flung it down at the pursuer. It caught the Somali on the chest and dropped him off the horse. A moment later, the horse stumbled and crashed down on the rocks.

Ki-Gor, his breathing labored from the fearful exertion of the extended uphill run, began to worry a little about the situation of the Maasai. He had not thought horses could come up nearly so far. That meant that Black Mike could bring his riflemen up the pass between the bamboos much faster than anybody had anticipated. They could swarm up to the plateau with the same advantage they would have held on the plains below.

He looked back every now and then as he stumbled upward, gasping for breath. What he saw confirmed his worries. The Somalis were halted below in a knot, waiting for the rest of their force to come and join them. Ki-Gor quickly estimated the breadth of the river bed and reckoned that twelve or fourteen men could walk up it abreast. Twelve or fourteen men could dispose of considerable fire-power.

There came a shout from up the hill, and Tembu George came plunging down to meet him.

"Whut's happenin', Ki-Gor?" the big Negro said anxiously.

Breathlessly, Ki-Gor told him, and told him of the gathering Somalis down the river bed.

"If you could have come up a little earlier," Ki-Gor gasped, "we could have sent warriors down here among the bamboos and ambushed them. But it's too late for that now."

A half dozen bullets sprayed the rocks near the two friends.

"You shouldn't have come down!" Ki-Gor cried. "You might get hit!"

"Nossuh, I is too lucky!" George replied gaily as they both scrambled up the increasing slope. "Anyways, the rivuh curves around up yere a little, an' they cain't see us. "Whut a man cain't see, he cain't shoot."

AS THEY rounded the turn, Ki-Gor looked upward and exclaimed.

"Ah! You built the dam!"

"Yeah, that was a great idea of youahs, Ki-Gor! Already quite a bunch of water has backed up. You wouldn't believe it, seein' this little bit of a stream."

The dam, Ki-Gor noted, had been well placed on top of a small falls. Scores of twenty-foot bamboo poles had been set upright side by side, and secured by other poles placed horizontally.

"She is pretty leaky," George cried, "but she holds plenty of water!"

They were scarcely fifty yards below the dam now, and Ki-Gor was beginning to bog down. He slowed to a walk, gasping.

"Take yo' time, Ki-Gor!" George urged. "You is safe now for a few minutes—ontil them devils come around the curve shootin'. Say, whut we goin' to do about them, anyways?"

Ki-Gor shook his head mutely. He was so exhausted, he could hardly think.

"Wait a minute!" George shouted, "I got it!"

Just then a horde of Maasai, headed by Merishu, poured down from both sides of the glistening dam. They shouted gleefully at Ki-Gor and brandished their spears.

"Where are the Somali?" Merishu demanded. "We are going to wipe them out!"

"Not while they got guns that shoot, you ain't!" George shouted. "You come with me—you got something else to do befo' you go down yonduh."

It took George precious seconds to bring the brawling warriors around to his point of view. But eventually, they trooped after him. And while Ki-Gor sat well back from the river bank, getting his breath, George and the Maasai began attacking the dam. The warriors slashed at the lianas which bound the bamboos together, and George stood at the base of the dam and swung his ax at the poles themselves.

In the middle of the business, there came the ominous crack of rifles. Ki-Gor jerked his head around and saw a phalanx of Somalis appearing around the bend in the river bed below. They were a dozen abreast and they were firing as they came.

One of the Maasai was hit and fell off the top of the dam.

"Get back!" George roared. "Get back under covuh! You finished yo' job—an' I c'n do the rest by musse'f!"

Reluctantly, the warriors withdrew from the dam, and George swung his ax at the foundations. The rifle fire grew hotter. Bullets began hitting all around the embattled American Negro. Ki-Gor sprang to his feet.

"George!" he shouted. "Come away! They'll kill you!"

"She's comin'!" George replied. "Jest two-three mo' little poles, an' then I'll scramble! Don't worry about—"

George did not finish the sentence. He stood as if in a daze, his hands hanging limp. Then his knees crumpled and he sagged down to the rocks. The Maasai cried out, and Ki-Gor was running up to the dam. Somehow he got to the prostrate form of his friend before anyone else did. A rill of blood was flowing down across the Negro's forehead.

"Carry him away," Ki-Gor commanded the Maasai. As they did, Ki-Gor picked up the ax and hacked at the spot George had been chopping. More bullets continued to scream and thud into the dam around him. But Ki-Gor ignored them as George had. If the dam could not be broken, they would all be at the mercy of Black Mike's riflemen.

There was a sudden welcome crackling sound. The column of water which had already been spurting out from the hole at the base of the dam, suddenly increased. Ki-Gor glanced up and saw the whole row of bamboos swaying out over him. He leaped aside and scrambled up the bank. He was not a moment too soon.

The bamboos toppled majestically over and crashed on the rocks below, and a wave of water ten feet high followed. Amid the frenzied shouts of the Maasai, the river temporarily came to life and boiled down its old channel spreading to both banks and carrying a mass of bamboo poles down upon Black Mike's Somalis.

There was only three days' accumulation of water behind the little dam but for a brief time it was effective as a three years' accumulation. The Somalis were spun off their feet and swept down the hillside through the bamboo forest, completely helpless.

"Merishu!" Ki-Gor called. "The guns will not shoot now—since they are wet!"

But Merishu and his warriors needed no urging. Like lean black avenging angels, the Maasai splashed down the river after the invader.

Ki-Gor turned and looked down anxiously at Helene who was bending over George's still form.

She drew her hand sticky with blood from George's head.

She smiled up, tremulously, at Ki-Gor.

"It was awfully close," she said. "Just a quarter of an inch lower and our friend would have been through."

"He's all right?" Ki-Gor demanded.

"I think so," Helene declared. "A scalp wound. See, he's coming to already!"

THAT NIGHT there was a feast beside the site of the destroyed dam. The warriors danced and sang of their exploits that afternoon. It was as Ki-Gor had said, Merishu marveled—the guns of Black Mike's men would not go, being wet. So there was great slaughter. Because without a gun, no Somali is a match for a Maasai. He, Merishu, was a little incensed to find a few Nandi at the bottom of the hill. He knew they were there because Helene had told him. But it enraged him to see the Nandi also slaughtering Somalis. It was like hunting in a game preserve that belonged to somebody else. He and Ashwana had had some words over the matter. Ashwana had pointed to his own dead Nandi, however, and Merishu could not condemn him then for getting revenge—even if it was on Maasai territory.

Ki-Gor brooded over the fact that Black Mike had apparently gotten clean away.

"My sakes!" muttered George sitting beside him, head bound up like an Arab. "Don't' worry about that fella. It's goin' to take him a long time to get so he is ever dangerous again. He is so well hated, he won't dare stay around yere without no Somalis to p'tect him. Nossuh, don't worry about him!"

Ki-Gor turned and looked at his wife. There was a shadow on her lovely face just below one eye, and it was not a shadow that flickered with the firelight. It was the bruise that Black Mike had left when he hit her.

"I am not worried about Black Mike," Ki-Gor said. "It is he who had better be worried about me."

STORY XIV

BLOOD PRIESTESS
OF VIG'NA

KI-GOR ROSE TO A kneeling position, his massive bronzed frame moving in one smooth continuous motion until he faced eastward. His high-cut sensitive nostrils dilated as they tested the hot breeze that swept toward him from the arid Central Sudan. Beside him, Helene watched him inquiringly—almost fearfully. Half-consciously, she rubbed her stomach. Her abbreviated leopard skin garment seemed to hang loose, her stomach felt so hollow.

"Don't tell me," she murmured, "that you smell game."

She smiled quickly so that Ki-Gor would not think she was being peevish. But it was a wan smile. Helene felt almost like crying. It seemed days and weeks since she had eaten a proper meal.

Ki-Gor put out a warning hand.

"There's a buck," he whispered, "upwind. A big one. But only one, I think."

Relief surged over Helene. If Ki-Gor's marvelous nostrils told him there was game nearby, why then there was game. And even if there were only one buck, she trusted Ki-Gor to bring it down. Her mouth began to water involuntarily at the very thought of an antelope steak.

Ki-Gor's huge right hand closed over the seven foot hunting bow beside him, and he eased himself up to a standing position. He stood motionless for several long seconds. Then as if by magic, a long hardwood arrow was notched to the bowstring, and he moved soundlessly away. Helene knew better than to follow him. Since she had settled down in Africa as Ki-Gor's mate, she had learned a great deal of jungle lore. She had learned stalking, for instance. But now, she knew that Ki-Gor would do his stalking without help from anyone. Too much depended on his getting that unseen buck for Helene to risk intruding her own comparatively inexperienced self into the hunt.

As he stole away, Helene looked after the giant white man and marveled at his tremendous physical co-ordination. Even though he was moving faster than an ordinary man could walk, he made not a sound, but seemed to drift over the ground like a vagrant ghost, his tawny body blending into the brown background of trees and canes and grasses.

When Ki-Gor scented the buck, they had just stopped up on the high bank of the great river they had been following upstream for several days. A few yards away another much smaller stream came in at right angles to the river, joining its waters at that point. A row of trees and undergrowth marked the course of this smaller stream, and it was along this row of trees that Ki-Gor moved now.

He had gone scarcely a hundred yards when he sank to the earth. Helene, who had not taken her eyes off him, lost sight of him completely. Then she saw him again slowly rise to his knees and lift the great bow to a shooting position. At the same time, she heard a faint sound of drumming hoofs and rustling bushes. A moment later, a small antelope sprang out of the undergrowth some hundred feet beyond Ki-Gor. It streaked out toward the open as if a squad of lions were after it. Helene watched Ki-Gor aim the arrow. Her mouth parted in suspense. It was not, as Ki-Gor had first supposed, a big buck, but it was plump and certainly big enough to assuage the gnawing hunger in her stomach and Ki-Gor's.

The first arrow sped through the air. But it was as if the fleeing antelope could see it overtaking him. He dodged away to his left, and went shooting off in a series of bounds.

Helene groaned. The antelope seemed to go as fast as Ki-Gor's arrow.

Then Ki-Gor shot again. This time the arrow went so fast that Helene could hardly follow its flight. Straight and true it whizzed after the antelope. Helene did not see the arrow hit the antelope. But she saw the creature suddenly bound straight up high into the air. The little buck landed on all four feet with a sickening jar, and for a fraction of a second stood still shivering.

Helene saw the feathered butt of the arrow then, sticking out from the left shoulder. And as she watched, another arrow snicked into the fawn-gray shoulder, hardly an inch away from the first one. Again, the antelope sprang into the air.

It came down staggering, and started off once more toward the

open country. And then a strange thing happened—so strange, that Helene could scarcely believe her eyes.

From somewhere in the undergrowth a long slim spear floated lazily through the air, tilted downward over the plunging antelope, and struck it just in front of the hindquarters. The antelope stumbled and crashed to the ground. Ki-Gor was already dashing after his prey. But so, apparently, was someone else.

A big thick-necked black appeared out of the undergrowth and lumbered shouting toward the twitching antelope. Ki-Gor stopped short.

"Hai! Brother!" he called out in the Hausa language. "Where do you think you are going?"

THE BIG black swerved and trotted toward Ki-Gor. His shouts died away in astonishment, and he came to a full stop as his eyes took in the details of Ki-Gor's appearance. Perhaps this Hausa had never before seen a white man. He certainly had never seen such a white man as Ki-Gor—huge and bronzed, with glinting blue eyes and a thatch of straw-colored hair, and dressed only in a brief loincloth of leopard skin.

At any rate, the Hausa stared long and hard at Ki-Gor, and slowly drew from his belt a nine-inch knife. Ki-Gor sauntered forward.

"I think," he said pleasantly, "we were hunting the same buck."

"Wah!" the Hausa exclaimed. "I know not about you. I have just killed a buck!"

"Come and look," Ki-Gor said easily, and moved toward the prostrate antelope.

"I can see from here," the Hausa snarled. "There is my spear."

Ki-Gor chuckled good-naturedly.

"Since when," he laughed, "did a spear in the rump of an animal ever kill him?"

"Stop!" the Hausa shouted. "Go no closer to my buck! I know not who you are, but I will take no insults from any man—least of all—"

"Stop, yourself!" Ki-Gor retorted, and turned slowly to face the Hausa. He held his great bow negligently in front of him, but there was an arrow ready and notched.

"I have known the Hausa many years," Ki-Gor said conversationally. "I have friends among them. Always, I have found them cheerful, courteous, good-natured people. They are proud and self-respecting, but they do not imagine insults where none were intended—"

"Hah!" the Hausa interrupted scornfully. "You talk like a white man. They think the only good Hausa is one who is good-natured and polite always. That is going to be changed—all going to be changed!"

Ki-Gor regarded the big black silently.

"Now the whites fight among themselves," the Hausa went on, "and the black man has a chance to take back his land. When the right time comes, you will see. You will see how good-natured the Hausa are. El Hakim will strike and the power of the whites will be forever destroyed!"

"Enough—enough," Ki-Gor said coldly. "I am not interested in your politics. I am hungry. I am going to cut some steaks from that buck which I killed. If you want the rest of the carcass, you may have it."

"Buck which you killed!" the Hausa screamed. "I killed the buck—as anyone can see! There is my spear!"

"Aye—sticking out of his rump, as I said before," Ki-Gor said dryly. "If you go closer, you will see two arrows of mine in the buck's heart."

"Tricks!" the Hausa snarled. And then, without warning, he whipped his right hand around and threw the long knife full at Ki-Gor's chest.

The Hausa was no more than twenty feet from Ki-Gor when he made the treacherous attack. The heavy nine-inch blade traveled like a bullet. Helene, walking toward the two men, screamed. Ki-Gor could not possibly have time to dodge the flying knife....

What happened then, Helene could not quite make out—because it happened so fast. But Ki-Gor's left wrist, holding the great bow, seemed to twist. The bow jerked and shivered. There was a clanking noise, and the heavy knife went spinning off to one side of Ki-Gor and fell harmlessly to the ground.

IT TOOK Helene two or three seconds to realize that Ki-Gor had used the bow as a shield, batting the flying blade aside as deftly as the Congo blacks from whom he had learned the trick. But if Helene was amazed, the Hausa was astounded. He stared with bulging eyes as Ki-Gor coolly inspected the bow. The tough wood had caught the flat of the blade and was hardly nicked. Ki-Gor looked up at the Hausa, and there was a cold gleam in his blue eyes.

"You tried to kill me," he said quietly, "and you failed. I could put an arrow through your heart in the wink of an eye, and it would be no more than just."

"Aye," the Hausa growled. "You have me at a disadvantage."

The black's face was defiant, but his voice trembled a little.

"How do they call you?" Ki-Gor asked unexpectedly. "What is your name?"

"Why—I am called Doogoo," the Hausa replied.

"Very well, Doogoo," Ki-Gor said. "Men call me Ki-Gor. If you have not heard the name before now—you will be likely to remember it for some time to come, after today."

Whereupon Ki-Gor dropped the bow with the notched arrow, and leaped forward at the Hausa bare-handed. The big black thrust out long ape-like arms instinctively and lowered his bullet head. Ki-Gor crooked his left elbow, and his forearm crashed down on the thick, black wrists like a bar of pig-iron. At the same time, his right hand hooked around and landed with sickening force on the Hausa's cheek just in front of the ear.

As was his custom, Ki-Gor struck with open palms like a gorilla instead of clenched fists. It protected him from fracturing his knuckles, and, furthermore, the blows hurt their victims more.

This blow drove the Hausa's head sharply aside. But before the black could collect his wits, Ki-Gor's left hand had hooked into the wide face. The hard palm smashed against the flat, spreading nose of the Hausa and split the skin like a ripe blackberry. The Hausa gave a strangled cry and staggered backward, flailing his thick arms futilely. But Ki-Gor pressed forward, those punishing palms raking the Hausa's head and face mercilessly.

Helene's heart was in her mouth as she watched the mêlée. She knew that Ki-Gor was able to take care of himself against almost any single adversary. Nevertheless, the Hausa was just as big and powerful as her mate, and was probably considerably heavier. The reckless fury of Ki-Gor's initial attack had bewildered the black man, but it had also laid Ki-Gor open to counter-attack.

As she watched, the Hausa went tumbling on the ground on his back. Ki-Gor poised over him for a split second. The black squealed and pumped his legs in blind terror. And then Helene moaned, as one of those legs lashed out and Ki-Gor recoiled, doubled up with pain. The Hausa's hard heel had apparently driven hard into Ki-Gor's stomach.

For a moment, the black did not see his advantage. Then, as Ki-Gor retreated two or three paces, arms clasped over his diaphragm, the Hausa gave a hoarse cry and scrambled to his hands and knees. Then the black sprang forward in a deep crouch, his hands barely off the

ground. He did not leap toward Ki-Gor—but past Ki-Gor toward the long knife which lay on the ground beyond the jungle man.

But, as the Hausa stormed past, Ki-Gor came to life and flung himself at the black figure in a flying tackle. Black man and white crashed to the earth, the Hausa raining blows on the back of Ki-Gor's head. Then Ki-Gor was somehow on his knees, his head drawn back out of reach of the Hausa's fists. His right hand suddenly snaked out seizing a black wrist.

There was a short howl of pain, and Helene thought she heard the sound of a bone snapping. Ki-Gor was on his feet and both hands dragged the Hausa upward. The big black's left harm dangled uselessly at his side. Ki-Gor hooked one more terrific blow across the battered, bleeding, black face, and the huge Sudanese sank moaning to the ground.

Doogoo, the Hausa, had evidently had enough.

Ki-Gor stood over him and glared down for a brief time, then he turned away and picked up the long knife off the ground. "I will keep this knife," he said, "to remember you by, Doogoo. As for you—you will not soon forget Ki-Gor."

The Hausa's only answer was an inarticulate groan. Ki-Gor sent a reassuring glance at his mate, and went straight toward the antelope. Helene followed suit, making a wide circle, however, around the vanquished Sudanese.

CHAPTER II

AN HOUR LATER—AND A mile away—Ki-Gor and Helene finished off their meal of antelope steak. Helene's jaws ached from the tough, freshly killed meat, but her stomach was comfortably full. She leaned back with a sigh against the trunk of a tree and closed her eyes drowsily.

"Oh dear," she murmured, "I would certainly like to stay right here for a while and digest that wonderful meal."

"We will," Ki-Gor said.

"Really?" Helene opened her eyes in surprise. "Shouldn't we go back to the big river and try and pick up the tracks of David Gray's safari?"

They had come up the smaller stream to cook their meal. Ki-Gor looked back down the fringe of trees that bordered the smaller river at their backs. He shook his head with a smile.

"We don't have to go a mile to find the tracks of the safari," he said. "They pass about twenty feet in front of us—over there."

"Why, I didn't know that!" Helene exclaimed.

"Didn't you?" Ki-Gor said comfortably. "You must have been too excited to notice them."

Helene made a little face at him. Then she became serious once more.

"You mean?" she said, "that David Gray turned off along this stream?"

Ki-Gor nodded. "And headed due east," he confirmed.

"Well," Helene sighed, leaning back again. "Do you think we'll ever catch up with him?"

"I don't know," Ki-Gor said. "It's an old spoor. I wouldn't have been able to follow it if this were not open country. The porters spread out as they marched. If it were a jungle trail, they would have followed the leader in single file, and the footsteps left by the white man in boots would have been covered up."

"Have you any idea how old the spoor is?" Helene asked.

"It's hard to say," Ki-Gor answered. "The message, as I got it, did not say when our friend started out on the safari. It just said that he was in trouble."

"I see," Helene said. "Oh, dear, and there was nothing in the letter David left behind to indicate when he had started out, or even when he intended to start out."

Ki-Gor stared at his feet in silence for a while. Then he looked up with puzzled eyes.

"This is bad country up here," he remarked. "I know, because I came up here once when I was a boy. Why would our friend have to come into it?"

"Well, he goes where he thinks he may find something interesting," Helene said in explanatory tones. "He is interested in strange customs, in ruins or anything which shows how men lived a long time ago."

"He didn't have to come all this way to find ruins," Ki-Gor objected. "There are plenty of those down near our home. Plenty of strange tribes, too."

"I know," Helene said, "but he found something which indicated to him that there might be something especially interesting up here."

She paused to arrange her thoughts. It was a little difficult to explain to Ki-Gor exactly what an anthropologist was, and why he did the things he did.

"You remember," she said, "how deeply interested David Gray was in that tribe of Bushmen we discovered? He said they were living the same lives and carrying on the same customs as men did ten thousand years ago?"

Ki-Gor remembered, but that did not explain anything. He had been puzzled at the time over the anthropologist's passionate interest in a tribe of very backward Bushmen.

HELENE WAS about to try further explanation, when she saw that her mate was staring off to the westward, the direction from which they had come.

"What is it?" she said.

Ki-Gor shook his head without answering. Then he stood up.

"I thought I heard something," he said. "But it's downwind, and the sound was very faint."

Helene followed the direction of his eyes.

"Look!" she cried. "There's somebody running."

"Yes," Ki-Gor said. "It's the Hausa who tried to kill me. He is running away from something."

"I should say he is," Helene exclaimed. "And for a man with a broken wrist he is running pretty fast. What is he frightened of?"

"I don't know," Ki-Gor confessed. "I thought I heard voices."

They watched the Hausa flee away almost out of sight. But just before he disappeared, there came several faint crackling sounds.

"Guns!" Ki-Gor murmured.

"Rifles!" Helene corrected. A moment later khaki-clad figures began streaming out of the undergrowth close to where the Hausa had been lying. A chorus of yelps could be heard from them, and some of them fired again at the distant figure of the fleeing Hausa. Soon they halted, evidently convinced that further pursuit was useless, and gathered in a little knot.

"Who are they, Ki-Gor?" Helene whispered.

"Askaris," Ki-Gor replied, and glanced behind him as if estimating the cover afforded by the growth on the river bank. Just then, the little knot of figures broke up with more yells, and started straight for the spot where Helene and Ki-Gor were standing.

"Say!" Helene exclaimed. "It looks as though they're coming after us!"

"They found our tracks," Ki-Gor admitted. "But I don't think we have to fear them. They may even be British. But whatever they are, there is a white officer with them."

As the group rapidly drew nearer, Helene saw that Ki-Gor's remarkable eyes had gathered at a distance what she only now began to perceive. The newcomers wore uniforms with cartridge belts, and carried military rifles, and to the rear of them walked a white man in khaki shorts and open-throated blouse and wearing a sun helmet.

Ki-Gor stood motionless as the group came nearer.

The askaris had approached to within a hundred yards before one of them caught sight of the jungle man and his mate. There was a shrill cry, taken up by the rest, and the whole group ran forward with their rifles at the ready.

Ki-Gor raised his right hand, palm outward, and greeted them in Hausa. They slowed up, exchanging doubtful glances among each other. Several yards away they halted, and one of them, a sergeant, came forward scowling.

"You are dressed like a heathen savage from the bush," the Mohammedan sergeant said. "You speak with a Kanuri accent. Yet your skin and features are as a white bwana."

"I am a white bwana," Ki-Gor said. "My accent and my clothes are nothing to you. I will speak to your officer."

The sergeant bristled. "My officer," he stated pompously, "is a most important officer. He cannot be—"

"Aye," growled Ki-Gor, "and you are a Swahili far away from home." With that, he dismissed the sergeant and called in English, "Who is in command of this detachment?"

The sergeant fell back in astonishment, and a moment later the officer, a lean, grey-mustached man, pushed through the crowd of askaris.

"Captain Creighton, King's Nigerian— Great Scott!" he broke off in astonishment as he got a good look at Ki-Gor and his mate. "Are you English?" he demanded.

Ki-Gor smiled. "My father and mother were British," he said. "I am Ki-Gor. This is my wife."

Captain Creighton looked a little bit stunned. His eyes roved toward Helene's scantily clad beauty, then moved quickly away.

"KI-GOR?" HE said. The comprehension began to dawn on his craggy face. "Oh! Ki-Gor!" he exclaimed. "Oh yes! I believe I've heard of you somewhere! So that's who you are! By Jove!"

The captain fell into embarrassed silence, peering nervously at the huge jungle man. Helene essayed to put the Englishman more at ease.

"We noticed," she said, "that your men chased that Hausa over by the river."

"Oh, yes! Yes, rather!" the captain exclaimed, grateful for a topic of conversation. "Skittish johnny, wasn't he? Ran away like the wind. All we wanted was information."

"He was not exactly friendly," Helene observed. "We ran into him a little earlier."

"Did you really?" the captain shouted. "Oh, I say—I wish you'd tell me about it. I mean to say—d'you think we could sit down somewhere? Have a bit of a chin? P'raps you could help me with some information. Tell you what—our launch is down on the river. Would you care to walk back and come on board? We might scrape together something to eat, who knows?"

"We've just eaten, thanks," Helene replied, "but we'd be glad to consult with you."

Once on board the military launch, Captain Creighton came quickly to the point.

"Fact is," he confessed, "I'm a bit out of our bailiwick, strictly speaking. These waters are definitely French territory. But the dear old French are sulking in Dakar, wondering whether to bite their old enemies or bite their old friends. In the meantime, the hinterland is rather going to pot. The natives are noticing the lack of control and they're getting the teeniest bit restive."

He paused and regarded Ki-Gor. The jungle man's face was expressionless. Captain Creighton resumed.

"All this is by way of explanation of why I'm here. You see, every so often, a patrol like this comes over the border to wander about and have a bit of a look at things in general, investigate certain rumors, and—er—give ear to certain other rumors."

The Englishman paused again.

"I thought possibly," he said, at length, "that you might have heard some rumors."

Ki-Gor frowned. "I don't think we can help you," he said. "We are strangers here, ourselves."

An expression of relief appeared on Captain Creighton's face.

"Ah—quite so," he murmured. "It seemed to me that I had connected your name with territory farther south and east than this."

Helene's eyes twinkled. "I think," she observed, "that Captain Creighton was a little suspicious of us, Ki-Gor. However, all he need do is radio Nairobi, or even Brazzaville, to be assured that Ki-Gor and his wife are loyal subjects of the Crown."

Captain Creighton's relief grew even deeper.

"Splendid," he murmured. "Then perhaps I can come out into the open. I'm looking up a chap called 'El Hakim.' You don't happen to have run into him, do you?"

Ki-Gor and Helene exchanged swift glances.

"Ah!" Creighton said quickly, "I see you have!"

"No," Helene replied. "But we heard of him—for the first time— just a little while ago. We heard of him, in fact, from that very Hausa your men were chasing back on the river bank.

"Tell me about it," Creighton urged.

Helene related the circumstances of the quarrel over the antelope.

"And before he threw the knife," Helene said, "he shouted some- thing about the whites fighting among themselves, and how that gave the blacks an opportunity to take back their land. I can't remember his exact words—"

"I can," said Ki-Gor. "He said, 'El Hakim will strike and the power of the whites will be forever destroyed.'"

Creighton smiled. "Sounds easy, doesn't it? Go on."

"Well," Helene said. "That is the extent of our knowledge of 'El Hakim,' I'm afraid. What do you know about him?"

"I'VE NEVER seen the blighter," Creighton said, reflectively. "But he must be quite a boy to have gotten the Hausa so excited. They're such decent, loyal blokes ordinarily—but now—" he waved a hand toward his askaris "—well, these chaps are all from other sections. I'm not taking my Hausa troops into this territory. Damnable, isn't it?"

"Who and what is 'El Hakim?'" Helene asked.

"Far as I can tell," Creighton said, "he's a Fulani. Mixed Berber- Negro, you know, and fanatical Moslem. They swarmed down here over a hundred years ago from God-knows-where and conquered the Hausa and Yoruba and set up an empire. It was the last great empire in the Western Sudan. But this fellow we're talking about might have some ideas of his own along those same lines. This sort of semi-open country with communications and so forth seems to encourage large empires or confederations—much more so than the jungle farther south. And if a man came along, especially one of the dominant Fulani race, and had the personality to weld together the tribes—there might be some rather interesting results."

"But doesn't Hakim simply mean 'doctor?'" Helene asked.

"Yes, it does," Creighton acknowledged. "But then in English we have Doctors of other things besides Medicine. We have Doctors of Philosophy, and Doctors of Divinity. So in Arabic a Hakim is not necessarily a physician. He might be a religious leader. And all through history, Mohammedans everywhere have been especially prone to military action behind a religious leader. Many a 'Mahdi' started out as a mere 'Hakim,' and that's just why we have the wind up so about this fellow."

"Well," Ki-Gor said. "We shall be in this region for a time. If we learn more about the—the—Hakim, we will look for you on our way back."

"By Jove! That would be splendid of you!" the captain cried. "By the way—er—precisely what are you doing here so far from your home?"

"We are looking for our friend," Ki-Gor said seriously.

Helene smiled at the look of incredulity on Creighton's face.

"Perhaps we'd better explain," she said. "Our friend is the anthropologist, David Gray."

"Ah!" Creighton murmured. "Ah yes! Scientific johnny. What is he after anyway?"

"It's a long story," Helene said. "But he's on the trail of some Viking remains."

"Vikings!" Creighton exclaimed. "You mean Norsemen, and all that sort of thing?"

"That's it," Helene nodded.

"Great Scott!" the Englishman cried. "Who'd ever think of looking for Norsemen in the Western Sudan!"

"Not Norsemen!" Helene laughed. "Just *remains* of Norsemen!"

"But good heavens!" Creighton expostulated. "Those Viking johnnies sailed about a goodish bit, but they didn't come this far, did they?"

"David Gray believes they did," Helene said. "According to a letter he sent us, he had discovered an ancient manuscript in Iceland that told of a Viking expedition far to the south to the land of black men. Furthermore, he had found some rocks inscribed with what might have been runes, the ancient Norse lettering, near the mouths of rivers emptying into the Gulf of Guinea."

"By Jove!" Captain Creighton exclaimed. "I've seen some curiously inscribed rocks myself along the Coast, but it never occurred to me that they were runic inscriptions."

"Apparently David Gray thought some of them were," Helene went on. "So he determined to go up one of those rivers to see if he couldn't find further traces of that expedition."

"Does he think the Vikings went up the river in their ships?"

"Apparently he does," Helene said.

"That's utter rot," Creighton said. "You can't sail across the bars at the mouths of half of these streams, and as for sailing clear up—"

"The Viking ships were shallow draft," Helene pointed out, "and they could be propelled by oars as well as sails."

"That's true," Creighton admitted. "But still and all, it's a pretty fantastic idea, don't you think?"

"I frankly don't know much about the thing," Helene shrugged. "I'm not an anthropologist, and David Gray is."

"Mm," Creighton murmured. "Well, every man to his taste. But I must say this David Gray chose a damned awkward region to explore at a damned awkward time."

"Yes," Helene said, "and that's just why we're here. We heard that David Gray was in some kind of trouble."

"HOW ON earth did you hear that?" Creighton demanded.

"The jungle telegraph," Helene said. "To be precise, the message was relayed many times through members of the Brotherhood of the Dog."

"The Brotherhood of the *Dog!*" Creighton shouted. "What on earth is that?"

"A secret society of which my husband is a member," Helene said serenely, secretly enjoying the Englishman's astonishment. "It spreads the length and breadth of Africa and communicates messages among its members by all sorts of means."

"I say!" Creighton murmured, running a hand around his damp collar. "Spooky sort of thing, rather, isn't it?"

"Many people think Africa is spooky," Helene said, smilingly.

"Well now, let's get this straight," the captain said. "You're out looking over this gigantic waste for a small scientific safari which is headed by a friend of yours. Have you any idea"—the captain addressed Ki-Gor directly—"of how you're going to find it?"

"Yes," Ki-Gor answered simply. "We are following the safari's trail right now."

Creighton's tired blue eyes bulged. "But, to the best of my memory that safari has been out at least three weeks," he said.

"We didn't know that," Ki-Gor replied. "I'm glad you told us. But I can still follow the spoor."

"Extraordinary!" Creighton muttered. "Simply shattering! Well, look here! After you've found your chap—and you know he's in trouble from your supernatural message—what do you propose to do?"

"Why," Ki-Gor said calmly, "we will get him out of his trouble."

The English officer thought a long time. Then he looked up with a beatific smile spreading over his craggy face.

"Now, I'm quite sure," he said, "that you are British."

Ki-Gor smiled back and stood up.

Creighton stood up with him.

"I'm under strictest orders," the Englishman said, "to return to our post before dark. Otherwise, I'd be tempted to trundle along with you. Just in case you ran into a situation which might be beyond powers of a single man."

"Thank you," Ki-Gor said. "Sometimes a single man can go where several cannot, and can do what many cannot do."

"Right you are!" Creighton said, shaking his head in mock despair. "By the way, in what direction does this spoor go that you are following?"

"Along the river—this smaller river—to the east."

"Does it really?" Creighton said with a little frown. "Then I can't be the slightest help to you. Funny thing, but I can't find this tributary on any of my maps. Specially odd, when you consider that it isn't a bad size body of water. One of these days, I think I'll turn the boat up into it, and see where it goes to. My maps are pretty vague about the country to the eastward, too. There are mountains and desert indicated, but no settlements or oases or anything of that sort. I dare say you'll find some jolly wild country over there."

Ki-Gor threw a look at his wife that was half-amused, half-embarrassed. Helene's mouth twitched.

"I don't think Ki-Gor is worrying much about that, Captain Creighton," she said. "You see, Ki-Gor is quite at home in what you call 'wild country.'"

Creighton's tired eyes swept Ki-Gor's mighty bronzed figure. Over his seamed, dignified face there appeared an expression that came as close to being sheepish as is possible in the face of a British colonial official.

"I shall say not one word more," Creighton declared, eyes twinkling, "except good-bye and good luck."

The jungle couple stood on shore waving good-bye to the genial Creighton and his askaris until the launch had disappeared downstream. Then they climbed the high palisaded bank to the place where they had originally halted that noon.

Out on the veldt a half dozen vultures were waddling obscenely about the carcass of the antelope. As Ki-Gor and Helene walked past, they hopped reluctantly away a short distance, clacking their huge bills defiantly. Ki-Gor paid them not the slightest attention, but Helene shivered a little as they passed the gruesome scene.

CHAPTER III

IT WAS NOW MORE than three years since Helene had left the life of a pampered society darling to live the life of brutal realities in Africa. And although she had become hardened in mind and body to a great extent, there were still some things, everyday occurrences in Africa, that she was slow to become accustomed to. Fortunately, she had been originally endowed with an athletic body and a fine intelligent mind, so that she had been able to adapt herself remarkably well to the rigorous life which Ki-Gor led. So that Helene shivered a little at the vultures, but the ugly sight did not stay long in her alert, sensible mind.

Although it was past the middle of the afternoon, it was ferociously hot, and Ki-Gor managed to stay pretty well in the shade of the trees bordering the stream. Every so often, he struck out into the open to investigate the grass and make sure that David Gray's safari had not deviated from its indicated line of march. After a while, it became pretty obvious that the safari had stayed near the river and Ki-Gor no longer bothered to check the spoor but maintained a brisk pace in the shadow of the trees.

Toward the end of the day, however, the shading trees grew sparser and smaller. As Ki-Gor and his mate had traveled northward, they had left the great forests behind and progressed through open grassy parklands. This open country, originally green and fertile, had become just a little dryer each day. By the time the jungle couple reached the spot where they met the Hausa, and turned eastward, the grass was short and brown, and here and there was burnt away altogether. A narrow fertile strip remained along the river bank, but even this seemed to be petering out. And the open country now began to take on quite a desert-like aspect. The grass gave way to gravel and here and there white sand. Even the river, itself, seemed to be shrinking. Certainly there was less and less water in it, although the broad banks indicated that once the river had been much fuller than it was now.

When there appeared to be about a half hour's daylight left, Ki-Gor halted and began to make dispositions for spending the night. It was a desolate enough spot. The flat plain stretched away for miles in all directions, the horizon line lost in haze. There was no sign of game or life of any kind except for the straggling vegetation. Fortunately, there were one or two date palms on the river bank, and Ki-Gor garnered some tough-skinned, dry dates for a Spartan meal.

Some instinct forbade Ki-Gor from kindling a fire for the night. The date palms were hardly suitable to sleep in. So he slid down the eroded sandstone river bank to look for a safe place to spend the night. He had not gone far along the pitted bank before he found a shallow cave some ten feet above the river bed. A few minutes work with the butt of his spear succeeded in deepening the cave and clearing it out. And as darkness folded over the land, he boosted Helene up into the cave and then climbed up beside her.

"It is not very good," he remarked, "but I think we will be safe enough. And anyway, we'll be sheltered from the dew."

"Oh, this is fine," Helene said loyally.

But she left unspoken a hope that the following night would find them in more comfortable quarters.

"I don't understand," Ki-Gor said, after a while, "about these people that David Gray is looking for."

"Vikings?" Helene said. "Well, I don't quite know how to explain them to you."

SHE HAD tried to explain the Vikings before without much success. It was difficult to explain historical things and people to Ki-Gor, because he had had no opportunity to read history of any kind, and, therefore, it was hard to find a starting point. Indeed, less than four years before, Ki-Gor did not even know how to read. When Helene came into his life, he had almost forgotten the English that he had spoken as a young boy, when his missionary father had been killed by a jungle tribe, leaving him to bring himself up in the seething depths of the African forest. Patiently, Helene had worked on his half-remembered mother tongue, and his alert, remarkable brain had responded with amazing results. So that Ki-Gor handled ordinary English as well as any of the dozen African languages he spoke. Furthermore, he had learned to write tolerably well, and to read the few books that Helene had obtained from outposts of civilization that they visited from time to time. But Ki-Gor's weak point was still history.

"Well, I told you," Helene said, "that these Vikings were just another of the many tribes of white men that lived far to the north. The main thing about them was that they were great sailors and great wanderers. They were big, blond men, for the most part."

"Like me?" Ki-Gor interrupted.

"Yes," Helene said. "They probably looked a good deal like you. In fact you probably have some Viking blood in you, yourself."

"But you said my father's fathers belonged to the Scottish tribe," Ki-Gor objected.

"That's true," Helene conceded. "But several different tribes went to make up the Scottish tribe."

"How can that be?" Ki-Gor demanded. "A tribe is a tribe. Their fathers all had the same fathers."

"Not always," Helene said. "Look at the Maasai. They are tall and thin and have thin noses like the Amharas of Ethiopia. But they have woolly hair, and black skin like the Buganda. So some of their fathers must have—"

"I see, I see," Ki-Gor interposed, hastily, granting the basic truth of the diverse origins of a race. "Tell me more about the Vikings. Did they have guns?" "No, no. They lived hundreds of years ago, Ki-Gor. Nobody had guns in those days. They had spears, and swords and things like that. As I told you before, they were very warlike."

Ki-Gor smiled. "David Gray had better be careful," he observed. "Because he is anything but warlike—and if he finds these people—"

"Oh, he doesn't expect to find them," Helene corrected. "They must have disappeared long ago. He is just interested in seeing where they might have gone to, and if they left anything behind that would point to their having been there."

Ki-Gor shook his head. It was quite beyond him why anyone

should be concerned with people who lived ages ago and died out. Ki-Gor was primarily concerned with the Present. The Future he felt capable of meeting, and the Past he felt was gone beyond recall, therefore he wasted no time on it. It was a practical philosophy and it had sustained him through a life of unbelievable rigors and fantastic dangers. He could not help but think of the man, David Gray, and his preoccupation with the past.

What good had that preoccupation done him? At this moment, it had apparently gotten him into some mysterious trouble.

Since the encounter with the Hausa, and the conversation with Captain Creighton, Ki-Gor was beginning to form an idea of what sort of trouble David Gray was in. The scientist had taken a small, and probably unarmed, safari into wild uncharted country at a time when a Mohammedan fanatic was evidently gathering outlaw bands together for an eventual projected uprising against the white men. Ki-Gor, who was nothing if not a realist, felt that it was quite probable that David Gray had been attacked by El Hakim's men. What the outcome of that attack, Ki-Gor had no way of knowing. He did think that Gray was most likely taken prisoner. If he had been killed outright, there would have been a different message through the Brotherhood of the Dog.

However, Ki-Gor realized, conjecture was useless. As long as the spoor of the safari remained visible, he would find out for himself what had become of David Gray.

AFTER AN uneventful night, the couple breakfasted meagerly on dates and proceeded on their way. Following the river, their direction veered gradually a little northward of the due east they had traveled the day before. The river began to have less and less water, and the country grew progressively more arid. The sun was fearfully hot and the sandy and gravelly earth sent up rippling waves of heat.

The ground itself was quite uneven, rolling off in all directions in low undulations. From the top of one of these low ridges Ki-Gor perceived to the northeastward a blue line of mountains on the horizon.

Helene was beginning to wilt under the desert sun, when Ki-Gor stopped at one of the last clumps of date palms and stripped off a quantity of the narrow leaves to improvise broad conical sunshade-hats for her and himself. As Helene plodded dizzily along, she wondered just how much good the headgear was, but then she reflected that she would probably be unable to travel at all without it.

The water in the river continued to shrink as the country grew dryer, and Helene began to wonder if they were not drawing near to the source of the stream. And when, toward noon, a sort of oasis appeared some miles ahead, Helene concluded that they had reached the origin of the river.

This, however, did not prove to be the case. It was not a true oasis, but a mere widening of the river into a sort of large, narrow pond fringed with trees. The jungle couple sank down gratefully in the shade of the trees to rest. After a short while, Ki-Gor got up and wandered around, coming back to report that the river continued onward at the upper end of the pond.

In any case, the place was a life-saver. Ki-Gor discovered that the pond contained some large, fat fish that were easily caught and made delicious eating. Washed down with the sweet juice from the crown of a palm tree, it made a refreshing and satisfying meal. A short rest followed, and then the couple resumed their march along the still distinguishable trail of David Gray's safari.

Ki-Gor observed a noticeable freshening of the hot northeast breeze. Furthermore, white fleecy clouds began to gather behind the mountains along the horizon. In a remarkably short time, those clouds had grown measurably larger and had come bouncing across the sky until their advance guard were well overhead. They afforded some temporary shade which was grateful enough, but Ki-Gor felt a vague uneasiness.

His experience with desert climate was limited, but he remembered that the desert could breed sudden storms of tremendous violence. And while he could not be sure that this breeze and these clouds portended a storm, he instinctively cast about in his mind for the best course of action in case a tempest should break. Helene broke in on his thoughts.

"Oh! Those blessed clouds!" she exclaimed. "How much cooler it's become! I feel as if I could actually breathe a little!"

Ki-Gor smiled absently at her, then moved straight over to the river bank. It had occurred to him that the best shelter in case of a storm might be that bank. Such a shallow cave as they had slept in the night before would shield them adequately. Ki-Gor looked back at Helene.

"I'll join you in a minute," he called, and slipped down the bank to the river bed. He was immediately encouraged. The bank was of the same soft rock, eroded and pitted, as it had been farther downstream. It would be the work of a mere moment to deepen any one of a score of existing indentations in the bank to make a shallow cave shelter.

The jungle man glanced up at the sky, and wondered if he had not been overanxious about the weather. There were plenty of low clouds scudding over, but still there were many patches of blue sky. And standing down on the river bed, he felt scarcely any breeze at all, sheltered as he was by the high banks. He strolled to the foot of the bank and prepared to climb up the shale, when his mate's voice was borne to his ears.

"Ki-Gor! Ki-Gor! Come quick!"

The giant white man scrambled up the bank like an agile-footed duiker. He moaned curses at himself for leaving Helene alone and out of sight of him in this strange, desolate country. What awful thing had happened to her now?

AS KI-GOR gained the crest of the bank, a thrill of horror went through him. Helene was standing off on a ridge hardly more than a hundred paces away, and ten feet distant from her danced a great gorilla. Even as Ki-Gor broke into a frantic sprint the animal waddled forward toward the terrified Helene. But Ki-Gor's mate retained enough presence of mind to retreat slowly backward from the fearsome beast.

It was when she turned to run that it happened. Some object on the ground, which Ki-Gor could not see at that distance, tripped Helene and sent her sprawling. The gorilla gave a grunt of animal triumph as it bent over the prostrate girl. The great hairy arms lifted Helene as lightly as if she had been a feather.

It was then that Ki-Gor struck. Diving forward in a desperate flying tackle the jungle man smashed the gorilla with all the weight of his mighty body. It was a measure of the gorilla's amazing power that, encumbered as he was with Helene's weight, he did not go down. He staggered; then, lifting Helene above his head with one gargantuan hand, he whirled to face the jungle man.

Ki-Gor circled the great beast warily. He had unsheathed his hunting knife as he ran, and this he held in his left hand. Thus he could slash a mortal wound to the left side of any animal he fought. He feinted once, like a boxer in the ring. The gorilla grunted viciously, and launched a terrific blow at Ki-Gor's head. If it had landed,

Ki-Gor's skull would have been crushed, but the giant white man weaved under it. Then, like lightning, Ki-Gor struck. His right fist thudded against the gorilla's hairy body and as the beast grimaced in pain, Ki-Gor's knife-hand swept up. The stroke was timed perfectly. Full into the matted chest the razor-sharp knife drove. The gorilla screamed once, then the sound changed into a horrible gurgle. The great arm holding Helene aloft collapsed, the giant frame shuddered. Helene tumbled to one side, but before she could touch the ground, Ki-Gor caught her. He whirled her out of danger as the great gorilla mewled in agony and sank to its knees. The eyes rolled in its head and then the beast slipped silently over and lay still.

"Ki-Gor!" gasped Helene, shaken now that the danger was passed. "Oh, Ki-Gor! How *awful!*" Her gaze fell on the dead gorilla and involuntarily she shuddered. Then Helene remembered something.

"Ki-Gor!" she said excitedly. "Here is what I was looking at when the gorilla came up behind me!" She disengaged herself from Ki-Gor's arms and ran down the slope. Ki-Gor followed.

"What is it, Helene?" he asked, as his wife came to a halt and looked down at something at her feet.

For an answer, Helene merely waved a beckoning arm, and looked back at her feet. Ki-Gor broke into an easy lope. In a few seconds, he had approached his wife close enough to see what she was looking at. It was the corpse of a Negro.

Ki-Gor gazed briefly at the huddled body, then shifted his eyes to the down-sloping ridge beyond—which he had been unable to see until he had come up to Helene.

"So this," he murmured, "is where David Gray met trouble."

There were two more corpses of Negro porters, and strewn about were empty packing cases hastily ripped open and robbed of their contents. The hard, gravelly ground was churned up here and there, indicative of the brief but intense struggle that must have taken place. Ki-Gor strode down the slope, his eyes darting over the tell-tale marks.

"There were horsemen," he reported over his shoulder. Then after a moment—"They came on them at night. I see some remains of camp fires. The safari was taken by surprise—they didn't have a chance."

"Who do you think were the attackers?" Helene asked. "El Hakim's men?"

"Who knows?" Ki-Gor replied. "They might have been."

"But aren't El Hakim's men Hausas?"

"Some of them," Ki-Gor said.

"Would they attack and kill David Gray's men—who were prob-ably Hausas?"

"I don't think that would make any difference," Ki-Gor said. "But at that, Gray probably had boys from the Coast, Yorubas. What surprises me is that only three of the safari boys were killed. The rest, I suppose, were carried off with David Gray himself as prisoners."

Helene looked around and shivered.

"I wonder what sort of man this Hakim is," she remarked.

"I have a good idea," Ki-Gor said grimly. "Before we get home, we will probably have a chance to see him."

"I suppose we will," Helene said, in a tone which showed no great impatience to look upon the mysterious personage. She stared at the bleak country surrounding, while Ki-Gor walked around the slope studying the mute evidence of the raid on David Gray's safari.

"Those mountains off to the east look much closer, don't they?" Helene said. Ki-Gor answered mechanically and went on with his detective work on the camp site.

"Maybe it's just that the breeze cleared away some of the haze," Helene went on.

"Maybe," Ki-Gor murmured, walking still farther down the slope. It appeared to him as though the raiders had come in from the south—at right angles to the river—and having accomplished their purpose, had gone back the same way. That much seemed fairly clear. One thing kept Ki-Gor searching, and that was that he could find no unmistakable boot-prints left by David Gray himself. On such hard, gravelly ground, they would be rare, Ki-Gor realized. But even so, he thought that he should be able to find a heel-mark somewhere in the vicinity.

"Ki-Gor!"

The jungle man looked up quickly at his wife. She was standing on the top of the little ridge, staring eastward toward the mountains.

"What do you suppose that is—way over there?"

She extended a slender brown arm, and Ki-Gor turned his head in the indicated direction.

"I don't think you can see it from down there," Helene said. "Come up here beside me. It's very curious—looks like the skeleton of a dinosaur or something."

Reluctantly, Ki-Gor left his spoor-reading to go and stand beside his wife. His eyes picked out twin rows of curved stakes in the distance that resembled nothing so much as the bleached ribs of a huge animal.

"Let's go over and look at it," Helene urged.

"All right," Ki-Gor said finally, glancing at the sky. "There is plenty of time to come back here and pick up the trail of those horsemen."

AS THEY hurried along the river's edge, Helene was full of theories. "Do you suppose it is the skeleton of a prehistoric beast of some kind?" she demanded.

"It might be," Ki-Gor conceded. "This climate is very dry and preserves bones and hard wood and things like that."

"Wouldn't that be exciting if that's what this thing turned out to be!" Helene exclaimed. "Can you imagine how excited David Gray would be if he saw that. Or maybe he wouldn't, at that. He would probably rather find something that had to do with his Vikings."

They dipped down on to lower ground at this point, and the undulating ridges ahead temporarily hid their objective from view. And when they finally climbed upwards again, they were much closer to the great skeleton and could see it very plainly. Helene stopped abruptly.

"Wait a minute!" she exclaimed softly. "Wait a minute!"

"What is it?" Ki-Gor demanded.

"*That* is something David Gray would go crazy over, all right," she replied. "It's a skeleton—but not the skeleton of an animal. That thing, Ki-Gor, was once a ship."

Ki-Gor gazed incredulously at the great curved ribs that rose out of the white sand. If there was a keel left, it was buried far out of sight, but at either end of the double row of ribs, great single timbers curved up and out, indicating bow and stern posts.

"Well, I'm really amazed," Helene said. "Up to now, I thought David Gray was a little touched in the head to believe that any Vikings ever came so far south as this. But that looks exactly like a picture I remember seeing in a history book—a picture of the remains of a Viking long-ship. Those same heavy ribs, the sharp stern, sloping stem post. The only thing different was that the one I saw in the picture had a big carved figurehead on the bow—a wolf or a dragon or something."

Ki-Gor stared off at the fossil ship in wonderment. Helene's remarks were all pretty much beyond him, innocent as he was of the main historical facts concerning the Norse sea-rovers of nine hundred years before. One thing, however, was perfectly plain to him, and that was that those bare timbers protruding from the sand had once been the framework of a ship.

"Let's go and look at it," he suggested, and walked forward.

"How on earth did they ever get it up this far?" Helene marveled. "Why we must be at least a thousand miles from the sea, here."

"Came up the river," Ki-Gor shrugged.

"Yes, but see—it is some distance from the river now," Helene pointed out.

"Rivers change their courses," Ki-Gor said, and Helene granted that that was a probable explanation.

The probability that this river had changed its course at one time or another grew more apparent when Ki-Gor and his mate found that the last hundred yards to the ship led through pure white sand. The ship itself was buried in sand at least half way up the gaping ribs.

"Oh!" Helene gasped. "If David Gray could only see this!"

"He has," Ki-Gor said quietly.

Helene whirled on him. "What do you mean?"

Ki-Gor pointed down to the sand beside him. Helene saw a vague depression. She looked up questioningly.

"David Gray has small feet," Ki-Gor said. "And he wears boots. The sand has blown over those prints a little, but not so much that I can't be positive that our friend left them."

Helene saw more of the time-dulled footprints now, a trail of them leading away straight toward the Viking long-ship.

"Well then!" she exclaimed. "Wasn't he captured?"

"I don't think so," Ki-Gor said. "Just about here, he began to run. He may have wandered over by himself just before the raid began. And when he saw what was happening, he ran to the old ship to hide."

Hurriedly, the pair followed the prints of the small boots to one end of the Norse long-ship. There they found a place where the sand had been scooped away to make a depression.

"He crouched here," Ki-Gor stated, "while the raiders hunted for him. They did not find him. See, his trail leads away now, eastward—alone."

Helene gasped. "Then he wasn't captured?"

"No," Ki-Gor said gravely. "It might have been better if he had been. A white man all by himself in this country could not live long."

"Of course, he couldn't," Helene breathed. "I see what you mean—no provisions, no water—Heavens!"

"Yes," Ki-Gor nodded. "We'll have to hurry—if we are to catch up with him, alive."

Helene appreciated the truth of that observation, and much as she would have liked to examine the Viking ship, she cheerfully followed Ki-Gor across the sand.

Just at that moment, the breeze, already fresh, began to grow stronger. Helene felt a little particle of sand sting her cheek.

DURING THE next two hours, Helene kept telling herself that anticipation—of anything, even a sandstorm—was far worse than the realization of the feared happening. Certainly the anticipation of the sandstorm that seemed to be gathering was fearful enough in itself. Ki-Gor set a tremendous pace, one that even Helene's hardened muscles found it difficult to keep up with. She knew why he was hurrying. The wind-borne sand was fast obliterating David Gray's footsteps, and Ki-Gor hoped to get as far as possible before they disappeared altogether.

There was one helpful circumstance. David Gray had apparently fled toward the river bank, and then followed along the edge of that bank. So that even when the swirling sand had all but hidden the boot-prints, Ki-Gor did not slacken his pace. And when all traces of David Gray had disappeared, Ki-Gor plunged along the river bank, confident that the little scientist had not changed his course, and was somewhere ahead of them.

Helene marveled at how gradually the storm mounted. At first, there were brief gusts that lifted pockets of sand knee-high and carried them a few yards before depositing them. The gusts became more and more frequent, and lifted larger pockets of sand and carried them farther. There came a time when Ki-Gor and Helene had to stop, turn their backs to the wind, and stand with both arms over their faces to protect themselves from the flying, stinging grains of sand.

And soon after that, the wind began to moan and shriek. The sun was blotted out by great clouds of sand. The full weight of the storm was about to descend. Ki-Gor led the way toward the steep river bank.

He soon found a cavity in the bank which he attacked with his spear butt. In a few moments, Helene crawled into the improvised cave, and Ki-Gor climbed in after her, shielding her body with his own from the bitter, cutting grains of sand. Helene drew a deep shuddering sigh.

"I thought you were never going to go in out of the storm," she said, her voice a little tremulous.

"I know," Ki-Gor acknowledged. "We should have stopped before now. But I wanted to get as far as possible from that ship."

"Why?"

"Because it's too good a landmark. Gray's safari was attacked within sight of it. The raiders might come back."

"I hadn't thought of that," Helene said. "But you were right, of course."

Helene was so weary from the battering of the wind and sand that she felt like dropping off to sleep immediately. But it soon became evident that the cave was too shallow for real shelter, and Ki-Gor's back was still too much exposed. There followed then another hour while Ki-Gor patiently dug farther into the bank. At the end of that time, Helene was completely exhausted, and fell into a deep sleep while the sandstorm raged outside.

CHAPTER IV

WHEN HELENE WOKE UP, she could not, for a moment, imagine where she was. She was lying in a cramped position in a low narrow space hardly wider than her body. Some dim reflected light from somewhere in the direction of her feet enabled her to see coarse shaly rock a few inches above her eyes. For a brief moment Helene was on the verge of panic. Then she remembered the sandstorm and Ki-Gor's digging out the shelter in the river bank.

She bent her knees and pushed back over her head with her hands. Her body slid toward her feet. Ki-Gor was not in the little cave. Evidently, it was quite late in the morning, and he had gone out exploring while she slept on.

She squirmed her way out feet first and finally sat at the mouth of the cave, her legs swinging free six feet above the river bed. Then she was astonished to find out how really late it was. The sun was quite high and hidden from view behind her back—the cave being in the south bank of the river. Ki-Gor was nowhere in sight.

She called out to him several times, but got no response. After a minute or two of silence, she was about to call him again. But, just then a great shadow loomed up on the river bed below her. She gazed fondly at the massive shoulders and legs silhouetted on the sand. He must be standing on the bank right above her, with the sun directly behind him. She pushed herself forward out of the cave and dropped lightly on to the river bed.

"Well," she said, turning around and looking up. "I guess I got enough sleep to last me for several days. Where have you been—"

Helene broke off in sudden terror. As she stared upward, the skin over her spine prickled.

The blond giant standing on the bank above, looking down at her, *was not Ki-Gor.*

She gave a frightened squeak and fell back two paces looking wildly around her. *Where was Ki-Gor?*

The huge blond man above her shouted some words in a language Helene had never heard. Quickly, another—a darker-skinned man—stepped up beside him, and still another. Helene gazed at the strangers in terror and bewilderment. Who were they and what was she going to do. Could she hope to run away from them? There was nowhere to run except up or down the river bed. She doubted if she could get up the opposite bank before the strangers could come down and catch her.

Still more of them had appeared now, until there were six of them ranged on the bank beside the blond leader—for so he seemed. As Helene looked at the strange group, she wondered how she could ever have mistaken the blond man for Ki-Gor.

His legs and arms and torso were bare, it was true, and he wore a leopard-skin breech-clout like Ki-Gor. The color of his skin was about the same, too, with the stranger's perhaps a little darker bronze—as if he had been out in the sun a little longer.

But there any true resemblance ended. The stranger's eyes were pale gray, and his hair, a dark blond, almost a faded green color, lay in tight waves over his small head. His nose was much shorter than Ki-Gor's, and the nostrils flared over a wide mouth with full, pouting lips. The six men with him were uniformly darker—a pale brown color, with heavily freckled faces, pale eyes, and dark wavy auburn hair. All seven wore curious sandals with long lacings that criss-crossed up their shins and tied just below the knees. All seven wore broad rawhide baldrics over their right shoulders. And attached to each baldric at each left hip was a prodigious long straight sword with a simple cross-hilt.

The design of those immense swords and the criss-cross leg lacings set Helene's mind to working furiously. She had seen something like them before—perhaps in the same history book which had the picture of the Norse ship in it. The swords and the footgear, Helene told herself, were certainly of Norse design. But these men—what were they?

Her thoughts were interrupted by the men themselves. At first, they had evidently been as astonished by the sight of Helene as she had been at seeing them. Now, the blond leader shouted something, while looking straight at Helene. His words were in no language that she recognized. He shouted again, not in a disagreeable manner, but rather as if he thought Helene were deaf.

WHEN HE got no answer, he suddenly dropped down, and swung his legs over the bank, preparatory to coming down. A wave of fear swept over Helene. She backed away, frantically trying to think of something to do or say. They must know Hausa, she reasoned. And while she was not too fluent in Hausa, she knew a few common phrases.

"Who—" she faltered, "who are you?"

The strangers seemed astounded. They stared at each other, and at Helene. Then the leader broke out into a torrent of words. They sounded something like Hausa, yet Helene could not understand their meaning. Helene fought to control her dread of the strangers. They were so big and so noisy. Where—oh, where was Ki-Gor!

The big leader held his sword up away from his body, and suddenly slid down the bank, landing heavily on the river bed some twenty feet away from Helene. She repressed an impulse to scream—made up her mind to appear as fearless as possible. The blond leader was coming grinning toward her. Helene stamped her foot and shouted at him.

"Who are you?" she demanded again in Hausa, "Speak slowly!"

Again the leader looked astonished, and the six auburn-haired giants on the bank suddenly burst into roars of laughter. The leader flushed and said some words. They sounded vaguely familiar to Helene but she could not make out their meaning.

"I can't understand," she cried. "Speak slowly."

Again the leader spoke and again Helene could not understand. Although his last phrase again sounded familiar.

"What name your tribe?" Helene began again patiently. "I can't—"

"Vig N'ga! Vig N'ga!" the leader cried in an exasperated tone, while his companions laughed uproariously. He went on then with that other phrase that sounded so familiar. And suddenly Helene understood it. It was merely a repetition of her own question—"Who are you?" The man was speaking Hausa, all right, but it was a most peculiar kind of Hausa. And Helene could not yet make out what "Vig N'ga" meant. That was a phrase she had never heard before.

"I am of the tribe of Americans," she said. "What is your tribe?"

"Vig N'ga!" the blond shouted.

"What means 'Vig N'ga?'" Helene demanded.

The stranger rolled his eyes helplessly. "Vig N'ga!" he repeated desperately. "My tribe name Vig N'ga!"

"Oh! Oh!" Helene cried, the light finally dawning. "Your tribe is Vig N'ga?"

"Yes! Vig N'ga!" the stranger beamed. "My name Haw Faw Ga."

Perhaps it was the open expression of his face, or it might have been the friendliness in his voice—at any rate, Helene lost all sense of fear toward him and his six companions. She began searching her mind for the Hausa phrases meaning "Have you seen my husband?" Her acquaintance with the Hausa speech was so limited, however, that she had some difficulty figuring out how to put the question.

In the meantime, the stranger—or Haw Faw Ga, as he called himself—had come and stood in front of her. His large gray eyes were frankly appreciative of Helene's face and physique. He reached out a huge brown hand and touched her lightly on the shoulder.

"We go now," he said. "You come."

Helene thought quickly. Then she nodded and smiled, and walked over to the bank. She managed to get up about four feet when her feet slipped, and she would have fallen back. But Haw Faw Ga was close behind her and placed a firm hand between her shoulder blades. One of the darker-skinned giants at the top hauled her over the edge.

SHE LOOKED about her quickly for some sign of Ki-Gor, but he was nowhere to be seen. She was surprised to see a group of horses standing not far away on the drifted sand. It was to these horses that Haw Faw Ga started to lead her.

Helene gently disengaged her arm from the blond giant's hand, smiling diplomatically. Then she stepped back and shouted at the top of her voice. "Ki-Gor!"

Haw Faw Ga and his companions exchanged startled glances. Once again Helene called.

"What are you doing?" Haw Faw Ga demanded. "You call someone?"

"Yes," Helene answered. "I call my man."

Haw Faw Ga flushed. "Where is he?" "He is nearby somewhere," Helene said. The strangers turned their heads and stared in all directions. Helene raised her voice to a scream.

"KI-GOR!"

The blond leader whirled and put out his hand. "Stop!" he commanded. There followed some rapid Hausa phrases that Helene did not understand—all except the last phrase, which she did understand all too well. It was, "You come with me!"

Helene, of course, had no intention of going anywhere with the strangers, however amiable they seemed to be. Sooner or later, Ki-Gor would return for her at the place he left her, and she intended somehow or other to be there when he came back.

So, as the blond leader moved forward toward her, she backed away protesting. Haw Faw Ga did not care for that, and a menacing frown gathered on his low brow. A little panicky lump gathered in Helene's breast. The strangers had been so friendly and genial—would they continue to be? She was afraid she could not count on it. A desperate plan formed in her brain.

She had backed away from Haw Faw Ga toward the horses. Those horses were scarcely two hundred feet away. She was a good horsewoman. Haw Faw Ga lunged at her, hands clutching. Helene leaped to one side, whirled around, and before the strangers realized what she was about, she was flying across the sand toward the horses.

Helene was swift of foot, and as her feet flashed over the white sand, she knew the huge strangers could not catch up with her before she reached one of the horses, threw herself on its back and galloped away to safety. There was an angry roar behind her and the ground shook as the strangers pounded after her. She thanked her stars that none of them had been armed with bow and arrows. All of them, she was sure, had worn only the huge swords.

Triumph mounted within her as she got closer to the horses. She could see the crude saddles clearly, with the round shields and conical helmets hanging from the pommels. There were not many more yards to go, and Helene was thankful for that. The desert sand contained a good measure of sharp stones as big as her fist, and her bare feet had encountered several of them during her headlong flight.

But she was almost there now, and was already deciding on which horse to use. The one closest to her was a little bit to one side, and she veered to her right to run toward it. Just at that moment, there was a smacking, thumping sound, and three of the horses reared up neighing. Helene shot a glance behind her. To her horror, the air seemed filled with stones. She saw the seven Vig N'ga giants stooping and picking up stones and flinging them as fast as they could. It was just a fleeting glance, but it told her the worst. One great stone was coming apparently straight for her head. She swerved and ducked to get out of its way. But another stone seemed to be hanging in midair right in front of her eyes.

Her scream was stillborn on her lips. She felt something hit her with pile-driving force—felt herself hurled backward irresistibly. The top of her head seemed to explode in yellow flame. The last thing she was conscious of was fearful pain....

CHAPTER V

IT SEEMED TO HELENE that she was having a hideous dream, the worst nightmare of her life. Ki-Gor was gone—where she did not know—and she was all alone among a great noisy crew of strangers. She was quite blind, and a band of iron was encircling her head, crushing her skull in. Somebody—she did not know who—was carrying her, and carrying her roughly. And there was loud talking in a strange language full of liquid consonants and singing vowels. These were fleeting impressions interspersed with long periods of darkness.

Later, a woman's voice rang out, shrill and clear and angry. And then, someone threw Helene into the sea where she floated helpless in the trough of mighty waves. And it seemed to her that she lay in the path of a great Viking long-ship with a towering figurehead representing a dragon. The ship was bearing down on her and there was no way she could get out of its way. She whimpered and shook her head to try and drive the dreadful picture away. Suddenly a man spoke to her in English.

"There, now," the voice said soothingly. "Are you coming out of it a little?"

Helene opened her eyes with an effort, and then shut them quickly as a hundred pains went shooting through her head.

"If you *can* wake up, it would be a good idea," the voice went on. "You've probably got a terrific headache and if you can just sit up for a minute, maybe I can do something for it."

The confusion in Helene's poor battered brain began to fade. The voice was familiar. Who was it?

"I have some water ready," the voice continued, "and some aspirin tablets. How about it? Do you think you could wake up now?"

Helene heaved a great sigh of relief. The voice belonged to David Gray.

Helene forced her eyes wide open and made an effort to smile into the anxious face of the little scientist.

"They threw stones," she said. "I guess one of them struck me in the head."

"Yes," David Gray said. "But I don't think any serious damage was done. You'll have a fine headache for a while, but when that wears off, I think you'll be all right." Helene put a hand on the ground beneath her and pushed herself up to a sitting position. She blinked and looked around.

"Where in the world are we?" she said. Then right over David Gray's head, she saw a monstrous object looming up. "Great Heavens!" she exclaimed. "What's that?"

But she knew what it was the moment she asked the question. It was the figurehead from the prow of a Viking ship—a huge bronze dragon's head.

"The figurehead!" she breathed. "From the ship."

"Ah," said the anthropologist. "Then you saw the ship?"

"Yes. We wondered whether you had seen it."

"Oh yes. I was at the ship when I first saw, and was seen by, these amazing people."

"Who are they, David?" Helene demanded, "and what is this place?"

"This," said Gray, "is the most extraordinary place in Africa— perhaps the most extraordinary place in the whole world. It's called Taw Loa Ga—or some such sounding name, and it's the—"

"It's full of Viking remains," Helene broke in. "I can imagine how happy you are. But what are these strange people? Berbers from the desert? They seemed to have found the Viking remains before you did."

"Berbers, nothing!" Gray exploded. "They're *Vikings!* Lineal descendants of the original band of sea-rovers who sailed hundreds of miles up from the Gulf of Guinea some nine hundred years ago."

"Lineal descendants!" Helene cried incredulously. "They can't be! How on earth could you ever be sure of a thing like that?"

"For any number of reasons!" The anthropologist was quite carried away by his enthyciasm. "Their own name for themselves. It is Vig N'ga. And Vig N'ga is an obvious corruption of 'Vik-ingr,' the Old Norse name for the men who lived in the viks, or fjords, of Skandinavia and Iceland. Furthermore, these Vig N'ga speak a language which is very little different from Icelandic. I've studied Icelandic and I can tell. I've also studied Landsmaal, which is the corruption of Old Norse still spoken in the back country districts of Norway. And from my studies in both languages, I am perfectly able to understand almost every word spoken by the people of this amazing place we're in."

"WHY, IT'S unbelievable!" Helene said, staring fascinated at the little scientist. "What did you say the place was called?"

"Taw Loa Ga," Gray replied. "As well as I can make it out. I am pretty sure it is just a corruption of Thor's Logr, or Thor's Lake."

"Oh, is there a lake?" Helene took her eyes off her companion for the first time and looked around her. She gave a cry of dismay. "What is this? They've got us in some sort of a—"

"It's a cage, my dear," Gray said gently. "A wooden cage. We're prisoners of the Vig N'ga. They don't know what to do with us, so they've put us in this cage underneath their dragon figurehead, while they make up their minds what to do about us."

"But—but that's awful!" Helene cried. "Where is Ki-Gor? What have they done with Ki-Gor?"

"Ki-Gor?" Gray echoed. "Why, I don't know. Did they capture Ki-Gor, too?"

"No!" Helene said triumphantly. "I remember now. He went away exploring or something of the kind while I was still asleep. And before he came back, I met up with the—the—"

"Vig N'ga," Gray supplied.

"Yes," Helene said, "I was trying to think of the leader's name."

"Irruk?" Gray said.

"No—a longer name. It was quite outlandish."

"Oh!" Gray said. "I know. Haw Faw Ga. That isn't his name—it's his title. It's a corruption of Haarfaager. The leader of the original band was a descendant of Harald Haarfaager—Harold Fair-hair—the first king of Norway. Apparently those descendants were very proud of that fact and kept the name as a sort of surname, or even a title, as in this case. Haw Faw Ga is hereditary head man of this colony. His own name is Irruk—obviously a corruption of Eric. I believe he is coming over to visit us, right now. The young woman with him is either his wife or his betrothed. Her name is N'grit."

Helene turned her head and saw a group of the latter-day Vikings coming toward the big cage in which she and Gray were confined. Haw Faw Ga, or Irruk walked at their head, and with him was a tall, rather beautiful young woman who was blonde in much the same way he was. Helene had just time to note that the surrounding country was no longer desert, but forested mountainside, when Irruk strode to the wooden bars and began talking in Hausa.

"Why did you run away from us?" he demanded wrathfully. "You were stupid. You might have been killed."

"You threw stones," Helene retorted.

"We threw stones at the horses," Irruk shouted. "You got in the way."

THAT WAS some consolation, Helene thought. At least, it justified to some extent her lack of fear of these huge primitive men. Awe-inspiring and ruthless as they appeared, yet they had not intentionally hurt her. Irruk glared at her through the wooden bars, but his expression was aggrieved rather than hostile. He then had a short muttered conversation in his own language with the woman at his side, as if discussing a point. At length, the two of them walked along the outside of the cage until they came to a gate or door—which Helene had not noticed up till now. They opened the door and walked in, coming over to where they sat on the ground.

Irruk bent over and felt Helene's head gently. The woman did likewise, and several remarks in Old Norse passed between them. Finally, Irruk addressed Helene in his curious broken Hausa.

"You come," he said. "We go."

Helene wonderingly took his outstretched hand and rose to her feet. She looked questioningly at David Gray.

"How do you feel now?" the anthropologist inquired.

"Not bad at all," Helene admitted.

"They're going to take you down to their Assembly Hall," Gray said. "That is, Irruk wants to—but the girl is not so keen about it.

However, I wouldn't move unless I felt like it. You had a nasty blow on the head, and you probably should rest a good long time until you recover from the shock."

"I really feel all right," Helene said. "My head aches but I feel perfectly strong. Why are they taking us to the Assembly Hall?"

"Taking *you*—not us," Gray corrected. "I don't know. They still don't quite know what to do with either one of us. Although, I think Irruk is a little taken with you."

"In that case," Helene said slowly, "I think it would probably be a good idea if you and I stayed together."

At this point, Irruk interrupted.

"You come," he said harshly, his hand closing over Helene's upper arm.

"Yes," Helene nodded, smilingly. She pointed to Gray. "He comes, too."

Irruk shook his head violently.

"No!" he stated. "He not come. You come."

"Don't argue, for heaven's sake," Gray said hurriedly. "Go along with them. I'll be all right."

"I'll do no such thing," Helene said. "You can speak their language—explain to them that we are old friends and that I intend to stay with you."

"No," Gray said. "I'm afraid that wouldn't do. As a matter of fact, they don't know I speak their language—they don't even know I understand it. I'm saving that in case I get into real trouble."

Irruk shook Helene's arm impatiently. She looked at him coolly, then deftly wrenched away from his grasp and sat down beside Gray.

"If he goes, I go," Helene said determinedly in Hausa. "If he stays here, I stay here."

Irruk looked extremely displeased, but a murmur of amusement came from his followers outside the cage, and the woman smiled inscrutably. There followed a short discussion, in which Irruk apparently gave in. He eventually waved Gray to his feet, and the two captives were both led out of the cage.

Now, for the first time, Helene began to look around and really see what sort of a place she was in.

THE CAGE was situated at the inner end of a steep-walled grotto, right under a huge projecting rock on which the bronze dragon head was mounted. Because of the high rock walls, the grotto looked smaller than it actually was. Probably three or four hundred people could have crowded into its boat-shaped confines. At the outer end, the walls grew less precipitous and the bare rock was clothed with thick moss and short shrubs.

The young Viking chief led the way down a gently sloping pass lined with trees and bushes. And after a short distance, this pass in turn opened out on to a high pasture.

Here, Helene paused with an involuntary sigh to gaze at an unexpected and beautiful panorama.

About a thousand feet below, a little jewel of a lake lay placidly twinkling in the sun. It was completely surrounded by green mountains that rose abruptly from its shores to form a great jade cup for it. Directly below, there was a modest extent of white sand beach, and off that beach were moored some half dozen sharp-sterned boats. These craft were all miniature versions of the Norse long-ships, each capable of holding perhaps ten men.

In shore from the beach, smoke rose from some half-hidden houses, and it was to those houses that Irruk, the Viking, now led the way.

"Thor's Lake!" David Gray murmured, as they descended from the mountain and proceeded down a short, narrow street that curved between a double row of wooden houses.

"Look at those houses!" the anthropologist said. "We might be in a fishing village in the Lofoten Islands. Lord, what a discovery! A culture of nine hundred years ago, preserved intact! It's unbelievable! If I can ever get away from here to tell about it!"

"Of course, you'll get out," Helene said. "There's nothing to fear from these people."

"I wonder," said Gray.

"And anyway," Helene said, "sooner or later, Ki-Gor will track us here and get us out safely."

At this point the people of the village evidently discovered the presence of the captives, for they erupted with loud cries from the houses on all sides. Men and women swarmed out into the little street, jabbering and staring. They were curiously uniform in coloring, being pale brown and heavily freckled. Almost all had auburn hair, and all had grey eyes. David Gray was obviously fascinated with them, but he had no time to indulge in any scientific observation, as Irruk and his corporal's guard hustled the two prisoners into the largest of the houses, a tall, long building that opened on to the beach.

They discovered themselves in a sort of hall, a spacious, high-ceilinged place that evidently was the community meeting-place. The men and women of the village poured in after Irruk and his party and crowded around the raised platform at the far end of the hall where the young chief took his place. Helene and Gray were made to sit down on the floor at the edge of the platform in full view of the crowd. Irruk stood a few feet behind them and addressed his people.

David Gray listened attentively to the young chief's words. Very soon the scientist's face grew grave.

"This is not so good," he whispered in Helene's ear. "They don't know what to make of us. We are obviously not their old enemies, the Negroes, and apparently they've never before seen white people. They think there might be something of the supernatural about us."

"That's wonderful!" Helene whispered back. "We ought to be able to turn that to our advantage, somehow."

David Gray shook his head, and listened to Irruk for several minutes. Then he interpreted again for Helene.

"That's it," he said. "It's you they're in doubt about. I suppose because you, too, have red hair. But me, because of my strange dress and my shortness, they think I'm a witch of some sort. 'Troll' is the word he used."

"Splendid," Helene murmured. "All we have to do is think up some way of terrifying them—"

"Unfortunately," Gray interrupted. "These people are afraid of witches—but not terrified of them. The usual treatment is apparently to burn them. That is what Irruk is touching on, now."

Helene felt an unpleasant little chill run up the back of her neck.

"HOWEVER," GRAY went on, one ear cocked to Irruk's speech. "It isn't decided yet, by a long shot. Apparently, the more Irruk talks, the more he is inclined to think that you, at least, are all right. Ah—but wait a minute!"

Irruk had stopped for the moment, and the tall young woman was talking. Her voice was deep and vibrant, and she was evidently quite excited.

"The woman, N'grit," Gray translated, "thinks Irruk is wrong. She believes you are a witch. I shouldn't be surprised if she were quite jealous of you."

Helene turned her head and looked up at the angry young woman. N'grit caught the glance. Color flamed in her haughty face, and she pointed a violent forefinger at Helene, bursting into a torrent of impassioned oratory. Helene turned her head quickly to the front and looked out at the crowd of freckled, auburn-haired giants. It seemed to her that their expressions showed disbelief at N'grit's words.

Eventually, the young Vig N'ga woman stopped, and there was dead silence for a moment in the hall. Then Irruk's voice spoke a few words in an interrogative tone.

"Ah!" David Gray whispered. "He is asking for opinions from the people."

The first to speak was one of the warriors who had been with Irruk when Helene had been captured. After listening to several sentences, David Gray smiled and translated.

"Witness for the defense," he murmured. "The young man says you could not possibly be a witch. That when they captured you, you did not try to throw a spell. You merely used woman's wiles, and then ran like a gazelle. Ah—and Irruk himself is confirming that statement."

Helene risked a backward glance at the young chief. It seemed to her that Irruk's face showed great relief. He suddenly looked down at her and stopped in the middle of his discourse. Then he strode toward her.

"Stand up!" Gray chattered. "He's all for you, and wants you to show how innocent you look."

Helene got to her feet. Irruk stood beaming beside her, and put one hand on her shoulder. An approving murmur came from the crowd below.

But there was one person in the hall who very evidently did not approve, and that was N'grit. She gave a choked cry and came storming at Helene, one hand outstretched. Irruk quickly thrust up one arm to ward her off. But she dodged under it and sent a raking hand down over Helene's face. Helene just barely did jerk her head back out of reach. Irruk swung around to handle N'grit. But the tall, young woman had the center of the stage and she used it to pour out what was obviously a torrent of invective directed against Helene.

"The woman's insane with jealousy," David Gray told Helene. "She's changed her tune. You are no longer a witch, but you are in league with the enemies of the Vig N'ga."

"But why?" Helene whispered back. "How could I be?"

"She wants you to explain what you were doing so close to these mountains—which have been the inviolable sanctuary of the Vig N'ga for time immemorial. Ah! Here it comes! You are a spy of the terrible El Hakim!"

N'grit unquestionably had better than average powers of oratory. But Irruk was not disposed to let her continue her denunciation of Helene. However, just as the young chief walked in front of her to stop her flow of invective, there came a sudden interruption to the whole proceedings.

A youth dashed into the rear of the hall from outside, shouting at the top of his lungs. Instantly, the crowd, Irruk, and N'grit—everyone in the hall—fell silent. The disorderly excitement of the moment before changed in a heartbeat to a tense stillness. Helene looked questioningly at David Gray. The anthropologist shook his head, signifying that he knew nothing of what had caused the change. The Vig N'ga seemed to be listening for something.

FROM FAR away came a tiny thread of sound—a scarcely audible wailing call. The crowd sighed, and Irruk snapped a question at the youth who had run in. The youth stammered an answer, and instantly Irruk shouted a brief series of orders. The crowd—or rather the men in the crowd—seemed to anticipate those orders and began pouring out of the hall. Irruk swung around to N'grit, barked a command at her, at the same time pointing to Helene and Gray. Then he leaped off the platform and ran out after the warriors. His gesture left no doubt in Helene's mind that she and the little scientist had been temporarily assigned to the tender mercies of N'grit.

"What's happening, do you know?" she asked Gray.

"Evidently that was a warning signal of an attack by a hostile group. It can't be too unexpected, because our friends seem to know what they are doing."

N'grit advanced on them, her face ominously calm.

"You come with me," she said in Hausa, and Helene did not at all like the expression in her eyes.

The two prisoners moved out of the hall on the heels of the crowd, their Amazonian guard stalking grimly behind them. Outside, the slanting rays of a setting sun reflected on a scene of orderly chaos. Warriors were running from everywhere, buckling on great swords, or fitting conical steel caps on their auburn curls. Some of the steel caps were ornamented with pairs of hawk or eagle wings.

All the warriors made straight for the beach, where they plunged unhesitatingly into the water and splashed out to the boats. These boats were moored in shallow water, and along each gunwale was a row of round shields. In a very short time, each boat was filled with warriors. Long oars were shipped, and with roars of defiance the warriors slipped their moorings. One by one the boats tore away across the lake.

A little knot of women who had gathered on the beach to watch the departure of the warriors now turned and came slowly back toward the village. As they passed N'grit and her prisoners, their eyes were cold and their faces grim.

"I don't like this, at all," David Gray said under his breath. "For a time we were getting on very well—thanks to Irruk, who seems to be definitely favorably disposed to us. Or you, at any rate. Then N'grit changed her tune and accused us of being spies for El Hakim. And right away an attack follows—probably by El Hakim's men."

"But I don't understand," Helene said. "Why should we be blamed just because somebody attacks them?"

"Apparently," Gray said, "there are several passes or gates into the valley here from the outside. One of them, at least, is very secret. It is called the East Gate. No enemy is supposed to dream of its existence."

"Well?"

"It is the East Gate which is being attacked now," Gray finished, simply.

"That's ridiculous!" Helene exclaimed. "How could I have led El Hakim or anyone else to the East Gate, when I was myself carried in here unconscious. I haven't the faintest idea what way they brought me."

"I'm afraid," Gray said, heavily, "that a jealous woman requires no logic to defend her accusations."

The events of the next hour certainly justified the little scientist's pessimism.

WITH THE restraining influence of Irruk removed, N'grit gave full rein to her bitterness. With mounting apprehension, Helene found herself and Gray being driven back up the steep path to the grotto where the wooden cage lay under the dragon's head. N'grit had a six-foot staff in her hand, and behind her came three other women of the Vig N'ga. All three of these other women carried bright shining little hand-axes, and lengths of rope.

"What do you suppose is on their minds, David?" Helene panted, as they toiled up the steep slope.

"Heaven knows!" Gray moaned.

Thwack!

The heavy staff crashed on the ground beside Helene's feet. Helene whirled, eyes blazing. N'grit jabbered something at her, and waved the staff threateningly.

"Come along," Gray pleaded. "For Heaven's sake, don't antagonize her any more!"

"If she didn't have a bodyguard, I'd do more than antagonize her!" Helene declared. But her good judgment quickly prevailed and she turned and proceeded up the hill again.

When the party arrived in the grotto, N'grit indicated clearly that the two prisoners were to go back into the wooden cage. The door slammed shut on them, and N'grit and her three grim handmaidens retired some yards, evidently to have a conference.

"Say, I don't like the looks of this, at all," Helene said.

"Shh!" Gray warned. "Let me listen to what they say."

Helene nodded. She realized now how valuable it was that Gray had not revealed to the Vig N'ga his knowledge of their language. As she watched the little man, she saw that he was turning pale.

"What is it?"

"Bad. Bad," Gray said. "There is no doubt in their minds that you are a spy of El Hakim's. The fight that is going on now is at the secret East Gate. And you were brought in through the East Gate. N'grit claims that you were faking unconsciousness, and that you left a trail of some sort so that El Hakim's men could follow."

"Oh," said Helene shortly. "As a matter of fact, if I had been conscious, that is what I would probably have tried to do. But not for El Hakim's men, of course."

"Wait a minute, wait a minute, what are they saying now?" Gray turned his head toward the Vig N'ga women. As he listened to their grating voices, his face—already pale—grew still paler. Helene could not but guess that he was hearing terrifying news.

Just then the council of war seemed to break up—as if they had decided on their course of action—and N'grit came over toward the cage. Her three henchwomen moved away toward the entrance to the grotto. Helene was more interested in their activities than she was in those of N'grit herself. One of the three started to hack at a straight young tree—the other two busying themselves gathering dry faggots off the ground.

Helene swung around to Gray.

"You heard them, David," she said. "What are they going to do?"

Gray's face was the picture of horror. His jaw hung slack and his eyes bulged. His mouth moved feebly, but no words came.

"What?"

Helene enunciated the one word and looked deep into Gray's frightened eyes. He shook his head as if to shut out a horrible sight from his vision.

"No, no!" he muttered. "It musn't be!"

"Come, David," Helene said firmly. "I'll know sooner or later. You might as well tell me now."

The scientist gulped and bent forward with closed eyes.

"They're going—going—to tie you to a stake," he said in a hoarse whisper, "and—burn you!"

An icy calm descended over Helene, She knew what Gray was going to say, even before he said it. His words merely confirmed what she had already guessed from the actions of the Vig N'ga women. She was mildly surprised at herself for not being frightened. For she felt not the slightest sensation of fear. The idea of being burned at the stake struck her as being too fantastic to be taken seriously. *It just couldn't happen to her.*

AT THE same time, she knew that the Vig N'ga women intended that it should happen, and that she, therefore, had to think of some means of defeating their dreadful scheme—or at least of delaying its execution. But what means could she think of? She was unarmed and outnumbered. She was doubtful of how much help David Gray could be. The little mouse of a man had flaming courage in one direction, but he was completely out of his element in any physically competitive way. As for fighting women—even to save his life—Helene doubted that he would be capable of it.

N'grit stood at the door to the cage, and Helene tried frantically to think of something. There was no lock to the cage door, merely a wooden bolt and hasp on the outside. But the door was solid wood, and the frame around it was solid for several feet, so that anyone imprisoned there could never reach through the bars and be able to touch the bolt.

Helene watched N'grit breathlessly. The tall Viking woman seemed undecided as to her next action. She looked over her shoulder at the other women. Then she turned back again, her mind apparently made up.

"You woman," she said in Hausa. "You come out."

She slid the bolt, and flung the door open, stepping back quickly and holding her staff menacingly to one side.

Helene took a deep breath. She wished she knew more words in Hausa so that she could reply with provocative insult. She still had no plan figured out, but she determined to improvise each moment as it came along. She stared coldly at N'grit.

"No," she said.

The Vig N'ga woman flushed. "Come out," she cried, "or I will make you come out!"

"Make me!" Helene replied steadily.

The gray eyes of the woman grew almost black with fury. She lunged forward through the doorway and into the cage. Helene had only time to note that the woman was holding the staff too far down by the butt—that there was not room enough in the cage to swing the staff. Automatically, Helene went into action. She skipped lightly to N'grit's left. The Vig N'ga woman swung the staff ponderously at her. The end of it hit the opposite side of the cage.

"Down, David!" Helene yelled. "On the ground!"

And then she flung herself at N'grit's legs in a football tackle.

IT WAS a desperate move—to risk physical combat with a woman so much bigger than she was. But Helene dimly realized that while N'grit might be five inches taller and thirty pounds heavier than herself, she was not necessarily any stronger. Helene's rigorous life as the mate of Ki-Gor had hardened and strengthened her naturally athletic body, and sharpened her already quick reflexes. And she had one advantage over the giant Vig N'ga woman—she was limb-free in her brief leopard-skin garment, while N'grit was clothed from neck to toe in a loose flowing gown.

Helene hit N'grit squarely at the knees. N'grit's momentum carried her body forward while her legs remained locked in Helene's desperate embrace. She toppled over and crashed to the earth like a neatly felled pine tree. In a flash, Helene gathered her feet under her and half rose. Then a split-second inspiration seized her. Her hands stabbed down at the heavy legs of the fallen woman thrashing in the folds of the robe. Snatching the lower edge of the garment just beneath one thick ankle, Helene hauled upward and forward toward the woman's head. Before N'grit realized what was happening, her powerful legs were hopelessly trussed in the folds of her own gown.

N'grit screamed with rage, beat the ground with her arms, and rolled over on to her back. Helene stayed with her, fought aside her arms and reached for a hold on that thick neck. She had a temporary advantage, and she knew it was just that.

"David!" she cried through clenched teeth. "Grab her staff and get out of the cage. Beat off the others if they try to get in here to help this—this—maniac!"

On the last words, N'grit managed to double her knees and bang them into Helene's back with terrific force. Helene gasped and then by way of retaliation whanged her right hand across the woman's face. The woman moaned, and Helene felt her sag beneath her.

Helene's hopes suddenly rose. Perhaps—perhaps this hardy Norse woman was not so hardy when she was hit in the face.

But Helene's rising hopes apparently were premature. From her supine position, N'grit hooked a vicious right hand into Helene's side and knocked the wind out of her. She fell away to one side, with the world momentarily going black before her eyes. The Vig N'ga woman heaved upwards and flung her completely off her body. If N'grit had not been tangled up in her gown, Helene would have been lost then and there.

As it was, Helene had a precious second to pull herself together and fling herself back at N'grit's head. She somehow got a knee on each of the big blonde's shoulders, and from that point of vantage, she poured blows onto the broad snarling face. A quick glance to one side showed Helene that David Gray had followed her instructions. He was standing outside the gate of the cage sweeping the air with N'grit's staff, while the three other Vig N'ga women screamed and waved their hand-axes helplessly at him.

Helene went to work on N'grit's face with renewed vigor. The Norse woman was sinking under the hail of blows, and Helene began to hope that perhaps she might pull out of the situation.

Suddenly, there was a despairing shout from David Gray. At the same moment, Helene heard the sound of chopping close by her ears. Two swift glances told her the story. The three Vig N'ga women had divided forces. While one of them threatened Gray at the door to the cage, the other two had run around to the other side of the cage, and had begun chopping the wooden bars through. Gray was up against an impossible dilemma. If he abandoned his post at the gate to chase off the women chopping at the bars, the third woman would slip through the gate to the aid of N'grit.

Helene's heart was pounding so from her excitement and exertions that she began to feel dizzy. She shook her head fiercely and desperately tried to think of some way out. The two women at the back of the cage were making swift progress at the wooden bars. The third woman stood off and taunted Gray as he stood helpless. *There must be some way out,* Helene told herself. *Ki-Gor would think of a way.*

Suddenly, she sprang to her feet. Of course, there was a way out!

"David! David!" she cried. "Run! Run at the woman! And then keep on running out of this place! Down the path!"

Gray was a little slow to catch on. But at least he had started just about the time Helene sped through the gate of the cage. The lone woman on that side was completely taken by surprise. She flung herself to one side on the ground, and Gray and Helene ran like deer across the floor of the grotto. Shrill cries of rage pursued them from the cage, but once again Helene's hopes soared.

WHAT SHE and Gray would do when they ran into other Vig N'ga women, she did not know. But she trusted to her wit to surmount that situation when she met it. The important thing was that, for the moment, she and Gray were escaping N'grit.

Some yards before they reached the top of the path leading out of the grotto, Helene became uncomfortably aware of a terrible weakness, an irresistible lassitude settling over her hard-worked body. Her heart was pounding furiously, even though she was running slightly downhill. Her head began to ache suddenly, too.

"David!" she panted. "What's coming over me?"

She stumbled and would have fallen, except that Gray turned quickly and caught her arm.

"What's the matter?" he demanded. "You're as white as a sheet!"

"I—don't know," Helene faltered. "But I suddenly feel terribly weak!"

"Good Lord!" Gray exclaimed, "I don't wonder! But try and keep going, can't you?"

"I'll try," Helene whimpered, stumbling forward. "But I'm—I'm afraid I'm going to faint, David. Run along—save yourself—"

Gray caught her by the waist and eased her to the ground. The last thing she heard was Gray saying, "It's the rap on the head coming home to roost! Delayed shock from the concussion—"

Helene did not hear N'grit and her three handmaidens pounding up. In fact, the next thing Helene did hear was the deep harsh voice of N'grit raised in a sort of triumphant chant.

She forced her eyelids open and saw the great blonde woman standing several feet in front of her brandishing a torch over her head. A sickening sensation swept over Helene. She tried to move her arms and legs. Then she found that they were securely bound—that she was tied to a stake in the middle of the grotto, under the leering head of the dragon. A pile of dry twigs was heaped up around her feet.

"This is the end, I guess," Helene told herself. "When she finishes that chant, she will bring the torch down to these twigs—and then it's going to be awfully hot—"

Higher and higher, N'grit's voice mounted, until it was like the neighing of a horse. Her chant was full of the word, "Taw," which Helene in her semi-stupor supposed was "Thor," the old Norse thunder-god.

"Thor," Helene mumbled to herself. "Thor is Thunder and N'grit is Fire. I suppose N'grit was originally Ingrid, hundreds of years ago. Has Ingrid any connection with Ignis, Latin for Fire? Thor for Thunder, Ingrid for Fire. I wish Thor would come. Fire is such a slow death."

Suddenly Helene came wide awake, with a paralyzing shudder. What was she talking about? Her own death? *It couldn't be!* It couldn't be! Where was Ki-Gor? Oh, Ki-Gor would come and save her! Where *was* he?

"Ki-Gor!"

CHAPTER VI

SIX HOURS BEFORE IRRUK first saw Helene down on the river bed, Ki-Gor was captured by El Hakim's men.

He had left the uncomfortable little cave shelter in the river bank to explore the country, and to see what the sand storm had done the night before. He had gone back to the ruin of the old Viking ship to make a more leisurely inspection of it.

The sand storm had played curious, capricious tricks. Here it had piled up sand—somewhere else, it had blown it away. Right away,

Ki-Gor noticed something which he had not seen in the skeleton ship before. Presumably it had been exposed by the driving wind.

It was a thick bar of iron standing straight up out of the sand in the middle of the ship. The bar was nearly three inches thick, was round, and showed about a foot above the sand. Ki-Gor gave it a tentative pull, but the nether end was apparently securely anchored. That interested the jungle man. He pushed away some sand from around the bar with his feet, exposing several more inches. Then he pulled again. The bar did not budge.

Now, Ki-Gor squatted on his haunches and regarded the iron bar in earnest. What made it so secure in that sand? It must be more than just a simple bar. There must be a curve, or angle or projection of some sort down out of sight which prevented Ki-Gor from hauling it free. Ki-Gor had prodigious strength in his arms and wrists, and even the casual force he had applied to the bar should have had more effect than it did.

The jungle man began scooping sand away from the base of the bar. It was close-packed and hard, and the job was more considerable than Ki-Gor originally supposed. But he kept at it patiently, exposing more and more of the bar as he worked farther into the ground. Presently, he had to make his excavation wider around the bar, because the sand was sliding back into the hole as fast as he scooped it away.

Eventually, his patience was rewarded. And by the same token, his judgment was vindicated. The bar was not a simple bar of iron. It was a three-foot long handle of a gigantic hammer. And now Ki-Gor saw the reason why he could not move it. The thick, blunt-ended head of the hammer was firmly imbedded in a crack between two ledges of rock. Ki-Gor pummeled the handle gently with the heel of his hand. The hammer made a faint deep thrumming sound along the handle from the fixed base.

Ki-Gor stood up with a faint smile. The hammer interested him. Further, it constituted a challenge. He intended to get that hammer free, or know the reason why. For the next ten minutes, he pulled and hauled and pushed and lunged. But nothing he did seemed to have the slightest effect on the hammer. It was completely immovable.

Ki-Gor squatted again, and began scooping more sand away from the hammerhead. Here, the sand was packed so tight that it defied even his hard-horny hands. He had to resort to the long knife which he had taken from the disagreeable Hausa. After a while, he had laid bare a considerable portion of the rock surrounding the crack in which the hammer was imbedded. And then Ki-Gor gave a grunt of satisfaction. He had dug down far enough to see clearly that the crack between the rocks widened imperceptibly below the hammer-head. The crack was in effect wedge-shaped with the base at the bottom. If the hammer were pushed or knocked downward, the head could be freed of the rock-vise and drawn out and up.

Ki-Gor stood up quickly, laid both hands on the butt of the handle and thrust down with all his weight. He still could not budge the hammer. However, he knew that all it needed was a sharp blow or tap to start it. He looked about him for a good-sized rock. Something made him look up. A murmur of dismay left his lips.

Four burly, coal-black Hausas stood scarcely a hundred feet away staring at him. Each one of the four held a modern rifle in both hands ready to snap to the shoulder in shooting position. One of them spoke, showing yellow teeth in a nasty grin.

"Be advised, O Yellow-haired One," he called. "If you behave—you are our prisoner. If you try to run away, or even make a strange move of any kind—you are a dead man. Our rifles shoot straight and they kill at a thousand paces. Take your choice, O Yellow Hair."

KI-GOR STARED coldly at them for a moment before he spoke. Then he spat contemptuously in the sand and ran his hand coolly through his wind-blown hair.

"Who are you who come with hard words to a stranger and point white men's guns? I have no business with you, nor you with me. Therefore go your way, and let us hope the next time we meet you will have learned better manners."

He turned his back on the black quartet with exaggerated disdain, and gazed off in the direction where Helene still lay asleep in the river bank. The spokesman for the Hausas laughed, not without a note of grudging admiration.

"Your words are as harmless as your arrows, O Yellow Hair. Why ask us who we are, when you speak our language as well as we do ourselves? It is for us to ask who you are that appears suddenly in our country all by yourself."

Ki-Gor noted with satisfaction that they apparently did not know of Helene's presence with him.

"Or perhaps," the Hausa went on, "you are no stranger—but come from the mountains."

The Negro pointed off to the range which yesterday had seemed distant, and today somehow appeared much closer.

"In any case," the Hausa said, advancing with his gun held ready, "you will come with us and answer the questions that our master will want to put to you."

"Who is your master? El Hakim?"

Then Ki-Gor could have bitten off his tongue in vexation for having blurted that name out. The effect on the Hausa was precisely what he was afraid it would be.

"Ah!" the Hausa smiled his ugly smile again. "So you are not a stranger! You know who we are!"

There was not the slightest use of putting up any resistance, and Ki-Gor knew it. He was covered by four rifles in the hands of men whose tribe made excellent warriors. These four, in particular, were matter-of-fact and cool, bespeaking competence in conflict. Ki-Gor shrugged and went along with them, suffering them to disarm him without doing other than commenting sarcastically on the whole procedure. They did not notice the Hausa knife which he had left on the ground beside his little excavation, and in fact paid no attention to the iron hammer. Evidently, they wanted to get him to their headquarters as quickly as possible and be rid of the responsibility of him.

As they marched him over the undulating dunes of sand and gravel, Ki-Gor saw how they were able to sneak up on him so effectively and take him so by surprise. The dunes offered excellent cover. They must have seen him from a distance, and then had silently come toward him, threading their way carefully along the series of little valleys between the dunes.

It was queer country, altogether, with one mile giving no hint of what the next mile might reveal. The direction the Hausas took was south-east, pointing toward the southern extremity of the mountain range. Quite soon after leaving the Viking ship, the ground began to fall away, and the march became consistently downhill.

The sun was fiercely hot, and Ki-Gor wondered how long these men intended to go across the desolate waste on foot. But again, he was due for a surprise. Hardly four miles from the Viking ship, the Hausas and their prisoner surmounted a slight rise and looked down on to an extensive oasis set deep in a valley below them.

It was a richly foliaged oasis, and evidently quite thickly populated, from the number of cooking fires that sent their smoke spiraling upward on the still air. On the other side of the valley, a long black line wound downwards in the direction of the oasis, looking like a column of driver ants. The Hausas were quite excited at seeing it and Ki-Gor gathered from their unguarded conversation that the column was a local tribe of considerable size called the Bobo-Haffa. The Bobo-Haffa were coming en masse to have a conference with El Hakim with a view to joining him.

"We will hurry," the leading Hausa said, "so that we may get our prisoner to the master before the Bobo-Haffa assemble."

Hope lighted Ki-Gor's brain for a moment. If the Hausas started hurrying, they might grow careless. It would not be the first time Ki-Gor had escaped captors in the very sight of the jail to which he was being taken.

But the hope was quickly dashed when the Hausas ranged themselves behind him and ordered him in no uncertain terms to run. They acted like professional soldiers who knew their business, these Hausas.

THE OASIS was thickly populated without a doubt, but Ki-Gor saw it was a city of tents. A small army seemed to be installed under the fringed date palms. Ki-Gor was taken immediately to the largest tent in the place—the tent, of course, of the commander of this army, El Hakim. The jungle man had time only to make two observations before he was thrust inside the tent. Both of the observations reflected, in Ki-Gor's mind, on the military capacity of the mysterious El Hakim. First, Ki-Gor noted vulnerability to attack of the spot El Hakim had chosen to install his force. It might be only a temporary location, but even so an attacking force could line the rim of the cup-shaped valley and make things very uncomfortable for El Hakim's men. Furthermore, the men in the oasis would have a steep climb to make with absolutely no cover before they could come to grips with such an enemy and dislodge him.

Secondly, Ki-Gor observed that the horses of the little army—and like most desert armies, it predominated in cavalry—were concentrated in one area at the lower end of the valley, where the walls were if anything steeper than anywhere else. To be sure, there was better grazing down there, but at the same time, some smart enemy might sometime make use of that concentration of the army's mounts.

El Hakim himself was a considerable surprise to Ki-Gor.

He had not known quite what to expect, although the English

officer's remark about the man's probably being a Fulani should have eliminated certain possibilities. The Fulani are a highly mixed people, containing elements of Berber and Sudanese Negro, and so present great variation in their physical types. However, Ki-Gor expected to see, at the very least, an impressive man as the head of this considerable band of renegade Hausas and related tribes.

Instead, El Hakim was an insignificant little yellow man with a thin cruel face and huge fanatic's eyes. He sat up on an enormous raised dais high above the tent floor and rasped at everyone about him in a harsh querulous voice. His clothes, once magnificent, were dirty—soiled robes that dwarfed him in their voluminous folds. On his head was a tall dark Tuareg turban that looked oppressively heavy over his thin bloodless face. Here was a man, Ki-Gor decided, who had few of the qualifications for becoming a desert conqueror, except the burning desire to be one.

"What have we here?" El Hakim snarled, as Ki-Gor was brought to the foot of his eminence. Then, as his eyes took in the details of Ki-Gor's figure and coloring, he sprang to his feet with a joyous cry.

"Hah!" he screamed. "A prize! A prize! Rewards a-plenty will go to you, my brave ones, who brought this prisoner in. A Vig N'ga! The first one to be caught alive!"

A murmur arose from the crowd of henchmen in the tent, and there was a great straining and pushing to catch a glimpse of the new prisoner.

"Come, tell us, O Brave Ones," El Hakim chortled, "how it was you were able to bring this monster from the mountains in to me!"

His huge eyes roamed from Ki-Gor to the four soldiers who had brought him in. The leader of the four shuffled his feet uneasily and stared down at the carpet.

"Come, speak up!" the renegade chieftain urged. "We await your story eagerly."

"O All-Wise Master," the Hausa began in a troubled voice, "at first sight, we too thought this man was of the Vig N'Ga—"

"What do you mean?" El Hakim exclaimed angrily. "Of course he is of the Vig N'ga! Just look at him!"

"Aye, he looks the part, O All-Wise Master," the Hausa said. "But when we came upon him, he behaved in a manner totally different from all the others of the Vig N'ga we have encountered."

"How is that?" El Hakim demanded. It was obvious that no matter what the Hausas told him, he would still believe Ki-Gor was of the Vig N'ga—mainly because he wanted so to believe.

"WELL—FOR—FOR ONE thing," the Hausa stammered, "he behaved reasonably with due allowance for the circumstances. We covered him with our rifles and called upon him to surrender. Whereupon he did so, with but little fuss and some insulting words—and few of them. It is well known to you, Master, that previously everyone of the Vig N'ga we have come upon have acted like crazy men. They have disregarded the advantage of our guns and have flung themselves in furious attack upon us. We have had to kill them to prevent being killed ourselves by their great swords or battle-axes."

"Where is this one's sword?" El Hakim demanded irrelevantly.

"He had none," the Hausa replied. "Only this great bow and the quiver of arrows strapped over his back, and this knife at his waist. There were other things, too, O Master. He spoke our language not in the uncouth way the men from the mountains do, but in the same way we ourselves do. Also, you have noticed he has no spots on his face."

"What of it?" El Hakim demanded petulantly. "Who is there to say that all the Vig N'ga have spotted faces! Perhaps this is one who is without spots. Where did you find him?"

"He was in the ruined ship—"

"Hah!" El Hakim cried, delighted to come upon one detail that confirmed his own opinion. "That is the great ju-ju place for the Vig N'ga! If you found this one there, isn't it proof positive?"

"O All-Wise Master!" It was a new voice from one side of El Hakim's pedestal. "Give me leave to speak! I can tell you something about the prisoner. I saw him before today. I fought him over on the bank of the Great River, and he broke my arm by treachery."

Ki-Gor glanced swiftly in the direction of the new voice, and felt a disagreeable sensation. There, his arm in a crude sling, stood the giant Hausa who had tried to kill him in the quarrel over the antelope.

"Speak, speak!" El Hakim said testily, as though he were afraid that this new testimony would weigh against his own prejudgment.

"Well, then," the man said, "I, too, mistakenly thought the prisoner was a white man—because he had no spots, and because he spoke our language in a different way from the Vig N'ga. I thought so even more when I lay in hiding and watched him go away with an

English officer. He spoke English—or so it sounded to me. Both he and the red-haired woman with him."

"Red-haired woman?" El Hakim shouted. "Where is she now?"

The leader of the four Hausa warriors looked uncomfortable and said he had seen no red-haired woman.

"That decides it!" El Hakim declared. "Everyone knows that many of the Vig N'ga are red-haired—"

He broke off and looked around him for approval. Then he turned his face down and addressed Ki-Gor for the first time.

"Ho, there, Wild Man of the Mountains! What do your uncouth friends call you?"

Ki-Gor stood silent for a moment, his blue eyes glinting dangerously. When he spoke, it was in purest Fulani, and it was in terms of complete equality.

"Peace to you, Commander of the Faithful. I think this has gone far enough. I am called Ki-Gor. And if you do not know that name, you should. Knowing nothing about me, you nevertheless say that I belong to some tribe called the Vig N'ga. I have never in my life heard of such a tribe. I, myself, am originally of the English. But I owe no man allegiance. I am a peaceful traveler through your country. I wish you no ill, nor will I do you ill—so long as you treat me with due courtesy. I ask you now to return my weapons to me, and I will go my way."

When Ki-Gor finished, there was a long astounded silence. El Hakim looked as if he could not believe his ears. He looked uncertainly about the great tent for a moment, then fixed his great eyes on Ki-Gor again. Then a crafty light crept into those eyes.

"Do not think for a moment," he began softly, "that I am fooled by these crafty words. Ki-Gor, Ki-Gor—it is an odd name, but it could be Vig N'ga, just as everything else about you could be. I think we are dealing with the cleverest, most dangerous member of the Vig N'ga here. But think not, O Ki-Gor, that you can fool El Hakim! I say you are of the Vig N'ga—and let there be an end to it!"

HE FAIRLY screamed the last words, and glared pouting at Ki-Gor. The jungle man returned his look coldly. He was considering the possibility of leaping up on to the dais and seizing the diminutive person of El Hakim before his followers knew what he was about. A quick side glance, however, changed his mind. Those excellent Hausas had their guns watchfully trained on him.

"Well, then—what do you want?" Ki-Gor snapped.

"Ah!" El Hakim murmured, with a crafty smile. "That is better! You know what I want! You know I want the bronze dragon."

Ki-Gor blinked. What was the little weasel talking about?

"I want the bronze dragon," El Hakim went on, "to set up in my tent. It will be the greatest ju-ju in the world, and all the tribes for miles around will come and acknowledge me as their chief."

Ki-Gor dropped his chin in thought. He had not the faintest idea of what this absurd little upstart was talking about. What sort of people was this mysterious tribe of Vig N'ga that he talked about?

And why should he, Ki-Gor, be mistaken for one of them? He did not especially resemble any of the white men he had met—especially dressed as he was, and with uncut hair. But at that, he resembled white men much more than any other people of Africa he had ever seen. Here, something buzzed in his memory. What was it? Helene, not long ago, had said something about his looking like somebody or other—who was it? A dragon, too. She had used the word just as recently. Ki-Gor cudgeled his brain to recall what she had said. Where had they been when she talked about those things? Ki-Gor suddenly remembered. It had something to do with David Gray. He had asked her what David Gray was looking for, and she had said he was looking for remains of a dead tribe who were big and blonde and looked something like him.

Ki-Gor sighed. He could not see that the recollection was particularly helpful, or had any bearing on his present predicament. The people he resembled were long dead. As for the dragon—it had something to do with that skeleton ship, and certainly did not connect up in any way with the strange demand of this little yellow man, El Hakim.

"Come, come, Ki-Gor—as you call yourself," El Hakim said impatiently. "Speak. Will you help me gain the dragon?"

"How," Ki-Gor said frowning, "can I help you?"

"You should know better than I," El Hakim snapped. "But if you want me to command you—then I will. You will lead the way tonight into your stronghold by the least-guarded route. If you meet any sentries it will be up to you to eliminate them quietly. If you don't—"

El Hakim broke off with a dramatic gesture, drawing a finger across his yellow throat. Ki-Gor all but snorted with contempt. It was a ridiculous plan—from the point of view of El Hakim. Ki-Gor wished with all his heart that he knew something about this tribe called Vig N'ga, and their mountain stronghold. It would have delighted him to appear to accede to El Hakim's plan, and then during the execution of it, double-cross him in any of the number of ways it could be done. Unfortunately, he could not agree to lead them to the Vig N'ga when he had not the faintest idea of where they lived. He was considerably perplexed about what he should do. Somehow, he could not take the little yellow man very seriously, although he guessed that El Hakim was capable of all kinds of treachery and all kinds of cruelty. But the renegade chieftain was, in Ki-Gor's opinion, of very low mentality and should not be too much of a hurdle to freedom. Disdaining to exchange tricks with him, Ki-Gor decided to insist upon the fact that he was not a Vig N'ga tribesman, and to demand his freedom.

SO, AS El Hakim snarlingly bade him to speak up, Ki-Gor restated his case in no uncertain terms, and continued to do so for the next twenty minutes. But to his increasing dismay, El Hakim obstinately refused to believe him, and instead grew angrier and angrier at what he considered Ki-Gor's defiant attitude. And finally Ki-Gor woke up to the ugly realization that he had gravely underestimated the absurd little yellow man.

"My patience is exhausted!" El Hakim screamed. "If you will not willingly cooperate with me, I have means at hand to reduce you to a more agreeable disposition!"

Too late, Ki-Gor realized that he was facing the probability—if not the certainty—of a prolonged session of torture. It was certain to come if he could not soon devise a means of escaping this insane little Fulani.

A blessed reprieve suddenly arrived in the person of one of El Hakim's lieutenants, who came in to report that a visiting tribe, the Bobo-Haffa, had all arrived in the oasis and were assembled at the lower end ready to be greeted by the chieftain himself. El Hakim looked distressed. He either had to forego the pleasure of torturing Ki-Gor, or risk offending a tribe whom he was cultivating with a view to absorbing them into his rising militant power. Worst of all, the man whom he wanted to torture held the key—so he thought—to the submission of the Bobo-Haffa, if he would only sensibly procure the mysterious fetish, the ju-ju dragon of bronze.

Then one of the Hausa—the one whose arm Ki-Gor had broken in the fight—went up on the dais and whispered in El Hakim's ear.

The little chieftain smiled wolfishly and nodded. The Hausa continued to whisper, and El Hakim broke out into satanic laughter.

"We shall have the torture!" he proclaimed. "It will be in public. Why shouldn't we give our guests, the Bobo-Haffa, the pleasure of seeing the obstinate Vig N'ga squirming and squealing!"

CHAPTER VII

EVENTS MOVED SWIFTLY, THEN—SO swiftly that Ki-Gor could scarcely keep track of them. He hardly believed his senses when he found himself standing alone with his back to the wide trunk of a large tree, while about him in a great semicircle hundreds of grinning blacks swarmed and pushed and jostled. In the middle of the semi-circle, squarely in front of him, about forty feet away, El Hakim sat on a raised stool. He looked more grotesque than ever in the brilliant sunlight. But his great eyes glittered in anticipation of the spectacle he expected to unfold. And Ki-Gor's brain began to get very busy on the question of how he was to get out of this predicament with a whole skin.

From all indications, his torture was to be a long-drawn-out affair, beginning with relative pinpricks and ending—who could say where? Ki-Gor wondered whether it would save him any pain if he gave in and became, for El Hakim's sake, a Vig N'ga. He suspected that it was too late for that. And anyway, even if he did give in, how on earth could he deliver the dragon?

El Hakim shouted loud and long, and the shout was taken up by his lieutenants and soldiers and echoed by the visiting Bobo-Haffa—even though the latter hardly knew what they were cheering about. Ki-Gor guessed that the time for the pinpricks had arrived. He looked swiftly about him and saw that the scene was plain at the lower end of the oasis. In front of him, and beyond the massed blacks around El Hakim, the horses of his little army grazed peacefully.

Behind Ki-Gor stood the great tree. Improvised fences had been set up for about twenty feet on each side of the tree, so that Ki-Gor, who was not yet bound hand or foot, would have no avenue of escape in that direction. Apparently, he was not to be tied up—at least for a while. El Hakim no doubt anticipated great sport watching Ki-Gor trying to run away from his tormentors, but being ringed in with his armed Hausas, and the fences on each side of the tree.

Three or four Hausas now approached El Hakim. One of them

was carrying Ki-Gor's bow, another his quiver of arrows. There was a brief moment of consultation, then the quiver was handed up to El Hakim. But to Ki-Gor's surprise, the man with the bow turned and came straight for him. His astonishment deepened when the man presented the bow to him and walked away. Ki-Gor stared at his beautiful bow—a deadly weapon, especially at short range—but of course completely harmless without arrows. He looked up at El Hakim. The chieftain plucked an arrow from the quiver, and cackled fiendishly.

Now, it became clear to Ki-Gor what was going to happen. Evidently the Hausa with the broken arm had told El Hakim of Ki-Gor's deflecting the thrown knife with the bow, during the fight by the big river. El Hakim, it appeared, thought it was a neat trick, and intended to throw his own arrows at Ki-Gor to see how many of them the jungle man could knock down and hit aside. The arrows that Ki-Gor missed would, of course, hit him. And Ki-Gor's arrows were three-foot shafts of heavy hardwood sharpened on the end to needle-points and then baked in hot ashes to make them as hard as steel. Tossed by hand ever so gently at a distance of less than forty feet, they would have the effect of so many marlin-spikes.

El Hakim shouted loud and long, standing up on his pedestal. The crowd of Hausas and Bobo-Haffa hushed appreciatively and watched the chieftain hold up the arrow by its feathered butt. Ki-Gor compressed his lips and gripped the bow at the center of the curved shaft. He had long ago played this game with the Bushongo of the central Congo. But with the Bushongo it was regarded as a harmless pastime. The arrows were light wands, and they were tossed gently at the man holding the bow, who was always given plenty of time to set himself before each arrow was cast. The Bushongo attained incredible dexterity and really made an art out of using their bows as shields. Ki-Gor thanked his stars that he had had good teachers.

El Hakim brandished the arrow in midair, screaming wordlessly. When he was sure he had the attention of everyone within sight of him, he balanced the shaft in his fingers, and suddenly threw it with all his force.

IT WAS a beautiful throw—whether by accident or not, Ki-Gor hardly had time to decide. The arrow came whistling straight for his heart. It seemed that the jungle man had barely time to jerk his body to the right and strike diagonally downward with the bow. His bow hand was too slow. The bow barely grazed the feathers of the arrow. The point snicked along the skin over the ribs of his left side, then went on and slapped quivering into the tree trunk. There was a concerted demoniac yell from the onlookers, and Ki-Gor whipped his right hand to his left side. The wound was a mere scratch, but he could feel the blood welling out and trickling down his side.

El Hakim was beside himself with triumph and glee. Ki-Gor's face was a grim mask, and yet he almost smiled. Whether the excellent cast of the arrow was an accident or not, certainly the fact that it nicked Ki-Gor was no accident. The jungle man had gauged the arrow's flight perfectly, and allowed it to graze him. Ki-Gor had come to the decision that he wanted El Hakim to throw arrows at him. Therefore, he had let him score on the very first throw to encourage him to throw more.

The second arrow Ki-Gor knocked deftly to the ground at his feet, but the third one grazed his left forearm, drawing blood, to the great delight of El Hakim and his men and his guests, the Bobo-Haffa.

Vindictively, the little yellow man began to throw arrows faster, and Ki-Gor needed all his coolness and magnificent co-ordination to keep the heavy missiles deflected from his body. Eight arrows came hurtling at him in rapid succession, and all eight were either knocked down or successfully dodged. There came a pause, while El Hakim gathered several arrows in his hand. Then one of them came shooting down low. Ki-Gor allowed it to graze his thigh, thus giving El Hakim the satisfaction of drawing blood for the third time.

To make the situation look worse for him, Ki-Gor pretended to be hurt considerably, staring at the wounded thigh. The piece of play-acting nearly cost him dearly. El Hakim flung an arrow swiftly on the heels of the previous one. Ki-Gor just did see it as it coursed straight for his throat. He fell away just barely in time to save a serious wound, but the arrow struck the fleshy part of his left arm just below the shoulder.

A wild yell went up on all sides. Grimly, Ki-Gor set himself for another quick arrow, and knocked it down successfully. Then he plucked the arrow out of his arm, thanking his stars he did not use barbs.

But now the arrows rained down at him as fast as El Hakim could throw them. The crowd was screaming insensately, as Ki-Gor, bleeding from four wounds, crouched and leaped and jerked his bow hand.

He slipped once and went on one knee. The crowd thought he had been weakened by loss of blood and roared for the kill.

Actually, none of Ki-Gor's wounds was at all serious. He had purposely smeared the blood that came from them all over his arms and legs, so that he would present the gory picture of a man staggering on his last legs.

El Hakim was throwing in a frenzy now, and Ki-Gor had his hands full to come out unscathed from the rain of arrows. He did not trust himself to be hit any more—it was too risky, when the arrows came so fast. However, he had been counting the arrows, and he knew that-El Hakim would shortly exhaust the contents of his quiver. He was not quite certain exactly how many arrows there had been in the quiver, but he was fairly sure there were more than twenty and less than twenty-five.

Nineteen—twenty—twenty-one—they clicked against the parrying bow and dropped to the ground. Two of them went down point foremost and joined four others near Ki-Gor's feet that were sticking vertically, feathers up.

There was a slight pause, and Ki-Gor saw that El Hakim had just two arrows left. The time for action was close at hand. El Hakim flung both arrows at once.

Ki-Gor had a bad moment. He could not shield himself from two arrows coming at him at the same instant. Luckily, one of them flew wide.

The jungle man saw all this in a split-second. He gauged the flight of the arrow that was coming straight at him—stepped to one side—and caught it. His right hand snatched it out of mid-air, and with a lightning motion swept it down and notched it in the bowstring. Before anyone realized what was happening, Ki-Gor had snap-aimed, drawn the powerful bow its full distance, and released the arrow.

EL HAKIM had just started to scream in terror when the arrow caught him in the throat. The scream turned into a horrible gurgle, as the three-foot shaft drove straight through the scrawny neck, and a gout of Fulani blood spurted four feet straight out into the air.

While the Hausas were still staring unbelievingly at their stricken chieftain, Ki-Gor had plucked another arrow from the ground at his feet and had sent it whining through the air at a rifleman beside El Hakim's pedestal. And even as the rifleman reeled backward clutching at the feathered butt just above his belt, still a third arrow slanted through the groin of another Hausa on the other side of El Hakim. Working like an automaton, Ki-Gor picked off three more men around El Hakim.

Only now, fifteen seconds after Ki-Gor notched the first arrow, did the crowd—Hausas and visiting Bobo-Haffa alike—awake to what was happening. And now, Ki-Gor backed to the tree trunk, and plucked arrows out of the bark without turning around. He shot even faster now, not bothering to aim, but simply discharging at waist-level all around the semi-circle of massed blacks. Only two or three of the Hausas went for the rifles lying on the ground in front of them. But by the time these few were in position to shoot, they were too excited or terrified to do so. The Bobo-Haffa were in a complete uproar, milling and surging in abandoned panic.

There were still a few scattered arrows lying on the ground around Ki-Gor, but he knew that he must take advantage of the initial panic. It would only be a matter of moments before the Hausas, veteran soldiers that they were, recovered from their surprise.

"A-a-a-rrrgh!"

Ki-Gor roared his great challenge and sprang straight forward toward the pedestal of the fallen chieftain. Two or three devoted Hausas moved over to intercept him. Ki-Gor slipped his hand down to one end of his bow, and slashed at them. As they fell away, he leaped past them into the crowd of terrified Bobo-Haffa. They fought and clawed each other to get out of his way.

As Ki-Gor flung himself into the struggling mass of Bobo-Haffa, a rifle spoke behind him. The Hausas were beginning to recover themselves! Ki-Gor knew he had somehow to prolong the panic, or he still might not be able to escape alive from the valley of the oasis. He was through the belt of Bobo-Haff now, and running toward the herd of El Hakim's horses.

Sudden inspiration seized Ki-Gor. He slashed at the nose of the nearest horse with his battered bow, and shrilled high and clear the hunting call of the leopard. The beaten horse screamed with pain and reared, flinging itself to one side. Instantly the entire herd, already made nervous by the noises of panic, broke into panic themselves. Ki-Gor pursued the nearest ones, flailing at their plunging rumps until his bow splintered in his hand.

But by now his purpose was accomplished, and the herd was stampeding. The affrighted animals dashed ahead of him at first and tried to gallop up the steep wall of the valley. Only a few were able to keep their feet, however, and the herd split into two waves which bent around and thundered away toward the opposite end of the valley. The twin stampedes carried right into the crowds of Bobo-Haffa and Hausa that were streaming away to safety.

For several minutes, the oasis was a bedlam of screaming men, neighing horses, and scattered rifle shots. Ki-Gor dug his feet into the soft sand of the steep wall at the lower end, following the handful of horses that had succeeded in getting up there. As he fled over the rim, he cast one swift backward glance at the chaos in the valley below. He was even a little astonished at himself for doing such a complete job, considering that it was broad daylight, and he had used no suggestion of supernatural aid to play on the superstitions of his tormentors.

However, as he loped over the sand, he realized that he was by no means out of all danger yet. It was just a question of time before the Hausas would pull themselves together, catch their horses, and come after him, thirsting for revenge. The fall of their leader would delay them considerably, of course, but eventually they would break into pursuit. It behooved Ki-Gor to be far away by the time that began.

As luck would have it, one of the horses that had climbed out of the valley ahead of him soon lost its fear and became curious. Ki-Gor called to it, and before the animal could run away, the jungle man had vaulted on to its back. No great horseman, Ki-Gor nevertheless kicked the brute into a gallop and guided it by its mane in the direction from which the Hausas had originally brought him. He was headed back for the Viking ship.

CHAPTER VIII

HE HAD FIRST OF all to find Helene, and secondly to procure some kind of weapon to replace his shattered bow and stolen knife. He knew enough about horses to save his mount for a long pull, and not to push it too hard. Even so, he reached the Viking ship in good time. Securing the horse to one of the ship's ribs by its long mane, he leaped off, found a good-sized rock. Holding the rock in both hands he smashed it down repeatedly on the handle of the great hammer. Soon, the head moved down under the impact of the blows, and finally slipped free. With beating heart, Ki-Gor disengaged the great maul, and pulled it from under the rocks. It was a ponderous thing to manage, but it was a weapon after a fashion—when handled with the strength of a Ki-Gor. The jungle man vaulted back on to the back of the horse and urged it up along the river bank. Keen scrutiny of the horizon revealed no sign of pursuing Hausas yet.

When Ki-Gor reached a spot on the bank about a hundred yards below where he judged Helene would still be in the little cave, he began calling her name. When she did not appear, he began searching the ground for signs of her footprints. He did not even have to dismount to see the evidence of her capture and abduction by strange, sandaled men, who had galloped off with her on horseback. They had left a broad unmistakable trail leading eastward directly toward the mountains.

Ki-Gor estimated the distance toward the mountains, and slowed the horse to a walk. He had a hunch that Helene had been taken to those mountains. She had not been captured by the renegades of El Hakim, and she had not been captured by their neighbors, the Bobo-Haffa. And those two groups between them had no doubt controlled the desert plain. Therefore, whoever had carried Helene off must have a protected hideaway in the only mountains thereabouts.

Mountain men! The thought struck Ki-Gor like a lightning bolt. El Hakim talked about them—insisted that Ki-Gor was one of them! What did he call them? Vig N'ga—that was it! The Vig N'ga—who had a mountain stronghold and kept in it a dragon of bronze. Ki-Gor stirred uneasily on the horse's back. What sort of people were these mountain men? Well, for one thing, they evidently looked enough like himself for El Hakim to mistake him for one of them. Could they be whites? Could there be in Africa a whole colony of Ki-Gors?

It was an exciting idea, and in a way Ki-Gor was relieved by it. He felt somehow that Helene would be considerably safer as the prisoner of such people than she would be among the Sudanese blacks. He continued to jog along at a good speed beside the trail of Helene's abductors.

The desert played tricks with the eyes—that Ki-Gor knew. Nevertheless, he was astonished at how rapidly he seemed to approach the mountain range. It was almost as if he were standing still, and the mountains were coming toward him at a tremendous rate of speed, growing larger and taller every minute. They rose abruptly from the plain, high and sheer. By some freak their slopes were covered with dense dwarf vegetation, in contrast to the dry plain. The foliage was not so dense, however, as to conceal the rugged quality of the slopes.

Here and there, great boulders and ledges could be seen amongst the stunted growth.

The spoor of the abductors bore Ki-Gor's guess out by going without deviation straight toward the nearest spur of the mountains. Indeed, after a while, Ki-Gor began to puzzle a little as to where the abductors went. The mountains loomed higher and higher over him, and yet there was no sign of a break in the slope ahead of him. There was no indication of any opening for a pass, or any trail up the rugged mountain side.

However, there was the evidence left by the horse's hoofs, and the trail led straight ahead. Ki-Gor came to within five hundred yards of the foot of the mountain, and had begun to suppose that the tracks must turn aside soon, when the mountain seemed to unfold before his eyes. A narrow, high-walled ravine suddenly appeared where a moment before there had been an unbroken slope. So narrow was the opening that Ki-Gor would never have seen it, unless he had been searching for something like that with his keen eyes. He stopped the horse momentarily to shift the burdensome hammer from his left to his right hand. At that moment, he heard a sound like distant thunder, and the ground trembled imperceptibly under him. He flung a glance behind him over his shoulder. Unconsciously, a deep growl sounded in his throat.

ABOUT A half a mile behind him, a large body of horsemen was riding toward him. They were blacks and there were several hundred of them.

Almost at the same instant, Ki-Gor heard a curious sound—a thin wailing sound that seemed to come from somewhere on the mountain ahead of him. Ki-Gor had never heard a sound like that in his life. But he did not doubt for a moment that it was a warning signal of some kind. These mountain men, these Vig N'ga, no doubt kept lookouts around their stronghold to sound the alarm when strangers approached. Whether this alarm was being sounded because of him, or because of the more distant Hausas, Ki-Gor had no way of knowing. But whatever the case, he himself was for the moment in a delicate position. He was squarely between two armed groups—for he supposed the mountain men were warriors.

He kicked the horse into a gallop, and headed for the narrow opening. He might have some trouble establishing peaceful relations with these unknown Vig N'ga, especially with time so short. But the

Hausa band were very definitely his enemies, so that there was no choice in the matter. If the worst came to worst, he reflected, he could abandon the horse and the pass, take to the brush, and thus avoid any embattled mountain men who came down to receive him.

As the horse clattered through the opening, Ki-Gor saw that he might be forced to abandon the horse shortly anyway. The pass—for it was a pass—led abruptly off to the right and started climbing precipitously. Rough and boulder-strewn, it was less of a path than it was a dry water-shed. Ki-Gor clung to the horse's mane manfully as the animal plunged up the rocky trail. It was marvelous that the horse kept its feet in such treacherous going. Between jolts, Ki-Gor reflected that a very few men should be able to defend the pass against any amount of invaders.

The horse soon began gasping for breath, and Ki-Gor knew it was cruel to stay on his back. But he was being carried up the mountain side faster than he could run, and every second counted with that band of implacable Hausas at his heels. There was no way of telling how near he was getting to the top. Presumably the trail crossed the mountain at its lowest point. But at any rate, the horse was still going strong when Ki-Gor estimated that he must be at least half way up.

But no horse could stand that strain for long. There had to be a moment when the horse would either keel over from exhaustion or grow tired and stumble. And that moment finally came. Ki-Gor was prepared for it, and slid off as the animal lost its footing and crashed forward on its nose. The left fore leg was splintered, and Ki-Gor paused long enough to swing the great hammer high and bring it mercifully down on the head of the agonized horse.

Far down the mountain side, Ki-Gor could hear the Hausas shouting. He was none too far ahead of them. He swung the great hammer up on to his shoulder and turned and trotted up the trail.

A very short time later, he found out how near he was to the top of the pass. A huge man barred the way, swinging an enormous two-handed sword. His face was pale brown, his eyes gray, and his hair auburn. So this, Ki-Gor told himself, was a Vig N'ga tribesman! He was prepared for something pretty odd, but even so he was amazed at the warrior's appearance. But there was no time to be astonished. Ki-Gor shouted a greeting in Hausa.

"I am your friend!" he added quickly. "Your enemies are behind me down the trail!"

The effect on the strange warrior of Ki-Gor's appearance was apparently extraordinary. He dropped the tip of the great sword to the ground, and stared at Ki-Gor open-mouthed.

"Come, come!" Ki-Gor said, still in Hausa, "there is no time to be lost."

Still the guardian of the pass did not move, but stood stock-still, gaping at jungle man. Ki-Gor thought of an urgent question to ask.

"Where is the young woman with the bright red hair?" he demanded. "She was brought in here not long ago."

THE VIG N'GA warrior brushed an incredulous hand over his eyes, then gulped. Then he pointed his left hand backwards over the crest of the pass, and spoke in halting Hausa.

"Across the lake," Ki-Gor thought he said, although he could not imagine a lake nearby. But before he could say anything more, the strange warrior gave a wild yell, and began jabbering in a perfectly strange language. He waved his arm, pointed at a shield lying on the ground, and finally took up the sword with both hands and lifted the point to the sky. Ki-Gor had not the faintest idea of what the man's words signified, but they were delivered in the most fervent of manners.

Finally, the warrior climaxed his wild speech with a thunderous roar and leaped down the trail. Ki-Gor leaped aside, swinging the hammer. But the warrior apparently no longer even saw him. He plunged past Ki-Gor and went crashing down the trail, a wild sort of song on his lips.

Ki-Gor blinked at the warrior's extraordinary action, and wished he had even a glimmering of what some of his gibberish meant. One word or group of syllables had been repeated often, and even now came floating back up the pass, as the warrior charged down to attack the Hausas single-handed. The word sounded like "Valhalla." Ki-Gor wondered what it meant, for the man was going to almost certain death.

Ki-Gor climbed a few steps and found himself looking off into a beautiful steep-sided valley. At the bottom of it was the lake the warrior had spoken of. Helene was somewhere the other side of that lake, and that could not be too far away, as the lake was scarcely a mile wide. The trail dropped down in front of him steeply, evidently leading to the lake side. Ki-Gor wondered how Helene was faring. Something within him seemed to believe, or want to believe, that she was in safe hands. If that warrior who had guarded the pass was a fair sample of the Vig N'ga, Ki-Gor was prepared to like and trust them. He suddenly felt an acute pang of conscience for letting the warrior go alone, armed with only a sword, to meet hundreds of black Hausas armed with rifles.

As the jungle man hesitated at the top of the pass, the sound of rifles came up to his ears, and a chorus of shouts. Ki-Gor looked down the pass, and then down the other side toward the lake. A column of men suddenly appeared below hurrying upwards toward him from the valley. Giants they were like the guardian of the pass. They looked like him except for the leader, whose hair was almost as yellow as Ki-Gor's himself. Evidently, they were answering the call to arms sounded by the guard. They too were armed with swords, but as they came leaping up the trail, Ki-Gor felt that somehow they would be a match for the Hausas, rifles or no rifles.

A sudden impulse seized Ki-Gor to join their fight. It was no doubt far too late now to save the first man. But he could contribute his strong right arm to avenging his death. He cupped his hand by his mouth and shouted toward the oncoming Vig N'ga. When they jerked their heads up to look, he raised the hammer high with his right hand, and beckoned urgently with his left.

To his dismay, the giants halted in their tracks and stared at him with awed expressions. Ki-Gor fumed and beckoned even more furiously. This was no time for these warriors to stand and gape at him! Then the blond leader began to shout. He raised his sword high and continued to shout one word, repeated over and over. The rest of the warriors took up the word with him, and the valley rang with rhythmic repetition of the monosyllable.

"Taw! Taw! Taw! Taw!" Still shouting, the leader started up the path, leaping and running, the rest following swiftly after him. They surged to the top of the pass, eyes ablaze with a fanatical fire. They would have rushed right past Ki-Gor, but as they reached the top, he leaped in front of them and thundered down the narrow trail at the head of the column.

In the meantime, the Hausas had been wasting no time. They were more than half-way to the top of the pass, when Ki-Gor, dashing around a bend, came upon them. The front rank seemed scarcely a hundred feet away, and behind them the pass was jammed with the black riflemen. Ki-Gor barely broke his stride, then. But, as he ran, he brought the hammer around and over his head, describing a great arc. When his outstretched arm was parallel to the ground, he let go the handle. Twenty-five or thirty pounds of iron hurtled through the air and hit the front rank of the Hausas shoulder high. The effect on the serried mass of blacks was exactly as if an old-fashioned cannon ball had been fired into them.

A GAPING gory hole was torn right down through the center of the invading column. And hard behind the terrible missile came a giant bounding figure who seemed even more terrible. Ki-Gor was upon the dazed and horrified Hausas before they could fire a shot. He wrested the gun from the nearest black, clubbed it, and laid about him in a cold fury. Behind him, the Vig N'ga cut and slashed with their great swords.

For a few short minutes the scene in the pass was indescribable. Because of the cramped quarters, no man who survived the fight had a clear idea later of exactly what happened in detail. For one thing, the Vig N'ga, possessed of a battle fury that exceeded even that of Ki-Gor, swarmed up the sides of the ravine and poured along both rims, leaping down into the flanks of the jammed and helpless crowd of blacks.

Ki-Gor's fury soon left him after his initial charge. He recovered his hammer and then stood still a moment to observe the irresistible Vig N'ga leaping and slaughtering. It was only too obvious that they did not need his help any more, if indeed, they had ever needed it. The tide of the battle speedily receded down the pass away from him as the Hausas melted away under the fury of the strange auburn-haired giants. Ki-Gor slung his hammer over his shoulder and trotted up the pass again.

His mind had gone back to Helene, and he was anxious to find her and make sure she was all right. He was not really worried about her. She was evidently in the hands of these very men who were performing such prodigies of reckless valor. Nevertheless, he wanted to find her.

He hesitated at the crest of the pass before dropping down into the valley. Across the lake he made out some dwellings tucked away under the trees. As he looked, he saw a tiny boat set out from the beach in front of those houses. His keen eyes made out a single figure in the boat, bending back and forth energetically over the oars. The little craft came rapidly but erratically across the lake toward the shore below Ki-Gor. Ki-Gor could not but think the lone occupant was a poor boatman who was nevertheless in a great hurry.

The foot of the trail ended at the lake shore, where a half dozen big boats were beached. For a startled moment, Ki-Gor realized they were built in the same fashion as the skeleton ship back on the desert. But he had no time to conjecture on that point, for the small boat with the lone occupant was spurting and splashing toward him. The boat was close enough now for Ki-Gor to make out the lone occupant. It was David Gray.

As the boat ran up on the beach, the little scientist, wild-eyed and disheveled, scrambled out and started to run toward the path. Then he saw Ki-Gor and an agonized cry left his lips.

"Ki-Gor! Thank Heaven! Quick—into the boat! There isn't a minute to lose! We still may be too late! Helene—" Later, Ki-Gor hardly knew how he made that boat trip, jerking at the unfamiliar oars in a frenzy as Gray in the stern stammered out the awful tale of N'grit's diabolic intentions toward Helene. Nor did he remember precisely running up the path to the grotto.

The picture which greeted his eyes as he surmounted the last rise and pounded into the grotto itself would always be etched horribly in his memory.

Helene, head back, calling his name—bound hand and foot to a thick stake—the dry wood piled around her feet. And the tall blonde woman in the long robe, dancing a slow horrible dance of death in front of her, holding aloft the flaming torch. Now, she was lowering the torch and dancing slowly toward Helene's pitifully struggling body. The malevolent white-robed figure was scarcely ten feet away from Helene, and Ki-Gor was two hundred feet from them both. But Ki-Gor swung the hammer and let it fly. The great iron maul sailed lazily through the air, turning over slowly. Ki-Gor held his breath and watched it fatalistically. For one awful moment, he was sure it was going to hit Helene.

But it missed Helene by about three feet and struck N'grit square-ly on her blonde head.

HELENE STIRRED and stretched on the high bed, and pushed the lion-skin covers away off her chest. She blinked and smiled up at the anxious faces of Ki-Gor and David Gray.

"I'm all right," she declared in a normal strong voice. "Really I am, Ki-Gor. I haven't any headache, my hands don't tremble—see?"

She held out a brown hand that trembled only slightly. Ki-Gor seized it and pressed it against his cheek.

"That's fine," David Gray beamed. "I think it would be a good idea, though, if you stayed on your back for another hour or so. Then you can get up and have some light nourishment. Thank goodness you have such a healthy and resilient nervous system. The average civilized woman who had spent a day like yours would be a jibbering idiot by now."

"Well," Helene smiled. "I don't think I'm any crazier now than I ever was. I was scared all right, and I didn't see how I was going to come out of that jam. But somehow I knew Ki-Gor would come."

"With about three seconds to spare," Gray murmured, shaking his head.

An idea seemed to cross Helene's mind, and she glanced anxiously around.

"Say," she said. "Everything seems perfectly peaceful. What about our dark-skinned Nordics—how did they take the violent death of N'grit? Isn't there going to be some trouble about that?"

"No," Gray said definitely. "It's a long story which I'll tell you some day. But N'grit violated the law of the Vig N'ga in attempting to execute a prisoner when the tribe had not decreed death. Besides, I think that the tribe in general and Irruk in particular were not terribly sorry that N'grit was killed. She had been making a nuisance of herself for quite some time, so I gather. She was madly in love with Irruk but she couldn't marry him because she was his cousin, being a descendant of the Haarfaagers, herself. But still she loved Irruk and was insanely jealous of him."

"Poor creature," Helene mused. "I can understand jealousy." She smiled at Ki-Gor.

"As a matter of fact," Gray went on, "Ki-Gor would be in no trouble if he had killed anybody in the place. The Vig N'ga are convinced that he is none other than Thor the Thunderer, the old Norse god of war. His size and coloring would have suggested it anyway, but when he showed up with that immense hammer, that clinched it in their minds. In the Norse cosmology, Thor always carried a great hammer and hurled it at his enemies—much to the detriment of his enemies."

"Well, where in the world did the hammer come from?" Helene demanded. Ki-Gor told her.

"I don't believe it," Helene said. "How could a piece of iron lie out in the open for eight or nine hundred years or however long it's been—and not dissolve away into rust?"

"Pure iron," Gray explained, "does not rust, or rusts very little, especially in that dry desert air. And this hammer was probably made out of that pure iron-ore that comes from those rich mines in the north of Sweden. And now why don't you rest a little while. I am writing a speech for Ki-Gor to make later in the evening."

"A speech?" Helene said. "But Ki-Gor doesn't know the language, does he?"

"I am writing it for him in Icelandic," Gray said with a smile, "and putting it into English phonetics for him. Then, we'll rehearse it carefully. Thank goodness, Ki-Gor has such a quick ear for language. It would never do, would it, for Thor the Thunderer to speak his own language haltingly?"

"My, my!" Helene murmured wonderingly. "But if Ki-Gor is Thor, who are you and I, David?"

"They still don't quite know what to make of me," Gray laughed. "But, as for you, Helene—Irruk suspected in the beginning, and now he and the whole tribe are sure that you are one of the Valkyrie!"

Helene drew a deep breath and grinned at one and the same time.

"My, my," said Helene. "This, I guess, is Africa—where the impossible always happens!"

STORY XV

THE CANNIBAL HORDE

KI-GOR SLANTED THE ROUND blade of the paddle into the water as far away from the gunwale as he could reach, then swept it around in a wide arc. The nose of the canoe swung around and pointed toward the north bank of the river. Helene in the bow lifted her paddle out of the water, and looked back over her bare shoulder.

"Are you heading for that little patch of beach, Ki-Gor?" she inquired.

"Yes, that's just inside Bambala country," Ki-Gor replied. "I'm going to leave you two there, You can float down the river, and I'll meet you at Otempa."

"But we'll get to Otempa long before you will, won't we?" Helene said, "if you travel overland?"

"Oah, Heavenly Days, *memsahib!*" exclaimed the third person in the canoe. "How fast are you contemplating propelling canoe by yourself—with fat Brahmin passenger doing absolutely nothing to help?"

The third person was Hurree Das, the plump Hindu doctor who was a fugitive from the authorities at Nairobi, but who had more than once demonstrated his loyalty and friendship to Ki-Gor and his lovely red-haired mate. The Hindu was an enthusiastic herbalist and had begged to join Ki-Gor and Helene on their expedition to the country of the Bambala in the south-central Congo region. The Bambala were famous iron-workers and weapons-makers, and Ki-Gor was going to them to replace weapons which he had recently lost or broken. Hurree Das had desired to come along "for lofty purpose of botanical research," as he had put it in his unvaryingly flowery English.

The canoe grated on the sand, and in a moment the three occupants stood beside it on the little beach.

"What do you think, Ki-Gor?" Helene persisted. "Won't we get to Otempa long before you will?"

"No," Ki-Gor said patiently. He squatted on his haunches and began to draw a rough map in the sand with his fore-finger. "This is the Mikenye River," he said, "flowing from east to west. Right about where we are standing, it curves south sharply. Then it turns all the way north again up to Otempa. There it heads straight west again."

Ki-Gor's forefinger had described a deep U in the sand. At the top of the right-hand shaft of the U, he put a dot, which indicated their present position. At the top of the left-hand shaft, he placed another dot to indicate the Bambala village of Otempa.

"See?" he said, "You will have to go down and all the way around this loop"—tracing the U—"while I go straight across"—he closed the top of the U with a straight line.

Helene glanced doubtfully back at the dense jungle that towered up from the river bank, like an impenetrable barrier.

"Even so," she remarked, "that doesn't look like very easy traveling to me."

"Easy enough," Ki-Gor grinned, "by the tree-route. I'll stop only a little while in Toli—that's a little Bambala fort just about half way to Otempa. I want to hear whether they know of the rumors the Tetela told us last night."

"A Bambala fort?" Helene said, frowning down at Ki-Gor's little map in the sand. "But I thought you said the river, here, was the northern boundary of the Bambala country."

"It is," Ki-Gor agreed, "except for this section here." He indicated the land contained within the U. "They never gave up this part to the B'Kutu cannibals. The boundary between the Bambala and the B'Kutu goes from here to here."

Again, Ki-Gor's finger traced a straight line across the open top of the U. It was the same line which he had indicated as his route overland to Otempa.

"Oh dear," Helene murmured. "Isn't that a little close to those nasty little cannibals? I'd hate to think of you—"

"Come now," Ki-Gor smiled. "You know you don't have to worry about me."

"Just the same," Helene said stubbornly. "Last night, those Tetela told us they thought the B'Kutu were about to attack the Bambala."

"You will always hear rumors in the jungle," Ki-Gor said. "And the Tetela admitted that the Bambala didn't believe that rumor."

Just then, Hurree Das, who had been poking around the edge of the undergrowth bordering the beach, gave a little cry.

"Oah! Most interesting discovery!" the Hindu cried. "Spent missile of savage blackamoor, no doubt!"

He turned and came down the beach toward them, the flimsy muslin *dhoti* flapping inadequately around his thick legs. His right hand was extended and held a small crude arrow. Ki-Gor glanced at it briefly.

"B'Kutu arrow," he said. "Be careful—the tip is probably poisoned."

"Indubitably!" Hurree Das said beaming. "Grant me a few moments while I scrape off some of the black gummy substance on tip. During some future leisure, I shall perform chemical analysis on same."

Whereat, he busied himself at the water's edge harvesting a sample of the arrow-venom, after which he scrubbed himself and the arrow vigorously with liquid from several bottles out of his little black bag. Eventually, he stood up beaming and offered the arrow, now perfectly clean, to Ki-Gor.

"Most amusing idea occurs to me— wait!" he said. He dived into the black bag again and came out with a bottle of iodine. He coated the arrow point liberally with it, and then offered the arrow again to the jungle man.

"Blackened tip appears menacing," he observed, "but in point of fact—ha-ha! pun!—in point of fact, arrow is now completely harmless. You could play great joke on some unsuspecting fellow by pricking his skin with this. Wound, of course, would be absolutely and entirely harmless, but poor fellow would be convinced of impending death from arrow-poisoning."

Ki-Gor took the little arrow with a reproachful grin. Nowhere in Africa did he know of a man, black, white, or brown, who would ever forgive the perpetrator of such a joke—but Hurree Das was a good friend, even if his sense of humor now and then verged on the child-like. Ki-Gor tucked the arrow through the band of bark around his upper left arm, Bambala-fashion, and prepared to leave his wife and friend.

"Paddle easily," he told Helene. "The river is deep and the current is slow. At Otempa, the banks get narrower, and the river flows faster. But the Bambala have a bridge across it at Otempa with vines hanging down. If you have trouble getting to the bank and the current sweeps you downstream, you can always grab one of the vines at the bridge."

"I don't think I'll have any trouble," Helene said, with a trace of asperity. "I've handled a canoe ever since I can remember."

"All right," Ki-Gor grinned. "Then you probably won't tip over. The river's full of crocodiles."

"Oah, Heavenly days!" Hurree Das ejaculated, wagging his plump jowls. "Most abominable idea! I am not caring at all to furnish hearty meal for hungry saurians. Sometimes I am having serious doubts concerning seaworthiness of this frail craft."

The Hindu stared dubiously at Ki-Gor's home-made canoe.

"Come on, Hurree!" Helene laughed. "You'll be perfectly safe. Ki-Gor made it from a sketch I drew of an Algonkian birch canoe— and he made it extra broad in the beam, just to fit you!"

Ki-Gor watched them until they had floated out of sight around the steep bend in the river. Then he crossed the beach, plunged into the undergrowth, and went up the trunk of the nearest tall tree. In less than two minutes, he was two hundred feet off the ground and swinging from branch to branch in his favorite mode of travel—the tree-route.

A LITTLE before noon, the jungle man halted to make a frugal meal of nuts and wild fruit. He judged he was not far from the little Bambala outpost of Toli, and he preferred to have eaten before he entered the village. Otherwise the hospitable Bambala would expect him to fill up on heavy manioc bread and the ever-present native beer.

It was much better this way, Ki-Gor thought, as he munched his nuts high up off the ground. The noon hush had closed in, and a cathedral-like stillness governed the vast cloistered jungle around him. The monkeys and the wild parrots were silenced, and even the shrill dreeing of the countless insects was subdued. Ki-Gor's keen eyes constantly roved about, penetrating the eternal gloom of the jungle below him. There was a light screen of undergrowth that hid the ground from him, except for patches here and there. But directly below his swinging heels, a broad elephant trail meandered off to the westward, presumably toward Toli.

Ki-Gor was accustomed to the silence of the African high noon, but on this day the jungle seemed to be more than ordinarily quiet. For all his giant frame, Ki-Gor was keenly sensitive to the moods of the jungle. And today, there seemed to him something foreboding, something fearful, in the flat stillness about him. It was as if the multitudes of little animals and birds were waiting breathless—waiting for something to happen.

Even after he had finished his meal, Ki-Gor lingered on his perch

high above the jungle floor, reflecting. His thoughts went back to the night before, when he and Helene and Hurree Das had been entertained royally in a Tetela village.

The Tetela were a husky, warlike nation, but at the same time they were straightforward and trustworthy, and represented a high type of the Bantu-speaking tribes of the Congo. They were capable warriors, and much too proud to descend to treachery—in great contradistinction to some of their neighboring tribes. At one time they had practiced cannibalism in a restricted, ritualistic form. That is to say, they sometimes ate the heart of a fallen enemy, in a religious way, to acquire that enemy's bravery. But nowadays, they did not even do that. And the Tetela detested their neighbors across the river, the B'Kutu.

The B'Kutu were still active and confirmed cannibals. They were a bestial, dirty, and degraded people, backward and treacherous. They were suspected of having Pygmy blood, and they used poisoned arrows

like the Pygmies. Unlike the Pygmies, they ate human flesh as often as they could get it—ate it because they liked the taste of it. They invariably ate their prisoners of war, and during extended periods of peace, they frequently resorted to eating their own slaves.

And the Tetela had said the B'Kutu were going to war against the Bambala!

However, the Bambala apparently had laughed at the idea, and

Ki-Gor hoped that the rumor was unfounded. He was very fond of the Bambala. They were civilized to the point of effeteness, but they were industrious agriculturalists, and skilled iron workers. At one time, they had been fine warriors, but long years of peace had softened them. Handsome and slender, they were inordinately vain, and spent hours dressing their hair, and daubing their bodies with clean red clay. But they were courteous, hospitable, and had a fine sense of humor. And effete as they were, they would still fight bravely, if attacked.

Ki-Gor hoped that the Tetela were wrong in their prediction of a B'Kutu attack on the Bambala. However, he knew that if the B'Kutu attacked anyone it would be the light-hearted Bambala. The little cannibals would never dare to try conclusions with the tough Tetela, and the next nearest neighbors were the Akela, an equally warlike nation.

Ki-Gor stood up on his precarious swinging perch and stretched. It was time he got along. It would be interesting to find out what the Bambala at Toli thought of the rumors of war. Suddenly, he stiffened.

Somewhere the fearful brooding silence of the jungle had been broken. It was a slight sound, which Ki-Gor had felt in his chest, rather than heard. But it grew a little louder, and Ki-Gor's ears picked up the sound, and identified it as the sound made by someone running.

He stood quite still, eyes fixed on the stretch of elephant trail visible to him below. In a short time, his vigilance was rewarded.

A lone man appeared on the elephant trail, running at full speed toward the west.

HE WAS a slender man, unarmed, and he acted badly frightened. His hair was elaborately dressed in five ridges along his long skull, and his body was daubed with red clay. He was unquestionably a Bambala.

While he was still in view of Ki-Gor, he suddenly checked his headlong flight, and stood quivering in the middle of the elephant trail. Ki-Gor almost called down to the man to ask him what he was fleeing from. But the Bambala was in such obvious terror that a strange voice would probably have only terrified him more.

The stranger hesitated only a few seconds. Then, with one last frightened glance around him, he leaped off the elephant trail and plunged into the undergrowth—headed southward.

Ki-Gor frowned. What had struck that Bambala? What was he running from in such abject terror? And why, having gone up the

trail, did he halt in his tracks, and then finally leave the trail altogether? Ki-Gor thought back on the last time he had gone via Toli
to Otempa. He had only done it once before, and on that occasion
he had taken the tree-route. He recalled now that on that occasion,
too, he had crossed this self-same elephant trail, and that it did not
go to Toli. It veered southward later, away from that village. This
recollection increased Ki-Gor's puzzlement over the conduct of the
lone Bambala. What was the man running from?

The jungle man waited patiently in his treetop, on the chance that
he might see someone or something pursuing the Bambala. But no
person or thing came along, and brooding silence once more gripped
the great jungle. Eventually, Ki-Gor decided that there was nothing
to be gained by waiting any longer, and that he would have to seek
the answer to his question—if there were an answer—in the village
of Toli. So he continued on his way.

However, some instinct caused him to go carefully, slowly, and
absolutely silently. His normal pace was rapid and rather noisy as he
leaped from one limb to another. But now, he stayed high in the
tangled tops of the trees, pushing his way noiselessly through the
damp leaves. He could see less of the ground than ever, traveling in
this manner, but something told him it was the thing to do. Every
now and then, he stopped and peered downward through open patches
among the foliage. For three of these brief halts, he saw nothing, and
after the third halt, he resumed his way almost convinced that there
was nothing to look for, and that he might just as well come down
lower and travel swiftly until he got to Toli.

But he decided once more to stop and look down, and when he
did, the skin along his backbone prickled.

At first, it seemed as if the light screen of undergrowth just above
the ground were moving—as if a light breeze were blowing down
there. But even as that impression was recorded in his mind, he realized that it was no breeze that was moving that undergrowth.

The jungle floor below him was alive with men.

Silent as death, a horde of wiry, naked blacks were creeping through
the undergrowth. Armed with long knives and short bows, they were
unmistakably B'Kutu.

Ki-Gor carefully let himself down some twenty feet where he could
command a larger area with his eyes. His amazement deepened.
Everywhere he looked, the forest was crawling with B'Kutu. They

seemed to be in endless numbers. And there could be no doubt as to where they were going. They were already in Bambala country, and they were headed for the Bambala village of Toli.

The Tetela were right.

And the Bambala, who had laughed at the rumor that the B'Kutu were going to attack them—would all too soon find out their mistake.

Ki-Gor's brain churned. He hated to think of the carnage that would soon take place at Toli, when the cannibals fell on the unsuspecting Bambala. What could he do about it? How could he prevent the surprise?

Two alternatives flashed through his mind. One was fling himself through the trees in a furious race toward Toli. The other was to shout at the top of his voice. Both alternatives meant that he would cast all caution to the winds, and reveal himself to the horde of creeping B'Kutu below.

But even as Ki-Gor debated with himself, a dreadful sound went up. It sounded far away at first, a distant savage wail, then spread like a grass fire through the jungle. In a few seconds, the B'Kutu underneath Ki-Gor sprang up from their concealment and joined the ferocious, man-eating cry. With a sinking heart, Ki-Gor realized that he was too late—that he could have done nothing, anyway. The first wave of cannibals had already attacked Toli.

CHAPTER II

ABANDONING ALL CAUTION, KI-GOR set off at full speed for Toli. Certainly the noise of his progress would never be heard over the unearthly screeching of the attacking B'Kutu, and it was doubtful if any of them would look up and see him swinging through the branches. The jungle man had little hope that he could do anything to help the little band of Bambala in Toli. They were probably no more than fifty of them at most, and they could not stand up long against the multitude of invaders.

As he swung along over their heads, Ki-Gor marveled at their numbers. There were more B'Kutu within sight of him than he had dreamed were in the entire tribe, and by the savage sounds that re-echoed through the cavernous jungle, there were many more that he could not see.

And even more remarkable than their numerousness was the fact that they had combined in a concerted action. The B'Kutu were so shy and so backward in any social organization that Ki-Gor would never have believed that they would ever have united like this, if the evidence were not right before his eyes. There must be some powerful and compelling force behind it all, Ki-Gor thought, to drive such primitive hunters into such unified action.

For obviously, this was no border raid. The fact that hundreds of the cannibals had circled around into Bambala territory to surround Toli demonstrated that they had intended to catch the entire Bambala garrison. No one was to escape from Toli to tell of the disaster and warn the Bambala nation that the attack had begun.

Ah! but one of the Bambala *had* escaped! Ki-Gor recalled the lone unarmed youth running for his life along the elephant trail. Had he gotten through? Ki-Gor devoutly hoped he had.

By now the jungle man was above the outskirts of Toli, and evidences of the success of the surprise attack were immediately evident. The Bambala, for all their lack of eagerness for war, did however construct their villages with a view toward their successful defense. Every Bambala village was surrounded by a ring of small two-man forts—and not one ring but three—built at some distance from the center of the village.

From his vantage point in the trees, Ki-Gor could see two of these advanced outposts. Their defenders had been killed instantly without loss to the attackers. And now B'Kutu were swarming over their dead bodies, screaming their blood-lust at the top of their lungs.

The next ring of forts had evidently had a few seconds of warning, and B'Kutu dead mingled with Bambala. But they had not held up the attack for long. The B'Kutu had poured over them in a resistless flood of screeching humanity, and had even passed the last and strongest set of defenses by the time Ki-Gor arrived over them.

And now the din mounted as the cannibals converged on the village itself, and the Bambala fought to the death against the overwhelming numbers of B'Kutu. Such a one-sided conflict could not last very long, and it was all but over by the time Ki-Gor came within sight of the village.

Heartsick, he watched a few scattered knots of Bambala fighting back to back in the midst of the torrent of blood-crazed cannibals which swirled around, and then—over them. They gave a good account of themselves, those gay slender Bambala, hacking and stabbing grimly until the last man was rolled under the roaring tide of B'Kutu.

With all his heart, Ki-Gor wished he had been a little earlier on the scene, although what he could have done, he did not know. Even his mighty strength and crafty brains would have been powerless against an attack so smartly planned and perfectly executed. Again Ki-Gor wondered who or what had organized the shy and dispersed B'Kutu into such extraordinary unity of action.

As he watched the shambles in the village of Toli, Ki-Gor suddenly felt a new astonishment. The swarming, screaming butchers down there were not all B'Kutu! There was a considerable group of Tono in amongst them. The Tono were cousins of the B'Kutu—a sub-tribe, in fact—and were equally savage, equally degraded. And there was still another tribe represented down there. They were the Tofoke, or Scarfaces, easily recognizable by the way their faces and necks were covered with rows of hideous ridged cicatrices.

And now Ki-Gor's puzzlement deepened. If it was unusual for the B'Kutu to combine amongst themselves, it was unheard-of for them to join other tribes in any action. What was the motive power, the driving force behind this?

Then still a new group of warriors appeared among the milling shrilling cannibals, and when Ki-Gor saw them, he nearly fell out of his tree with astonishment For these newcomers were not natives of the Congo region at all. They were big brown men who towered over the stunted blacks around them, and they were armed with throwing sticks, and long assegais, and carried coffin-shaped shields of buffalo hide. They had the haughty carriage and the graceful kilts of the Ama-zulu, and Ki-Gor recognized them instantly as belonging to that independent branch of the Ama-zulu—the Kara-mzili. And the King of the Kara-mzili was Dingazi, Ki-Gor's friend!

Ki-Gor was astounded. What were Dingazi's mighty warriors doing here in the Congo-Kasai basin, hundreds of miles from their home south of the Great Lakes? And why would they be allied with these filthy cannibals, and attacking the inoffensive Bambala?

Just then there was a tiny rustle of leaves close by Ki-Gor's perch in the tree. Without turning his head, Ki-Gor rolled his eyes. An unpleasant thrill went through him. Scarcely ten feet away on a neighboring limb, a B'Kutu was crouched. His little bow was raised and a poison-tipped arrow was notched in it and pointed at Ki-Gor.

THE CANNIBAL had evidently spotted Ki-Gor and climbed up after him. For several seconds, Ki-Gor did not move a muscle. The savage apparently thought Ki-Gor did not see him and Ki-Gor let him cherish the error.

But the jungle man's skin twitched at the thought of that deadly arrow pricking him. He stood up with elaborate casualness, and pretended to be preoccupied with the scene below in the village. But his eyes were slits, and under cover of the heavy lashes, they did not miss a move the B'Kutu made.

Evidently the savage was pondering whether to try to get closer to his quarry before discharging his arrow. The B'Kutu were notoriously poor archers, being unable to hit anything except an elephant farther than twenty feet away. And apparently, this B'Kutu even had doubts of making his mark from a distance of little more than ten feet.

Confident that Ki-Gor was unaware of his presence, he lowered his bow and crept out a little farther on the bough. It was all the opportunity Ki-Gor needed. Without so much as a preparatory twitch of his muscles, the jungle man sprang off his perch.

It was a standing jump across empty air with the ground a hundred and fifty feet below—an exacting feat under the best of circumstances, but an almost impossible one under these circumstances. Fortunately, the other limb was slightly lower than the one Ki-Gor leaped from.

The B'Kutu's reaction was swift. As Ki-Gor took off, the little savage perked up his bow and let fly the venom-tipped arrow. In mid-air Ki-Gor doubled both knees, and saw the arrow flit beneath him. He could not be sure the tip did not graze his skin—but there was no time for that, anyway. The B'Kutu's hand flew back to his quiver, as Ki-Gor landed lightly on the bough beside him.

Out came the filthy black hand clutching another arrow. Ki-Gor's left hand shot out, gripped the B'Kutu's wrist and held it high in the air. The cannibal gave a bleat of terror and tried to fling himself off the bough. But Ki-Gor's right hand was at his throat, supporting him.

But if Ki-Gor thought his battle was won that easily, he was mistaken. The B'Kutu's unwashed hide was slippery as an eel's, and Ki-Gor's powerful fingers could not hold the grip on that scrawny neck. Whipping hie wiry body like a mongoose, the B'Kutu was suddenly free—all except the hand holding the deadly arrow. Without relaxing his grip on the wrist of that fatal hand, Ki-Gor grappled frantically with his other hand. The B'Kutu was screaming now at the top of his lungs, but Ki-Gor had no time to look and see whether the screams could be heard over the tumult in the sacked village. Grimly holding the arrow hand far away, he strove for a firm grip on the B'Kutu's greasy neck.

The cannibal fought like a mad dog.

Apparently he had no hope or desire of surviving the fight himself—but was bent only on killing Ki-Gor if he could. Recklessly he leaped into the air, flailing his heels against Ki-Gor's thighs. And suspended by the one wrist, he twisted from one side to the other, throwing his weight about in a savage attempt to pull Ki-Gor off balance and send both of them hurtling off the limb to the ground below.

For a moment, Ki-Gor thought he had succeeded. The little savage sprang straight out into the air. The incredible swiftness of the maneuver dragged Ki-Gor's huge frame to one side. And for an awful moment, the jungle man teetered on the brink of death. The twisting, screaming savage dangling at arm's length was hauling him inexorably off balance. Instinctively, Ki-Gor bent his left knee, and kicked his right foot out into the air on the other side of the limb. The sweat started out on his bronzed forehead, and his upper lip was drawn tight over his teeth, as he strained and fought his way back to an even keel.

Then, with knees bent in a half crouch, he looped his right hand over and down in a short arc. The hard palm crashed down on the B'Kutu's frizzy skull, and the cannibal went limp.

Nerves jangling, and body trembling, Ki-Gor backed cautiously to the trunk of the tree. His left hand still held the B'Kutu's wrist in a death grip, even though the deadly arrow dropped out of the nerveless black hand. As Ki-Gor felt the rough bark of the tree trunk against his back, he shook his head vigorously as if to shake off a bad dream.

It had been a close call.

A brief inspection showed that the B'Kutu's neck was thoroughly broken, and that if he was not already dead, he would probably not return to consciousness. Ki-Gor looked out over the mob scene in the village. He could nowhere see a single face uplifted toward him. It did not seem possible that such a bitter frantic struggle could have gone unnoticed by anyone down below. It had taken place in full view of hundreds—if any of them had happened to look up. However, it was an indication of the single-minded bloodlust of the B'Kutu and their allies.

However, now that the last of the Bambala had been slaughtered, an anti-climactic lull began to settle over the scene. The tall foreigners—the Kara-mzili—had something to do with creating the lull, too. Ki-Gor could see them efficiently pushing the squalling cannibals out of the center of the village and clearing a space there.

And now with renewed impact, the question of these Kara-mzili reasserted itself in Ki-Gor's mind. What were they doing here? And why did they fight with the B'Kutu against the Bambala?

Just then, the milling crowd parted and a litter was borne into the cleared space on the shoulders of four strapping Kara-mzili. Ki-Gor recognized the fat, yellow-skinned young man in the litter, and his questions were answered.

The fat young man was Mpotwe, the traitorous nephew of Dingazi, King of the Kara-mzili.

KI-GOR HAD been with Dingazi when Mpotwe had led an unsuccessful uprising against the old king. If Ki-Gor had not been with Dingazi, the rebellion might have succeeded, and the treacherous Mpotwe might have become king over the murdered body of his uncle. But Ki-Gor had performed some feats which had convinced the Kara-mzili that he was a mighty ju-ju. The rebellion, in consequence, had failed, and Mpotwe with a few followers had fled the kingdom with a price on his head. The malevolent young prince had somehow escaped being captured, and disappeared leaving no trace.

Evidently—Ki-Gor reflected, as he stared contemptuously down at Dingazi's nephew—Mpotwe had put many miles between him and his vengeful countrymen, and had finally taken refuge in the dank Congo forest. It did not take much imagination to reconstruct what had happened since then. The scheming Mpotwe had come within an ace of becoming ruler of a powerful, martial nation—he would not long remain content to cower in the perpetual twilight of the B'Kutu jungle. He had somehow overcome the suspicions of the beady-eyed little cannibals and induced them to act as a group instead of individuals as they always had from time immemorial. From there on, the traditional efficiency and organizing powers of the Kara-mzili had taken over and welded an army out of the B'Kutu and their cousins, the Tono, and the scarfaced Tofoke.

Right in front of Ki-Gor's eyes, that Kara-mzili organization demonstrated itself. The blood-crazed cannibals were herded off into groups by the handful of Kara-mzili warriors, and some semblance of order was brought about. Under ordinary circumstances, the B'Kutu would still have been running around in a delirium of excitement, hacking and butchering the dead bodies of their enemies. But now, the uproar was gradually stilled—even though the cannibals were obviously reluctant to leave the prized corpses of their Bambala victims.

A mound of stones and earth was quickly piled up in the center of the clearing, and the litter on which Mpotwe reclined was set on top of it. Evidently Mpotwe intended to address his triumphant army.

Ki-Gor wondered what the renegade Kara-mzili prince would say. It was unlikely that Mpotwe would rest with taking Toli. More likely the surprise of that outpost and the annihilation of its defenders was just a prelude to much wider action. But what was that wider action to be?

Suddenly, Ki-Gor knew. Before Mpotwe opened his mouth to speak, Ki-Gor guessed what he would announce. It would be a swift and secret march on Otempa—Otempa which straddled the Mikenye River, sprawling on both banks, and connected by a sturdy bridge between the two halves. The B'Kutu were notoriously afraid of the water, so that Mpotwe would lead them across the bridge at Otempa into Bambalaland proper. Mpotwe would never be satisfied to rule over a savage wilderness peopled by ignorant cannibals, when right at hand were the rich gardens, and tobaccolands and busy foundries of the Bambala.

But now Mpotwe began to speak, and his first words showed bow closely Ki-Gor had guessed.

"O brave B'Kutu, Tono, Tofoke! This is no time for feasting on the bodies of the conquered! There will soon be many more bodies! You have taken the first outpost, swiftly, magnificently! You have permitted no messenger to escape and warn the Bambala! We must strike again—swiftly and silently—like the cobra! In a short time we will be at Otempa! Much bigger than Toli is Otempa—but it will fall as quickly! Then—across the bridge! Hear me now, your chief, Mpotwe the Great—"

But Ki-Gor stopped to listen to no more. He lifted the body of the B'Kutu on to his shoulder and began to climb high into the tree, out of sight of all the thronging cannibals in the ravaged Bambala village.

He knew what Mpotwe and the cannibals did not know—and that was that *one messenger did get away!* The Bambala at Otempa would be warned of the treacherous attack that was about to be launched upon them. But forewarned as they would be, Ki-Gor knew that the Otempa warriors could not withstand the swarming numbers of the invaders or the crafty tactics of their Kara-mzili leader. There simply were not enough of them. And it would take a certain amount of time for help to be sent to Otempa from the other parts of Bamhalaland. The easy-going, talkative Bambala would be sure to waste precious hours and even days debating among themselves as to the best way to meet the emergency. In the meantime, Mpotwe's hordes would have forced the passage of the river and would be swarming southward, ravaging and slaughtering.

Somehow, Ki-Gor told himself, the cannibals must be stopped on this side of the Mikenye River. The Otempa garrison must be given as much time as possible to prepare for the attack—and to give them that time, Mpotwe must be delayed in starting from the ruins of Toli—as long as possible.

There was only one person who could conceivably cause any such delay, and that was Ki-Gor. He did not know exactly how he was to accomplish that delay, but he had to find a way—and find it soon.

For if Mpotwe and his cannibals were to leave Toli at once, they would arrive at Otempa at about the same moment that Helene and Hurree Das would float unsuspectingly downstream to the bridge. There would be fighting, and Helene and Hurree Das would be squarely between the opposing forces.

CHAPTER III

AS KI-GOR CLIMBED THE tree, he set to work with his knife on the great bundle of lianas that followed the treetrunk straight up like a cable of interwoven ropes. It was no great task to cut the clinging tendrils and loosen the lianas from the supporting tree. In a short time, Ki-Gor had yards and yards of tough, dependable rope, firmly knotted together. Coiling the rope over one shoulder, and still carrying the dead cannibal on the other, he descended the tree again to the lowermost bough.

Mpotwe was still orating, and growing more and more impassioned. The B'Kutu and their allies listened attentively—even though they had to get Mpotwe's thoughts at second-hand. Mpotwe spoke in Kara-mzili Zulu, and a man standing below him translated it into Chituba, the trade dialect of the Congo region.

But, at least, everyone was far too preoccupied to notice Ki-Gor fastening one end of his long cable of liana around the branch of the tree. Nor did anyone notice as he stealthily let the other end, which was looped in a small foot-loop, toward the ground. Not until Ki-Gor himself was halfway down the rope, the B'Kutu corpse still on his shoulder, did a few of the listening cannibals stare unbelievingly at him.

He had still a few seconds before these ignorant savages would credit their eyes and give the alarm. And a few seconds was all he needed. Even before he slipped one foot through the loop which hung scarcely six feet off the ground, he had begun to set the long rope swinging. And by the time the first cry of alarm was uttered, he was swinging back and forth through an increasingly longer arc.

As frightened shouts went up on all sides, Mpotwe broke off his harangue with a yelp of terror. He struggled up to a kneeling position and goggled at Ki-Gor. The jungle man swung toward him and with a surge of his mighty shoulders pitched the dead B'Kutu out on to the air. The limp body flew through the air and landed in a grotesque heap on the ground about fifteen feet in front of Mpotwe.

A quick, horrified gasp went up from the cannibals, and then there was a desperate babbling sound as those nearest to the tumbled corpse suddenly tried to go elsewhere in a great hurry. On the next swing of the long rope, Ki-Gor kicked his foot out of the loop and let go. His great bronzed body lanced through the air, back arched and feet together.

It was an appalling distance to drop, even for Ki-Gor, but his iron frame and prodigious muscular co-ordination were ready. He landed on the balls of his feet and sank down almost to a squatting position, the muscles of his legs acting like coiled-spring shock absorbers. Instantly, he sprang up again lightly, his feet almost leaving the ground, and ran forward several steps until he stood beside the dead cannibal.

Mpotwe gave a despairing shriek and flung a fat arm over his eyes.

"The ju-ju white man!" he cried. "It is Ki-Gor!"

The litter was none too well balanced on its improvised pedestal of rocks, and as the gross fat young prince shrank backward, it careened over with his enormous weight. The fear-struck Mpotwe made a feeble attempt to save himself, an attempt which was spectacularly unsuccessful. With a helpless shriek he rolled off the tilting litter on to the hard-packed ground.

A low moan went over the crowd, and died away into a breathless silence as Ki-Gor strolled over to the groveling chieftain.

"I come in peace, O Mpotwe," Ki-Gor intoned in Kara-mzili, and repeated the phrase in Chituba. "Cross me not, nor attempt to harm me, and you need not fear me."

With that he suddenly straddled the lumpy mass of flesh, bent over and lifted Mpotwe up by his armpits. The nephew of Dingazi must have weighed close to three hundred pounds, but Ki-Gor swung him up into the air as if he were a feather-pillow. Mpotwe was too terrified to utter a sound. Then with feet braced and biceps bulging, Ki-Gor set the astounded Kara-mzili prince back on his litter—the litter that required four men to carry it when Mpotwe lolled on it.

A dozen Kara-mzili warriors were moving forward protectively, but reluctantly. Ki-Gor swung around and glared at them. Trembling, they raised their spears.

"Touch me not!" Ki-Gor growled. "Or I will turn you into braying bull-frogs! Be warned of my mighty ju-ju!"

The Kara-mzili hastily lowered the spears and backed away precipitously. And beyond them, the B'Kutu who had been goggling at Ki-Gor's impressive demonstration of his physical might surged backward once again. Ki-Gor turned to Mpotwe. The fat prince, he noted, seemed to have rapidly regained composure—no doubt because he found himself quite unharmed at a time when fearful death seemed to have threatened.

"Oh, mighty Ki-Gor!" Mpotwe said in a subdued voice. "We did not expect to see you over here in this wilderness. What do you do here?"

"You know what I mean," Ki-Gor accused. "My ju-ju has told me that Mpotwe is up to new treacheries."

"No!" Mpotwe protested. "It is no treachery! The B'Kutu make war on the Bambala, and they chose me to lead them."

"Why should the B'Kutu make war on the Bambala?" Ki-Gor demanded. "The Bambala have done them no harm."

"The Bambala refuse to trade with us—with the B'Kutu," Mpotwe said. "They will not sell their good spears."

That was probably quite true, Ki-Gor reflected. Knowing how the Bambala detested the cannibals, it was not unlikely that they would refuse to have any trade relations with them.

"And so," Ki-Gor said, "you treacherously surrounded and butchered a whole Bambala village without warning."

"That is war," Mpotwe defended.

"Your kind of war, perhaps," Ki-Gor said scornfully "But let me tell you something—you won't surprise Otempa the same way."

Mpotwe's fat face expressed wary surprise. He was silent for a long moment, evidently thinking over Ki-Gor's last statement. Finally his heavy-lidded eyes flicked back over the jungle man.

"Your ju-ju," he said, "found out Otempa was the next place we were going. How does it know there will be no surprise?"

"There will be no surprise at Otempa," Ki-Gor said flatly.

There was another pause. Then Mpotwe said, "Not a single Bambala got away from Toli. Who could warn Otempa?"

Ki-Gor thought of that lone Bambala he had seen fleeing along the elephant trail. Unquestionably, that man had been outside the ring of cannibals that surrounded Toli. Ki-Gor was willing to gamble that he got through to Otempa with the news of the invasion. However, Ki-Gor was not going to tell Mpotwe about him. He had a better idea.

"I," said Ki-Gor. "I warned Otempa."

"You!" Mpotwe exclaimed, fear casting a shadow over his eyes. "How could you warn Otempa?"

"Ask not too many questions," Ki-Gor warned. "By my ju-ju, I made a sending. And this minute the Bambala are gathering their defenses at Otempa. When you get there with your loathsome cannibals, you will find the Bambala ready and waiting for you."

FEAR AND incredulity struggled for supremacy in Mpotwe's fat face. Ki-Gor began to assay his own position. He stood alone and—except for the knife at his belt—unarmed in the middle of a silent throng of ruthless, treacherous cannibals led by a ruthless, treacherous renegade from Kara-mzililand. There could be no doubt that Mpotwe feared him deeply and believed him capable of tremendous feats of magic. However, he knew that Mpotwe was afraid only of his magic. There was no question of Mpotwe and his men regarding Ki-Gor as anything but a very gifted human being. He was no god, or even a demigod. He was simply a mortal who, as long as he lived, could command supernatural weapons against them.

Behind Mpotwe's heavy eyes, Ki-Gor knew the renegade prince was probably trying to figure out some way of killing him without risk to himself. Once Ki-Gor was dead, Mpotwe no doubt felt he would be safe from that deadly magic. But—reading Mpotwe's mind further—who would take the fearful risk of attempting to kill Ki-Gor? Mpotwe and his Kara-mzili had once before seen Ki-Gor's ju-ju in action, and a terrifying experience it had been.

But—and Ki-Gor emphasized this in his own mind—the cannibals had never before seen Ki-Gor. The B'Kutu and their cousins the Tono and the scarred Tofoke had no evidence of Ki-Gor's magical powers. To be sure, they had seen an exhibition of his tremendous physical strength when he lifted the mountainous Mpotwe off the ground up onto his litter. Otherwise, they saw only a lone, half-naked white man whom the Kara-mzili seemed to fear for some reason. Ki-Gor guessed that Mpotwe was trying to find a way to induce the cannibals to kill Ki-Gor—induce them without Ki-Gor knowing he was doing it.

Now, as Ki-Gor watched him narrowly, the fat prince seemed to have decided on a plan of action. He folded his thick arms in a composed gesture and stared coldly at Ki-Gor.

"It is not given to many to be able to make a sending," he said coolly. Mpotwe was quite evidently trying to show the B'Kutu that he did not fear this Ki-Gor so very much after all. Ki-Gor picked up the challenge promptly.

"You think I did not make the sending to Otempa?" he demanded. "Then, continue to think so! But—don't be surprised when you attack Otempa and find the defenders ready and waiting for you!"

Ki-Gor was well aware that this was none too strong a retort. But, evidently it worried Mpotwe to some extent. The fat prince dropped his eyes and thought in silence.

Suddenly, Mpotwe raised his head and his face was contorted with malevolent rage.

"That was an unfriendly act, Ki-Gor!" he shouted. "To warn my enemies against a surprise attack from me!"

He raised both fat arms upward as if in imprecation. A warning signal buzzed at the back of Ki-Gor's brain. This sudden change in Mpotwe's demeanor was purely for effect. What was the purpose of it?

The jungle man spun around. A little B'Kutu arrow was floating through the air toward him. Deliberately, Ki-Gor stepped aside. The venomous dart dipped lazily past him and hit the ground at the very base of Mpotwe's pedestal.

Quick as thought, Ki-Gor whipped the B'Kutu's arrow out of his armband, the arrow which Hurree Das had cleansed and then coated with iodine. Holding it up, he shouted out in Chituba to the ring of B'Kutu who were furtively notching arrows.

"If you want to kill your leader," he cried, "I care not. But, be warned that your poisoned arrows will have no effect on me. My ju-ju gives me special protection against them. Watch!"

He held out his left arm and jabbed the iodine-smeared arrow point into the flesh above the elbow. A concerted gasp went over the B'Kutu, and then an expectant silence hung on the air. The tip of the arrow was well embedded in Ki-Gor's left arm. He let go of the shaft and let the arrow dangle from its tip. A thin stream of blood trickled from the wound.

"Already the poison is mingling with my blood," Ki-Gor shouted, pointing his right forefinger at the breathless crowd. "But it will have no effect on me—none at all. Watch now, and you will see how my ju-ju will conquer your deadly venom!"

It was a quite unnecessary admonition. The fascinated B'Kutu could not take their bulging eyes off him. For unless this strange white man had a ju-ju the like of which could hardly be imagined, he would very shortly show the well-known symptoms. His arm would begin to swell, his breathing would grow short and labored, and inside of twenty minutes, he would fall down dead.

Ki-Gor well knew the power of suspense. For a full five minutes he said not a word, but glared watchfully at the ring of bestial faces around him. He had a bad moment when the arrow-wound began to smart ferociously. Could something have gone wrong? Had some of the venom stayed on the arrow-tip in spite of the Hindu's careful cleansing? Then he remembered that once before Hurree Das had put iodine on an open wound of his, and that the iodine had stung like the sting of a scorpion. His face, however, did not betray his momentary doubt, and he took heart as the smarting gradually eased away.

The minutes crawled by in dead silence.

SOME STARING cannibals began to shift their feet uneasily. By all rights, this strange white man should have begun to show some effects from their fearful arrow venom. The blood had stopped flowing from his wound, and the little trickle had begun to dry on his arm. Yet there was only a slight reddening and swelling around the blackened tip of the arrow. There was no general angry swelling. His mighty chest rose and fell in an even cadence. His piercing blue eyes glared about with undiminished brightness. Cold fear began to close over the hearts of the cannibals. Never before had they seen man or beast survive their carefully concocted arrow venom.

Eventually, Ki-Gor reached deliberately across his chest and plucked the arrow from his left arm. He held up the point glistening with his own blood, so that all could see it. Then he strode over to the crumpled body of the B'Kutu he had killed in the tree.

"Hear me now, *O Basenji!*" he spat. *Basenji* meant bushman, savage, primitive jungle creature, and even though the word described the B'Kutu perfectly, they resented the term.

"O Basenji!" Ki-Gor repeated scornfully, "This mate of yours"—he stirred the dead body with his foot—"tried to kill me. But as you have seen, the arrow venom had no effect on me. What's more, the moment the point touched me, he fell dead. You can see that there are no wounds or marks on this body. Be warned, O Basenji!"

Swiftly, he tucked the arrow back in his arm-band, bent down and picked up the limp carcass of the B'Kutu. Then without warning he flung the body straight into the mass of B'Kutu in front of him. The savages promptly fell into the wildest confusion. Shrieking with terror, they fought with each other to get away from the horrid, contaminated carcass. An irresistible spirit of mischief seized Ki-Gor. He flung his arms in the air and gave vent to a tremendous roar of triumph.

To the already panic-stricken B'Kutu, this was the last straw. The rear ranks broke and streaked away, and the rest followed with howls of terror. Inside of three minutes, the entire pack of cannibals had melted into the jungle surrounding Toli. Ki-Gor followed them to the edge of the village, shouting and waving his arms and generally enjoying himself like a small boy stampeding a flock of chickens.

He stood for a moment triumphant at the far end of the village, his hands on his hips, watching the last of the grimy savages disappear into the gloomy forest. Unconsciously, his right hand slipped over and touched his upper left arm. Something was missing. Quickly, he looked down and saw that the arm band was gone. It had evidently snapped and fallen off while he was so energetically thrashing his arms around. Ki-Gor was slightly vexed with himself. He had tucked

Hurree Das' arrow back into that arm band, and now it had fallen to the ground somewhere behind him.

He turned, eyes on the ground, searching for the valuable arrow. Something made him look up. And his eyes met a very disagreeable sight.

While he had been chasing the cannibals out of Toli, Mpotwe had not been idle. The fat Kara-mzili prince had apparently come down off his litter and saved a panic among his own tall Kara-mzili warriors. And now he stood not ten yards away from Ki-Gor, his big spearmen ranged protectively about him. Their spears were leveled menacingly, although fear lurked in their eyes.

But there was no fear in Mpotwe's fat face. His heavy lidded eyes, on the contrary, glittered with enmity as he stared at Ki-Gor. Worse still he held a B'Kutu arrow in his hands, and Ki-Gor instinctively knew it was the one with iodine on the tip.

"Stay where you are," Mpotwe snapped. "Don't move—unless you want twelve spears through your guts. I'm beginning to think your ju-ju is not so mighty, after all. I'm beginning to think your ju-ju is no ju-ju at all, but just a neat little bundle of tricks."

Ki-Gor said nothing, but his face was a grim mask as he folded his arms expectantly over his chest.

"You can fool those ignorant Basenji," Mpotwe went on. "But you cannot fool me. This arrow did not poison you, because you took the poison off it, beforehand."

Mpotwe glared at Ki-Gor.

"Isn't that true?" he demanded.

Ki-Gor allowed a thin smile to appear on his lean face.

"What Mpotwe thinks," he said carelessly, "is no concern of mine."

The fat prince scowled furiously.

"Answer me!" he cried. "Or I will find ways to make you answer me!"

"Think what you please, O Mpotwe," Ki-Gor replied coolly. "And do what you please. If you are right and I really have no ju-ju—then you will be safe in doing anything to me you please. *But*"—and here Ki-Gor bared his teeth in a fierce grimace—"if you are wrong, the consequences may be terrible for you!"

Mpotwe hesitated just long enough for Ki-Gor to suspect that the fat prince was not quite so sure of himself as he wanted to seem. For a fleeting moment, the jungle man toyed with the idea of running an extra bluff with that arrow—of daring Mpotwe to try it on himself. If it worked, and Mpotwe was afraid to prick himself with it—then Ki-Gor's mastery of the situation would be maintained. However, if it did not work, then everything would be lost, and Ki-Gor would have absolutely no protection against Mpotwe. Ki-Gor decided against the idea.

It was not good having Mpotwe suspicious that his ju-ju was mere trickery, but as long as Mpotwe was not quite sure, Ki-Gor still had a chance of regaining the upper hand at some time or other. When Mpotwe finally spoke again, Ki-Gor's hope rose. For the Kara-mzili prince evidently had decided to postpone the issue, and Ki-Gor could wish for nothing better. Time, at this point, was Ki-Gor's ally.

"I will dispose of you later," Mpotwe said finally. "There is too much to be done right now, for me to take the time to deal with you in the way you deserve."

"It is good," said Ki-Gor with a crooked grin. "There will be plenty of time after you discover that the Bambala at Otempa are ready and waiting for you."

Mpotwe looked startled, and Ki-Gor followed his thrust up.

"You will wonder, O Mpotwe!" he jeered, "how Otempa could have been warned. For if my ju-ju is just a bag of tricks, then I could not have made a sending to Otempa."

The fat prince suddenly turned aside and began screaming commands at his Kara-mzili bodyguard. Evidently he did not choose to prolong the battle of wits.

Four of Mpotwe's biggest warriors now came forward and surrounded Ki-Gor, carrying more than a hint that he was to consider himself a prisoner. However, the jungle man was not too badly satisfied. The situation could have been a lot worse. As long as there was a tiny thread of doubt in Mpotwe's mind concerning Ki-Gor's magical powers, he had some sort of hold over the fat prince. There was, of course, the chance that Mpotwe would try out that arrow to find out whether it was harmless or not. Not on himself, that was certain, but on one of his own men, or one of the cannibals. If that happened, and the arrow was proved to have no venom—it would make Ki-Gor's position precarious.

But apparently Mpotwe considered that his first and most important job was to rally and collect his scattered army of cannibals. He set about this with typical Kara-mzili efficiency, sending out his warriors in pairs to scour the jungle, while four drummers kept up an incessant rhythm on two giant double-headed tomtoms.

EVEN SO, it was a long time before any of the B'Kutu or their allies could be persuaded to return to the village. Several times Ki-Gor caught Mpotwe looking longingly in his direction, and Ki-Gor surmised what was going on in the fat prince's crafty mind. If Ki-Gor's dead body could be exhibited to the B'Kutu, the cannibals would be convinced that it was safe for them to come back.

But evidently Mpotwe would not take the risk of trying to kill Ki-Gor himself, and none of his warriors was brave enough to try it, either. This was tremendously encouraging, and the jungle man squatted happily in the middle of his quartet of nervous guards, while the drums hammered away and the rest of the Kara-mzili beat the jungle dispiritedly for their cannibal allies.

Eventually, a few of the B'Kutu were discovered and caught and brought struggling back into the village. Mpotwe lectured them severely, while they cast frightened glances behind them at the imperturbable figure of Ki-Gor.

But the wily Mpotwe now played a winning card by commencing preparations for a cannibal feast. It was a sickening sight—as much for the Kara-mzili as for Ki-Gor—but it finally brought the B'Kutu and their cousins out of hiding. Warily they came at first, one by one, and then two by two. But after a while, as the cooking fires blazed up higher, and the bodies of the fallen Bambala were gathered and butchered, the cannibals began to swarm in.

Fighting down his rising gorge, Ki-Gor told himself that his ultimate object was achieved. He had set out to delay the immediate march of Mpotwe's army on Otempa—and he had succeeded. The afternoon was well advanced, and the cannibals would be in no state to move from Toli until the next day. That should give the men of Otempa plenty of time to arrange their defenses.

But now a new worry arose to assail Ki-Gor's mind. What about Helene and Hurree Das? They would arrive at Otempa in the canoe on schedule that evening and they would find no Ki-Gor. When he had left Helene, she had already been uneasy about his traveling so close to the border of the B'Kutu country. She would be bound to fear that the worst had happened to him when he did not show up at Otempa at the time he had promised to.

There was nothing to be done about it, however, but trust to Helene's good judgment in the matter. Even if he could make a break for freedom, Ki-Gor knew that he would be stalked by the B'Kutu—and he acknowledged that they were magnificent stalkers. They would be less inclined to fear him if he were running away, and he might receive in his flesh an arrow which had not been cleansed of its poison.

As long as Helene stayed put in Otempa and did nothing rash, Ki-Gor knew there was nothing to fear—for the present. It would be up to him the next day to figure out some means of ensuring her safety. As long as she stayed put—but Ki-Gor suddenly realized he had overlooked one factor.

Otempa would have been warned of the attack on Toli. Helene knew he was going to Toli. Helene would be in a state. And with that thought, worry settled down anew on Ki-Gor's mind. Helene had great faith in his ability to take care of himself, but in a situation like this she would be fearfully anxious about him. If she would only keep her head, Ki-Gor prayed, and not run out into the jungle to try and find him single-handed....

CHAPTER IV

IT WAS A GRUESOME evening. The Kara-mzili warriors were as disgusted with the nauseous scene as Ki-Gor was, and withdrew to a great campfire of their own. The jungle man saw that Mpotwe's men did not intend to relax their vigilant guard of him, so he philosophically curled up and went sound asleep amidst the obscene revelry of the cannibals.

As a result, the next morning Ki-Gor was probably the most refreshed individual in the shambles that was once the border village of Toli. Mpotwe sent his haggard and harassed Kara-mzili among the bloated, sluggish B'Kutu to try to rouse them for the march on Otempa. It was a prodigious task, for the cannibals had no sense of discipline and were extremely disinclined to move from their gruesome surroundings. In the resulting confusion, Ki-Gor saw an opportunity to make a clean getaway.

He ignored it, and stayed right where he was.

If Ki-Gor had been of a reflective nature, he might have been surprised at himself for such an action—or lack of action. But he had wakened from his long sleep with a well-defined plan for the day, a plan which he hoped would remove the threat of danger from Helene and Hurree Das, and which would incidentally benefit the easy-going and peace-loving Bambala nation. The only way that plan could be put into operation was by his staying close to Mpotwe.

The fat prince was in a savage mood at the interruption in his schedule that Ki-Gor had caused. It was well along in the morning before he could finally get his force under way—a delay of some eighteen hours of his march on Otempa. And even then, his motley horde of savages did not move with their accustomed speed.

Ki-Gor was ordered to walk beside Mpotwe's litter—an order he did not mind at all, as it gave him an idea of how the renegade prince ran his army. But for the duration of the march, Mpotwe constantly addressed veiled threats at Ki-Gor—little asides that hinted that Ki-Gor had no magical powers, at all, but was a mere trickster, not to be feared by any Kara-mzili. To all of these, Ki-Gor smiled grimly and returned one answer—"Wait until you get to Otempa!"

It was about two hours after the noon sun when Mpotwe was informed that the first wave of B'Kutu were within reach of the outer defenses of Otempa—that is, that part of Otempa which was on the near side of the river. Most of the town was on the farther side, the southwest side of the river in Bambalaland proper, but in the course of years a considerable number of Bambala had moved across the vine bridge, and a sort of residential suburb had sprung up behind the three rings of defense shelters.

Ki-Gor thought it probable that Helene and Hurree Das would have landed on the far side of the river, and, therefore, would be safe from any preliminary fighting. However, he could not be sure of that, and he determined to put his plan into action immediately. For his plan—if it succeeded—would stop hostilities even before they began.

"Go back to those B'Kutu quickly," Mpotwe was telling his messenger. "Tell them to lie still until all the rest are close up behind them. Our full force must strike without warning. Go! Hurry!"

"Wait!"

Ki-Gor's voice was twice as commanding as Mpotwe's. In spite of himself, the messenger paused. Ki-Gor turned on the astonished prince before he could say a word.

"Your B'Kutu," he stated in a tone that brooked no disagreement, "Your B'Kutu are in for a bloody surprise. Scores of them will be killed and you still won't take Otempa!"

Mpotwe's neck swelled. "What surprise?" he bellowed.

Ki-Gor half-closed his eyes wearily, as if his patience were wearing thin. "How many times have I told you, O Mpotwe," he said, "that the Bambala are ready and waiting for you. I warned them. I made a sending to Otempa from Toli."

"You made no sending!" Mpotwe shouted wrathfully. "You cannot make a sending! You have no ju-ju! You are a fraud!"

"Silence, Mpotwe!" Ki-Gor shouted back. "I am getting tired of your insults! I gave you more than fair warning! I warned you of my ju-ju—I warned you of its consequences. I was about to suggest a plan to you whereby you could accomplish your aims without risking the lives of your B'Kutu. But you will not listen. Instead you insult me! Go, then! Throw away your warriors! Throw them into a bloody ambush! When they stagger back, bleeding and shattered, from the Bambala steel—then remember that Ki-Gor is no fraud!"

Mpotwe glared ferociously at his prisoner. But there was hint of fear in his close, secretive eyes.

"Go on!" Ki-Gor taunted. "Send your messenger! See? He stands here twiddling his thumbs while the great Mpotwe tries to make up his mind about Ki-Gor's magic!"

Ki-Gor threw his head back in derisive laughter.

IT WAS a brave front. More than that, it was a desperate gamble. Ki-Gor was gambling that that lone Bambala he had seen streaking through the jungle before the attack on Toli had gotten safely through to Otempa with his warning. If the Bambala had not gotten through— and Mpotwe attacked and found the garrison unready—Ki-Gor's stock would be low indeed. Therefore, Ki-Gor was trying to bluff Mpotwe out of even attacking at all.

The renegade prince sat irresolute for a moment, while his messenger awaited his commands. For a moment, Ki-Gor thought his bluff was going to prevail. Plaintively, Mpotwe spoke.

"What is this plan?" he said. "How can I obtain my objects without fighting?"

"Send an embassy to the Bambala," Ki-Gor said promptly. "Tell them your demands, and see how many of them they will grant rather than fight you."

The jungle man held his breath as he waited for Mpotwe's repercussion. But fate intervened before the fat prince could utter an opinion. Another messenger arrived, a B'Kutu who had been sent back from the advance guard.

This second messenger was obviously not the bearer of good news.

He was a petty B'Kutu chief, disheveled and blood-flecked. Breath-lessly, he told of how that advance wave of cannibals did not wait for orders from Mpotwe, but had crept right up on to the outer row of defense shelters. These appeared not even to be manned, and the B'Kutu were emboldened by this seeming carelessness on the part of the Bambala to keep right on going toward the next line of defenses.

To their amazement and dismay, they were suddenly and fiercely attacked from behind. There had been Bambala aplenty, but they had stayed hidden until the cannibals had unsuspectingly gone past them. A shower of spears had taken a fearful toll of the B'Kutu, and then the Bambala had leaped vengefully into close quarters. It was with the greatest difficulty, the messenger reported, that the B'Kutu had extricated themselves from the ambush, and their losses were very heavy.

Mpotwe shot a frightened glance at Ki-Gor, and Ki-Gor heaved a discreet sigh of relief. The fat prince could not help but believe now that Ki-Gor had made a sending to Otempa warning them to be ready for an attack. The jungle man tensed himself for the next development.

But the next development went far beyond anything Ki-Gor had expected. Mpotwe began screaming and babbling at the top of his lungs.

"Attack! Attack!" he yelled. "With everybody! Or everything is lost! Everyone—attack!"

As he screeched his orders, Mpotwe put both fat legs over the side of the litter, and jumped clumsily to the ground. He threw one last terrified look over his shoulder at Ki-Gor, and then lumbered away heavily, as if he were desperate for his life.

"Keep him off!" Mpotwe shrieked. "Keep him away from me! He is a great ju-ju!"

Ki-Gor's guards backed quickly away from him, and then, while he was still too astonished to do anything, they turned and fled precipitately after their master.

Ki-Gor stood for a moment in perplexity watching the flight of the Kara-mzili away from him. He assumed that Mpotwe's cries of "Attack!" meant that his whole force should attack the defenders of Otempa. It was the logical thing to do, the surprise having failed. Sheer weight of numbers crushingly applied must now take the place of surprise.

The jungle man turned and snaked up a tree-trunk. Arrived in the lower branches, he set off by the tree-route in the direction of the Mikenye River, which he estimated could not he very far away. Mpotwe's precipitate flight, and his orders for a general assault had temporarily upset Ki-Gor's plan for instituting negotiations. Ki-Gor had hoped to create a lull in the hostilities during which he could seek out Helene and Hurree Das and remove them to a safer place. As matters stood now, there was no lull, and he had to find them while a pitched battle was going on around them. And while the forewarned Bambala had scored in the first round, Ki-Gor doubted that they could long hold their ground against Mpotwe's surging hordes. They must be fearfully outnumbered, and while they could probably give a good account of themselves against the cannibals, they would be outmatched by Mpotwe's strapping Kara-mzili if he chose to throw them into the fray.

The sounds of battle grew in Ki-Gor's ears as he swung tirelessly and swiftly through the trees. Ki-Gor visualized the jungle hordes swarming up to the Bambala defenses all along the semicircular ring. He quickened his pace, and soon emerged on to the bank of the river.

Less than a quarter of a mile downstream he could see the vine bridge that connected the two halves of Otempa—or rather which connected the main part of Otempa with its outpost across the river. The bridge was crowded with black figures streaming over to the main town away from the fighting zone. Ki-Gor's keen eyes made sure that the figures were almost all women and children making a belated evacuation—they were most certainly not Bambala warriors.

Where, Ki-Gor asked himself, were Helene and Hurree Das?

IT BEING just before the rainy season, the Mikenye was quite low, and there was a narrow strip of muddy beach all along the bank down to the vine bridge. Ki-Gor set off down this strip at a fast lope, hoping that the fighting had not extended quite to the river bank. He was not a moment too soon.

Half way to the bridge, a little knot of scarfaced Tofoke erupted from the undergrowth beside Ki-Gor. The jungle man saw them a fraction of a second before they saw him. Hardly slackening his pace, he leaned over and scooped up a ten-pound rock. Just as the bestial Tofoke caught sight of him, he flung the rock hard into their midst. One of them never knew what hit him, and the rest scrambled back shrieking into the undergrowth.

The din of battle mounted higher and higher as Ki-Gor swept into Otempa. The great open square at the end of the bridge was crowded with women and children and old men, all frantic to get safely across the river to the main part of the town. So dazed by the shock of the attack were they that Ki-Gor caused scarcely any comment from them as he pushed through their midst. Here and there, Ki-Gor saw wounded warriors looking equally dazed. He went up to one of them.

"Where is your leader, the Chief Kwete?" he demanded of the warrior.

The man regarded him stupidly for a moment, and then said, "Ah! You are he who is called Ki-Gor! Have you brought us help? For we sorely need it."

"Maybe I have," Ki-Gor replied, then repeated his question. "Where is Kwete?"

"Out the North Trail," the man said. "I just left him. It's our strongest point—if we can hold it. They need more arrows, though. That's what I came back for—"

The man's voice trailed off into a mumble. His eyes closed and his head nodded. Ki-Gor caught him as he started to sag to the earth.

"You are hurt," Ki-Gor said gently. "Where are the arrows? I will take them to Kwete."

The sinking warrior gestured feebly behind him. Ki-Gor stared over the heads of the crowd and saw several bundles of arrows piled against the base of a tree. The jungle man looked down again at the Bambala.

"Rest easy, brother," he said. "I will take the arrows along."

The blood had drained out of the warrior's face, and under the coating of red clay, it was a ghastly color. He was quite evidently dying. Yet there seemed to be something else he wanted to tell Ki-Gor. The jungle man bent his head to catch the faint whisper.

"The Red-Haired One"—he heard—"your woman—with Kwete—"

An ugly thrill went through Ki-Gor.

"What was that you said, brother?" he demanded. "My woman?"

But the warrior was dead.

CHAPTER V

KI-GOR CARRIED THE LIMP body over to the tree where the bundles of arrows lay. He laid it down gently and looked around to see a small group of curious Bambala watching him. There was another wounded warrior among them carrying a bow. At Ki-Gor's request, the warrior handed over the bow, and Ki-Gor slipped it up over his arm and on to his left shoulder. Then he picked up three of the bundles and set off up the North Trail.

There must have been about a hundred iron-headed arrows in each bundle, and awkward and heavy they were to carry. A lesser man might have found himself unequal to the task, but Ki-Gor swung all three bundles over his right shoulder, curled his arm over them to balance them, and broke into a rapid trot.

All these actions, however, were more or less automatic and mechanical. Ki-Gor's brain was burning with the Bambala's dying words. There could be no mistaking what he said, and Helene must be somewhere ahead of him along the trail in the thick of the fighting. It was a rude shock, for Ki-Gor had hopefully come to believe that Helene would have stayed away from danger until he arrived, at least.

If he had not been so worried about Helene, Ki-Gor would have been considerably annoyed. Because she must have known she was walking into danger—the garrison at Otempa were warned of the B'Kutu attack as evidenced by their readiness for it when it came. But Ki-Gor was too anxious for Helene's safety to be annoyed very long with her. And his anxiety increased with every rapid step forward along the trail.

As he left the last houses of the town behind and plunged into the jungle, the noises of battle became louder and louder, the high-pitched venomous scream of the cannibals echoed throughout the cloistered forest and was answered by the defiant yelps of the Bambala. The ground thudded under the heels of hundreds of hurrying blacks, and the undergrowth crackled under the weight of grimy bodies. And, as if the sounds were not in themselves sufficient indication of the desperate conflict in progress, Ki-Gor met every now and then wounded Bambala stumbling back along the path. One of them was hacking at his arm with a knife. Evidently, the warrior knew of no other way to treat a wound made by a poisoned arrow.

There was no need for the jungle man to stop and ask how the battle was going. Some of the wounded men were too far gone to do anything but stare dully at him. But others hailed him feebly and urged him to hurry forward with the arrows.

"We're outnumbered up there," they told him, "but we can hold them off as long as our arrows last."

"Where is Kwete?" Ki-Gor asked one of them.

"You will come to a place," he was answered, "where the trail crosses a stream by a footbridge. Turn off the trail there to your left, and follow the stream a short distance. You will come to one of our strong points, and you will find Kwete there."

It was not many minutes later that Ki-Gor arrived at the stream. Before turning off to his left he halted. The battle sounds had suddenly died down for no reason that Ki-Gor could think of. The shrill shouts which had filled the air a moment ago had now stilled, leaving an ominous silence that was broken only by the occasional scream of a wounded man.

What had happened?

Ki-Gor could not believe that Mpotwe's men had been beaten off—not that easily. There were too many of them. Just then, the ground under his feet hummed a little, and a moment later a dozen or so Bambala came tumbling down the path toward him. They came from the direction of the enemy and were evidently an advanced post in retreat.

Ki-Gor stood grimly in the middle of the path and waited for them to come up to him. As they panted toward him, their clay-smeared faces showed mild astonishment.

"Where are you going?" Ki-Gor demanded bluntly.

"The posts on either side of us gave way," one Bambala explained. "Without support we would have been surrounded and killed. We took advantage of the lull to get out."

"How far back were you going to go?" Ki-Gor asked.

The leader of the little group looked sheepish. He glanced around him as if measuring the possibilities of defending the footbridge. Then he said, "We will go no farther. Give us some arrows and we will stay here and protect Kwete's flank."

Ki-Gor grunted approval and dumped one of his bundles on the ground.

"What does the lull mean?" he asked. "Were they beaten off?"

"No," the Bambala said emphatically. "They were breaking through everywhere—but they were taking heavy losses. And for some reason, they just turned and ran away."

"What makes you think they will attack again?" Ki-Gor asked.

"Twice already they have attacked and retired," the Bambala said, "and then attacked again."

That was unusual, Ki-Gor reflected. Battles in the Congo—indeed in most of Africa—conformed ordinarily to a single pattern. A tribe attacked—bravely, even recklessly. If the attack succeeded, the battle was won. If it failed, the battle was lost. Few tribes even of the best fighting stock resisted attack for long, or persisted in pressing for long an unsuccessful assault. The great exception to this rule were the Kara-mzili. And unquestionably the secret of the Kara-mzili's military success was the rigid discipline which sent them attacking again and again opponents who beat their first charge.

Ki-Gor watched this little group of Bambala distribute the arrows and then take up positions around the footbridge. Then he plunged down into the stream and waded off in the direction of Kwete's position.

Before he realized he was anywhere near the Bambala chieftain's defense post, a spear went whizzing past his head and voices rose in challenge.

"Save your spears for the enemy!" Ki-Gor roared. "It is Ki-Gor—with arrows for you!"

Instantly, three Bambala rose out of the undergrowth with contrite faces.

"Shame on our heads, O Friend—" they began, but Ki-Gor brushed off their apologies and told them to take him to Kwete. A moment later, he held Helene in his arms.

"Oh Ki-Gor!" she whispered, "I've nearly gone crazy! I should know by now that you can take care of yourself, but—"

"I'm here, aren't I?" Ki-Gor said gently, and patted her back. "Now, there's no time to lose—"

He looked swiftly around. Kwete was coming toward him, and beside the chieftain Hurree Das stood up. The Hindu had evidently been doctoring a wounded warrior. His umbrella was open and lying on its side sheltering the head of the warrior from the sun.

"My goodness gracious, Ki-Gor!" Hurree Das called out gaily.

"Most unexpected pleasure—having you dropping in like this! What is general outlook for all in your opinion?"

Ki-Gor grinned noncommittally and took Kwete's extended hand.

"The arrows will save our lives, Ki-Gor," the chieftain said.

"Will they attack again, you think?" Ki-Gor asked. "Without doubt," Kwete said grimly.

THE JUNGLE man looked out beyond the wicked breastworks that enclosed the miniature fort. The position was well-chosen in a little copse surrounded on three sides by a wide tobacco field. At the rear a natural covered runway of underbrush led off to the wooded stream from which Ki-Gor had come. It was like most of the Bambala "strong points" in commanding open fields. Any enemy would have to attack without cover, exposed to the arrows of the defenders.

This tobacco field was dotted with black shapes, and a score or more of grimy B'Kutu bodies lay in grotesque positions in front of the wicker breastwork. Ki-Gor turned back to Kwete.

"How soon can help come from the south?" he asked.

"I sent to King Masolo the minute I heard the B'Kutu were attacking Toli. I should have had word from him before now. But"—Kwete shrugged—"I haven't." Ki-Gor shook his head. Well he knew the easy-going Bambala and the intolerable slowness with which they were quite likely to meet even such a serious emergency as this. Bluntly, Ki-Gor inquired of Kwete how many men he commanded around Otempa. The answer was discouraging—the Bambala were prodigiously outnumbered by Mpotwe's invaders.

"Without immediate help," Ki-Gor told Kwete, "you can't possibly defend Otempa this side of the river."

A frown of disagreement appeared on Kwete's handsome face.

"You probably won't be able to withstand this next attack," Ki-Gor pursued. "We threw back the others," Kwete pointed out.

"Not everywhere," Ki-Gor said. He told the Bambala chief about the group he had met retreating along the North Trail, and their story of being left unsupported. And even as Ki-Gor spoke, a wounded Bambala arrived from another direction with the news that two other defensive posts had been abandoned to the left of Kwete's position. For a moment, the chieftain looked dashed. Then he raised his head dramatically.

"We will stay here and defend the place to the last," he declared. "We will die fighting."

"No matter how heroically you die," Ki-Gor observed drily, "it will not necessarily save Otempa—or prevent Mpotwe from crossing the river and carrying the war into Bambalaland. And if that happens"— Ki-Gor shot a keen look at Kwete—"all the Bambala warriors will not be able to stop him."

Kwete looked distressed.

"What about your neighbors, the Bushongo?" Ki-Gor asked. "Would they come to your help?"

Kwete shook his head. "They are blood-kin to us," he replied, "but they have always been jealous of us. It's more likely that they would jump in and start grabbing on their own account."

"Then your situation is serious, and your responsibility great," Ki-Gor said. "You have to keep Mpotwe from crossing the river. And you have to find a means quickly—before this next attack begins."

The jungle man moved toward the breastwork and stared across the tobacco field at the edge of the forest beyond. Kwete followed him.

"What do you think I should do?" he asked plaintively. "Retreat across the bridge now?"

"That would be disastrous," Ki-Gor said. "Your enemies would overtake you and cut you to pieces while you were doing it."

"What shall I do, then?"

"You should count yourself lucky," Ki-Gor replied, "if you can get your people back across the river without loss of life."

"How will I do that?"

"Consent to a parley with Mpotwe."

"What?" Kwete looked at Ki-Gor aghast.

"Let me explain," Ki-Gor said. "Mpotwe does not know just how strong you are now. He probably thinks you are stronger than you actually are. If he could gain to the river's edge without any more fighting, he might consider that a sufficient profit."

Kwete looked shocked. "You would have me abandon territory without a fight?"

"You need time more than territory," Ki-Gor pointed out "If you can get safely across the bridge with what men you have left—then you can hold it until help arrives. But"—Ki-Gor made an impatient gesture—"you have no time to argue about it. If you want to do it, I will go and talk to Mpotwe, but I have to do it this minute, before he launches his final attack. So decide quickly—whether to die bravely, but uselessly, or to save what you can of Otempa."

Kwete glanced across the tobacco field at the border of the jungle. There were unmistakable signs of renewing activity over there. The Bambala chieftain sighed and shook his head.

"I don't know how you can accomplish it," he said. "But if Mpotwe calls for a parley, I will discuss terms with him. Not directly—I will not speak face to face with the cutthroat—but through you as an intermediary."

Ki-Gor wheeled and walked toward Hurree Das. He had committed himself to a desperate errand, and he was not quite as sure how he was going to accomplish it. But Hurree Das's big black umbrella had given him an idea.

"My friend," he said to the Hindu, "you and Helene must go back over the bridge right away. I may succeed and I may not, but Kwete will grant that you two should be sent to safety. I am going over to talk to Mpotwe. Will you give me that thing?"

Ki-Gor pointed to the umbrella, and received a prompt and voluble acquiescence from the learned Hurree.

FORTHWITH THEN, the B'Kutu and Tofoke who were gathering on the far side of the tobacco field for a final and supreme assault on the Bambala were treated to an unexpected and wholly unwelcome sight.

The great White Witch who had struck such terror to their hearts back in Toli suddenly appeared from the Bambala position. He was walking coolly across the tobacco field toward the forest all by himself, apparently totally oblivious to the thunderstruck savages watching him. In his right hand, he carried a Bambala spear with a tuft of grass waving from the tip—the sign of peace. His left hand was supporting an extraordinary instrument the like of which none of the B'Kutu had ever seen before. It looked like a black shield, round and dish-shaped, held horizontally over the Witch's head by means of a slender pole.

The B'Kutu stirred uneasily and immediately sent a messenger to Mpotwe informing him of the reappearance of Ki-Gor. And as Ki-Gor came closer and closer to them, they prudently retired through the jungle before him.

Mpotwe, as it happened, was not far away. In fact, he was on his way to the very group of B'Kutu who sent him the messenger. With him were his own Kara-mzili warriors whom he was planning to throw in to battle behind the initial assault of the cannibals against Kwete's position. When the messenger arrived telling of Ki-Gor, the fat prince flew into a rage.

"Superstitious fools!" he cried, "to be afraid of a single man!"

And he urged his litter bearers to put on speed and carry him to the cowering cannibals as quickly as possible. In a short while, he was among the retreating B'Kutu, screaming curses at them. But a few moments later, a voice broke in on his imprecations—a powerful deep-throated voice shouting his name.

"Mpotwe!" Ki-Gor roared. "O Mpotwe! Stop your shouting! Listen to Ki-Gor's words and profit from them!"

The renegade prince suddenly became as still as his B'Kutu savages. His pale face grew paler and he cowered on his litter. The Kara-mzili clustered protectively around him and stared off at the lone white giant who picked his way toward them through the light undergrowth. The B'Kutu all around retired even more briskly, their pointed faces sullen masks. Only one of them was brave enough to turn and stand in front of Ki-Gor.

"Shoot! Shoot!" Mpotwe murmured.

The B'Kutu lifted his bow and released the string. A tiny deadly dart floated through the air. Without relaxing his stride, Ki-Gor swung the umbrella downwards. The envenomed arrow tip glanced off the ferrule and barely pierced the fabric beside it. The watching B'Kutu gave a moan of dismay as Ki-Gor lifted the umbrella over his head with the little arrow dangling by its barb.

"That should be enough," Ki-Gor said sternly. "Stay your murderous hand for a moment now, Mpotwe, and hear what I have to say. It will be to your benefit."

Fear and incredulity struggled for supremacy in Mpotwe's fat face, but he said nothing and awaited Ki-Gor's next words.

"I told you the men of Otempa were warned and would be ready for you," the jungle man said, "but you wouldn't believe me. You have lost heavily in unsuccessful attacks. You are about to launch another one. This attack will be beaten off, too. And when it is, your B'Kutu will melt away. You will have gained nothing."

Ki-Gor paused. For a moment he was tempted to go much farther than his original plan. Just that little trick with the umbrella, an unfamiliar object to these primeval savages, had put them in such awe of him that he might be able—at that moment—to chase them all far away from Otempa. But, Ki-Gor reflected, it was a possibility and not a certainty. And as long as there was a chance that too daring a move might fail, he could not risk it. His immediate task was to stop all hostilities, and he had better limit himself to that.

"To save your face, Mpotwe," Ki-Gor said, "you have to win at least a partial victory. Call for a parley, and you may get some of what you want without spilling any more blood for it."

Mpotwe's black eyes glittered craftily.

"You just came from the Bambala," he said. "Did they tell you to tell me this?"

"No," Ki-Gor said promptly. "In fact, Kwete, their chief, said he would not talk to you face to face. But if you call for a parley, he will talk through me as a go-between."

Mpotwe looked away in silence, as if he were thinking the proposition over. Ki-Gor suddenly could not help but feel that his plan asked a great deal of Mpotwe's credulity. To his surprise, however, the Kara-mzili prince swung around with a gesture of decision.

"Very well," Mpotwe said, "I will call for a parley. It can do no harm. If Kwete will not grant my demands, I can still attack him."

Ki-Gor was so pleased with this unexpected acquiescence by Mpotwe that for the moment he forgot to be suspicious. The fat prince acted with great promptness, sending messengers along his lines to tell his jungle warriors to stay quiet until further orders. Then Mpotwe ordered his litter moved to the edge of the jungle where he could see the Bambala strong point across the tobacco field. And presently, Ki-Gor strode back over that field with a formal request from Mpotwe to Kwete for a discussion of peace terms.

THE JUNGLE man was to cross and re-cross the tobacco field many times that day in his capacity as intermediary, but he did not mind it in the least. The most important thing was that his plan seemed to be working even better than he had ever hoped.

Kwete's first counter to Mpotwe's original request was a demand that the attacking forces be withdrawn a half mile from the positions they then occupied. Mpotwe assented without a word, and the parley was on.

Mpotwe first demanded that all of Bambalaland be surrendered to him. Kwete's answer to that was the unconditional surrender of Mpotwe and his forces. Neither commander had the slightest expec-

tation that these demands would be accepted. They were merely ultimate aims, and each commander fully expected that they would be
whittled down to the point where they approached each other closely
enough so that a meeting of minds might be near. Hours of haggling
and bargaining and counter-bargaining went by while the whittling
process went on. Patiently, Ki-Gor went back and forth across the
field, hard put to it, sometimes, to keep a straight face as each chieftain received the other's latest proposal and denounced it in the
strongest terms.

At long last, a compromise was reached. It was precisely what
Ki-Gor had recommended to Kwete in the beginning. The Bambala
were to evacuate Otempa on the west side of the river, retiring un-
molested across the bridge. Mpotwe promised no further aggression
until another series of talks was held concerning whether the Bambala
should sell the B'Kutu any weapons.

Kwete was jubilant over the outcome. Now that he and his surviving warriors were safe across the bridge, he admitted that he could
not have held out against another B'Kutu attack—particularly if it
had been followed up by a charge of Mpotwe's own Kara-mzili
bodyguard. Ki-Gor was satisfied that his plan had finally worked out
and that he had been able to stop fighting as long as Helene and
Hurree Das were in the fighting zone and in danger of being involved.
About the future of the Bambala, Ki-Gor was not so optimistic.

"I'm afraid," he told Kwete, "that your fighting has only just begun."

"Ah, but wait until our reinforcements arrive," Kwete said. "The
little cannibals can't stand up to us, man for man."

Ki-Gor was not even sure of that. The B'Kutu had shown desperate courage that very day, and although no one could have been braver
than the Bambala that day, they were still too civilized to fight with
the same zest as the cannibals.

"Have those reinforcements begun to come in yet?" Ki-Gor inquired.

The Bambala said they had not, but that they ought to at any
moment. Ki-Gor had his private opinion about that, knowing the
Bambala habit of procrastination. And yet, for the safety of all Bambalaland, the Otempa garrison should be reinforced, and reinforced
heavily as quickly as possible. For the wily Mpotwe would observe
the armed truce just so long as it suited his own purposes, and not a
minute longer.

"What will you do, Kwete, if Mpotwe tries to cross the river before the reinforcements come?" he asked casually.

"The only way he can come is across the bridge," Kwete answered. "If he does that, we can defend this end easily—or even cut the bridge if we are too hard pressed. There is no other way he can come. The B'Kutu are terribly afraid of the river. They would never dare swim across, and they have no boats. So, for the moment, we are perfectly safe. Later, I hope we'll be strong enough to go back across the river ourselves and reconquer the land we surrendered today."

Ki-Gor in his heart did not like to hear Kwete sound so complacent. Although he could not deny the logic of the chieftain's words, he felt that something was being overlooked. Mpotwe was not the sort of man you could merely shut up on the other side of a river, and then forget about. Mpotwe should be watched—carefully, vigilantly.

However, the jungle man felt that he had done his share in helping the gallant but improvident Bambala. It behooved him now to take his wife and their friend the Hindu doctor and go away from there as soon as he politely could. That proved to be not very soon.

The Bambala were determined to have a great feast that night, with Ki-Gor as the guest of honor. He had not the slightest desire to stay so long, but there was no way out of the situation. The Bambala would have been mortally hurt if he had walked out on them. One thing encouraged him a little, and that was the arrival of a contingent of fifty warriors from the interior of Bambalaland—the first, so they said, of large reinforcements.

The rest of the day was given over to elaborate preparations for the feast. The cleanly Bambala washed themselves scrupulously clean, and then daubed their glistening bodies all over with fresh red clay. After that, they spent hours doing each other's hair in the complicated coiffure that was so distinctly theirs.

No more reinforcements arrived that afternoon, but Ki-Gor was apparently the only person in Otempa who was bothered by the fact. The gay Bambala were completely absorbed in their festival, and seemed to have all but forgotten the existence of the B'Kutu menace just across the river. It was only after the most strenuous pleading by Ki-Gor that Kwete eventually provided a strong detachment to guard the bridge while the feast went on. The detachment was to be relieved at short intervals by new groups, so that no one would be deprived of the fun of the party.

This, of course, did not help the vigilance at the bridge. Each new group relieving was more intoxicated on beer than the one preceding. And in the end, it was Ki-Gor of all the people in Otempa who kept the sharpest watch on the farther bank of the river.

The surrendered portion of Otempa provided a sharp contrast to the riotous scenes of revelry in the main town. There were campfires, many of them, as Ki-Gor observed. But there was an unusual lack of activity of any kind. Ki-Gor liked the whole situation less and less.

At three o'clock the next morning, most of the Bambala were lying snoring in beery slumber. A few die-hards were singing and carousing here and there, but they were too happy to pay much attention to Ki-Gor as he walked past them with Helene and Hurree Das following sleepily. The jungle man led the way down to the river where the canoe was beached. By the light of the few campfires still alive, the trio launched the canoe and set off in the pitch blackness upstream. Only then did Ki-Gor heave a sigh of relief.

CHAPTER VI

WHILE THE MIKENYE RIVER was deep and sluggish all around the great U which Ki-Gor was retracing, the current was swift enough to cut down the normal speed of the canoe by nearly half. It was nearly noon by the time the canoe with its three occupants neared the base of the U where the river, from going southward, would turn sharply east, and then equally sharply north.

All during that time, Ki-Gor had been thinking about his happy-go-lucky Bambala friends. He was sure that Mpotwe would attack them sooner or later, and that they would not have the resources to withstand him. They should have called on the Bushongo, or the Tetela. They had not done so, and Ki-Gor was sorely afraid that they would need somebody's help, and that soon.

"Let's go ashore," Ki-Gor said abruptly, and swept the bow of the canoe toward the south bank. Helene raised her paddle and looked back in surprise.

"What are you going to do, Ki-Gor?" she asked.

"I think I'll leave you two again," Ki-Gor said with decision, "and travel overland. This going upstream is a little slow, and I've decided I ought to get to the nearest Tetela settlements as soon as possible."

"Tetela?" Helene echoed, wonderingly.

"Yes," Ki-Gor said. "I've decided that somehow they have got to help the Bambala—whether the Bambala ask for their help or not."

"Well, you know best," Helene said doubtfully. "But, do you think the Tetela will go to the help of the Bambala?"

"I've got to persuade them to, somehow," Ki-Gor said.

"Aha!" exclaimed Hurree Das, silent up till now. "Personally, I am inclining to wagering small amount on success of Ki-Gor's enterprise. Ki-Gor has astonishing powers of persuasion, don't you know?"

Helene grinned. Hurree Das did that to her with his flowery English. Furthermore, there was something to what he said—concerning Ki-Gor's powers of persuasion.

"Well, thank goodness," Helene said, "you're going to travel on the opposite side of the river, this time, from those dreadful cannibals."

"Yes," Ki-Gor smiled. "But, as a matter of fact, even if I did go on the other side of the river, I don't expect I'd see any B'Kutu."

"Yes, of course," Helene said. "I suppose Mpotwe will keep them close to Otempa while he figures his next move."

She reached her paddle out ahead as a fender as the canoe approached the bank. Ki-Gor swung the stern around, then stepped out in the shallow water and held the canoe steady. To the accompaniment of anxious murmurings from Hurree Das, Helene then moved back to the stern position. Ki-Gor released his hold on the canoe and straightened up.

"From here up," he said, "the current is very light. If you keep going steadily, you should be able to make it to the first Tetela village by sundown. I'll be there to meet you."

"Are you sure?" Helene said mischievously. "The last time we made a date to meet somewhere, it seems to me you were delayed."

"Who knows the future?" Ki-Gor said, with Arabic simplicity. "But I'll try to be there, this time." He swung himself up on to the bank and looked back with a grin. "Be careful of the crocodiles," he said, and disappeared into the undergrowth.

As Helene paddled upstream, she felt singularly light-hearted. The matter of Ki-Gor being involved with the B'Kutu had frightened her more than she had admitted to her stalwart mate. She, herself, had once been a captive of a cannibal tribe—in fact, Ki-Gor had arrived only in the nick of time to save her from their stew pots. And ever since then, she had had an awful dread of the very idea of cannibals.

But now, she and Ki-Gor were well out of the fight between the

Bambala and the invading B'Kutu, and she was thoroughly glad of it. To be sure, Ki-Gor still had to induce the warlike Tetela to go to the help of the Bambala. But Helene made up her mind that she was going to put her foot down on any further participation of Ki-Gor's in the war. If he could send the Tetela against the B'Kutu—well and good. But that was as far as she wanted Ki-Gor to go. She dug her paddle into the water hard, to emphasize her thoughts.

"Dearie me!" exclaimed Hurree Das. "Are we not fairly flying along! My gracious goodness, dear lady! Is it not too close to middle of day for such display of energy? Surely, you are not lasting whole distance going at such furious a speed!"

Helene laughed. "You're right, Hurree, I won't. I'll slow down, don't worry."

"Ah!" Hurree said, "only thing worrying me is my present status of fat, helpless millstone around your neck."

"Oh, come now!" Helene said. "You're nothing of the kind!"

"Dreadfully afraid I must differ to the contrary," Hurree Das said mournfully. "When I regard my tremendous bulk sitting here doing nothing, I am filled with contrition. Least thing I could do would be to hold umbrella over your head for affording shade against sun's rays. But alas! Am mortally afraid to move even fraction of an inch, for fear of upsetting this frail craft."

"Never you mind," Helene consoled. "You just aren't the athletic type, Hurree."

"Oh, by no means, whatsoever!" Hurree shuddered, closing his eyes at the thought.

"But you make up for it," Helene went on, "by being very good company, I tell you what you can do—you can tell me a story."

"Ah! Delighted to!" Hurree said brightening. "I shall tell you story of Ramayana, great Hindu epic, whose twenty-four thousand verses I once read in original Sanskrit."

"Twenty-four thousand verses!" Helene gasped.

"Oh, do not worry!" the Hindu chirped. "I will condense greatly to prevent utmost boredom on your part. Let us say I will merely venture to give you highlights of beautiful story—in my own words."

"I'll love it," Helene said. "Begin when ready."

"Very well," Hurree Das said, folding his plump hands in his lap. "Prince Rama was the son of Dasaratha, King of Ajodhya, and in consequence of a palace intrigue, he was driven into exile with his beautiful wife, the Princess Sita—"

Helene found herself enchanted with the old story of the exiled couple, and their adventures and tribulations. The Hindu's melodious voice went on and on without hesitation. Hurree Das must have read the Ramayana more than once, Helene reflected, because he never had to pause to collect his thoughts, or to remember the correct order of events in the long narrative.

So absorbed in the Hindu's story was Helene that she became almost oblivious of everything but the mechanical business of paddling and keeping the canoe on a straight course close to the bank of the river to stay as much as possible in the shade. She came out of her reverie suddenly with a start to find that the canoe was now in the blazing sun.

SHE HAD not changed her course, but the river had. They had arrived at the base of the U, and the Mikenye was beginning its long deep curve. Helene interrupted Hurree Das.

"Excuse me, Hurree," she said, looking quickly about her. "But we seem to be out in the sun all of a sudden, and I've got to decide what I'm going to do about it."

"So sorry my umbrella is of no use—" the Hindu began, but Helene broke in with a laugh.

"Oh, we don't need it," she said, "I'll just cross over to the other side of the river. The tall trees there will shade us for a while. And, if we need to—we'll just come back to this side, later on. Now"—steering the canoe into midstream—"go on with the story. I'm enjoying it ever so much."

"So glad you are," Hurree Das said gravely. "Well then, Rama and his brother, Lakhsmana, consulted with each other about what means to employ to rescue Sita from the cruel giant, Havana—"

And Hurree Das was launched again on his tale.

A few moments later, Helene thought she heard some faint sounds from the jungle beside them—human voices, possibly. But she heard no repetition of the sounds, and she hated to interrupt Hurree Das again to listen for them. She decided that there was nothing to worry about, and continued paddling, as the Hindu resumed his story.

From there on, Helene kept her eyes pretty much in the canoe, only occasionally casting absent glances ahead to see that she was paddling a straight course.

Just when Helene awoke to the fact that she and Hurree were not alone on that part of the river, she could never say. She must have seen the B'Kutu—or rather looked at them—some time before her brain grasped what her eyes were telling her. And by that time she had already passed the first raft full of cannibals and was drawing abreast of the next one.

A sudden icy fear clutched at her heart. She stopped paddling and stared stupidly at the raft. It was incredible! It was full of B'Kutu! And yet it couldn't be! The B'Kutu were far away down at Otempa!

Then full realization smote her. She gave a little cry, and started paddling furiously away from that bank, diagonally toward midstream.

"Gracious goodness!" Hurree Das exclaimed. "Whatever is the matter?"

"B'Kutu!" Helene hissed. And just at that moment, a felonious yell broke out from the little blacks on the rafts, and echoed up the bank.

"Oh, Lordie! Oh heavens! Woe is us!" the Hindu moaned. "Wherever did they come from?"

"I don't—know!" gasped Helene, redoubling her strokes of the paddle. "But—we'd better—make some time—or—"

She broke off as she saw another raft, a third one, issuing from the bank farther upstream. The river was curving sharply now, and with every few feet, it seemed, more rafts came into view. Glancing swiftly along the shoreline, she counted seven of the hastily rigged craft, and each one of them held about ten of the fearsome little blacks.

But by now, by dint of her hard paddling, she had sent the canoe out of reach of any of the rafts she could see. And even with her heavy passenger, she should easily be able to slip upstream before any of the rafts could pole across to intercept her.

"Don't worry, Hurree," she muttered, still stroking hard, "I think we'll get past them, all right."

"Oh, dearie! Sincerely hoping you are right!" the doctor said fervently. "Cannot bear the thought of my tender flesh going down beastly gullets of such loathsome blackfellows! Very idea gives me jimmywillies!"

Helene snickered a little hysterically, in spite of herself. But she quickly sobered when she realized that Hurree Das was being perfectly serious about a very serious situation. But she began to take hope as the canoe glided past the seventh raft, well out of reach of it.

The B'Kutu were keeping up a furious din now, as if enraged that the canoe should be so close and yet just beyond their clutches. Helene was moved to yell defiantly back at them. Now that she seemed to be moving out of danger, Helene began to marvel at these despised B'Kutu and at their leader, the renegade Mpotwe.

How the Bambala had underestimated them and him! While the Bambala had been reveling at Otempa, they had supposed Mpotwe was resting on his laurels across the river from them. But now it was evident that the wily Kara-mzili had lighted campfires to give the impression of his occupancy. But actually, he had marched far up the river to plan and launch a flank attack. The Bambala had been confident the B'Kutu were much too afraid of the water ever to cross the river by any other means than the bridge. But somehow, Mpotwe had persuaded them to ferry across the river with these rudely constructed rafts. Much as she hated Mpotwe and his despicable little warriors, Helene was forced to admire his energy and the malevolent brilliance of his mind.

She rested a moment panting, and looked back down the river. The raft farthest away was by now more than half way across. The rest of the rafts were strung out in a sort of loose echelon. Helene shivered a little. She would hate to be forced to turn around now, for any reason, and try to get through that formation of rafts. Probably, she reflected, she would not make it. But she thanked her stars that she had got past the terrible danger. Now, it was just a matter of paddling as swiftly as possible to the rendezvous with Ki-Gor at the Tetela village.

She turned her head forward, scanning the bank to her left with a swift glance. The bank was alive with B'Kutu, running along, brandishing their bows and shouting. Helene waved the paddle derisively at them, and then dug the blade into the water. As the canoe shot forward, she glanced automatically over at the other bank to her right.

A disagreeable sinking feeling came over her then. There were cannibals on that bank, too.

How did they get there? None of the rafts she had seen had made the complete crossing yet. Were there still other rafts that she had not yet seen?

Then, as the canoe followed the great curve of the river, she saw the other rafts. They were ahead of the canoe, upstream, and they stretched all the way across in an unbroken line. What she was looking at now was not so much a group of ferries, but a rude pontoon bridge.

The string of rafts were made fast to one another, and a long row of shrieking cannibals danced on them from bank to bank.

CHAPTER VII

HELENE STOPPED PADDLING IN dreadful dismay.

"Oah gracious! Dear lady," Hurree Das exclaimed. "What now, please?"

"We're in bad trouble, Hurree," Helene said soberly, "and I don't know just how we're going to get out of it."

For a moment, Helene did not know what she was going to do. With cannibals on both banks, it was hopeless to think of putting ashore and trying to escape that way. The river was completely closed ahead of her, and all but closed behind her. She sat for a moment helpless, her mind paralyzed with the awful, all-enveloping danger.

Then she plunged the paddle into the water and swung the head of the canoe around. If there was no escape in three directions, and only a slim chance of escape in the fourth—why then, she had to try for that slim chance, even if it meant running the gauntlet of those seven rafts downstream.

"Can you swim, Hurree?" she inquired, keeping careful control of her voice.

"Can swim—after a fashion," the Hindu quavered. "But not in this river. Very thought of crocodiles already paralyzes my legs."

Helene had forgotten the crocodiles, but the idea by now had no impact on her. If she was going to die, it didn't really much matter whether she died from a poisoned arrow or from a lurking river-monster. If anything, she supposed the poison would be less terrible.

Aided now by the current, she drove the canoe down upon the flotilla of rafts. Concentrating everything on her danger-studded course, she slanted off to her left, along a diagonal line parallel to the echelon of rafts. She had room enough almost all the way to keep sixty feet away from each raft. Remembering what Ki-Gor had said about the short range of the light B'Kutu bows, she estimated that sixty feet would keep the canoe well out of arrow-shot from the rafts. And there was water enough to her left to keep sixty feet from every raft—but the last one.

The water rippled and gurgled under the canoe as Helene thrust it forward with long powerful strokes. She could have gone faster without Hurree Das sitting gray-faced and mute in the middle of the canoe. But his very weight lent momentum to the light craft, and enabled her to turn it sharply.

It was this last fact that gave her an idea of how she might get past the last raft. She had shot past five of them now while the B'Kutu aboard them shrieked in impotent rage. She had to go very close to shore to pass the sixth one, and the seventh was squarely in her path. There was hardly thirty feet of open water between the seventh raft and the river bank.

But the last raft was a good hundred feet beyond the sixth raft. She might—if she could turn sharply enough—dodge outside that last raft. It would be like reversing her field like a football player on a touchdown run. Her hopes of escape suddenly rose high.

The clamor on the next to last raft was deafening as she sent the canoe boiling past it. She shot a grim glance in that direction and saw the cannibals lifting the long poles high out of the water as she went by. Another glance ahead to the last raft, and she prepared herself for her swift maneuver.

"Sit low in the canoe, Hurree!" she commanded, "and hold tight! We are going to make a very sharp turn!"

Exultantly, she gave one last prodigious stroke. Then she flipped the paddle over her head and plunged it into the water on the other side of the canoe and braked hard with it. Hurree Das gave a squeak of terror as the craft heeled dangerously. Quickly, Helene twisted the paddle, and the canoe gained an even keel, though it rolled terrifyingly. The bow had not come quite far enough around. Helene whipped the paddle to the other side and stroked hard before the canoe could lose too much momentum.

She was dimly conscious that the yells of the cannibals had taken on a new note. They all seemed to be screaming the same words.

"Gandu! Gandu!"—or so it sounded.

Not knowing the Congo dialects, Helene supposed it was a word signifying rage or frustration. A joyous wave surged over her. Her maneuver was going to work! They were going to get away!

A lightning glance at the last raft showed her that the cannibals aboard were desperately trying to reverse the direction of their slow-moving craft. They were digging their poles toward shore and pushing away madly. But they would be too late, Helene told herself exultantly! She only had to keep paddling straight out into the main current of the river, and she would soon be far out of reach.

Thirty seconds more and she and Hurree Das would be safely on their way back to Otempa!

The B'Kutu were still yelling, *"Gandu!"* and the endless repetition of the word suddenly began to ring a little bell in Helena's memory. She remembered hearing the Bambala using it. Did it mean "crocodile?"

At that moment, she saw the swirl of water just a few feet in front of the canoe. Instantly, Helene braked with her paddle. But at the same moment, two froglike eyes rose out of the water, and then a long ugly snout—right athwart the canoe's course. Under Helene's desperate paddling, the canoe swung around. But there was not time or room to avoid the unsuspecting saurian.

A split second later, the canoe's prow hit the crocodile a glancing blow behind one frog eye. The great lizard gave an astonished bellow and instantly went into action. Helene did not know it then, but the brute was just as frightened as she was, and his actions now were purely defensive. But defensive or not, they were just as calamitous in their results as if the crocodile were attacking the canoe.

The whole thing was so sudden that Helene never did have a clear picture of what actually happened. She had a brief glimpse of churning water under the bow of the canoe. Then there was a fearful shock as the crocodile crashed his mighty tail into the side of the canoe. Hurree Das gave a howl, and the canoe skittered sideways over the water for ten feet.

Helene just caught a glimpse of Hurree Das grabbing for his little bag and his umbrella as the canoe capsized. Then she twisted her body to meet the water.

HELENE HAD no plan of action, now, and her movements were purely instinctive. When her head came up out of the water, she found herself making for the nearest raft full of cannibals. Dimly, she felt them less of a menace than the crocodile. Her left hand still grasped the paddle. Without letting go of it, she still made good time with two legs and one arm.

But how she made it safely to the raft, she did not know. One of the long poles used for propelling the raft crashed into the water inches from her face. Without hesitation, she seized the end of it and pulled frantically. There was a scream and a splash and the cannibal at the other end toppled into the water.

Then she shoved the pole hard, without letting go of it, and kicked her legs hard, following it up. In a moment, she gripped the pole higher up. Unmindful of two other poles crashing at the water near her head, Helene worked up the pole until she was at the edge of the raft. Then she dropped the pole, and swinging the paddle in her left hand, slashed at the legs of the nearest B'Kutu. They backed away in astonishment, and Helene flung a leg over the edge of the raft.

Before the astounded cannibals could recover, she was on her feet and was gripping the paddle in her right hand. With a shrill cry, she sprang at the huddled group of B'Kutu, cutting from side to side with the paddle.

Two of the grimy little savages went down under her unexpected attack. But then the rest of them closed in on her with demoniacal yells. It seemed as if a hundred filthy hands were clawing at her.

Both legs were imprisoned, and her left arm. And one of the little brutes jumped on her back trying to get his hands around her throat. But Helene was not conquered yet. She ducked her head, and the encircling hands raked her face and eyes. Flailing her free right arm, she staggered away toward the edge of the raft. She teetered there for a split-second, fighting off the swarming cannibals in a frenzy.

Then, somehow, she was free of them for a precious moment. She turned and hit the water in a shallow plunge. But, as her head broke the surface a second later, she almost wished she had stayed on the raft and been killed. For unbelievable pains were shooting through both eyes. She shook her head and looked around her. To her growing horror, she found she could not see.

Her hand flew up to her eyes and felt a gummy substance on them. Sickening horror went through Helene. Those savage hands that had smeared over her face—were they covered with arrow-poison? Whatever it was, it was making her eyes feel as if red-hot pokers were thrust into them. She dared not rub them or do anything but keep them tightly closed.

Almost insane with despair, Helene thrust her head down and went into a furious racing crawl. She knew she was swimming downstream and away from the rafts, but that was all she knew. What would happen to her now, she could not even guess. She was really acting in a complete panic, with the dim hope somewhere in the back of her mind that if she kept on swimming the water might somehow wash the deadly poison out of her eyes.

Sometime later, it might have been seconds, or minutes, or hours,

Helene felt her knees strike bottom. She stopped swimming and stood up thigh-deep in the water. Her eyes were certainly no better for the washing she had given them. Behind her the cannibals screamed and splashed. Acting on a sudden decision, she rushed out of the river on to the bank, and flung herself blindly into the undergrowth.

And now came an interminable flight into the jungle, stumbling, tripping over roots, caroming off tree-trunks, screaming as trailing lianas slithered over her shoulders—were they lianas or were they snakes? Helene brought herself up short.

The pain was subsiding in her eyes, and with it some of her terror. She still could see nothing, but her mind was beginning to emerge from her blind panic. She groped about her until she felt a tree-trunk take shape under her hands, and there she stood trembling, taking stock of her situation.

She could not remember ever having been in such a terrible position. All alone, in a strange country, unarmed, and finally—quite blind. What was going to happen to her?

Then, as Helene's sanity returned to her, she began to feel a burning shame. She asked herself what Ki-Gor would have done under the circumstances. One thing he would not have done—she told herself—was to give way to such a panic. Nor would he have deserted Hurree Das, poor helpless Hurree Das, the way she did. What had become of him? Had he been killed by the B'Kutu?

She could still hear the babble of the cannibals in the distance—and it was not too great a distance at that. Evidently, in her blindness, she had circled and come to a stop not very far from the river. Instinctively, she felt around the tree-trunk for a column of vines. Even if she was blind, she still ought to be able to climb up to a safer position.

Just then, she heard something coming toward her through the undergrowth. She froze and listened over the pounding of her heart. Nearer and nearer it came. Whatever it was, it was no B'Kutu—it was making far too much noise. With mounting terror, Helene could only guess it was a large animal of some kind. Her trembling fingers groped hurriedly for vines to grasp. But within her reach the tree-trunk was quite smooth. She moved hurriedly around it, cursing her helplessness.

But Helene was destined never to climb that particular tree. Her foot caught in a surface root, and she crashed noisily to the ground. She lay still, frozen with fright.

Whatever the unseen thing was that had been approaching her had heard her fall and had stopped to listen.

There was no sound.

THEN A human voice called out of the jungle—a familiar voice—and Helene burst into tears of relief.

"Hulloa, *memsahib!*" called Hurree Das. *"Memsahib!* Are you there?"

"Yes, Hurree," Helene quavered. "Over here! Under a big tree. Come quickly, Hurree, oh—I never was so glad to hear anyone's voice—"

A moment later, the Hindu doctor was kneeling solicitously beside Helene, patting her on the back.

"Dear gracious! Dear lady, what is the matter?" he said. "Your eyes—"

"I've gone blind, Hurree," Helene sobbed. "Those filthy little cannibals had arrow-poison on their hands, and they rubbed it into my eyes."

"Oah, now—it may not be so bad," Hurree Das said, soothingly. "Come, just sit down now, and relax. Hurree Das will take care of you."

"Oh, it's awful, Hurree!" Helene moaned. "Do you think it will be—I'll be permanently blind?"

"At time like this," the Hindu said, firmly, "patience is greatest possible virtue of all. Let me make quick examination first. Ah! that is more like it! Relax properly! Remember, you are in hands of first-rate physician!"

The plump fingers explored Helene's eyes tenderly to the accompaniment of sympathetic little clucks. She heard the Hindu rattling in his little bag, and wondered vaguely how he had ever got the bag ashore from the overturned canoe. Then it suddenly struck her as astonishing that Hurree Das himself got ashore! How did he do it?

But now a wet cloth was being wiped over her eyes, wiping away the poison.

"What do you think, Hurree?" Helene asked tremulously. "Do you think I'll ever see again?"

"Oah yes," the Hindu answered cheerfully. "Without slightest shadow of doubt you will see—you will see very shortly."

"Really!" Helene gasped. "Oh, I can hardly believe it! I thought surely that arrow-poison would—

"In first place," Hurree Das broke in, "arrow poison would have no effect on eyes unless it contained snake venom. I analyzed this B'Kutu poison, you remember, and found it to consist only of vegetable poison—strychnine, mainly, from plant called *Strychnos Icaja Baill.* Evidently, B'Kutu blackfellows do not mix snake venom in their arrow poison."

"And the strychnine would have no effect on my eyes?" Helene said in bewilderment.

"Not the very slightest," Hurree Das said firmly. "So you see, dear lady, it was not arrow-poison on dirty hands of blackfellows."

"For heaven's sake, what was it, then?" Helene demanded.

"A sort of turpentine," the Hindu replied, still bathing the swollen eyes, "They had been doing considerable primitive lumbering for purposes of making rafts. Long poles for poling seemed to be especially gummy sort of wood. This gum got in your eyes, causing severe pains, no doubt—"

"They were," Helene said grimly.

"—and temporary blindness," Hurree Das concluded. "However, nothing to worry about. I have removed all foreign substance now, and I will bathe the eyes with boric solution, and shortly, dear lady, you will see out them just as clearly as ever."

Helene was silent for a minute. Then she said very humbly, "I think I've been all kinds of a ninny—"

"Not ninny at all!" Hurree Das denied indignantly. "You had not medical or botanical education—you could not know you were not permanently blinded!—"

"Well, anyway," Helene said, "I feel pretty rotten for the way I deserted you."

"Deserted me!" Hurree Das cried. "What are you meaning? You did not desert me. On the contrary, it was cowardly Hindu doctor who deserted you!"

"Tell me what happened," Helene said.

"Well," Hurree Das said, "as soon as I ascertained that canoe had struck crocodile, my mind became scene of utmost confusion, I can tell you! Only mere instinct told me to seize my bag and umbrella. Next thing I knew I was floundering in water. But to my utmost astonishment, water was shallow—only up to my shoulders. This was great consolation, but I perceived I was by no means out of danger.

Possibly crocodile was still lurking about, waiting chance to nab my leg!"

Helene turned her face away quickly, lest Hurree Das see the smile she was trying unsuccessfully to suppress.

"Worse still," the Hindu went on excitedly, "was provocative attitude of B'Kutu. They were seeming to think they had me at disadvantage—and for once, I was in complete agreement with them. But I am typical Hindu, and if Hindu people are not distinguished for active qualities, at least they have survived four thousand years, by some hook or crook or other."

Hurree Das paused. Helene said, "What did you do, then?"

"Unlike Mahatma Gandhi," Hurree Das went on, "I did not offer mere Passive Resistance. Under circumstances, I perceived that something more than Non-Co-operation was called for. I was holding bag and umbrella in right hand, high above water, to keep same from getting wet—"

"Yes," Helene said breathlessly.

"—And I waded farther in toward shore, until water was only at large portly waistline. Whereupon, B'Kutu made concerted rush at me from both sides. I turned around then, reached up with left hand and opened and closed umbrella rapidly at them. Once I escaped attack of mad dog in such fashion."

"And it worked against the B'Kutu?" Helene said incredulously.

"Dear lady, you cannot imagine extraordinary effect of my deadly umbrella on superstitious savages. They were thrown into utter panic. So, seeing them in this condition, I made my way safely to dry land."

HELENE COULD hardly contain herself at the picture Hurree Das painted of himself. She would have given anything to have seen him holding a pack of murderous savages at bay with nothing more than an umbrella, and then wading, dripping but sedate, to shore.

"Well, I think that was simply marvelous, Hurree," she said, "and I guess only you could have done it."

"So far," the Hindu broke in, "I have told you only good news. But now comes reverse side of picture."

"What do you mean?" Helene said.

"Cannibals on river," the Hindu said, "likewise, cannibals on shore. These I do not fear, thinking to disperse them with umbrella, too. But these dry-land cannibals are not alone. Down river bank comes procession of big, tall Kara-mzili with fat prince who is leader of all."

"Mpotwe!" Helene gasped.

"Same fellow," Hurree Das said sorrowfully. "And this Mpotwe is not scaring so easily. So quickly, I explained to him in Swahili I was medical man and could patch up any wounded men of his army. So he immediately retained me as Army Medical Corps. So far, not so bad. But now comes worse."

"Worse?" Helene echoed apprehensively.

"Mpotwe demanded to know whereabout of you. I confessed ignorance. He then said you had disappeared in bush, but that he was sending B'Kutu to hunt you down. Naturally, I was horrified, but I did not let him know it. Instead, I told him you were dangerous woman of superhuman strength, and that it would be safer for everyone concerned if I, myself, came to look for you. Luckily, I was able to find you in very short time."

The Hindu paused, and Helene felt that he was embarrassed.

"And what is to happen now, dear lady," he concluded in a very tired voice, "I do not know."

And now it was Helene who was silent while she digested the full importance of the Hindu's story. The more she thought about it, the more did a growing fear tug at her heart.

At length she said, "Then Mpotwe knows you went out to look for me?"

"Yes," Hurree Das said sadly.

"Did you give your word that you would bring me back to him?"

"Oah no," the Hindu said wearily. "Not necessary to. I was followed by whole regiment of B'Kutu."

"You mean they followed you here?"

Helene exclaimed, her voice rising.

"Oah yes. They are squatting all around us now. Silent little beggars, are they not?"

"Oh, Hurree!" Helene groaned. "Then we didn't escape."

"No—thanks to blundering fool of crocodile."

"But—but what are we going to do?" Helene said desperately.

"I am not knowing, dear lady," the Hindu said. "At present moment, I can only lead you back to Mpotwe. If not, sundry cannibals around us will simply make pincushions of us with little poisoned arrows."

"Well—" Helene struggled to stand up—"then we'd better go. We may be prisoners now, but it won't be for long. It's just a question of time before Ki-Gor finds out what has happened to us. And I've learned to rely on Ki-Gor to come through."

She put her hand on the Hindu's arm, and the two of them began to make their way slowly through the jungle.

"Possibly so," Hurree Das, the gambler, said. "But track odds are lengthening against our champion in race against time. Has it occurred to you, dear lady, that Ki-Gor will be waiting for us to arrive at Tetela village far up river? While Mpotwe will be taking us in completely opposite direction, toward Otempa."

Helene had been trying to put that very thought out of her mind.

"That is to say," the Hindu added, "we will be lucky if Mpotwe takes us with him—alive." Then, in a voice that was professionally cheerful, he said, "Bye the bye, how are the eyes feeling now?"

"They're mending fast, Hurree. The pain is all gone, and the left eye is opening a tiny slit."

"Excellent! Excellent!" the doctor said heartily. "I would say situation is excellent—as far as eyes are concerned."

CHAPTER VIII

MPOTWE SAT ON HIS litter like a gross, thick-lipped Buddha. His eyes were half-closed and inscrutable, but Helene could feel the black pupils fixed on her. The renegade chieftain spoke to her directly in Swahili.

"I first saw you a long time ago at the court of my uncle, King Dingazi. That was when my attempt to seize power failed—because you and Ki-Gor interfered. But even then, I liked your looks. You found favor in my eyes, even though you are so thin. I still like your looks, O Red-Haired One, and considering that I brought no wives with me, I would like you for a wife."

The skin along Helene's back prickled, but she suppressed the gasp that rose to her lips, and looked stolidly ahead.

"But," Mpotwe continued, "I must deny myself the pleasure. The B'Kutu have recognized you as Ki-Gor's woman, and they have demanded your person. They are hard to handle, at best, these Basenji, and it would be unwise of me to refuse them this request."

There was a long pause. Then Helene cleared her throat.

"What," she asked, "do the B'Kutu want to do with me?"

"They want to eat you," Mpotwe answered impassively, and a great numbness settled over Helene's brain. As if from a great distance, she heard Mpotwe.

"They are afraid of Ki-Gor," he said. "They think Ki-Gor is a great witch. But you live with Ki-Gor—you are his woman. Therefore, you must be immune to his witchcraft. So they believe that if they eat you, they also will become immune to any of Ki-Gor's spells."

Helene shook her head as if to wake herself up from a nasty dream. But the dream would not leave her. Mpotwe's voice went on in a monotone.

"These savages are not used to discipline, but they have submitted to a number of strange and unfamiliar commands of mine. It would not be well for me to carry my authority too far. Besides, if they eat you and then are able to face Ki-Gor without fear—that is to my advantage. We are moving on Otempa on this side of the river. This time it will be a complete surprise. The stupid Bambala will never expect us. But if Ki-Gor is there—and I assume he is, since he is not with you—he might pull some trick to cheat us out of our victory, as he has already done."

Hope stirred momentarily in Helene's leaden heart at the mention of Ki-Gor. She almost cried out that Ki-Gor was not in Otempa, but she just caught herself in time. If Mpotwe did not know where Ki-Gor was, there was no point in setting him right. There was certainly no point, Helene told herself bitterly, in telling Mpotwe that Ki-Gor was patiently waiting for her in a Tetela village twenty-five miles up the river. Worse still, she realized as she thought about it—he probably had not even arrived there yet. It was early afternoon, and Ki-Gor had agreed to meet her at sundown. He would not even begin to miss her for another five hours to come!

"How—how soon does the—the banquet begin?" Helene said, trying to smile at her own ghastly joke.

"They would like to have it here and now," Mpotwe began—and something snapped in Helene's brain.

"You cruel beast!" she flared. "You come from a civilized nation—the great Kara-mzili—and yet you join these hideous cannibals in making war on a helpless woman, a blind woman at that! Hurree Das!" Helene cried, "Oh, Hurree Das! Where are you?"

"Right beside you," the Hindu's voice said quietly.

"Oh, Hurree, did you hear?" Helene sobbed.

"Yes, I gathered what was said," Hurree Das said, "even though I just came from attending some wounded."

"Oh, what am I going to do?"

Mpotwe's voice broke in, speaking Swahili. "You did not let me finish, O Red-Haired One. The B'Kutu want to have their feast now. But I have forbidden it."

"Forbidden it?" Helene cried, suddenly aflame with hope.

"I have forbidden it now," Mpotwe said with a sardonic laugh. "The feast will be held at sundown, at the end of the day's march."

Helene reeled. To be apparently reprieved, and then to have the reprieve quickly snatched away—was almost more than she could stand.

"If I allowed the feast now," Mpotwe said, "there would be no marching for the rest of the day. And before sundown, I intend to be within striking distance of Otempa, so that I can launch the attack at dawn tomorrow."

Helene groped for Hurree Das' hand and gripped it. The renegade prince went on talking relentlessly.

"But I have promised," he said, "that nothing will prevent the B'Kutu from eating you at sundown, and they have agreed to that. So you see? I am not so cruel—I have given you an extra half day of life."

With Mpotwe's savage laughter in her ears, Helene fainted.

CHAPTER IX

KI-GOR LOOKED WITH TREMENDOUS satisfaction at the great assemblage of Tetela warriors that thronged the bank of the Mikenye. His self-appointed mission had succeeded far beyond his wildest hopes. It had succeeded, too, in much shorter time than he had thought was possible. Here it was only mid-afternoon. In a few short hours he had visited five villages and aroused the warriors in each of them to follow him.

To be sure, his job had been much easier and simpler than he had thought it would be. The Tetela had heard of the sack of Toli and of the unprovoked attack on Otempa, even before Ki-Gor told them. They were in an ugly mood toward the despised cannibals, and only needed the slightest of urging to set them on the war-path.

But whatever the motives, Ki-Gor was well-satisfied with the results. Nearly a thousand of the toughest, best warriors in the whole Congo-Kasai Basin were ready to descend upon the rear of the B'Kutu at Otempa. Ki-Gor had explained the situation at that town, and how the Bambala were supposedly watching Mpotwe's army, and were ready to repel them. But how little confidence he placed in the vigilance of the easy-going Bambala, he also went into, and the Tetela agreed with him.

But they were less inclined to agree with his outlined strategy for dealing with the B'Kutu. He had proposed to the Tetela that they cross the river right there and go overland—across the top of the U—taking the B'Kutu in the rear and completely by surprise. The Tetela granted the wisdom of the strategy but rebelled at the idea of the long overland march through the heavy jungle. They would much prefer, they said, to race down the river in their many canoes. The mileage was much greater but with twenty and thirty paddles to a canoe they would make much better time than they ever could crawling through the bush.

When Ki-Gor pointed out that going by water would probably lose the surprise-quality of the attack on the B'Kutu, the Tetela scoffed. The Tetela didn't need the help of surprise, any time they fought those dirty little cannibals. The B'Kutu were simply not a match for them under any circumstances. That was undoubtedly true, and Ki-Gor admitted that to the Tetela, but he could not convince them of the danger that lay in Mpotwe's brilliant tactical mind. They had never come up against the Kara-mzili and had no idea of their advanced military tactics. So that argument did not sway the Tetela. "Who was this Mpotwe?" they asked. A mere foreigner—to be wiped out with his despicable B'Kutu allies.

If he had pressed the matter, Ki-Gor knew, he could have prevailed on the Tetela to take the overland route. Unfortunately, he was in a bad position to press the matter. For he did not intend to go with the punitive force himself. He had promised Helene that he would wait for her at the village on the river, and he felt that he should keep that promise, after the scare Helene had had over the sack of Toli.

So, unless he went with the Tetela, he could hardly insist on their taking a route they did not want to follow.

The Tetela leader came and stood beside Ki-Gor. He was evidently a little embarrassed at going athwart Ki-Gor's expressed wishes, and wanted to justify the Tetela choice of routes.

"It is better this way, O Ki-Gor," he said. "We are no Basenji to go wriggling through the jungle at a fast rate. We could never make it to Otempa overland before nightfall. But by water, our great war canoes might take us there only a little after sundown. We can land a little upstream of the B'Kutu and storm their camp in the dying light. Because—and you can depend on this, Ki-Gor—once we come to grips with those devils, it won't take us long to dispose of them."

Ki-Gor nodded with a grin. He knew the Tetela confidence in themselves was well justified, and he conceded that they would probably do as their leader promised. Then, Ki-Gor sighed. He wished he could go with the avenging force.

"If I had not given my solemn word to my wife," he said, "I would love nothing better than to join your attack. I bear the cannibals no love, nor the treacherous Kara-mzili who leads them."

"If you gave your word, you cannot go back on it," the Tetela leader said politely. "It is too bad, though. We would dearly love to have you with us."

The jungle man was torn between his desire to go with the expedition and his fear of the scolding he would get from Helene if he did.

"There is this," the Tetela said, suddenly hopeful. "If we go by water, and it is pretty sure that we will, we will meet your wife coming up the river. You could see her and get her to release you from your promise."

"It is an idea," Ki-Gor said slowly.

"Why, certainly!" the Tetela said, enthusiastically. "There is the river! We must go down it, she must come up it! You can't miss seeing her!"

"No," said Ki-Gor, "Unless she happens to have pulled over to the shore to rest." And renewed doubt hit him. "That could very well be. She might even see your fleet of war canoes coming and be afraid. She might think you were some unfriendly tribe and hide along the bank."

"We could all keep our eyes peeled," the Tetela offered. "I will order everyone who is not paddling to watch the banks carefully."

Ki-Gor hesitated, his eyes roving over the embarkation going on all around him. Canoe after canoe was taking on its load of strapping warriors. On this exciting dash down the river, he was afraid the Tetela would be in no mood for scrutinizing the banks for a lone canoe with two occupants.

But—and here a thought struck him—if *he*, Ki-Gor, were watching those banks, he would never miss seeing Helene. His keen eyes would certainly pick out the canoe, no matter how cleverly Helene might hide it.

"Wait a minute," Ki-Gor said to the Tetela leader. "Let one canoe go in advance of all the others. And I will go in that canoe."

The Tetela leader gave a shout of joy, and it was quickly taken up by a thousand throats as Ki-Gor stepped down to the water's edge.

CHAPTER X

THE FOUR STOCKY SCAR-FACED Tofoke carrying Helene in the improvised litter stopped abruptly, and then dropped the litter rudely to the ground. The swelling around Helene's eyes had gone down enough so that she could see out of both of them, now. She looked over her right shoulder. Through the screen of leaves she could see mellow slanting sunbeams dancing on the wavelets of the river. What had caused the halt? Helene asked herself. It was not yet sundown—not by at least an hour and a half. Mpotwe had said they would march until sundown.

The bushes crackled up ahead, and presently Hurree Das came panting toward Helene. His face was pale and his jowls trembled. Helene noticed irrelevantly that he was wearing his rubber gloves, and carrying a little bottle full of some colorless liquid.

"Oh, dearie me!" the Hindu moaned. "Best laid plans nearly going awry on account of capricious jungle monarch. Mpotwe has decided to go no farther today. Already close enough to Otempa to make attack tomorrow at dawn."

Apprehension crawled down Helene's back.

"You mean," she said, "they aren't going to wait for sundown for the festivities?"

"I'm afraid they are planned for very near future," the Hindu said, wetting his lips.

"Well," Helene said, suddenly feeling very cold all over, but retaining a grip on herself. "It begins to look as if they're going through with this thing."

"Oh Lordie!" Hurree Das groaned, "If only Ki-Gor were near!"

"I might as well face the facts, Hurree," Helene said. "Ki-Gor is a good many miles away and he isn't even coming in this direction. He is sitting there, 'way up the river, waiting for you and me to come poking along in the canoe."

She looked despairingly around at the Tofoke litter bearers and the B'Kutu squatting beyond. Then she looked back at Hurree Das. The sweat was pouring off his round face, and he pulled a corner of his *dhoti* up to mop it off. Then he took his black pill-box off and held it in his trembling hand a moment.

"You have had no ideas, lady?" he asked.

Helene shook her head. "What ideas are there?" she said. "I'm only just getting back the use of my eyes, and I'm sitting here in the midst of swarms of cannibals."

"Yes," Hurree Das nodded, his jowls shaking again. The little black hat suddenly dropped from his fumbling fingers, and he stared at it resting on the ground at his feet.

"If Ki-Gor could only have missed me before now," Helene said evenly, "then I might have some little hope. I have tremendous faith in him. But"—she glanced at the sunlighted river again—"he won't even know we were delayed for at least another hour and a half. And by that time—I will be resting in little bloody pieces in the B'Kutu stew pots."

"Same reasoning as my own," Hurree Das said, in a voice far less controlled than Helene's. "Therefore, I perceived necessity for postponement of—of ceremonies. They must be postponed at all costs."

There was no hope in Helene's eyes and but little interest as she regarded the sweating Hindu.

"If they could only be persuaded," the doctor went on, "to wait until morning—that would give Ki-Gor all night to come."

Helene sighed. "Naturally, you couldn't persuade them."

"Naturally," Hurree Das agreed. "I tried hard with Mpotwe, but all the time getting nowhere. He has feeling you are dangerous, and he wants you out of way as soon as possible."

Helene winced, and a film came over her eyes.

"Oh, Hurree!" she cried, "why torture me with what might-have-been? If I've got to die—at least, I want to be able to die bravely—"

"Wait a minute, *memsahib*," the doctor said. "If B'Kutu cannot be persuaded to postpone slaughtering you—they might be frightened, somehow. I have been racking poor incompetent brains for some means of frightening them."

"Frightening them?" Helene said, as a little thrill went through her. "What do you mean, Hurree?"

The Hindu bent over and picked up his hat. Helene's eyes followed him, saw his hand drop the bottle on the ground beside the litter before it groped for the hat.

"Do not stare at the bottle, *memsahib*," Hurree said, replacing the hat on his black curls. "It is only hope of postponement we desire so mightily. Do not interrupt me now while I explain. There is so little time. But follow my directions about bottle. Do not hope too much—but it might secure postponement."

"But what, Hurree?" Helene said frantically.

"Listen carefully," the Hindu commanded. "You have to do this for yourself. I cannot do it for you, or these people would suspect something was up. It will hurt you like very devil—but better transient pain than certain death. In that bottle is juice from poisonous vine. It is powerful vesicant—it will raise painful blisters on your skin if it touches it."

The savages around the litter suddenly stood up chattering. Helene looked around and saw Mpotwe's litter being carried toward her. Hurree Das quickened his words.

"Smear that juice on each thigh and each upper arm," he instructed. "Make rough design if possible—something like crocodile in shape."

He started to move away.

"Forgive me pain it will cause," he said, over his shoulder. "And forgive me if results are not as I hope. It is all poor, inadequate Hurree Das could think up."

The Hindu was walking rapidly away as Helene reached out and snatched the bottle off the ground. Mpotwe's litter was halted some distance away and the Kara-mzili bodyguard crowded around their prince. The cannibals grinned wolfishly at Helene and began a soft little chant.

HEART POUNDING, Helene uncorked the bottle close to her thigh. She glared back at the cannibals and hoped against hope they were not watching her hands. Stealthily, she tipped the bottle slightly on to the finger tips of her right hand. Then she smeared the colorless liquid the length of her left thigh. If there had been pigment of some kind in the liquid, the smear would have shown a design more or less boat-shaped. Or it might have represented the long, narrow body of a crocodile. Two quick swipes crossways would represent the stubby pairs of legs.

While a great hubbub went on around Mpotwe, taking the attention of the cannibals, Helene repeated the operation on her right thigh, and then on each of her upper arms. The liquid felt cool, almost cold, on her skin and carried no hint of future blistering. She replaced the cork in the little bottle and peered down at her thighs. There was nothing to see, except the faint water glistening of the liquid. Nothing to see, nothing to feel—as yet. And Helene had an unpleasant thought. What if Hurree Das had been wrong? What if he collected the wrong kind of vine? It wasn't probable, she admitted, because the Hindu was a fine botanist.

Nevertheless, Helene's heart was falling as she looked around for something to take the fluid off her fingers. If the stuff really was a vesicant, she did not want her fingers burned, too.

The Tofoke litter-bearers had moved away several yards and were squatting, watching the commotion around Mpotwe. Just at the end of one of the litter poles stood a crude earthenware water bottle. Helene put her feet on the ground and calmly took three steps to the bottle.

Instantly some B'Kutu shouted. Helene's heart sank further. The cannibals were taking no chances on her trying to make a break. She bent over the water bottle and tipped it over on her hands, washing them and the little bottle of vesicant. Then she slipped the little bottle down inside the waist band of her brief leopard-skin trunks.

By this time she was surrounded by a half dozen B'Kutu, all yammering at her. She glared at them briefly, then turned her back and sat down on the litter. The bottle pressed hard into her stomach, and she hoped it would not make too noticeable a bulge. She sneaked a quick look down and saw that it was not too noticeable as long as she sat leaning forward. When she stood up, it might be a different matter.

Helene also sneaked a look at her thighs. The ivory-smooth skin had not the slightest blemish showing, and she began to worry a little. There was as yet no sensation of burning, or irritation of any kind. Could Hurree Das have made a mistake?

Several big Kara-mzili were coming toward her now, undoubtedly attracted by the commotion of the B'Kutu. Helene watched them dully as they approached. The hopes that Hurree Das had aroused in her when he gave her the bottle of vesicant and told her what to do with it were fast receding. Suddenly, she asked herself what the purpose of smearing the stuff on her was, anyway? What did Hurree Das have in mind? He might perhaps have explained to her, but his conversation had been cut short by the appearance of Mpotwe.

The Tofoke litter bearers, apparently under orders from the Kara-mzili, now came back and picked up the litter. The Kara-mzili ranged themselves on each side of the litter, and Helene was carried straight toward Mpotwe.

Now what? Helene asked herself. Is the slaughter to take place immediately— before the vesicant gets a chance to work?

But the litter was set down directly in front of Mpotwe's litter, and the Tofoke moved away. Mpotwe leered down at her. Helene looked helplessly about for Hurree Das. She finally spotted him some two hundred feet off to one side, talking earnestly to one of the tall Kara-mzili.

"It is unfortunate for you, O Red-Haired One," Mpotwe rasped in Swahili, "that we came to the end of our march so soon—and you come to the end of your life so soon. I promised you you would live until sundown, but now I see we cannot wait that long. If I can give you life, I can take it away again."

Helene gazed up at the bulbous face without knowing what to say. It was so unbelievable, somehow, that anyone should be telling her she had only a little while more to live. In a queer sort of way, it made her doubt the possibility that she was going to die.

"You still have a little while," Mpotwe said indulgently, "while the tribes make a rough camp and build some fires."

Even that shocking statement left Helene strangely unmoved. She began to realize that her previous awful dread of the fate Mpotwe was so confidently predicting had completely gone. She even had the impulse to smile impudently up at the fat prince. Absently, she started to scratch her left arm above the elbow. Then a thrill shot through her and she stopped her right hand in mid-air.

The skin of her left arm above the elbow was beginning to itch like fury. Likewise her right arm and likewise both thighs. Hurree Das had made no mistake in his plant juices! It was beginning to work!

She threw a swift sidelong glance at the spot where she had seen Hurree Das. The Hindu was talking to another Kara-mzili warrior now. And the first Kara-mzili, the one he had been talking to a moment before, was standing to one side looking very thoughtful. Helene pulled her eyes away lest Mpotwe notice her interest in the Hindu. Bitterly she regretted that Hurree Das had not been able to finish explaining his plan to her. If she only knew a little more of what he had in mind, she could govern herself accordingly.

"Well, then, Red-Haired One," Mpotwe said with heavy mockery, "are you not afraid to die—and to be eaten by these dirty little men?"

Helene looked up steadily at the beady little eyes. It would certainly do no harm to appear confident, she reasoned.

"No, I am not afraid," she said. "Because I am not going to die."

The renegade prince threw back his head and laughed a short, nasty laugh.

CHAPTER XI

HELENE'S MIND CHURNED. WHAT was Hurree Das' plan? Obviously the vesicant was intended to raise blisters on her arms and thighs—but what then? How would that save her life from the cannibals? Then a thought struck her. The blisters would certainly give her an extremely unwholesome appearance. Could it be that Hurree Das wanted to make the B'Kutu afraid to eat her—for fear they would be poisoned?

Her arms and thighs were beginning to burn in earnest now, but a quick glance down at them was disappointing. There was only the faintest sign of blistering, a mere pinkness appearing where she had smeared the plant juice. Again she looked cautiously toward Hurree Das. Now he was talking to two B'Kutu with two Kara-mzili listening beside him.

The Kara-mzili had taken charge of the business of making a camp and were handling it with characteristic efficiency. One large group of savages were clearing a great space, in front of Mpotwe's litter, of all undergrowth. Half of them were cutting bushes, and the other half carrying them away. One detachment had evidently been assigned the job of collecting dry wood for the fires, while still another group was engaged in building the fires themselves, with the rings of small rocks and the green-wood trestles to hang the stewpots on.

So well organized was the activity that it seemed no time before a dozen fires were blazing, and the B'Kutu were trooping down to the river bank to fill their crude vessels with water. It was a sight not calculated to increase Helene's newly restored confidence and hope. Nevertheless, she clung bravely to her hope, and found that it helped her attention on Hurree Das' mysterious activity among the Kara-mzili, and even more, among the B'Kutu themselves.

Mpotwe seemed to have forgotten her existence for the time being and immersed himself in conferences with his Kara-mzili captains, presumably discussing the business of the next morning's attack on Otempa. Helene considered this a blessing at first, for it not only meant that she did not have to endure the fat prince's mocking words, but also she could watch the Hindu without attracting the suspicion of the dull-eyed B'Kutu who squatted around her.

The speed of the preparations for the feast appalled her. The sun was still on the river when the cooking-pots hanging over the fire began to steam. And yet the plant juice had hardly raised any color at all on her skin where she had applied it, even though her arms and legs were burning and itching fiercely. She could see that Hurree Das, too, was a little worried about it. Twice he went past her, saying no word but glancing sharply at her thighs. His large round eyes shadowed with apprehension each time he saw no appreciable blistering.

Suddenly, there was a purposeful hustling and shouting of orders. Helene realized with an ugly shock that the B'Kutu were ready for their grisly banquet. The stew-pots were bubbling and the cannibals were yapping expectantly. In a horrified daze, Helene watched the savages range themselves—with incredible swiftness, it seemed to her—around the newly made clearing. Her litter was carried to a spot twenty feet in front of Mpotwe's litter, and for the first time, Helene noticed a crude sort of altar fashioned out of a dozen or so straight saplings laid across two piles of stones. Underneath the parallel poles was a wide-mouth earthenware pot of Bangongo workmanship. Helene's scalp prickled as she realized that the pot was intended to catch her blood as it spouted out under the sacrificial knife.

Even before any actual ceremonies began, the B'Kutu began a soft little chant, repeating it over and over.

"Aba-a-a N'kutu! Nyam nyam! Aba-a-a N'kutu! Nyam nyam!"

Helene well knew the meaning of *"nyam nyam."* In all Bantu dialects it meant, "fresh meat!"

Hurree Das stumbled toward her, his face a picture of horror.

"Have faith, lady! Please to having faith!" he cried hoarsely, staring at her arms and legs as if by sheer force of willpower he could raise the blisters there which had so far not developed. "They are so quick!" he moaned. "They have made everything ready so quickly! I should have given vesicant to you sooner! But have faith—"

He hurried away toward Mpotwe. Helene looked helplessly after him. She knew he was as helpless as she was. His plan to protect her depended entirely on the visible effect of the vesicant on her skin. As yet, there were no visible effects. And at the rate the business was proceeding, there was not much time left to have faith—

Suddenly, a sharp cry came from some savages still on the river bank. They came stumbling in toward Mpotwe. Helene caught the word, "Tetela," and her heart leaped. Mpotwe quickly rasped some orders which were promptly repeated by the Kara-mzili moving among the fires. Swiftly and silently the savages tipped the boiling stew pots over on to the fires, and one by one the fires hissed and smoked and fizzled out.

Helene gathered that Tetela had been seen on the river, and that Mpotwe was determined that the Tetela should not see the cannibal force. At first, Helene could hardly believe her good fortune. Not only were the ceremonies postponed, but the chances were that Mpotwe could not hide his savage minions in time.

Then, the more she thought about it, the more her hopes soared. Hurree Das appeared beside her, eyes gleaming.

"Tetela are speeding down river in canoes," he whispered. "Undoubtedly Ki-Gor is with them. I will go and watch."

Helene's heart gave a great bound at Hurree Das' words. Of course, Ki-Gor would be with the Tetela! Mouth open with excitement, she watched the Hindu ambling rapidly toward the river bank. Then a little chill struck her, as she saw two Kara-mzili stride up to Hurree Das' plump figure and seize him. And a moment later two more Kara-mzili stepped up to her, and pinned her arms to her sides. A large black hand was clapped over her mouth.

Mpotwe was taking no chances of an outcry from his prisoners.

FOR A few seconds, Helene struggled against that great horny hand clamped over her face before she realized that it was quite useless. And the next ten minutes seemed an eternity. Her back was to the river, so she could see nothing of the Tetela canoes that were sweeping downstream. But against the sepulchral silence of the camp, she could hear the Kara-mzili muttering. And out on the river she could hear the carefree shouting and singing of the Tetela as they paddled all unsuspecting past the hidden army of invasion.

After she had discovered the futility of fighting to cry out, Helene had to fight herself to preserve her sanity. There, within a hundred yards of her, went an unknown number of potential rescuers! It was a maddening situation. She concentrated on translating to herself the muttered comments of the Kara-mzili.

"Twenty canoes," one said.

"War paint and weapons, too," another said. "Are they going to attack Otempa before we can?"

"Who knows?" the first one murmured. "I always heard they hated our little friends here, the B'Kutu."

"Good fighters, too, *I've* always heard," the second Kara-mzili whispered.

There was no mention of Ki-Gor, Helene noticed, and her heart sank even farther. When the Tetela were first reported in sight, she had hoped Ki-Gor would be with them. If he had been, she knew he would never have passed the B'Kutu so innocently. His alert senses would have divined their presence somehow. But then she thought of the promise Ki-Gor had made—"I'll try to be there, this time," he had said—and she visualized Ki-Gor sitting patiently in the Tetela village miles away, waiting for her and Hurree Das to appear. And it was not yet even sundown!

But time eventually takes care of the most intolerable situation, and eventually the army in hiding relaxed as the singing of the Tetela died away in the distance. The Kara-mzili relaxed their grip on Helene and she heaved a bitter sigh. Then Hurree Das was at her elbow.

"So full of exasperation," he said gloomily, "I can hardly talk. However, mere presence of Tetela helped us in one way."

"How?" Helene asked dully.

"Caused postponement," the Hindu pointed out. "Now, fires have to be lighted all over again and—ah!"—he broke off and pointed—"vesicant is having time to do its work."

Helene looked down at her burning thighs. A bright red crocodile stood out in bold relief on each leg!

Hurree Das's eyes shone purposefully as he moved away. Mpotwe began rasping orders again, and the B'Kutu resumed their soft, spine-tingling chant.

"Aba-a-a N'kutu! Nyam nyam! Aba-a-a N'kutu! Nyam nyam!"

A score of the savages flung fresh wood on the steaming fires. And in a moment they began to flicker, and presently burst into flame. The hissing pots were replaced on the trestles, and the atmosphere seemed to thicken about Helene. Then, above the chant of the cannibals, came the voice of Hurree Das.

"Stand up, *memsahib!* Stand up and hold your arms high above your head!"

A group of B'Kutu all carrying long knives came toward her litter. With her eyes fixed on them, Helene rose and lifted her arms. Then Hurree Das' voice continued. But he was no longer speaking English— or even Swahili. Helene could not understand his words, but they sounded remarkably like B'Kutu, itself! Here and there, she caught familiar words. "Ki-Gor"—"*gandu!*"—"*nyam nyam.*" Once he broke into English, giving her directions—

"Walk straight toward nearest fire— and then turn around—so all can see crocodiles!"

Helene followed his commands, and the B'Kutu chant broke off into a low concerted moan.

AROUND AND around she turned so that no one could miss seeing the fearsome red welts on her limbs. Hurree Das went on in his strange high voice, and Helene could not even guess what he was telling the cannibals.

But the group of B'Kutu who had started for her with drawn knives had halted irresolutely and were staring at her with a horrified fascination.

But now a guttural cry broke out from Mpotwe.

"What are you telling them, Yellow Man?" the prince demanded in Swahili. Quickly the answer came from the Hindu, likewise in Swahili.

"I am telling them that Ki-Gor has bewitched his woman! Ki-Gor is a mighty witch, and even from a distance can he cast a *kissi!* If you do not believe my words, look at her yourself—and see the crocodiles that Ki-Gor's mighty ju-ju has caused to stand out on his woman's arms and legs! Anyone who is brave enough to eat her now will be eaten in turn by a hundred thousand crocodiles who will rush out of the river behind you!"

"Silence! You fool!" Mpotwe cried. "There is not a word of truth in what you say! Ki-Gor can send no *kissi* to protect his wife when he does not even know his wife is in danger!"

"He knows, O Mpotwe!" Hurree Das replied, but his voice faltered, and Helene's heart skipped a beat.

Mpotwe screamed some orders in Kara-mzili, and his warriors started for Hurree Das, and others made for Helene.

"Fool of a Yellow Man!" Mpotwe shrieked again in Swahili. "You should have preserved your life! But by trying to cross my will, you have only sealed your doom! The woman shall die and you with her! You cannot make me fear Ki-Gor when Ki-Gor is far away!"

The tall men of the bodyguard were making straight for their victims when a new voice broke in—a fearful, deep-throated voice.

"Ki-Gor is never far away when his wife is in danger!"

Helene half turned with a sob in her throat, and saw the giant bronzed form leaping over the heads of the ring of B'Kutu, a long Bambala spear glittering in his right hand.

In a split-second the whole camp was a bedlam, with Mpotwe mouthing commands. But Ki-Gor kept coming.

"You, Mpotwe!" he roared, and his words could be heard over the screams of the B'Kutu. "You, who did not believe in my ju-ju—you will never have another chance to test it. Witness! All of you! And be warned!"

The great muscles tautened as Ki-Gor's right arm shot back over his shoulder. The spear seemed a live thing as it poised in his hand. Then he heaved. Swift as an arrow the spear, and as straight. Mpotwe gave a choked cry and flung up a fat arm. But the spear had already found its destination in the folds of his fat throat.

For a slow heart's beat, no one in the clearing moved. And during that sickening moment, Helene asked herself what would happen to Ki-Gor and Hurree and herself now. She knew that if the Kara-mzili attacked, Ki-Gor could not—single-handed—save the three of them. It all depended on whether the Kara-mzili were too shocked by his sudden appearance to do anything.

She started running toward Ki-Gor to be by his side, and as she did, she saw the Tetela.

They swarmed into the clearing from all sides with yells of triumph. Helene had a brief vision of their spears dipping among the panic-stricken cannibals, before she flung her arms around Ki-Gor's neck and fainted.

THE THREE sat in the best house in Otempa whence they had gone with the victory-drunk Tetela to tell the amazed Bambala of annihilation of Mpotwe and his verminous army.

"I know one thing, Ki-Gor," Helene said, "I never want to go through another moment like the one when the Tetela went right past us on the river—and never knew we were there."

"They knew you were there," Ki-Gor retorted. "They pretended they didn't. They went past on the river so that they could land downstream. It was less than half the Tetela force. The rest of them followed me along the shore, and the two forces carefully surrounded Mpotwe's camp and waited for my signal."

"But my dear old fellow," Hurree Das said, lifting a cup of Bambala beer away from his mouth, "how in name of Brahma, Vishnu, and Shiva did you know where we were?"

Ki-Gor half-smiled. "I nearly did not come," he said, "but that does not matter, what matters is that I did come. The B'Kutu were careless about hiding the rafts they crossed the river with. And they never did hide your canoe. I saw it washed halfway up a sandbar. One side was stove in. We landed then and guessed what had happened."

"Most extraordinary!" Hurree Das cried, accepting another cup of beer from a Bambala girl "But by Jove! Jolly good job you're arriving when you did!"

"In connection with that, Hurree," Helene said, "I didn't know you could speak B'Kutu."

"Before tonight I could not," Hurree Das replied. "Perhaps you noticed me talking with Kara-mzili and B'Kutu while camp was being prepared?"

"Yes, but don't tell me you learned B'Kutu in that little time," Helene said.

"Most indubitably and without any question," Hurree Das said luxuriously. "I learned enough words to make speech about Ki-Gor's magic. You see, we Indians are good linguists. I, for instance, speak my native Gujerati plus Mharathi, Rajasthani, Punjabi, Bengali—and English! Did I ever tell you, dear lady, that I took honors at Bombay University—in English?"